THE FLORENTINE DECEPTION

THE FLORENTINE DECEPTION

A Novel

CAREY NACHENBERG *3/22/18*

Ethan,
Go on to be great! And
enjoy the adventure!
Carey

OPEN ROAD

INTEGRATED MEDIA

NEW YORK

Cover design by Sony Nguyen

ISBN: 978-1-5040-2741-0

This edition published in 2015 by Open Road Integrated Media, Inc.
345 Hudson Street
New York, NY 10014
www.openroadmedia.com

To Mom, Dad, Papa, and SP

I would like to thank the dozens of friends, family members, coworkers, editors, and literary agents who read my manuscript—in many cases multiple times—and spent untold hours giving me valuable feedback. I'd specifically like to thank (in alphabetical order) Leonardo Blanco, Brian Chang, Dan Chen, Phyllis Cohen, Grace Coopman, Rob Crouch, Martin Dang, Cameron Feng, Jenya Gartsbein, Ari Horn, Bradley Kraemer, Sue Kwon, Silas Lam, Shawna McCarthy, Betsy Mitchell, Gail Mullen, Patrick Mullen, Andrea Nachenberg, Leon Nachenberg, Sony Nguyen, Daniel Nieh, Arlene Robinson, Neil Rubenking, Clint Sand, Bob Thixton, and ShiPu Wang.

Foreword

It is often said that "truth is stranger than fiction." Thus, an interesting story might well be based on reality—and many of the best ones are.

You are about to read Carey's first novel. He has drawn on both his experience and imagination to craft an engaging story grounded in reality. Herein you will find items that you might find in the real world around you, if you knew where to look:

- There is a hero who is driven to solve a puzzle.
- There is his loyal best friend.
- There is a possible love interest.
- There are some bad guys willing to hurt others to advance their selfish agendas.
- There is international intrigue.
- There is at least one mysterious treasure.
- There is a mechanism in play that could destroy civilization as we know it.

Wait, what? Didn't I say the story was grounded in reality? Wouldn't something like that be science fiction?

No, it's not—it is fiction that is entirely plausible based on how the world has developed around us. It seems far-fetched only by people who don't understand all of the components . . . but you will, after you finish reading this tale.

Without revealing the details here (and spoiling part of the story), I'll simply say that the rapid advance of some forms of technology in the last few decades has been carried out without appropriate consideration of safety and security: too many parties have valued getting things done quickly (and most profitably) than they have in getting them done safely. Thus, we have a world where the wrong set of factors coming together, either by accident or under the direction of those with evil intent, could prove catastrophic.

How do I know that? For 30 years I have been working on advanced topics in security and cyber crime, including in this field. As one of the most senior scientists in the field, I direct one of the world's foremost academic research centers studying threats from (and solutions for) advanced technologies. Carey's story resonates with things I had been studying many years ago and am still worried about (a little more on that shortly).

Carey himself has been at the forefront of some of these issues as well, and that is why his story is so believable. As a leading researcher and executive with a high-tech security firm, Carey has had direct, on-going experiences countering malicious activities; he did not have to stretch much to imagine portions of the threats he describes in his story. He has fleshed them out so a non-expert can appreciate them, and then surrounded them with a cast of interesting characters, resulting in this novel.

Thus, as you read the story, you might want to reflect on the possibility that some of the story could have happened in recent years . . . or may yet happen. As you do that, you may think that the government *must* have stepped in with regulations to prevent such a catastrophe. Were that the case!

It's not as if there haven't been warnings. Almost 25 years ago, while Carey was still a student at UCLA, I first started thinking about the technology problems at the heart of his novel. After a few years, I wrote a short white paper that had a Defense-specific view of the problem. I briefed that paper to senior personnel from several government agencies and commercial firms at the conclusion of a specialized study program. Most of that audience was polite, but their universal reaction to my paper was absolute certainty that it was "science fiction" and could not happen. I tried for several years to get some attention for the problem, to no avail. Eventually, the paper went into my archive and was mostly forgotten as I moved on to other topics of research.

Fast forward to the present. Carey and I met years ago, and our paths sometimes cross when our professional lives intersect. When I learned he was writing this book, I offered to read an early copy. Imagine our mutual surprise when we each learned that he had independently identified some of the same technological weaknesses I had outlined two decades ago!

Once you finish this book and have thought about its various twists and turns, if you are curious about my original take on the problem you can read it online. It is available as http://ceri.as/think, complete with original typos. Don't read it before Carey's story, however—you'll spoil some of the surprises. Plus, it doesn't have such a rich set of characters and action!

I'm sure you'll find Carey's novel entertaining and thought-provoking. Don't be in a rush reading it, though: haste is at the root of several of the problems in his book . . . exactly as in the real world.

Eugene H. Spafford, PhD
December 2014

THE FLORENTINE DECEPTION

Chapter 1

Microsoft Campus, Building 5—Redmond, Washington
2004

Vadim "V-man" Bulgakov stabbed his finger at his monitor's on-off button and spun his chair to face the door.

"Yes?" he said bluntly.

The door cracked open and an acne-scarred junior engineer poked his head in. "Hey V-man, the guys are going for some drinks. Want to join?"

Vadim relaxed his grip on his armrest and eased back into his chair. "Oh," he said, bringing his index fingers up to his temples, "no thanks. I've got a severity-one defect that I've got to fix by tomorrow morning or I'll be on Barry's shit list." Vadim pressed the pads of his index fingers against his head and began rubbing in concentric circles. "I'll try to join you guys later."

"Good luck," said the engineer empathetically. "We'll be at Daman's Bar if you finish early enough."

Vadim nodded with a grunt, then swiveled back to face his monitor. "Do me a favor and change my door tag to red. I need to concentrate."

"No problem." He flipped over the laminated cardboard circle outside Vadim's office and eased the door shut. Then from outside Vadim's door, he yelled, "V-man's not coming. Wait up and let me grab my coat."

Vadim waited for the muffled voices in the hall to subside before he took one more glance over his shoulder and powered his monitor back on. Earlier that evening, he'd received yet another last-minute order from Moscow via a dead-drop email account, and if he were going to make the necessary modifications in time for tomorrow's deadline, he was going to be up all night. He took a sip of overly sweet, lukewarm coffee and refocused his eyes on the C code that filled the screen.

"*Yebat!*" he cursed, paging back and forth through the code. After more than an hour tracing through thousands of lines of programming instructions, he still couldn't decide how or even where to best make the change. And he was now way behind on his official task list. That was the last thing he needed. That, and more scrutiny from his boss.

Vadim scrolled down a few more lines and ran his finger down the code.

Finally.

He'd found the section of logic he'd need to modify. In the latest communication from Russia, he'd been asked to introduce a subtle flaw into his project's authentication subsystem. According to the email, the flaw had to meet three specific requirements—each, no doubt, of paramount importance to the geniuses back in Moscow—yet be subtle enough that it wouldn't be discovered by one of Vadim's unsuspecting team members. And should the modification be discovered, it had to look like an honest mistake, a gaff that any engineer might make after a typical all-nighter at the office. At least that wouldn't be a problem. He'd been slaving away nonstop on his official work assignments since nine the previous morning.

Vadim stared at the code segment for several minutes, took a deep breath, and began typing.

Chapter 2

Alex Fife's House—Northridge, California
August 20, 2015

"WHY DON'T YOU JUST ASK HER OUT?"

"Now's not exactly the best time to be discussing my love life, Potter."

"You're not even at the hard part yet," Potter said. I shot a quick glance down; Potter stood far below, his chalk-covered hands outstretched and hovering protectively.

"That's reassuring." I inhaled, locked my left hand onto a peanut-sized outcropping, then delicately eased my right foot up into a shallow niche just below my hip.

"All right, back to business," he said. "Take it nice and deliberate."

I nodded absentmindedly, my focus on the overhanging rock above. The next hold sat four feet north of my head, well out of reach. I considered my options, but with each second of hesitation my biceps weakened, my body peeling farther away from the sheer face.

"Talk to me," Potter said. A trickle of sweat ran down my cheek.

"I'm going to throw for it." Ignoring the burn in my arms, I rocked onto my right foot, pulled my left shoulder in close to the face, and launched upward. My right index and middle fingers caught the rock just as my feet cut from the wall.

"I'm losing it," I said, my legs sprawling in midair.

"Feet, Alex! Get your feet back on."

I tensed my abs and swung my feet toward a narrow ridge. The tip of my right shoe skidded across the hold, caught, then slipped, sending my legs floundering violently backward.

"I'm gonna pop!"

"Hold it together!"

"It's not—*aaaaahhhh!*" My fingers gave and I plummeted. . . .

———

Potter's nimble hands caught my shoulders mid-fall and shifted me squarely over the padded vinyl mat; upon impact, a cloud of dust erupted from my chalk bag and settled on my face.

"You caught some serious air!" he said, offering me a hand.

"Thanks, Potter." I wiped the powder from my face and tousled my wavy brown hair until it stopped snowing chalk, then grabbed Potter's hand and pulled myself upright. Davis Potter, a lanky five-eleven with a perpetually clean-shaven face and a scalp to match, was the consummate climbing partner—technically adept, levelheaded, and always sporting a genuine smile.

"How was the right handhold?" he asked, wiping the sweat from his face. The sun had just cleared my roof and it had to be pushing ninety degrees.

"Pretty thin," I said. "You want to try?"

"Nah. It's way above my pay grade. You know, I can't remember the last time I climbed on your wall. I like the new routes." He gazed appreciatively up at the twenty-foot-high artificial rock wall I'd had custom-built and bolted onto the back of my house.

"Thanks! Speaking of new routes, when are we going to check out that new cave in Ojai?" I reached for my water bottle and drained its last few ounces.

"Give me another month to finish my master's thesis and I'm totally game. It's supposedly got some unbelievable crystalline stalactites."

"Next month works. And if Linda's interested, we'll have a quorum."

"Don't hold your breath," he said. "She's been working tons of overtime at the hospital. Never seems to have time to climb anymore."

"Don't worry. I'll guilt her into it."

"Well if anyone can, it's you." Potter hesitated a second. "Hey Alex, hear me out now that you're down."

My stomach clenched.

"I'm telling you, Potter, she's not interested." *Not to mention I get a panic attack every time I think about asking her out.*

"All right, all right." Potter put his hands up in mock self-defense. "Just give it some—"

The phone rang. I rolled over to the left edge of the mat and grabbed the handset.

"Hi Alex. Got a minute?" It was my dad, no doubt calling to check in on his directionless son.

I held up a finger to Potter and mouthed "one second."

"Yeah," I said, "What's up?"

Potter tapped his watch, waved goodbye, and headed toward my back gate.

"Just wondering if you had a chance to clean up that old PC for me yet?"

"Crap. I totally forgot." I'd been putting it off. "Can I get it to you next week?"

"Actually," he hesitated, "I was hoping you could finish by tomorrow. Father Magruda was planning to give it to the Guatemalan family we've been sponsoring. Could you get it done by then?"

"Yeah ... I'll do it this afternoon."

"Thanks, I really appreciate it." My father cleared his throat. "So, any new projects? Promising startup ideas?"

"No. Nothing new to report." I knew he meant well, but the nagging was starting to get to me. Truth be told, I was bored out of my mind. I just couldn't find anything to do that excited me. Other than climbing.

"So where'd you get the PC from?" I asked, changing the subject. "Garage sale?"

"Nope. An estate sale," he said, taking my diversion in stride. "Got it in a box-lot for twenty bucks."

Since Dad's retirement, he'd become quite the do-gooder. Computers, toasters, portable gas stoves, anything he could rummage from a friend's attic or find at a local garage sale, he'd buy, fix up, and offer to a needy family sponsored by the church.

Which led me to my exciting afternoon chore: delousing an old PC for his adopted family. It's a routine familiar to all "computer people." Everyone from third cousins to old high school teachers expect that since you're a computer guy, you can fix virtually any problem with their PC. Parents were the worst offenders: "I'm sure Alex can fix that problem. I'll have him drop everything and give you a call."

In any case, this was one favor I'd agreed to do.

I said goodbye and trudged up the stairs and into the shower. After a few seconds fidgeting with the temperature, I turned on my shower radio.

". . . heat wave, SoCal Edison says there's a five percent chance of rolling blackouts today. So pitch in and reduce your electricity usage during peak hours," it crackled. "In other news, one of our own local Angelenos may soon shoot the moon! After forty years of fruitless treasure hunting, a feisty octogenarian from Chatsworth believes she's finally located the burial site of the Wellingsworth fortune. Ruth Lindley stumbled upon Wellingworth's diary at a local garage sale in 1966 and has been hunting for the millionaire's treasure ever since. Until now."

Interesting. I wondered if she'd finally found it. I'd been infatuated with buried loot, treasure maps, and one-eyed pirates since devouring *Treasure Island* in the eighth grade, and had even done some poking around Wellingsworth Canyon myself as a teen. I didn't find any treasure but did pick up a nasty case of poison oak.

I upped the volume.

"Want to hear more about Ruth's most recent find, and the sordid history behind the treasure? Tune in to *ABC 7 Local News* tonight at eleven."

Of course, just a teaser. I made a mental note to google later for the details.

I finished showering, toweled off, and looked in the mirror. Just one day without shaving and I was already getting scraggly. No good. I might be a slacker, but I sure as hell wasn't going to look like one. I grabbed my Braun and went to work, then finished off the stragglers with a disposable razor. I'd gel my hair later, just before the party.

All right, what to wear? For computer cleanup detail? Grunge. I threw on a pair of comfortable blue jeans and a passable "*No, I will not fix your computer*" t-shirt from the hamper.

Reluctantly, I dragged the still-sealed cardboard box from my closet. A brief inspection revealed a chassis, grimy keyboard, small LCD monitor, standard three-button mouse, and a rat's nest of cables.

I disentangled the wiring, laid each neatly on the carpet, and then began connecting components. It took just a few minutes, but this was the easy part.

I planted my thumb firmly on the power button and stared expectantly at the monitor. After what seemed like an hour-long boot-up, Windows decided to make an appearance.

The login screen greeted me with a single account name: *Richard*.

Holding my breath expectantly, I prayed to the computer gods that Richard's account had no password. That would make things so much easier. With an exhale, I clicked on his login picture.

Windows prompted me for a password.

What was I expecting, anyway? All right, I'd turn it into a challenge—could I hack in within fifteen minutes or less?

No problem.

I'd start with the low-hanging fruit; I began guessing passwords.

"password" didn't do it. Neither did "Richard" or "richard." Nine out of ten people use easy-to-guess passwords.

"qwerty"? Denied. A few more failed guesses and it was time for the nuclear option.

"123456"? Definitely top five. Rejected.

"12345678"? No.

"abc123"? Fail.

"letmein"? Nope. "111111"? No.

Enough guessing—time was running out. I rummaged through my nightstand and snagged an old thumb drive, then grabbed my laptop and booted it up. It took a few seconds to find a website hosting the latest version of OphCrack—it had been the top password-cracker when I was at ViruTrax. Assuming Richard hadn't encrypted his hard drive or picked a super-long password—and most people didn't—this'd get me in within five minutes.

I downloaded and installed the password-cracking program onto the thumb drive, then inserted it into an empty USB slot on the front of Richard's computer and rebooted with the "boot-from-USB" option. After about ninety seconds and a whirlwind of scrolling text, the OphCrack program popped up.

"Please wait . . ." it said. Following a few moments of analysis,

OphCrack indicated that Richard's hard drive wasn't encrypted and that a password-crack was possible. Things were looking up.

I selected Richard's account name—the only one on the list—and clicked "Go." A little hourglass appeared as the program began generating and validating hundreds of millions of passwords until it found the one that matched Richard's. I visualized the process—"aaaaaa," "aaaaab," "aaaaac," . . . "aaaaba," "aaaabb," "aaaabc"—hundreds of thousands of guesses . . . and failures . . . every second.

The hourglass turned over and over. One minute. Two. Three. The guy must have picked a long password. Four minutes. Five.

I began sweating. If this didn't work, I'd have to go in, locate the proper system password files by hand, and reset Richard's account. A year ago I wouldn't have blinked at the prospect. But that was a year ago. Not to mention I'd blow my fifteen-minute goal.

Finally, after seven minutes of brute-force guessing, OphCrack issued a ding. The password "r1ch4rd" appeared on the screen. I issued a sigh of relief.

"Take *that*, Anonymous."

The PC had all of the must-have apps: a word processor, spreadsheet, Minesweeper, and more than likely a venereal buffet of computer viruses. Minus the viruses, whoever was to receive this computer should be happy. The background picture on the desktop showed a beautiful Impressionist painting, maybe a Van Gogh, I thought. I'd leave it for the new owner.

A few clicks revealed antivirus software last updated during the last presidential election—this machine was going to need some serious detox. Twenty minutes later, I had a freeware antivirus+firewall package installed and scanning away. It was a smorgasbord all right; the scanner unearthed and removed two dozen infections.

Step 1: Completed.

Step 2: Remove all personal information from the machine. Financial records, documents, pictures (all types of pictures), music files, and home movies—such private information, and yet so often forgotten. It never ceased to amaze me how often people forget to remove personal data before discarding a computer. I'd started by searching the hard drive for JPEG picture files when my bedroom door creaked open.

"What's up, slacker?"

"Who . . . ?" I spun around.

"Gotcha!"

"Jesus! You scared the crap out of me!" I growled. "How the hell did you get in?"

"I used my old key." Steven shoved aside a pile of glossy open-house flyers and plopped onto my futon. His otherwise-uniform helmet of curly brown hair had been marred by a razor-shaped trough above the left ear.

"Hillary give you a haircut?"

"Look good?" Steven adjusted his glasses and shot me a sultry look.

"Go look in the mirror." I grinned.

"Dammit," he groused, showing no desire to verify for himself. "She was watching some new-age vegan show while she was buzzing away. Whatever. Hey what's this?" he asked, picking up the top sheet from the stack of flyers. "Whoa, four-point-five mil!"

"Nice huh? Twenty-foot-high walls of glass overlooking the Pacific. It's in the Santa Monica Canyon."

"That is one serious chick magnet!" He winked suggestively. "Are you going to buy it?"

I shook my head. "I haven't decided yet. It's got some layout problems. But it's on my top-five list right now."

Steven dropped the flyer back onto the pile and leaned back against the wall, perching his hands on an increasingly prominent belly.

"So what's the latest?" he asked.

"Not much. I'm stuck cleaning up a donated PC for Dad's adopted family." I pointed at the dusty computer.

"Man, that family lives better than I do." Steven wiped his forehead with his arm. "Hey, got anything cold to drink? It's like an oven outside."

"One second." I socked him in the arm, then traipsed downstairs to check the fridge. Steven was my best friend, actually more like a brother. We'd lived together since our freshman year at UCLA, until he got hitched.

"Here," I said when I returned, handing him a bottle. Steven had already managed to click up a tasteless picture from Richard's hard drive.

"Wow, this computer cleanup thing isn't nearly as bad as I thought. It has some real perks." He grinned.

I rolled my eyes. "Glad to hear it. Then you can do the rest of it."

"So what are you up to later?" he continued, ignoring me. "Want to catch *Dead Alive II*? Hillary's doing girls' night tonight, so I'm a bachelor." Steven took a gulp and clicked on another picture.

"Sure. When's it playing? I need to head over to Tom and Gennady's place around six." I took a swig.

"I was thinking of going at seven, but I'll bet there's an afternoon matinee."

Steven clicked on the Internet Explorer icon and pulled up Google. A few keystrokes later he consulted his watch and said, "It's playing at the Winnetka 21 in . . . thirty-seven minutes." A (temporarily jobless) rocket scientist, Steven was habitually precise.

"Okay. Let me finish this and we can go." I'd reached for the mouse when the newly installed firewall software popped an alert onto the screen:

> **Firewall Alert:** *Unknown program WINCALC.EXE is attempting to send an email to address: OXOTHИK@flavmail.ru.*

It offered two buttons: "Block" or "Allow," about as meaningful as a poorly translated fortune cookie. Only unlike a fortune cookie, this type of prompt encouraged people to call their computer-expert-sons for help. WinCalc, huh? Since when did Windows calculator programs send emails to strange Russian email addresses?

"What's that alert mean?" asked Steven.

"Not sure. The firewall software I installed is grousing about some calculator program on the computer trying to send email over the Internet."

"Calculators sending email? That makes no sense."

"Agreed. My guess is it's a spyware program, maybe an email virus. The antivirus scan I ran totally missed it."

"Think it's an entirely new virus?" he asked.

"Wouldn't surprise me," I said. "The last year I was at ViruTrax we discovered something like thirty million new strains."

"Jesus." Steven's jaw dropped. "So can you figure out what it does?"

"I'm a bit out of practice but it probably wouldn't be too hard."

"Why don't you take it apart, Mr. Virus Expert?" he chided.

"Skip the movie?"

"Why not? I've always wanted to see how a virus ticks."

"All right. Let's do it."

Chapter 3

My buddies in the lab at ViruTrax could dissect a new computer virus in ten or fifteen minutes, determine how it spawned, what data it tried to steal (most likely your credit card number), and how to exterminate it. During your first few dissections, the process was utterly confusing, like reading Shakespeare for the first time. After a dozen, you started recognizing idioms, familiar techniques. After a few hundred, you began recognizing familial relationships between different strains, much like historians can identify the artist of an unknown painting based on its brush strokes, composition, and structure.

My eight months of retirement had made me a bit rusty, but what the hell. I inserted a second thumb drive into Richard's computer and, after a bit of hunting, located and copied the enigmatic WINCALC. EXE file over to my laptop.

"Just bear with me, I haven't done this in a while."

"No worries. So how do you figure out what it does?"

"I'm going to run it through a disassembler," I said.

"A disassembler?"

"It's a tool that produces a human-readable listing of the program's computer instructions, its underlying logic. Then we get to slog through them all to see what they do. That's the tricky part. It's like reading a mystery novel and fitting all the clues together until you see the bigger picture. Give me about an hour and I should be able to give you the CliffsNotes overview."

By five, we had most of the particulars nailed. Richard's computer was home to a species of garden-variety spyware. This particular organism recorded and archived every keystroke typed by the user into a hidden file. Once every day, it emailed the latest transcripts to its master, owner of the mysterious Russian email address.

"So it records everything you type?" asked Steven.

"It looks like it. Had it not been for that firewall alert, our Russian friend would know what movies you were looking up at the Winnetka 21."

"Scary," he said with unusual sincerity.

It took just a few minutes to disable the spyware from Richard's PC now that we knew how it ticked.

"Feeling voyeuristic?" I asked. "Want to see a transcript of this guy's last minutes?"

"What do you mean *last minutes*?"

"My dad picked up this PC at an estate sale. That means that the owner's dead. Deceased. Pushing daisies. That spyware wiretap file probably has the last words he ever typed in his life."

Steven's eyebrows rose. "Seriously? What do you think we'll find?"

"Who knows? Probably nothing." I glanced over my shoulder conspiratorially and lowered my voice. "But maybe, just maybe, the directions to the Wellingsworth treasure."

"Wellings-what? Treasure? Really?"

"No, not really." I laughed. "It's probably just a list of the last few porn sites the guy visited."

I slid the mouse back over to the file, but a fraction of a second before I could open it, the lamp's filament flared and popped, and the power to the house died.

"Perfect timing." Speaking about timing, I looked down at my watch. It was 6:45 p.m. "Crap! I need to go. I'm late for Tom's party!"

Chapter 4

"Tom!" yelled Gennady, "Alex is here." Gennady grabbed me in a bear hug, then stepped aside for me to enter. "Long time no see!"

"Hey Gennady."

"Come on in. What do you want to drink? *Wodka*? Jäger?"

"Jäger? I feel like I'm still in college. I'll take a Diet Coke and save the shots for later. Thanks."

I walked down the hallway to the kitchen. A half-dozen people, most with familiar faces but unfamiliar names, were mingling around the living room with red party cups. Pink Floyd's *Dark Side of the Moon* was playing in the background.

"Hey Alex!" A hand waved from behind the refrigerator door, then a second later, Tom popped his head up. "One sec, I'll be right over."

Tom finished his rummaging and returned holding a can of Pabst.

"Happy birthday, man." I handed him a bag of Reese's Pieces.

"Epic—just like old times! Thanks!" Tom ripped open a corner of the bag with his teeth and tipped a handful into his mouth.

"And here's the real gift." I placed an envelope in his hand. "Don't forget to open it or you'll regret it."

Tom gave me a quizzical look and placed the envelope with the others on the counter.

"Thanks. I won't. Follow me," he said, walking over to the other guests. "You remember Vic and Letty, right?"

"Hey guys," I said, "good to see you again." I had no recollection whatsoever who they were.

"And this is Cindy." Cindy was a well-endowed brunette, very good looking.

"Hi, nice to meet you. I'm Alex." I shook her hand. "How do you know—"

"And her girlfriend Vivian," interrupted Tom, strategically.

"Oh. Hi Vivian, nice to meet you too."

"The other two are Gennady's friends from Russia." Tom issued a

16

polite smile and nodded. "They don't speak much English, but boy can they pound the vodka."

"Hello," I said, nodding as well. The pair smiled.

Tom motioned me back to their red leather Bugatti couch. "Take a seat."

"So what's up? Word is that you bailed from ViruTrax?" said Gennady from the kitchen.

"That word is right," I said, shoving aside a bag of chips and taking a seat. "That was a while ago. When did we last talk?"

Tom, clearly well on his way to inebriation, stared up at the ceiling and considered.

"Don't remember," he said, taking a gulp.

"I do. Camping last November in Sequoia."

"Sue!" I hopped up from the couch to give her a hug. "How are things?"

"Good! I started a new job last week, and Gennady and I are heading to Maui next month, so I've got nothing to complain about."

"Excellent! Come sit with me." I sat back down and patted the couch. "I want to hear all about your job." Sue sat down and wrapped her arm around me for a second hug.

"Anyway, why'd you leave?" continued Tom. "All your options vest?"

"Nah. Things just got too political."

"Like he needed the stock options," said Gennady, handing me a red party cup. I took a sniff. Just Coke, no *wodka*. "Now on the other hand, we could have used the options."

I nearly choked on my drink. "You missed your calling, Gennady. You should have gone into standup."

Gennady and Tom had been employees number two and three at my college cyber-security startup. I'd invented an entirely new approach to detect computer viruses, but didn't have the mathematical background to make it work, or the business acumen to make it a success. Gennady, a brilliant applied mathematics major, and Tom, a physics major and business savant, were the perfect partners. I, of course, did all the programming.

After about twenty-four months of stealth R&D in Tom's parents' guesthouse, we shipped a new crowd-sourced antivirus technology that put existing security products to shame. Word spread, and the product was free, so within nine months on the market, we'd reached one hundred and sixty million users, surpassing ViruTrax as the world's most popular antivirus vendor. In a bout of desperation, ViruTrax offered us seventy-five million for our company; we settled for two hundred and ninety. Gennady and Tom had wisely cashed out and declined employment, but I promised to stay on a year as a condition to close the deal.

"So how's the new startup going?" I asked.

Tom looked at Gennady and smirked.

"Kaput," said Gennady. "Our VC funding ran out, and neither of us is willing to put any more of our own cash in."

"Not to mention that the product sucks," said Tom, just a little slur in his voice.

Gennady glared at Tom a moment, then nodded grudgingly. "It's true. So basically we're trying to figure out our next project. So what have you been up to, Alex?" he asked. "Traveling the world in a private mega-yacht? Ascending Mount Everest?"

I thought a moment. "Climbing, eating, sleeping." I took a drink. "And I think I'm having a midlife crisis too."

"Wow—you've been busy," said Gennady in his odd Russian-Texan accent. "Midlife crisis? At what, twenty-six?"

"Twenty-five."

"Same difference." He picked up a tumbler of some opaque alcoholic concoction from the coffee table and sipped. "Try buying a dacha in St. Petersburg and getting a new nineteen-year-old girlfriend. That worked for my dad."

I pulled out my smartphone and pretended to scrawl with my finger on the screen. "Nineteen-year-old girlfriend. Check. Vacation home in former Soviet Union. Check." I nodded. "Got it. Thanks man."

Sue began giggling.

"Let's create another startup," said Tom. "Nothing like ninety-hour workweeks to give your life meaning."

It wasn't a half-bad idea if I could just find a project I was passionate about; I needed something challenging to do soon or I'd die of sheer boredom.

"I'll give that some thought as well," I said, gazing around the room at Tom and Gennady's slovenly home-slash-headquarters. Why the two of them still lived together like college students when both could buy mega-mansions—for cash—was an enigma. Then again, who was I to judge; I lived in a tract home on low-fat microwave burritos and slept on a purple IKEA futon.

"How's Julie," asked Sue, changing the subject.

"Ummm . . . She dumped me two months ago."

"Sorry, Alex." Sue squeezed my hand, then said, "I didn't like her anyway. No big loss."

"Brutal," said Gennady, shaking his head. "I think we need to go on a bender to fix Alex up."

"Ben-der!" yelled one of the Russians from behind.

"Nah, I'm good. I'm just in a lull."

The doorbell rang.

"Be right back." Gennady made his way to the door. "Pizza's here," he yelled.

"Oh, before I forget," said Tom, "there's a letter for you on my desk."

"A letter?"

"Yeah, from Sheila."

"Why did she send it here?"

"No idea." Tom shrugged. "Maybe she lost your address. She's been backpacking in India for the past seven months. You know, I used to have a major thing for her."

Tom disappeared upstairs and returned with an envelope covered in colorful Indian stamps.

"Thanks," I said. I folded the letter and shoved it into my back pocket.

"Wow that smells good," said Tom, sniffing the aromatic deep-dish. The other guests had already grabbed plates and were snagging slices.

"Here you go, Alex. Dig in." Gennady handed me a paper plate and a napkin, then grabbed a slice for himself.

I eyed the pizza longingly, then put down the plate. "No thanks."

Gennady took a bite. "Dude, you've got negative body fat and your muscles have muscles," he said through a mouthful of pizza. "You can afford a slice."

"Not going to happen."

"All right folks, it's time," said Tom. "Grab your chow and take a seat, because we're going to start the movie in five." Every year on his birthday, Tom invited his friends to watch *Back to the Future* on his big-screen. There was only one hitch: any time a character said "McFly," you had to take a shot.

Tradition was tradition.

"Let's do it," I said. "But I'm stopping at three shots. And I'm only drinking Stoli—none of the cheap stuff."

"Lightweight," said Gennady.

Three hours later, after all the other guests had left, Gennady and the two drunken Russians gave a rousing rendition of "The Power of Love" by Huey Lewis. A second later, Gennady curled up on the couch and began snoring. Sue gently laid a blanket on him.

"It was great to see you, Alex," she said.

"Thanks for coming, man," Tom added.

"Wouldn't miss it for the world. Happy birthday!"

Chapter 5

WELL, AT LEAST THE POWER WAS BACK ON.

Ignoring the half-dozen flashing clocks, I worked my way to the kitchen and opened the freezer. I definitely needed to go shopping. A lone low-fat, low-sodium TV dinner box stared at me from the top shelf.

Good enough for government work.

I removed it, tossed the packaging, and threw it into the microwave on high.

While the food was spinning away in the oven, my mind wandered back to the computer upstairs and its late owner. So who was this Richard guy? And what was he thinking, or at least typing, in the final days before he died? A love letter? A suicide note? I felt mildly guilty prying into something so personal, but technically the guy was dead, and the curiosity was killing me.

A few moments later, a glass of water and the steaming tray in hand, I headed upstairs, flipped on my bathroom light for illumination, and eased down onto the floor in front of the old computer.

Once the computer had completed its glacial boot-up, it took just a minute to locate the spyware's concealed wiretap file. Ideally, the transcript would contain both Richard's keystrokes and a recording of the computer's screen as Richard typed: as if a spy were videotaping the monitor. Unfortunately, most spyware doesn't have this level of sophistication and Richard's was no exception. All I had was a recording of Richard's keystrokes, a one-sided conversation with the computer.

The spyware archived its recordings in chronological order, with the earliest entry in the file from April 6, and Steven's Google search at the rear. Surprisingly, minus the keystrokes that Steven and I had contributed, the entire listing contained only a handful of lines; Richard was a light computer user. The first day's recording began predictably:

R1CH4RD
r1ch4rd

He must've accidentally hit the CAPSLOCK key before logging in. I continued down the listing:

www.amazon.com
Hephaestus
shazam

Not much to go on. Another challenge. I double-clicked on the Internet Explorer icon and surfed to the Amazon homepage. Once the page rendered, I found what I was looking for: just below the web page's banner, Amazon.com welcomed Richard Lister back and recommended several new books he might be interested in. Like thousands of other websites, Amazon.com sends compact tracking beacons called "cookies" down to each customer's computer to track their shopping habits and deliver personalized recommendations. Just what the computer sleuth ordered. I jotted Richard's full name on my handy college-rule notepad.

What were Amazon's recommendations for Mr. Lister today? Healing Crystals and Gemstones: From Amethyst to Zircon for $16.98 and *The Heartless Stone: A Journey Through the World of Diamonds, Deceit and Desire* at the discount price of $25.72. The magnificent Mr. Lister was a morgue-meandering mineralogist. I jotted down the titles.

From the main Amazon screen, I clicked on the "Your Account" tab and then clicked on the "Manage Address Book" link. As I'd feared, Amazon balked and immediately popped up a login page asking for Richard's password before allowing me to see the goods. On a whim, I keyed in "Hephaestus," the first of the two password-like keywords in the spyware's log, and hit Enter. Remarkably, Amazon accepted the password, and after a brief delay, displayed its Billing and Shipping page containing Richard's address:

651 Latigo Canyon Road
Malibu, CA 90265

Score two points for the Fife-meister. I jotted this down, navigated back to the Account page and clicked the "Change Name, Email-address or Password" link. Amazon promptly delivered Richard's registered email address, antique1@yahoo.com, which I also scribbled onto my notepad. In two minutes and fifteen seconds, I had Richard's full name, his home address, his email account, and his taste in books. Such is the power of the Internet and user-friendly online shopping.

Just who was Richard Lister? Obviously a gem-hound. Wealthy enough to live in Malibu. Even spots in the trailer parks there cost millions. I searched for Richard's full name and in about a tenth of a second, Google delivered sixty-two different matching websites. The first hit, a back-page story in the *Los Angeles Times*, looked interesting: "Malibu Man Acquitted of Antiquities Smuggling." It read:

> "After a sensational four-month court battle, Richard Lister, 52, of Malibu, California, has been acquitted of four smuggling charges. Last year, the retired archaeology professor and his brother, Ronald Lister, were charged with importing more than two dozen Iraqi archeological artifacts, a violation of federal law under the 1970 UNESCO Convention. The artifacts, a set of cylinder seals used to sign clay tablets, were believed to be between 4,500 to 5,500 years old, and were allegedly stolen from the Iraqi National Museum during the opening salvo of the 2003 war. Both men were found not guilty on four charges of smuggling; however Richard Lister was indicted on one count of transporting artifacts already illegally imported into the United States. Mr. Lister has been released on bail and has already filed an appeal, with his case pending hearing by the Ninth Circuit Court of Appeals."

The next few screens of search results were references to the same proceedings, and bore little additional information.

Next, I decided to reconnoiter Richard's email account. Consulting my notepad, I keyed "yahoo.com" into the browser. Just as with Amazon.com, Yahoo used tracking cookies to remember Richard, and welcomed him back. Unfortunately, it appeared that Richard had logged out since last reading his email, and Yahoo also requested a password to access his account. Hoping for a Daily Double, I tried Richard's "Hephaestus" password with no success, then keyed in "shazam." This also failed. After half a dozen more guesses, Yahoo displayed a stern warning explaining the legal ramifications of hacking, and locked Richard's account. Defeated, I stood up to stretch.

The phone rang.

"Hello?" No response. "*Heeelloooo?*"

Just as I was about to nix the call, Steven started yelling. ". . . wait, wait, hello . . . my mute was on. Hello?"

He was calling from his car. I delivered a well-deserved berating, then proceeded to fill him in on my detective work.

"So neither password worked with Yahoo? Are you sure you typed them in right?"

He annoyed me sometimes. "Of course I am."

"Hmmm. Maybe the *shazam* thing wasn't a password?"

"What else could it be?"

"Well if it was a password, how come he didn't type in a website or his username first?" Finally Steven was onto something.

"Good point. Hold on a sec." Richard could have easily selected a website from his web browser's History list or Bookmark list and surfed to it, eliminating the need to manually type in the full web address. I clicked on the browser's History button and scrolled down the list.

"What are you doing?" inquired Steven.

"Just hold on." Scanning the list, one web address excited me: www.zeusmail.gr. Perhaps Lister had two email accounts? I clicked on the link and ZeusMail's login screen greeted me; the site recognized Richard's computer and had pre-filled his email address, antique1@ zeusmail.gr, in the user-name field. With some trepidation, I keyed in "shazam" and clicked the "Login" button.

"Well, what's happening?" whined Steven.

"One second!" I reprimanded. The small rotating globe at the top of the browser spun around maddeningly for a good twenty seconds. Then, as I was about to give up, the screen refreshed and displayed Richard's inbox.

"Bingo!"

Chapter 6

THIRTEEN MINUTES LATER, Steven was by my side panting from his sprint up the stairs.

"You waited, right?"

"What choice did I have? Ready?"

Steven sank to the floor Indian-style and motioned for me to proceed.

Richard's inbox held a single message, as yet unread, dated August 16, 2015, four days ago. I clicked. The email read:

> From: Spirited One <khalimmy@freemail.com>
> To: Antique Collector <antique1@zeusmail.gr>
> Subject: RE: delivery of your goods
>
> where the hell were you? $5M isn't enough? you're a dead man.
>
> On April 2nd, Antique Collector <antique1@zeusmail.gr> wrote:
>
> >Per our discussion, I will delay delivery of the
> >florentine until 12am on August 16th
> >to give you time to secure the required
> >payment. Meet at the agreed-upon location.
> >No more $$ excuses or I'll unload on another
> >buyer. Do not attempt contact before the drop.

"Holy shit! This is getting interesting," said Steven, rubbing his hands together. "Shady million-dollar deals, midnight drops, and dead archaeologists."

"He must have died just after he sent the original email," I considered out loud. A quick Google search confirmed my suspicions; the *LA Times* online obituaries noted Richard's death on Wednesday,

April 7. Cause of death: heart attack. So much for the death threat. Richard's heart had beat him to the punch.

"So what's this Florentine deal?" questioned Steven. "Google it."

I obliged. The first few results were not encouraging:

Delicious Italian Recipes: **Florentine** Cooking
www.italiancookingforall.com/florentine.html
Learn Italian recipes from the **Florentine** chef masters, . . .

Florentine Chicken Extraordinaire
www.easyitaliancooking.com/recipes/flor_chix.html
The **Florentine** Chicken dish is a favorite at Italian restaurants, but with this easy recipe, you can recreate the magic at . . .

Italian Dishes for the American Palette
www.atozrecipes.com/f/florentine_lasagna_recipe.html
This recipe is one that I discovered while visiting Florence during my honeymoon last year. Here's the list of ingredients . . .

"Worthless." A dozen more pages turned up more recipes. "It must be a codename of some sort."

"Maybe it's stolen property," conjectured Steven, "a famous Italian painting, pottery from an Italian archaeological site?"

It was worth a try; I googled "stolen Florentine painting" and was rewarded with a barrage of Mona Lisa hits.

"The Mona Lisa was stolen in 1911 from the Louvre. According to the page, Mona was from Florence," I offered. "They found it two years later when the thief tried to sell it to a Florentine art dealer. Maybe it's gone missing again."

"No way," said Steven, "if someone had stolen the Mona Lisa, it'd be front-page news. And even if it had been stolen, no one's going to sell it for five mil."

He had a point.

I broadened my search to "stolen Florentine," and this time we hit pay dirt.

The **Florentine** Diamond
www.famouslostdiamonds.com/florentine_diamond.html
The diamond had been in her family since the end of World
War I (the **Florentine** was stolen in 1918). She reminisced
that the diamond was of a very unusual shape . . .

I waggled my finger at the result.
"You think it's a diamond?" he asked incredulously.
"Fits the profile." I pushed my notepad to Steven and pointed to
Lister's most recent Amazon purchases.
Clicking on the link, we learned more:

*"According to legend, Charles the Bold, Duke of Burgundy,
wore the 137-carat Florentine Diamond into battle in 1467.
After Charles's death, a foot soldier discovered the gem on the
battlefield, and taking it for a worthless piece of glass, sold it
for a florin. In 1657, the stone again surfaced, this time in
Austria within the coffers of the Grand Duke of Tuscany. After
the fall of the Austrian Empire during World War I, the Florentine was spirited away by the imperial family to Switzer-
land, where it remained until its theft in 1918."*

Midway through my reading, Steven smeared his index finger
on the LCD display and read: "The diamond hasn't been seen since,
although rumors have been circulating for nearly ninety years of its
demise," then continued, "your Mister Lister had a one-hundred-and-
thirty-seven-carat diamond. And now he's dead. The question is: did
the bad guy ever get the diamond?"
"I don't think so." I considered. "I'll bet it's still missing. Whoever
sent that email didn't know that Richard had already died. He didn't
know where the gem was or he wouldn't have made the threat."
Steven became quiet. I think we were thinking the same thing, or
at least I hoped so. For the first time in a long time, I'd actually enjoyed
myself; I'd found the day's hours of sleuthing intellectually mesmer-
izing. And the prospect of a treasure—buried or not—titillated me.

A prepackaged adventure had been dropped in my lap, reviving my childhood treasure-hunting obsession. I could already see myself crawling through musty passages in abandoned mines, hunting for the diamond.

Back to reality.

I punched Richard's Latigo Canyon address into Google to get a map. To my surprise, Google responded with a "house for sale" web-page at the top of the search results.

"His place is for sale," I said. Steven was still zoning out.

"Steven?" I roused him from his stupor. "Richard's house is for sale. And no one knows about the diamond except us and our mysterious emailer-slash-jewel collector-slash-psychopath."

"Okay, and?"

"And I think it's at least worth some investigating. What do you say we take a midnight visit to Richard's house?"

Steven looked up.

"You're crazy, fool! You want to break into the guy's house?"

"Not break in, just walk around outside. Get a feel for the place. C'mon, we'll do a little detective work. The place is for sale and the guy is dead. It's got to be empty. We'll just take a look through the windows. I'll give you ten percent if we eventually find it, just for joining me for a walk."

"That's called trespassing, Alex. Last I heard it's illegal. Plus Hillary would kill me."

"Nothing bad's going to happen."

"That's what you said senior year in the Boelter basement." Steven was referring to our near-calamitous excavation of UCLA's Boelter Hall basement in search of a supposedly buried copy of computer legend Alan Turing's PhD dissertation. We ended up empty-handed, and, had it not been for some fast-talking by my Computer Science mentor, Amir Taheri, we would have been charged with felony vandalism.

"That was the adventure of a lifetime and you know it. Plus it all turned out fine."

"Only because Amir played bridge with the campus police chief." He shook his head. "Look, it's one thing to do that when you're in college. It's another thing for two guys in their mid-twenties to go skulking around on private property, in the middle of the night, because of random emails." He shook his head again. "I don't know."

"A, we're not going to get caught. And B, we're not going to do anything wrong. We're just going to look around a for-sale house. Thirty percent?"

Another headshake, but I could tell I was getting closer.

"Forty?"

"Fifty-fifty or I'm staying here and playing Minecraft. And I'm not going into any house. I'm not going farther than the front door."

"Sold!"

Riding on the excitement, I bounded over to the closet and threw on a navy UCLA tshirt. The jeans I was wearing were fine. I glanced at Steven; he was wearing a bright orange Jethro Tull shirt and a pair of wrinkled beige shorts. I threw him a black t-shirt.

"Camouflage. Put it on."

"Uh huh," he said. "Where are the walkie-talkies, Nancy Drew?"

"Good point! Our cell phones might not work in the hills."

I slid open my mirrored closet and pulled out a dusty shoebox. Inside were a pair of one-mile-range walkie-talkies and an unopened package of AA batteries. I threw them to Steven on the futon and began searching my nightstand.

"Pepper spray." I beamed, holding up a small bottle.

Steven rolled his eyes. "Make sure to set the radios to the same channel."

Chapter 7

Tallinn, Estonia
Six months earlier

RICHARD LISTER WAS NO STRANGER to paranoia—as a smuggler, distrust was table stakes—but today, his sense of danger was off the chart. Glancing once more over his shoulder, he nervously inserted his left hand inside his slacks pocket and wrapped his fingers around his Walther PPK. No taking any chances.

The lead had come to him through a contact he'd made in Iraq during a smuggling operation in the first Gulf War, and while the object was way outside his area of expertise, and the seller way too jumpy, if he understood correctly—and he thought he did—the opportunity was just too good to pass up.

Lister took a deep drag from his dwindling cigarette, letting the smoke warm his body against the early morning chill, then tossed it on the ground and knocked on the door.

The keyhole darkened.

"*Кто э́то?*" Who is it? The voice was shaky, anxious.

"Arkady," responded Lister. "Let me in, I'm freezing," he continued, in Ukrainian-accented Russian.

Lister heard a security chain slide open and the thunks of two deadbolts. A second later, the door edged open.

"Come in." He motioned Lister in, a World War II-era revolver in-hand, then quickly closed the door.

The man was five-eight with greasy, thinning brown hair atop a gaunt face with sunken, bloodshot eyes. *He hasn't slept in a while,* thought Lister. That meant he was edgy, and edgy was bad. Lister's fingers tightened on his pistol.

"Viktor?" asked Lister evenly, his eyes fixed on the man's gun.

"*Da.* Do you have a weapon?"

31

Lister hesitated.

"Do you have a weapon?" Viktor repeated anxiously.

"*Da.*"

"Please remove it slowly and place it over there," instructed Viktor, motioning toward a scarred table.

"There's no one else here?" asked Lister.

"No. Just me."

"May I take a look?" said Lister, his eyes fixed on Viktor's, his body perfectly still.

Viktor considered, then waved his revolver toward the door. "Go ahead."

Lister slowly removed the miniature pistol from his pocket, careful to aim it away from Viktor, and approached the apartment's only door. Using his foot, Lister eased the door open, then scanned the small bathroom.

"Satisfied?" asked the Russian. "Now please put your gun on the table."

"Together? As a gesture of trust?"

Viktor nodded, and eyes locked onto eyes, the two men laid their guns on the scarred pine table.

"Good," said Viktor, still visibly uneasy, and now covered in a patina of tiny beads of sweat. "Have you heard from Slava?"

"*Niet.* He has disappeared," responded Lister. "It's been several weeks. But he'll surface. He always does."

"Well, all we have is his mutual trust. Are you prepared to transfer the funds?" probed Viktor.

"*Da.* Do you have the Florentine?"

"*Da.*"

"How do I know it's authentic?"

"I can demonstrate this to you in just a few minutes. Sit." Viktor pointed toward the apartment's lone sofa.

Richard stepped over to the lumpy, threadbare couch and hesitantly sat down on the least stained of the cushions. The demonstration took seven minutes.

"Satisfied?" asked Viktor.

"Yes. How did you get hold of it?" asked Lister while he stood and extracted an iPhone from his breast pocket.

"You know not to ask those kinds of questions, Arkady." Viktor handed him a slip of paper. "Here are the BIC and IBAN numbers for my account."

Lister nodded, tapped in an international number, and placed the phone next to his ear.

"Make the transfer," he said. He hesitated, listening, then said, "Yes." Then he read the digits from Viktor's paper. When he finished, Viktor, too, made a phone call.

"As promised?" asked Lister.

"Yes." Viktor handed him the small box. "I don't ever want to see you again."

Lister nodded, then under Viktor's watchful eyes, slowly picked up his gun and walked to the door. "That won't be a problem."

Chapter 8

Malibu, California
Present Day

As we snaked up the old Kanan Road from the valley toward Zuma Beach, a leaden fog enveloped the car. I found it strange that there should be fog on such a hot day. Unaccustomed to the lack of visibility, I slowed to fifteen miles per hour and toggled my high beams around the turns. LA's mountain roads are notorious for midnight motorcycle riders and occasional rockfalls, so I didn't want to take any chances.

"Getting close," I said, slowing.

Steven roused from his thoughts and straightened.

A second later, a red stop sign materialized out of the mist. After a pointless check for oncoming cars, I turned right onto the Pacific Coast Highway and accelerated northbound.

"What if someone sees us?" he asked nervously.

"Holmes," I lowered the window, allowing wisps of fog to drift into the car. "In this? We'll be lucky if we can see each other. Stop worrying!"

Steven grunted.

"C'mon, it'll be just like old times!"

"That's what worries me."

Latigo was a constricted two-lane road straddled by overgrown California scrub and chaparral. About a quarter mile away from our mark, I eased my Outback onto a wide dirt shoulder and killed the headlights; the fog offered just meters of visibility.

We reached Richard's driveway minutes later, a Coldwell Banker sign offering confirmation. Steven's feet crunched on the gravel as he walked over to the sign and withdrew a crumpled flyer from the plastic for-sale box.

"Oh look, there's a phone number for the broker, I bet you could call and get a tour scheduled by Monday."

"Oh stop being such a wimp," I whispered. "We're here already. We've got to at least take a quick look."

"Tell that to the Malibu *poh*-leece when they've got you pinned on the ground," he retorted. "Officer, you know how fast these houses are selling these days, I just couldn't wait for my broker."

The home was set back a few hundred yards along a deteriorating asphalt drive from a hairpin bend on Latigo. Overgrown vegetation, covered in a species of what must have been invasive ivy, shrouded the driveway as we padded up.

"Did you bring a flashlight?" he asked.

"Crap. Of all the things. There's one back in the trunk."

Steven dug into his pocket and pulled out a hefty key ring. Fingering through the keys, he singled out a one-inch-long, diamond-shaped LED flashlight. "Lithium. Lasts twelve hours on a single watch battery. Ten-ninety-nine plus shipping and handling." Steven winked, now a bit more relaxed. He aimed the beam onto the pitch black a few feet in front of us and we continued through the mist up to the main property.

Like many Malibu homes, Richard's was surrounded by a formidable iron gate and a twelve-foot-high stucco wall, similarly covered with dense ivy. I pointed to the right and Steven trained his flashlight along the overgrown enclosure. We proceeded eastward around the wall toward the back and were soon completely obscured from the street.

"You want to take a look?" I whispered.

"No way. If you want to, that's your business."

I nodded vigorously.

"I don't know what makes me do these things." Steven placed his key ring on the ground, and with the help of a twig, angled the LED toward the lower part of the wall. He then clasped his hands together and motioned for me to vault from them. Using Steven for support, I launched upward and grasped the wall's ridge; ivy, lichen, insects, spiders—I didn't know what exactly—squished under my hands. Ignoring the mush, I hauled myself up and straddled my legs on the wall. Given the haze, I couldn't see much of the backyard. I promptly wiped the muck from my hands on my jeans.

"Grab the light and I'll pull you up."

Steven shook his head. "No way. I'm staying here." He bent down, snatched up the key ring, and, receiving my acknowledgement, tossed it up. The light arced upward, through my flagellating hands, and down into the shrubs. The beam extinguished.

"Crap," I hissed. "I'm going to jump down and get it. I'll take a quick look around and then find a place to climb back over."

"Okay. I'll meet you by the gate."

I rotated and dropped both legs onto the inside of the wall, scraping my feet against the stucco in search of a protrusion. None was to be found, so I relieved my arms and dropped as cat-like as possible down to the base of the wall. Cat-like indeed. My left leg landed in a bush, my right foot on a sprinkler, and I collapsed backward into the damp earth.

A few moments passed amidst the dirt and shrubs before I regained my breath and wits and did an inventory; everything was still intact with the exception of a gash under my knee. It stung nastily.

"I'm okay," I muttered. There was no response.

Sitting up, I trawled my hands through the dirt and mulch at the base of the wall in search of the keys. Minutes of increasingly paranoid searching bore little fruit; the desire to just find a tree along the wall and escape the yard was overwhelming. Hoping for another pair of hands to help locate the keys, or at least some moral support, I flicked on the walkie-talkie and whispered, "Hey, are you there?" I ratcheted up the volume until it hissed white noise. A little louder: "Hello?" Steven didn't have the damn thing on.

Increasingly consumed by paranoia, I groped for a reasonably weighty rock, and rotating several through my fingers, found a substantial one and convinced myself of its defensive qualities. My imagination at the moment was electric, and it wouldn't have surprised me if a couple of aliens came from nowhere and dragged me into a hole. The rock would make them think twice.

I knew the keys had fallen somewhere close. If they weren't on the ground, they had to be caught in a bush. I began to alternately waggle nearby bushes and hold my breath, the former to elicit the jangle of keys and the latter to monitor for approaching aliens, burglars, and wild animals. Neither event was realized. We'd have to go back to the car, grab the flashlight, and come back for the keys later. A minute or two of deep breathing calmed me and I had enough presence of mind to at least look around the backyard before finding my escape tree. From the little I could see, Richard's yard was like a jungle. I shoved through the nearby bushes and, covered in dead leaves, stumbled onto a pebbled walkway. Organized more like a botanical garden than a typical backyard, the path was flanked by an array of ferns, monstrous shrubs, and bamboo thickets. Improvised weapon in hand, I snaked toward the house, mindful of my crunching steps.

The back of the house opened onto the garden via a grid of six-inch square glass windows. Maybe my eyes were getting used to the dark or perhaps there was a nightlight in the house; either way, I could vaguely make out the interior. Moving closer to the grid, I cupped my hands around my eyes and pressed my face up to a pane. The room was incredible; spanning three levels, it sported a recessed fireplace nook, a midlevel conversation area, and a library loft with requisite spiral staircase and built-in mahogany bookcases. The place was totally empty. The source of the light—there was definitely a dim light inside the house—came from around the bend of the hallway.

A few moments more of my cupped-hand-gazing fogged the window, so I shifted to another pane to get a better view of the adjoining rooms. For whatever reason, the hallway light that had illuminated the room a second earlier had extinguished; it must have been on a timer. Robbed of my view, I bent down to check my gash and let my eyes adjust to the darkness for a second look. This was truly the craziest thing I'd done in a long time, definitely since college, and while I considered myself an adventurous person, this was definitely pushing it. The thought occupied me for a few restless seconds. Eyes acclimated, I re-cupped my hands to the second pane, only to find it fogged as well. I was surprised at that. I'd only hovered in front of it earlier for a second or two. I pulled up my t-shirt and wiped the pane. The hair on my arms prickled; the condensation wasn't on the outside.

The realization took a few seconds to gel. The subsequent *"schunk"* of an unlocking deadbolt settled it. I catapulted headfirst into the nearest cluster of bushes and then, as stealthily as possible, tried to lose myself within the densest part of Richard's jungle. Reaching a niche behind a dense hedge along the north wall, I spun my back to the wall and froze, my heart's violent pulsations deafening me. I immediately started taking quiet, deep breaths to calm down, slow my heart rate, and restore my hearing.

While I waited, I heard the vague crunch of decaying leaves. Whoever it was remained quiet—no "I'm going to call the police," no "Get the hell out of my backyard." He was hunting me. I didn't know who "he" was, but it sure as hell wasn't a real estate agent hosting a midnight open house. I tightened the grip on my rock. A few seconds later, the footsteps subsided. I couldn't honestly tell if the guy had found me and was standing inches away from the hedge, waiting to shoot me, or if he'd left to search another section of the garden. Either way, I needed to see where I was and I needed to get out. I waited two more minutes, barely breathing and ears perked for the slightest snap of a twig. Nothing.

The prolonged quiet bolstered my courage. I edged my head around the side of the hedge and scanned the area. Other than the huge dark ferns, I couldn't see a thing, and a brief pause revealed no movement whatsoever in the bushes. Turning my attention to the wall, I looked west for a means of escape. No cooperative trees or rocks stood along this stretch of wall, so I retracted my head, and as slowly as possible to conceal my presence, shifted to the other side of the hedge for a look. My heart jumped. Not ten feet away, a rock fountain installation abutted the wall. I paused to listen. Again, nothing. I crept from behind the shrub and hurled my rock house-ward. The stone cracked against a window, and as if choreographed, I heard my adversary sprint. I darted for the fountain, the porous lava rocks provided excellent handholds, and reaching the top, I swung over and dropped blindly into the chaparral.

After a few minutes of bush-dodging, I chanced upon a shallow gully that was out of earshot and eyeshot of the house. I switched on the walkie-talkie.

"Tell me you're there?" I asked of the ether.

"Yeah. What happened? I heard a crack."

"Just go back to the car. Now. As quickly and quietly as possible, and keep your eyes open. There's someone else on the property."

"What? I—"

"Go!" I spun the dial and took off.

Minutes later we were careening down Latigo like a bat out of hell.

"What the hell happened?" he asked.

"There was someone in the house."

"Someone, as in, the owner?"

"No way. The owner would have flipped on all the lights when he saw me and called the police. This guy slipped out a side door in the dark and began hunting me."

"Jesus. You think he was after the diamond too?"

"Why else would he be there?" I asked.

"How should I know? This whole thing was your brilliant idea."

I grunted.

"How did you esc—oh, before I forget, where are my keys?"

"Umm," I stammered.

"Umm what? Where are my keys?"

"They got lost in the bushes when you tossed them up to me."

"Lost? You lost my frickin' keys? Now how the hell am I going to get them back?"

"We'll get them tomorrow."

"Tomorrow? Another midnight visit with a psychopath? No thank you. And what if we're caught trespassing by some celebrity Malibu neighborhood watcher? Lovely. I always wanted to be raped in prison."

"You're not going to prison. We can pick them up at the open house tomorrow."

"Open what?"

"Open house. Look at the flyer." I stabbed a finger at the crumpled page. "They're having an open house tomorrow. It's Sunday. We can go look at the house, and while I'm talking with the real estate agent, you can go bushwhacking in the backyard for your keys."

It was Steven's turn to grunt.

"Look—all I know is there's something to this whole Florentine

Diamond thing, and we're going to find out what it is." Steven opened his mouth to say something, but I cut him off. "Just trust me."

Chapter 9

AFTER A HEARTY SUNDAY BRUNCH at the Malibu Denny's, Steven and I paid our second visit to Chateau Richard. This time Steven drove, using a spare key. Obsessed with engine specs, fuel injection kits, and ram-air intake valves, Steven was the engineer's engineer. Our drive up the coast included a series of obligatory roller-coaster take-offs, screeching stops, and a fishtail turn onto Latigo, accompanied by lively speculation about the prowler and Steven's current wish list of potential engine upgrades. This time we parked inside the open gate.

Steven reached for his door handle, then diverted his hand into his pocket. "Almost forgot! This one's for you." He held out an inch-long flashlight like the one we'd used in last night's reconnaissance.

"How come? Thanks man!"

"No problem. Consider it this and next year's birthday gifts."

I laughed. "Okay. Back to business," I said, adding the miniature flashlight to my own key ring.

"According to the flyer, the place has three bedrooms, two stories, and three thousand square feet. All for a bargain two-point-seven million."

"I can believe it. Hillary'd love a place like this. But then her parents would want to move in with us. So I guess I'll have to pass."

I rang the doorbell. About a minute later, a twentyish woman opened the door. She was on her cell.

"Hold on a sec."

She was chomping on gum.

I whispered to Steven, "The real estate agent must have her daughter babysitting the open house." Steven nodded. A few minutes later, Ms. Bubblegum returned, still on the phone.

"Hi guys, feel free to take a look around. Do me a favor and sign in." She tapped annoyingly on an empty guest book with a three-quarter-inch-long green fingernail.

Steven made a beeline for the backyard. I started on a self-guided tour. Ms. Juicy Fruit continued her conversation.

I looked around. The fifties-era house had been completely overhauled by someone with lots of money and nineteenth-century inclinations; the interior looked more like a British manor than a chic Malibu crib. I found the entryway particularly impressive—an inlaid marble mosaic covered its floor while the walls were adorned with rich cherry wood paneling and capped in crown molding. The three bedrooms were equally impressive, each one with a unique shape—one hexagonal, another with a curved ceiling, another with its own loft—and each had its own fireplace and exposed wood-beam ceilings. On a lark, I sauntered into the glorious master bathroom, looked over my shoulder—twice—and popped the top off the toilet tank expecting to find the Florentine wrapped in plastic next to the Ty-D-Bol chlorine tablet. No such luck.

Completing my circuit, I arrived in the kitchen. An otherwise peaceful view of the backyard was marred by a large spider-crack in the picture window above the sink, no doubt the fruit of my excellent midnight shot put. I shifted my gaze away guiltily. "What's the asking price?" I asked the masticator.

She shot me a condescending look that said, "You're way too young and too poor to afford this place," then picked up a flyer and read: "Two-point-seven million."

"Thanks. Anyone living here now?"

"No." She shot a quizzical look at me. "Why do you ask?"

"I was just wondering if I could move in immediately," I lied.

"Oh, no problem. It's totally empty and move-in ready. The family finished clearing the place out weeks ago." So much for the family member-acting-as-caretaker theory. That someone from last night was hunting for the diamond.

"Thanks. I'm going to look around some more."

She didn't seem to mind, and by the time I'd turned my head, was dialing another number. Walking down the hall, I noticed an obscure door on the left of the main entry hall just outside the kitchen. I wouldn't call it a secret door, but it was obviously designed to be inconspicuous, matching the rest of the cherry paneling and sans a doorknob. In lieu of the knob, it offered a flat brass ring-pull, set flush into the wood and matching in color. I dug my teeth-trimmed fingernail beneath it and after three attempts, succeeded in prying the ring from its hollow in the wall. The door opened with a bit of resistance and then a click. Behind it, a surprisingly rickety-looking stairway descended into what must have been a wine cellar. Excited by the prospect of another diamond nook, I flicked on the light switch just behind the door and started down the staircase.

"Excuse me."

I descended a few more steps, hoping the interjection wasn't for me.

"Excuse me. Please don't go down there," the babysitter reiterated.

I turned around. "I'm sorry?"

"The staircase isn't safe. A few weeks ago, a fat guy put his foot right through a step during an open house."

"I'd really like to see the cellar if I'm going to consider buying the place."

"It's scheduled to be fixed in about three weeks. If you'd like to see it before then, there's a 3-D tour on the Internet."

"Okay. Thanks. I'll just look around the backyard then."

I wound my way to the three-level great room in the back and stepped out the side door—the one with the deadbolt—and into the backyard. The garden was even more beautiful bathed in sunlight, and reminded me of a domesticated tropical jungle.

Steven crunched up the pebble-covered path, his wiry brown hair disheveled and strewn with leaves. He had a sarcastic "nice job" look on his face.

"You didn't find them?"

"I did, but it required some serious hedge diving."

"It shows." I paused. "Well, I didn't find any diamonds. But she wouldn't let me look in the cellar." I filled him in on the details.

"So we're done, right?"

"No way. Aren't you curious?" I prodded.

Steven gazed at his reflection in my glasses and brushed a few dry leaves from his hair. "Sure, but what're we going to do? Buy the house for a few mil and x-ray the walls?"

"Why not?" I grinned back. Steven stared, dumbfounded.

"In college you were just foolish, now you're rich and foolish—rich plus foolish equals dangerous. Need I remind you again of Boelter?"

"This isn't even in the same league, and admit it, you were just as into it as I was."

Steven pretended to ignore me.

"You're going to buy this house for a crazy treasure hunt?" he reiterated. "What if you're wrong? Hey, what's a few million dollars anyway, right?"

"You know I've been looking for a second place, and this one is amazing. Plus, I'm not necessarily going to buy it. I'm just going to make an offer."

Steven grimaced. "And then what?"

"Listen," I pulled closer, "the diamond's got to still be up for grabs, or that prowler wouldn't have been skulking around. I can put down an offer. If they accept, I'll have an inspector come in and check the place out."

"And?"

"And that's where you come in," I winked, "Inspector."

"Are you crazy? You've definitely lost it."

I ignored him. "You'll have access to the whole house: the basement, the attic, everything. If you don't find anything interesting, we cancel the sale. Worst case, I lose a deposit, or if we find something, I'll end up with a new house." I'd almost convinced myself.

"Isn't it illegal to hire a fake inspector?"

"I don't think so. It might not be smart, but I don't think it's illegal."

"But the girl will recognize me." He was trying hard.

"She's just the house-sitter. Once I make an offer, we'll deal with the agent. Nothing to worry about."

"How . . ." Before he could whip up any additional objections, I spun around and headed back into the house. It took a few minutes before I found Blondie blathering on the phone in the master bathroom.

"One sec." She cupped her hand over the phone and gave us a "yes?" look.

"I'm interested in making an offer. But if you're busy . . ." I raised my eyebrows inquiringly.

That did it. Fifteen minutes later, she had the listing agent on the phone and we were in business. We had an appointment set for nine a.m. Tuesday, just enough time to do a little research on recent home-sale prices.

Chapter 10

MONDAY PASSED WITHOUT INCIDENT and I had ample opportunity to plumb the Malibu market using the online Los Angeles-based real estate listing service. Three comparable homes had sold in the last six months on Latigo and Castro Peak, an adjacent road, between $2.4 and $2.6 million. Richard's was priced high and the market was still soft, so I figured I had some serious leeway.

I arrived a few minutes before nine and parked right outside Richard's main gate. Just as I engaged my parking brake, my smartphone vibrated. I'd received a text. From Linda.

LindaR: Been climbing recently, cowboy?

A transplant from Montana, Linda had her own hybrid Midwest-LA dialect.

Alex: Heading to Echo Cliffs in an hour. Can u make it?

LindaR: No can do. Working. Potter txted me about the Ojai cave next month. I'm totally in.

Alex: Oh cool! Gonna play hooky, huh?

LindaR: Nah. $$ dried up. No more OT for ER nurses.

Alex: All right, gotta go. Real estate agent's here.

A middle-aged woman in a gleaming silver Jaguar had pulled up next to my car. Regina Flowers, no doubt. From the looks of her wheels, business had obviously been good.

LindaR: What?!? U buying a house?

46

Alex: :) It's a long story. g2g.

LindaR: Catch ya later cowboy.

"Hello," said Regina Flowers, an annoyed look on her face. "Can I help you?"

"I think so. You're the broker, right? I'm Alex Fife."

Regina did a double take.

"Oh . . ." she stammered. "Alex . . . It's nice to finally meet you!" An irritating toothy grin beamed from a mouth wider than Julia Roberts's.

"Nice to meet you," I said, shaking her hand.

"Sorry about that—to be honest, I didn't expect you to be quite so young."

"Yeah, it's a little unusual, I guess. But don't worry, I'm serious about buying."

We stepped inside and after a half-hour of small talk and form-filling on a folding table, I submitted my offer of $2.45 million. The Julia Roberts smile withered. Apparently my offer didn't meet her Jaguar-class expectations.

"I'll give you a ring as soon as the seller's had a chance to review your offer."

"Thanks." And that was that.

After hunting fruitlessly for a Subway, I picked up a hideously expensive free-range chicken sub (on sprouted wheat) from a chichi sandwich joint on PCH, then worked my way up the curvy mountain roads to Echo Cliffs. For me, climbing was exercise, social mixer, and stress reducer all rolled into one. Now in my seventh year of the sport, I'd become so familiar with the local rock—its curves, pockets and projections—that I could zone out and climb in a practically trance-like state. Some of my friends had gym memberships and others had yoga—I had the rock. And Potter and Linda were my partners in crime.

At seven, after a full day tackling an overhanging climbing route called "Crash and Burn" with Potter's buddy Jamie and a few of his out-of-town friends, I headed over to Steven and Hillary's place, a bottle of muscat dessert wine and a hamburger squeezy-toy rolling around on my passenger seat.

Hillary greeted me with a warm hug, then stepped aside and motioned me in. Instantly, Pippin, their beagle pup, scampered over and sat in front of me. The dog had a sixth sense about squeezy-toys. Or maybe it was the fact that I brought one every time I visited. Pippin seized the orange plastic burger from my outstretched hand and took off.

"Are you losing weight?" I asked, closing the door. Attired in a yellow tank top covered in sunflowers and a matching yellow sundress, Hillary looked unusually svelte.

"You can tell?" She beamed. "I'm eating vegan every other day."

"The pork-and-vegan diet." I nodded approvingly. "I like it."

I glanced around.

"Where's what's-his-name?"

"Still in the shower."

I handed her the bottle and stepped in close. "Whaddya say you and I run off and leave Steven with his rockets?" I shot my eyes left and right in a conspiratorial display.

Hillary tossed her shoulder-length brown hair back seductively, then said in a deadpan voice, "I don't think so."

"Brutal." I shook my head. "So what's the latest?"

"Oh, you'll see soon enough." She rolled her eyes.

A few minutes later, Steven made his entrance.

"You look like a postman," I quipped. Steven was dressed in a beige button-up shirt and a pair of matching shorts, not unlike a UPS deliveryman.

"I'm a home inspector, foolish flunky. I found them at the Goodwill store. Not bad for twenty bucks, right? Of course, I expect my cut of the treasure to be increased quadratically."

I nodded vigorously. "Of course."

"Of course, every inspector needs props." He held out a clipboard with a stack of official-looking forms. I flipped through them.

"Where'd you get these?" They looked like official home inspection forms to me.

"I scanned in a copy of my parents' home inspection report and cleaned it up in Photoshop. It's five years old, but it'll pass. And . . ."

"There's more?"

He pulled out his wallet and handed me a business card.

"Unbelievable."

"I can't take credit for these. Hillary's the artistic one." She curtsied, as if on cue.

"Where did you find her, Steven? Hill, got any sisters?"

Hillary gave my shoulder a squeeze and beamed with pride. Five years ago, she'd stumbled on the two of us in the Boelter basement mid-excavation, and after a grueling Q&A session, threatened to spill the beans if we didn't add her to the roster. Steven fell in love instantly and three weeks later, the two were engaged.

"So when's the inspection?" asked Steven.

"Don't get your shorts bunched up just yet. I still haven't heard from the agent." I continued, "Hill, I was fearing you'd put the kibosh on my little adventure."

"We're both skeptical," she replied, "but you're the one putting up the venture capital, so what the hell."

What a woman.

"Do you really think you'll find the diamond?" she said.

"I'm hoping we'll have a better idea once your hubby canvasses the place."

After dinner, we moved to the family room for some muscat and tug-of-war with Pippin. Mid-tug, my cell phone vibrated.

"One sec Pip." I dropped the rope.

"Hello." It was Regina. Pippin had a different idea and began playing tug-of-war with my shorts.

"Hi Regina."

"Alex, I think you're going to be very happy. The seller's reduced his price by one hundred thousand. He's countering for two-point-six million, I faxed the counter-offer to the number you gave me."

I cupped my hands over the phone. "They're countering for two-point-six." Then I went back to Regina. "Thanks Regina. Let me think about it and call you back tomorrow morning."

"No problem Alex."

Steven and Hillary gave me a "So?" look.

"It's a fair price." I faux-stroked my chin. "I think I'll accept."

"So what's the game plan?" inquired Hillary.

"Steven's going to case every inch of that house for diamond nooks—the attic, closets, and especially that basement. Who knows, maybe you'll find a hidden safe." I gave him the "you never know" look. "If we don't find anything interesting, Mr. Inspector, we go with the termite-eaten-stairs excuse and I withdraw the offer. If you find something, I buy a new house and hire a safecracker."

"You're really going to buy if he finds something? What if it turns out you buy, and there's nothing in this hypothetical safe of yours?"

"Then I've got a beautiful new house. But this isn't about the money—that diamond isn't going to make any difference to my finances. Neither will the house. This is about adventure." *About breaking out of the damn rut I'm in.*

Hillary looked skeptically at Steven, who shrugged, a Machiavellian grin on his face.

She said, "All I know is, this time I'm not bailing either of you out of jail."

That night I had trouble sleeping. Whether it was the heat, anticipation of buying a new home, finding a lost treasure, or conning Regina into a fake inspection, I didn't know, but I woke at 4:45 a.m. and tossed for two hours.

By 7:45, I couldn't wait any longer, so I called Regina and told her I'd like to accept the counteroffer. Later that morning, I stopped by her Coldwell Banker office to sign the offer paperwork and drop off the deposit.

"Regina, I'd like to have someone inspect the house as soon as possible. I'm currently considering purchasing another home and if there are any problems with this one, I'd like to move quickly on the other."

"That shouldn't be a problem."

"I'm concerned about the basement stairway." And then my out: "I hope that's not termite damage. That would be a deal-breaker for me."

"Alex, it's nothing. The seller has offered to fix it before the close of escrow. But if it doesn't work out, do you need an agent to help with the other house?"

Sleazy agent. "No, I'm covered."

"So when would you like to have the inspection?"

"If possible, tomorrow?"

"Let me check my iPhone. . . . No problem. I can be there any time between eight and noon."

"It's a deal. I'll call the inspector and see you at eight."

Chapter 11

Richard Lister's House—Malibu, CA
Five months earlier

"DID YOU FIND ANYTHING ON THE COMPUTER?" the brawny Russian asked.

"*Niet*. None of the forensics tools found a thing."

"*Der'mo!* Where the fuck did you hide it, Richard?" The big Russian grabbed Lister by the collar, jerked him forward, and then slammed him hard into the chair.

Lister stared stoically up at the two men from his kitchen table. "I told you, I have no idea what you're talking about," he responded calmly. "I deal in antiquities."

"That's bullshit," said the first man. "That's not what Viktor had to say."

"Viktor?" A tiny bead of sweat coalesced on Lister's forehead, just below the hairline.

"Viktor would be so disappointed, Richard. He certainly remembers you, or rather your alter ego, Arkady. At least after we helped refresh his memory." A pause. "And we know you've been trying to sell it, Richard. So don't bullshit us."

"Florentine? Is that what you called it?" asked Lister. He ruminated momentarily. "I haven't purchased any Italian artifacts in years."

The second man stepped in to slap Lister, but had his hand arrested.

"*Niet*. Not yet," admonished the first.

"No more bullshit, Richard. We need you to return the Florentine and tell us who else knows about it."

"Listen, I wish I knew what you were talking about. But I don't." Lister hesitated, a nauseous feeling overtaking him. He steeled himself. "Who do you work for? Yuri? You work for Yuri, don't you?" He shook his head. "Tell Yuri that I don't have this Florentine thing he's looking for. And tell him . . . tell him that next time he wants to accuse me of stealing his antiquities, he should be man enough to do so himself. This is an insult."

Lister tried to stand up. The burly man instantly stopped him.

"I'm going to ask you nicely once more," said the man. "Where is the Florentine?"

Lister shook his head. "I told you, I don't know what you're talking about. But look, whatever Yuri's paying you, I'll double it. Two year's worth of salary to forget you found me." He hesitated as a wave of nausea passed. "Just tell Yuri you didn't find me. I don't have this Florentine thing anyway."

"You're a poor bull-shitter, Richard," said the first. Then, to the other man, he said, "Get the tools."

The second man nodded and left the kitchen.

"Why don't you just give us what we want and avoid the pain and suffering?" said the man.

Avoid the suffering. Right. You're going to kill me either way, you fucking Slav bastard. Lister's mind raced. If he could just get to his gun he might have a chance.

"Okay, okay, I'll give it to you."

The man shot a distrustful look at Lister.

Lister pointed upstairs, noticing for the first time a painful tightness in his right arm. He winced.

"It's in a floor safe in my bedroom," he continued through the discomfort, "I'll go get it."

The man looked at him warily, then took a step back, retrieving a steel-gray automatic pistol from inside his jacket. Lister rose unsteadily to his feet, and, receiving a nod from the man, began walking down the hall and up the stairs, stopping every few steps to catch his breath.

What's wrong with me? he wondered through increasing brain fog. *Something is not right.*

Lister eased his master bedroom door open and plodded over to his bedside table. Placing one hand on the nightstand and the other on the bed, he lowered unsteadily to his knees. The shotgun was just inches from his knee, under the bed.

"Nothing funny," said the man from the doorway.

It was now or never. Lister tried to thrust his hand toward the gun, but his arm refused to obey as a seizing pain gripped his chest. And with a sudden, final certitude he knew his life was over.

Richard Lister slumped backward to the floor, dead.

Chapter 12

Latigo Canyon House—Malibu, CA
Present Day

REGINA WAS LOST IN A COPY OF *MODERN BRIDE* and drinking a soy latte in her Jag when I arrived. Steven was nowhere to be seen. It was 8:05 a.m. So much for the punctual engineer.

"Getting married?"

"Oh," she said, startled. "Hi Alex. No, my daughter's getting married next spring. I'm playing wedding coordinator."

Ms. Bubblegum! "Was that nice girl watching the house the other day your daughter?"

"That's her."

"That's one lucky guy." I nearly choked on my own sarcasm.

"Yes, he is lucky. So when are you expecting the inspector?" she raised her hand and eyed her long nails with just a hint, ever so slight, of annoyance.

"It won't be long," I prognosticated, and just a few seconds later I heard a truck pushing up the driveway. Upon Steven's arrival, Regina threw the *Modern Bride* on the passenger seat, emerged from the Jag, and proceeded to unlock the front door.

Steven burst from the pickup with the overzealousness of a second-rate actor who'd just landed his first role at a Renaissance fair. Clad in his brown UPS ensemble, a handyman utility belt, and a hideous fake moustache, it took my entire self-control to prevent a fit of hysterical laughter. Steven bounced up to Regina, issued a cheery "Good morning ma'am," and extended a business card. "I'm Steven Crouch of Crouch Home Inspections."

"Good morning," Regina replied and carelessly shoved the business card into her purse.

She pushed the front door open, and turning her back on the

two of us, walked into the house. "Mr. Crouch, please feel free to start as soon as possible. I hope you don't mind, but I've been asked by the seller to oversee the inspection." She didn't sound too enthusiastic.

"That shouldn't be a problem ma'am." I gave Steven a finger-slashing-the-throat gesture and shook my head. Steven responded with a dismissive wave of the hand, and followed Regina in.

"Ma'am, I have a few questions. Does this house have a basement or an attic?"

"Both."

Steven scratched a few marks on his form. "Thanks. Can you please show me where I can access the attic?"

"I have no idea."

"No problem ma'am. How about the basement."

"That's over here." She walked over to the recessed door and pointed. "But you won't be able to go down there. There's some temporary damage to the stairs and it's too dangerous."

"Thanks ma'am, it shouldn't be a problem. I'm insured."

She seemed unconvinced.

"Does the house have any hidden features that I should know about?"

"Hidden features?" she asked, baffled.

"A panic room, wall safes, secret passages—these all need to be inspected."

"No. I'm not aware of any secret passages," she rolled her eyes, "or panic rooms in the house."

"Or wall safes?"

I gave Steven a dirty look.

"Or wall safes. No wall safes. The seller would have disclosed it."

Steven then proceeded to the bathroom off the entry hall with the two of us in tow. Upon arriving, Regina leaned against the wall and pulled out an emery board.

Steven advanced to the toilet. "These models are sometimes problematic," he offered authoritatively to no one in particular, and removed the top of the tank.

With his face just inches above the open tank, Steven began a

series of flushes. After each flush, Steven placed a tick on his inspection form, for what purpose, I had no idea.

"Ma'am, does the house have a septic system or a sewer line?"

"It's a septic system. The tank was replaced two years ago."

Steven placed his ear against the tank and listened, motionless, for
what seemed like two minutes, before Regina interrupted: "I'm sorry,
what exactly are you doing?"

"Trying to detect septic gas leaks, ma'am. This shouldn't take more
than ten or fifteen more minutes."

Regina issued an audible sigh and finally, exhausted of her patience,
abandoned the room after seven farcical minutes of intimacy between
Steven and the toilet tank. "I'll be out in my car. I have some calls to
make."

"Happy?" asked Steven, a huge grin radiating from beneath his
bristly brown moustache.

"Very. Let's get down to business."

Steven stepped out of the bathroom and after surreptitiously
checking for Regina, gave me a nod.

Less than a minute later, we'd slipped through the basement door
and flicked on the overhead light. The narrow stairwell led down
about twenty feet, surrounded on either side by cinderblocks covered
in chipped, graying paint. Two-thirds of the way down, the stairs' oak
planks became noticeably brittle and discolored, undoubtedly the
consequence of a prior basement flood. Here, two stairs had caved in,
exposing a crisscross of spider webs anchored between the stairway's
structural beams.

"Give me your hand," requested Steven. I obliged, and he gingerly
placed a foot onto the plank below the cavity. "It feels sturdy enough."

Once safely on the lower stairs, Steven stabilized me and I duplicated
his descent. A quick scan of the void beneath the stairs revealed little
reason for excitement in our diamond hunt, so we descended the last
few steps to the limestone cellar floor. A humid mustiness greeted us.

Upon the right wall at the base, we found another light switch,
which Steven toggled several times to no effect. It was difficult, therefore, to gauge the extent of the cellar, for the single bulb of our narrow
corridor illuminated only a small circlet of limestone at the top of the

stairs. Steven pulled a flashlight from his utility belt and, turning the corner, panned the light around the room. He handed me a second, smaller flashlight.

"Not much to get excited about," I commented. With the exception of a row of built-in, riveted-steel shelves along the wall farthest from the stairwell, the room was entirely empty and surrounded by the same dingy cinderblocks—not much opportunity to hide a safe or a secret room. I walked the circumference of the room and, playing Sherlock Holmes, tapped each of the walls with my fist, hoping to find a secret door or perhaps a façade covering a safe. I avoided looking back at Steven, fearing the look he was probably giving me right now, and not for the first time, I was beginning to doubt the perspicacity of my treasure hunt. But, being a kid at heart, I quickly banished the idea and continued my sonar.

"Do me a favor and check the floor stones too," I suggested.

The remainder of my inquiry yielded no fruit, so I walked over to Steven who was hunched over, minutely investigating a pair of grubby stones next to the shelves.

"Got something?" I asked hopefully.

"There's a fossil clamshell embedded in the limestone over in the corner."

"Wonderful."

"And this stone is definitely loose. And there's no grouting around it."

"Can you move it?" I asked.

"I'll need a screwdriver. I don't think I can lift it with my . . ." Steven dug his fingernails between the two stones and grunted, "fingers."

"Don't you have a screwdriver in your Batman belt?" I asked.

"Dammit Jim, I'm a home inspector, not a handyman."

"All right, McCoy—"

"Excuse me."

I turned in horror.

"Excuse me," repeated the stern voice above us.

Steven walked to the base of the stairs. Regina was standing at the top of the stairway, bathed in the harsh glare of the hanging bulb.

"Yes ma'am?"

"Is Mr. Fife down there with you?"

I turned the corner. "Hi, Regina. I was just watching Mr. Crouch inspect the basement."

"I'm very sorry, but I told you—you can't be down here. The seller doesn't want any injuries and the last thing he needs is a lawsuit."

"I'm sorry. I'll be right up."

"Turn on your walkie-talkie. I'll call you if I find anything," said Steven in a low voice.

With Steven's aid, I bypassed the chasm and joined Regina at the top of the stairs.

"I'll be up in just a minute, ma'am. I need to finish documenting the damage down here."

Regina frowned. "Like I said, Alex, the seller will be patching up the staircase before the sale. It's nothing to worry about."

"I know," I said. "I just wanted to see the space once more before I make my decision."

"I understand. Sorry for the trouble."

"It's okay. I think I'll take another look at the backyard."

"Be my guest."

Without another word, I proceeded out the back door and flipped on the walkie-talkie.

Chapter 13

FOLLOWING THE GRAVEL PATH to the rear-left side of the property, I found a small, hand-built wooden shed set amongst a thicket of bamboo. An imposing padlock prevented entry. Gardening supplies, probably. But it could be an unassuming place to hide a small safe too. I lowered onto my haunches to peer through a knot about a foot from the gravel.

"Breaker breaker," squawked the speaker. Startled, I jerked, nearly toppling backward. I steadied myself then pulled the walkie-talkie from my pocket.

"You find something?"

"Maybe. I need a little help. I plotted the dimensions of all the second-story rooms on my graph paper." Chirp. "Now I'm in the attic, and I'm having difficulty figuring out what's where. These rooms are so oddly shaped, it's not easy."

"So what do you need me to do?" I asked, my stomach tensing in anticipation.

"Walk through the rooms and tell me which ones have recessed lighting. I can see the backsides of the fixtures popping up through the insulation, so once you tell me how many lights are in each room, I should be able to reconcile."

"I'll be right there."

Regina, lost in her magazine, ignored me as I passed through the kitchen.

"I think I'll take a look at the upstairs rooms again. I really like the master," I said nonchalantly. Regina looked up, delivered a wide, toothy smile, nodded, and then returned to her matrimonial planning.

Steven had placed a ladder in the middle of the second floor hallway, just beneath the hatch to the attic.

"Where'd you get the ladder?" I voiced into the walkie-talkie.

"Just what kind of business do you think Crouch Home Inspections is? A *full* service operation. I brought it in the truck."

"Impressive." I lowered the volume and continued. "Okay. I'm here. What next?"

"I'm standing right next to the light fixture about twenty feet west of the hatch. Do me a favor and figure out what room it's in."

"One sec." I walked down the hall and looked into each of the two smaller bedrooms.

"The hexagonal bedroom has a ceiling fan with lights. There's nothing in the other room."

"Turn it on for a sec."

I yanked the fan's chain and it began to whir.

"Yeah, that's it. One second," squawked the walkie-talkie. "Okay. From here, about thirty feet north of the fixture is a group of, let's see, nine, ten, eleven—eleven recessed lights. See if you can find which room they're in."

"I think that's near the back of the house."

I proceeded downstairs and into the tri-level den. Scanning the room, I saw eight large bulbs sunk into the ceiling. Fearing that Regina would hear our exchange, I stepped into the hallway bathroom and eased the door shut.

"There're eight big recessed lights in the den, and the ones closest to the backyard are about six feet from the back wall."

"Hmmm. That's strange," said Steven.

"What?"

"You're sure there are only eight bulbs?"

"I'm sure. Just the eight."

"So where are the other three? I'm looking at one parallel group of three and two groups of four sticking out of the insulation."

"Maybe the other three lights are in an adjoining room? Isn't the master bedroom on the other side of the living room wall?"

"I'm a little confused about this part of the floor plan," he admitted.

"I'll go check the master. Give me a second." I slipped out of the powder room and back upstairs to the master bedroom.

"No recessed lighting here either," I squawked into the mic. "Wait a second."

I noticed that the master had a sliding closet door against the library wall. I slid the dark-stained maple door open. Hanging from the ceiling was a lone, 50-watt bulb.

"Nope. There's a single bulb hanging in the closet, but no recessed ones."

"That doesn't do me any good. I can't tell where the hanging bulbs are. The wiring is covered by insulation. Give me a minute and I'll come down and take a look."

Steven descended the ladder, tool-belt jangling, and gave both the living room and the master bedroom a thorough examination.

"Well, those are definitely the right lights. Same layout and everything. You see the bulb closest to the bookshelves?" He pointed to the leftmost of the eight recessed lights.

"Yeah."

"That bulb is about five feet away from our three mystery bulbs. So if I had to guess, the other three are in between the master and the bookshelf."

The thought electrified me. "You think there's a passage between the two rooms?"

"Either that, or when they added the bookcases, they cut some corners and left the old lighting intact to save money."

"Excuse me, Mr. Crouch."

I nearly jumped at Regina's voice.

"When do you think you'll be finished? It's already been an hour and a half."

"Just being thorough ma'am. I shouldn't be more than another twenty minutes. So far, so good."

"Oh . . . oh, good." Regina gave her best Roberts smile and returned to the kitchen.

Looking over my shoulder, I whispered, "Why don't you go back up and see if you can't poke a hole through the ceiling and see what's under those mystery lights."

Steven grinned widely and, turning his back to the kitchen, pulled out a tiny monogrammed Swiss Army knife. "I'll be right back."

Five minutes later, he took a seat on the bottom stair and finished filling out his forms; if he'd found something, he wasn't showing it.

"Well?" I questioned, looking over my shoulder.

"Well what?"

"Tell me."

"Excuse me sir, I can't divulge the results of my inspection until I finish writing my report."

I peered again over my shoulder. Regina was walking over.

"All done Mr. Crouch?"

"Yes ma'am. The home looks just fine with the exception of the water damage in the basement."

"That'll be fixed by the seller."

"The entire stairwell or just the two broken steps?" I asked. "The entire base of the stairwell needs to be fixed. It's rotten to the foundation. I'd like that in writing."

"I'll talk to the seller and get back to you, Alex."

Steven signed and handed a copy of his forms to me. "Here you are sir. The only problem I found was with the staircase, as you pointed out. Everything else is in good condition."

"Thank you, Mr. Crouch," I said, shaking his hand.

"No problem, sir. That'll be $550.00 even. You can make that out to Crouch Home Inspections." He started upstairs. "Excuse me, I need to retrieve my ladder."

Chapter 14

My six calls to Steven's cell phone during the drive into Santa Monica went directly to voicemail. I wasn't sure if he'd forgotten to turn on his mobile or was just torturing me. Thirty minutes later, we were sitting at Norm's ordering lunch from an eighty-year-old waitress in a muumuu and hairnet.

"Out with it," I said.

Steven took a faux-furtive look around and leaned in. "There's a secret hallway between the bookshelves and the closet."

"I knew it! What could you see?"

"Not much. The hall runs parallel to the bookshelves and stops at what I'm guessing are a set of stairs. I couldn't really see down that far. At the other end of the hall—behind the leftmost bookshelf—there was some type of door. Maybe one of the bookshelves slides out of the way. Even if we can't open it, we can always drop through the ceiling."

I could feel my heart palpitating.

"Oh, and I couldn't remove the floor stone from the basement."

"I totally forgot about that," I admitted. "We can dig it up later. I think we've got ourselves a treasure hunt."

"So you're going to buy it?" he asked as our waitress arrived with the first three of his six plates.

"Are you kidding? There's no question."

"Fifty-fifty on any find, right?"

"Absolutely."

"Well in that case, how quickly can we get the keys?"

"Good question. I'll have to call Regina."

While Steven's final plates arrived, I punched in Regina's number on my cell and stepped outside next to a couple of newspaper vending machines on Colorado Boulevard. Regina picked up on the third ring.

"Hi Regina. Well, everything looks good."

"Of course. It's a great house!"

A homeless man walked up to the vending machine containing

one of the triple-X rags and started cursing at the spread-eagle-legged woman on the front page.

"Excuse me?" Regina prompted.

"Sorry, I'm standing outside a restaurant and it's a bit noisy. Regina, how soon can I get the keys?"

A pause. "Alex, usually we wait until after escrow before the buyer gets ownership of the house. So, it'll be a little under a month."

"Is there any way I can move in earlier? I'd like to move in as soon as possible."

"I'll have to talk with the estate trustee." She paused. "You see, there are legal liabilities with this type of thing."

"I'd appreciate it if you could chat with them. I'd be happy to pay rent if that helps. I really need to vacate my current house."

"I'll call them and get back to you."

"I'd appreciate it."

A minute later I sat back down in the booth. My food still hadn't arrived. I scanned the room for the waitress.

"I just asked her—it'll be here in a minute," Steven said. "So?"

"She's going to check with the seller. I'm betting we can get the keys within a few days."

My pocket began to vibrate. I snatched the phone and clicked the talk button.

"Hi, Regina. What did the seller say?"

"Who's Regina?"

"Oh. Hey, Tom. Sorry about that. Regina's a real estate broker. I thought you were her."

"A broker? Are you buying a new place?"

"Something like that. I'll fill you in next time we hang. Anyway, what's up?"

"Dude—I just wanted to call and thank you for the tickets. That's unbelievable. How the hell did you score second-row Lakers season tickets?"

"I know a friend who knows a friend. I'm glad you like them."

"One sec, it's going to be a bit noisy. I just got home." I heard a garage door lowering in the background and a bunch of keys jangling.

"One minute," he continued, "let me unlock . . ." I heard the door open, then a pause. "Oh shit. What the fuck?"

"What happened?"

"Holy shit—our place has been totally ransacked." A pause. "Gennady?" he yelled. "Gennady?"

"Jesus. Are you okay?"

"I'm not sure. They might still be here. Alex, I'll call you back." The call cut out.

"Was that Tom Chien from your startup?" Steven waited a few seconds, then tapped me on the shoulder. "Alex—who was that?"

"Sorry." I focused back on Steven. "Yeah, it was Tom. Somebody broke into his house."

"Shit."

"Yeah. He lives a few miles from here. I'm going to head over. Do me a favor and pick up the tab for my food. I'll call you later."

I arrived at Tom and Gennady's place ten minutes later.

The house was in shambles. Every last cushion, pillow, and mattress had been slashed, their batting removed and strewn in cloud-like tufts. All the closets had been tossed as well. Everything—literally everything: clothes, suitcases, shoeboxes—had been removed, scoured, and tossed. Even the vacuum cleaner bag had been slashed and was hemorrhaging dust.

"You okay?" I asked Tom.

"Yeah, whoever broke in is long gone." He gazed down at his watch and sneered. "I'm just waiting for LA's finest to arrive."

"Did they take anything?"

"I don't know. . . . Not that I can tell."

"So then why—"

"I've got no idea. It's not like we have any expensive hardware here. No cash. No drugs." He shook his head, then said, "Gennady's going to blow a gasket."

"Sorry, man."

"It's okay. Nothing to do about it now." He sat down on the curb.

"Yeah. Well, hopefully they can lift some prints or something."

"I'm not holding my breath. Speaking of that, I need a smoke." He pulled a pack of cigarettes from his pocket, removed one, and shoved it into his mouth.

"Those are going to kill you."

"That's what Sheila always used to say." He lit the cigarette and took a puff. "Speaking of Sheila. What did she have to say?"

"Sheila?"

"The letter I gave you the other day—Sheila's letter from India."

I'd completely forgotten her letter given the exploits of the other night; in fact, I had no idea where I'd left it. It was probably still in my jeans.

"No idea. I haven't read it yet. Sorry."

"No problem. I was just curious." Tom took another drag, then stood up. "Here they are."

Chapter 15

FOUR HOURS LATER, I jumped in the shower, closed my eyes, and relaxed under a near scalding stream of water. I did some of my best thinking in the shower, and the events of the last few days had given me plenty to reflect upon. Somehow, deep inside, I knew the diamond was in Lister's house. And the challenge of finding it made me feel alive. More alive than I'd felt in years. I'd forgotten what it was like. The rush of the challenge. I craved the challenge. I decided then that no matter what happened, I'd see this through.

Toweling off, I noticed the LED on my smartphone blinking. I pulled up my voicemail app, tapped the top item on the list, and wedged the phone against my ear with my shoulder.

"Hi Alex. It's Regina Flowers. I've talked to the estate trustee and he's willing to let you move in early if you're willing to pay rent until escrow closes. The rent will be ten thousand per month, prorated of course, for the twenty-three days you have left in escrow." A pause. "Give me a ring and tell me what you want to do."

That was one problem solved. I tossed the phone onto my bed, and, after failing to find any clean pants in my closet, grabbed the comfy jeans I'd worn the other night from the top of the hamper. Which reminded me—I still hadn't read the letter from Sheila.

I fished around in my back-right pocket and came up empty; the left pocket wasn't much better, producing nothing but dried leaves. Overwhelmed by momentary obsession, I dug through my laundry pile and then bounded downstairs to excavate the strata of receipts, wrappers, loose change, and paper napkins in the crevice next to my car seat.

No letter.

I knew I'd had it when I'd left Tom's place the other night; I'd stuffed it in my pocket, and the pants had been sitting in the hamper ever since our trek to Lister's house. In fact, they still prickled with thorns from the chaparral.

I plucked out a burr and stared at it. The moment of reflection fundamentally disturbed me. I'd lost the letter in Richard Lister's backyard, and that man had found it.

He'd come after me—he thought I had the Florentine.

Fuck.

I picked up my phone and dialed. Steven answered on the first ring.

"Dude, I know who broke into Tom and Gennady's place."

"What? How?"

"The night we went out to Richard Lister's house, I lost a letter in his yard."

"I'm not following—you lost a letter in his backyard?"

"Yeah. With Tom and Gennady's address on it."

"Why did you have a letter addressed to Tom and Gennady?"

"It was addressed to me, but had their street address on it."

"What? Why?"

"It doesn't matter. The point is, I stuffed that letter in my pants when I left their place, and I can't find it anymore, and the only place I could have lost it was in Richard Lister's yard. And a few days later, their house is sacked."

He hesitated. "You really think that guy found your letter and came after you?"

"If he thought I had the diamond. Or knew where it was. He might." I gritted my teeth. "Fuck!"

"And you're *sure* you lost it in the yard?"

"There's no other possibility." I looked up at the ceiling and considered. "Unless . . ."

"What?"

"I took a pretty big fall into the chaparral when I jumped the wall to escape. I could have lost it there, or in the gully behind the house."

"For both our sakes, let's hope that's what happened." He paused a few seconds. "Alex?"

"I'm thinking," I said. "Yeah, I guess I could have lost it there."

"Maybe we should just call the whole thing off."

"What good would that do?" I growled. "If the guy did find the letter, then he's after me whether or not I decide to stop the purchase. Fuck."

"You don't know that," he said. "The guy obviously didn't find anything in Tom and Gennady's place, so maybe he'll lay off, think it was a false lead."

"I hope you're right. Either way, I understand if you want out, but at this point it's too late for me. If the guy found the letter, I'm fucked whether or not we stop." I shook my head. "I'm seeing this through."

Steven was quiet for a good five seconds.

"What the hell." He sighed. "You're my best friend, and hell if I'm going to let you get yourself killed."

"Are you sure?"

"No. But that never stopped me before."

"Thanks man."

"Just don't say a word to Hillary," he said. "If she had any idea there was any danger at all, she'd kill us both. This guy would be the least of our worries."

"Oh lord. Here we go again," I said.

"Buckle up."

Chapter 16

I SPENT THE NEXT TWO DAYS holed up in my house, a borrowed pistol from Gennady in hand, peering through my master-bedroom shutters for any sign of a stalker. Both nights, Steven arrived at about eleven—how he managed to con Hillary into this I still don't know—and we took shifts sleeping and keeping watch. Thankfully, my paranoia was misplaced, and our only visitor was the mailman.

I'd arranged to meet Regina at ten a.m. that Sunday to do a walk-through and hand her the rent check. She arrived right on time, and by eleven, I had the keys. An hour later, Steven, Hillary, and I were fed, geared up, and ready for our campaign, Hillary none the wiser about our earlier madness.

Things were somehow looking up.

Steven donned his leather utility belt and a pair of heavy leather gardening gloves. His implements included two flashlights strapped to either side of his belt, a heavy-duty Leatherman knife, a twenty-foot coiled nylon string, a Craftsman hammer, a roll of duct tape, and a flathead screwdriver. Vintage Steven.

I had a crowbar, my climbing headlamp and, concealed within my pocket, Gennady's loaded Ruger pistol. Better safe than sorry.

"Let's search the basement first," I said, motioning to the inconspicuous door. Hillary, determined to document our hunt, began filming with her iPhone's video camera while I popped up the brass ring-pull and unlatched the basement door.

"Be careful as you go down," I said, pulling the chain to the light. "Dammit. The bulb's busted."

"Pretty spooky," commented Hillary.

"Easy, Velma," said Steven.

"Flashlights?" I prompted. I depressed the small button on my headlamp, and instantly, a narrow beam burst from its trio of LED bulbs. A squall of fine dust particles danced through the light as I descended the stairs to the basement level.

"To the left," I said, once we'd reached the bottom. "And against the back wall." Steven panned his light over. "Now down. There's our first dig site."

The limestone slab was exactly as we'd left it, with the imprint of Steven's knuckles still discernable in the thin layer of dust surrounding the stone.

"Holmes, stick your knife right here." I motioned to the edge of the dusty, two-by-two-foot gray tile. Steven handed his flashlight to Hillary and inserted his blade in the gap next to the tile. I followed suit with my crowbar, and with a coordinated heave, the edge of the stone rose a few centimeters above the other slabs. Steven insinuated his glove-clad fingers into the gap, raised the stone several inches, and then grabbed it squarely. As he lifted, bits of damp earth and mold filaments tumbled from the underside of the stone and onto a yellowing plastic bag the size of a legal notebook.

"Eureka!" I said.

"Any bets?" inquired Hillary while zooming in on our treasure.

"Five bucks it's full of savings bonds," replied Steven.

"You're on." I brushed a few clumps of dirt from the package and removed it from its plot. It was sealed with a curling strip of duct tape.

"Heavy. I'd say there're at least fifty pages in it." I carefully removed the tape, unfolded the flap, and extracted a paper-clipped wad of sheets.

"And the verdict is?" asked Hillary.

"It looks like a will," Steven offered, grabbing the pile from me and flipping through a few more pages. "Dated June of last year."

"Worth anything?" asked Hillary.

"Not unless you're named in it," said Steven. "So much for the bearer bonds."

"All right," I responded, slightly dejected. "We've still got plenty of exploring to do." Steven inserted the stack back into the bag and started for the stairwell.

"You brought the ladder, right?" I asked, once we'd reached the main level.

"*Yah vol, mein herr.*"

"You mules go do the heavy lifting," said Hillary. "By the time you're back, I'll have found the latch to the secret door." She pointed toward the library. "You said the door was up there, right?"

"That's our best guess."

The two of us took off for the ladder outside. A few minutes later, we rested it up against the wall by the attic trapdoor and rejoined Hillary in the library.

"Any luck, Hill?" asked Steven.

"I'm pretty sure there's no secret door here. I've pushed and tilted everything, but nothing gives."

I scanned the cabinetry. The built-in shelves were separated into four vertical sections, in total about fifteen feet wide and ten feet high, and made of an antique mahogany inlaid with teak vines. A newer, sliding mahogany ladder was set into a sunken guiderail along the floor.

"Have you tried looking on the top shelves, or on top of the bookcase?"

"That's where I started."

I climbed the ladder and, gripping the bookcase, slid myself back and forth along the rail, scanning the top of the cabinetry.

"Just dust and spider webs, right?"

"Yeah . . . wait." I slid the ladder to the leftmost bookshelf. "There's a footprint on this one. Did you walk up here?"

"Does it look like I could walk up there?" responded Hillary. Not likely, given that the top of the case was less than four feet from the ceiling.

"Well that's a bit of a mystery," I said. "Hmmm. Maybe I'm thinking too much like a tall person."

I crouched down to inspect the woodwork on the underside of each of the lower shelves, running my hands along each surface in search of buttons or other mechanical switches. Steven, similarly inspired, initiated an assault on the sconces flanking the shelves, twisting, pushing, and pulling each fixture.

"Wait a second!" he said.

I popped to my feet.

"I think," he grimaced as he twisted the leftmost fixture, "this might be it!"

The right sconce resisted a beat longer, then cracked and came off into his hand.

"Oops." He grinned sheepishly.

"That's coming out of your share," I said, shooting him a dirty look. "All right, let's try the attic before you destroy the place."

A few minutes later, the three of us had ascended Steven's ladder and were perched upon the attic rafters, flashlight beams crisscrossing across the pink fiberglass insulation.

"Where to, Inspector?" I asked, wiping perspiration from my forehead.

Flashlight in hand, Steven teetered from plank to plank through the oppressive heat before stopping at a section of fiberglass batting about twenty feet away.

"Here are the three missing recessed lights." He sidestepped right a few feet. "So the hole I made . . ." He squatted and dislodged a corner of the insulation. "Is right here."

We cautiously followed, and, reaching an adjacent set of planks, I stooped down to peer through his makeshift opening.

"It's a hidden hallway, all right," I said, withdrawing my flashlight. "I'm betting we can enlarge the hole pretty easily. Give me a hand."

With Hillary manning the cam and a flashlight, Steven and I began stripping the large wad of insulation from between the rafters. After a minute of tugging and a typhoon of noxious particles, we'd cleared the three-by-five-foot strip and exposed the underlying gray mineral-fiber ceiling board.

"What do you say I take out the whole quadrant?" Steven asked.

"It'd make it easier to get through," I agreed. "Go for it."

I rose to my feet and stood next to Hillary.

Steven popped the snap on his holster, withdrew his knife, thrust it into the exposed ceiling board, and began sawing along the beams. After several minutes of hacking, the board began to sag.

"Just a few more inches," he said, his knife still engaging the plaster-like interior of the board.

All of a sudden, the sheet cracked and fell toward the floor, ejecting a miasma of powder and filaments. Steven, his hand wrenched by the plummeting mass, lurched forward and down through the cloud. Before the horror could register, we heard a thud and a groan.

"Steven, are you okay?" Hillary screamed.

A languid, breathless, "I think" drifted through the dust.

Adrenalized, I grabbed hold of the beams on either side of the hole and lowered my body until I was dangling a few feet above the floor. Leaning forward through the thinning cloud, Hillary trained her light through the hole and onto Steven's body, allowing me to drop safely beside him.

In a miraculous and most likely accidental feat, Steven had landed flat on the ground, face up, his knife and tools sitting inches from his head. How he'd managed such a landing after falling headfirst, I had no idea. I crouched beside him.

"You okay?" I asked. He tried to sit up.

"I think so. I got," he paused, "the wind knocked out of me."

"Anything broken?"

He took a few seconds to consider, moved each of his body parts, and shook his head, still clearly dazed.

"Honey, we've got to get you out of there," Hillary stared down helplessly at me. "How are we going to get him out?"

"Give me a second." I swept the surrounding walls with my head-lamp.

"One sec. I think there's a light switch here." In fact, there were two switches, one of the common up-down style and the other a red button, both unmarked. I stepped around Steven to the end of the hall and flicked the up-down switch; instantly, three recessed lights along the hallway ceiling flickered to life and bathed the walkway in a harsh yellow light.

"Better. Steven, let's move you away from the bookcase wall."

Steven took my hand and stood up slowly, wobbled for a second, and then steadied himself against the wall opposite the bookshelves. A trickle of blood had slid down the side of his face and onto his t-shirt.

"Okay?" I asked.

He gave me slightly foggy all-clear eyebrows.

"All right guys, grab hold of the beams for a second. I think I found the button for the door." I paused. "Ready?"

Hillary grabbed a rafter and nodded. I pushed the button.

Chapter 17

Russian Safe House—Downtown Los Angeles
Present Day

"WHAT DID YOU FIND IN THE HOUSE?" asked the brawny man.

"*Nichego.*" Nothing.

"Shit! We're running in circles."

"Calm down. I think—"

"Calm down? If we don't clean this up before Internal Affairs finds out, we're dead. They'll make fucking borscht from our testicles. Don't tell me to fucking calm down." The brawny man hammered back a shot of vodka and carelessly wiped his chin on a hairy forearm.

"Listen, Sergej. Listen. I may have another lead."

"What lead?" Sergej slurred.

"After I finished searching the house, I did a background check on the name from the envelope—Alex Fife."

Sergej shook his head. "And?"

"This man is the former chief engineer at ViruTrax, the cyber-defense firm."

"A computer security expert?"

"*Da.* His SVR dossier is nearly two hundred pages long."

"Quite a coincidence." Sergej closed his eyes and tried to concentrate. "You think he's after the Florentine?"

"Why else would he be casing Lister's house?"

"How could he possibly know about it? Lister wouldn't sell to a white hat."

"I don't know. Perhaps someone in the underground tipped him off?"

"*Niet.* We'd be locked up in a Moscow interrogation facility right now if there were any mention of this in the hacker circles. But I can't see how else he would find out." He took a deep breath. "We need to interrogate him."

"Too messy. He's a wealthy man. That could attract unwanted attention, and we can't afford that until we've secured the Florentine."

Sergej stared at the ceiling in thought. "This is true. Perhaps it makes more sense to surveil him and see what he knows. Then we can decide how to proceed."

"That sounds more prudent."

"Either way, the moment we secure Lister's copy, if this man has any knowledge of the program, he will have to be liquidated."

Chapter 18

Latigo Canyon House—Malibu, CA
Present Day

WITH LITTLE MORE THAN A MECHANICAL WHISPER, the leftmost bookshelf sank straight down and into the floor. About ten seconds later, the top of the bookshelf, dust, footprint and all, sat flush with the library floor, allowing brilliant afternoon light to flood through the aperture.

"I guess there weren't midgets after all," Steven said weakly.

"I'll climb down the ladder and meet you in the kitchen," said Hillary anxiously.

I grabbed Steven by the arm and led him through the opening, down the stairs and into the kitchen. A moment later, Hillary had him sitting in a folding chair and was swabbing his forehead with a wet paper towel.

"Does it hurt?" she asked. Steven brought his hand to his head and prodded it gently.

"A little. I banged it against the wall going down."

Hillary fumbled through her purse and a moment later presented him with a wrapped chocolate truffle.

"I'm feeling better already."

I believed he was.

While Hillary tended to his wounds, I took a seat in a folding chair and picked up the pouch containing Richard's will.

"Okay, time for a bit of Richard Lister trivia." They both stared at me expectantly.

"Richard also included a life insurance policy in his packet. For five hundred dollars, how much did Richard insure himself for?"

"Half a million," guessed Hillary. I looked at Steven.

"Who knows?" he croaked. "A million."

I issued a buzzing noise.

"Two million. Okay. Next question. What did Mr. Lister specify should be done with his body when he dies? Or rather, when he died."

"That's in the will?" asked Hillary.

"He's got some other paperwork in here too."

"Cremation?" guessed Hillary.

I delivered another buzz.

"Preserve it in plastic?" asked Steven goofily with a slightly steadier voice.

"Close," I said. "He donated his body to the UCLA Medical School."

"Ewwww," said Hillary, dragging a faux scalpel-finger down Steven's chest. "How'd you like to be dissected, hon?"

"Anyone want to take a second stab at the passage?" I looked to Steven, who seemed to be improving rapidly post-truffle.

"I think I'm feeling good enough to at least take a look."

Hillary considered Steven, then nodded and helped him up from the chair.

"Can you stand on your own?" she asked.

"Yeah, I'm okay now."

"Good," she said, and the three of us walked back up to the bookshelves.

I was the first to step over the bookcase and into the hidden hallway; by this time, the sun had lowered, leaving only a thin beam of light to illuminate the top of the newly revealed entrance. The hallway lights were on and Steven's tools were on the floor, just as we'd left them.

We walked the length of the hallway, all of about fifteen feet, to the end. Instead of a stairwell as Steven had guessed, a steel ladder descended vertically down a shaft of about twenty-five feet, illuminated overhead by a dangling 60-watt bulb.

"What if there are traps?" asked Hillary as she leaned over the shaft and aimed her iPhone camera downward.

"I can't imagine the guy booby-trapped his own home," I said.

"Well, if the guy was crazy enough to build a secret passage, he might be crazy enough to booby-trap it," said Hillary, a little miffed.

"I'll take my chances." I grabbed hold of the ladder, which was bolted into the back side of the library wall, and started down. Unlike the hallway, the shaft hadn't been finished and was framed by exposed two-by-fours and batted with the same pink insulation we'd seen in the attic. A bundle of wires ran down the length of the shaft, cinched to the beams every few feet with plastic cable ties.

After about five feet, I called up, "Why don't you stay up there until I reach the bottom and can take a look around."

Neither of them objected, so I descended cautiously. About halfway down the ladder, the wood frame terminated and was replaced by a chimney of gray cinderblocks. The block-lined shaft continued another ten feet and ended at a familiar-looking limestone tile floor.

"I've hit the bottom."

I loosened my grip on the ladder rungs, palms sticky from a combination of increased heat, humidity, and anticipation, and pivoted to survey the space. The narrow shaft opened up into a wider cinderblock hallway that led away from the ladder and toward the front of the house. The bundle of electrical arteries exited from the shaft and ran along the top of the corridor, sprouting glowing 60-watt bulbs every five feet through the rest of the passage, which ended in another wall of cinderblocks.

"It's okay to come down," I yelled. The pair engaged in a barely audible but obviously energetic discussion, and a second later, Hillary came clambering down the ladder. Seconds later, Steven followed, with Hillary filming his descent down the shaft.

"Shall we?" I pointed down the hall.

"What's down there?" asked Steven.

"I've got no idea. I waited for you to find out." I gestured to Steven. "After you."

Steven took the lead down the passage, and, reaching the end, turned left at the corner and shouted, "I think we found the mother lode."

I turned the corner and was equally impressed—just feet from the bend stood an imposing steel wall hung with a vault-like steel door. Mounted on the door were a ten-digit, phone-style keypad and a thick steel handle. An equally imposing grille covered an air vent about a foot from the ceiling and directly atop the door.

"It's a panic room," said Hillary.

"A panic room with a hundred-carat diamond inside," added Steven.

"What's this for?" asked Hillary. She pointed at a dinner-plate-sized mirror mounted face-height next to the door.

"Maybe the guy was a narcissist and liked to check his hair before he went to count his gems," said Steven.

"Maybe he wanted to make sure no one was behind him when he opened the lock," I suggested.

"Well, for now it's a mystery," said Hillary.

Tired of the current conversation, Steven shifted his attention to the keypad and began tapping keys. After every six buttons, the keypad emitted two reproaching beeps and then flashed its backlit keys.

"Let me try," I said, and I strained to remember Richard's password. "If I recall correctly, Richard's password was R, followed by the digit one, then C, H, 4, R, and D. We can enter the letters digitally just like on a telephone."

"That password's never going to work," said Hillary, panning the iPhone's camera between the keypad and me.

"Why?" I asked.

"The pad beeps after six digits. It takes a six-digit code, but R1CH4RD is seven long."

"Crap."

"Shazam!" exclaimed Steven.

Hillary shot a quizzical look at Steven and looked to me. "It must be the bump he took to the head," she said.

I grinned.

"Woman!" Steven rejoined, "*Shazam* was the password Richard used for his email account." He looked at me eagerly. "Let's try it!"

It was worth a try.

"Okay." I consulted my phone's keypad. "S is 7. Hit 7." Steven complied.

"H is 4. A is 2. Z is 9. Then 2 again. And then 6." The three of us looked hopefully at the keypad as Steven entered the final digit. Alas, the keypad rebuked us with the same two angry beeps.

"Any other ideas?" asked Hillary. "How about getting a locksmith out?"

Still focused on the keypad and oblivious to our conversation, Steven took his phone from my hand, and consulting it, began entering sequences of six digits.

"No way. I'm doing this myself."

"Seems like a waste of time to me," she said. "You could have this thing cracked open this afternoon."

"I'm not so sure," said Steven, rapping his knuckles on the steel door. "I don't think the average locksmith would have a chance against one of these things. You'd probably have to call in a specialist or someone from the company that built it."

"At least let me do some research and see if we can't find a way in," I said. "I wonder who manufactured it, anyway." I began scanning the surface for tags or logos, but the perfectly smooth, shiny steel wall was devoid of markings.

"You think you could get in through the air vent?" asked Hillary.

I looked up. The grille covering the duct looked pretty tough, but it was worth a try.

"Maybe. Steven?"

Steven looked up from the keypad questioningly. "Huh?"

"Do you think we could pull that grille off with your hammer, or maybe the crowbar?"

Steven backed up and stared at the grille. "Maybe. Give me a leg up."

I stepped up to the door, braced myself, and cupped my hands. Steven grabbed Hillary's arm and my shoulder and placed his right foot into my hands, then stood up. He stared for a second, then grabbed a flashlight from his belt and flicked it on.

"I could have the grille off in thirty seconds," he said, shining his light down the duct. "But there are half a dozen one-inch-wide steel bars right behind it that aren't going anywhere."

I sighed. Steven re-holstered his flashlight and stepped to the ground.

"Well, it was worth a shot," I said.

"At least the former owner was kind enough to leave us with some movies to watch," said Hillary, pointing to a pile of VHS tapes stacked against the wall. We must have overlooked them in our excitement. I picked up the top tape and spun it in my hands. No labels or markings.

"Homemade shag movies?" asked Steven.

"As good a guess as any. You guys have a VCR?"

Hillary looked at Steven.

"Nope," he said. "Our last VCR broke years ago."

"I bet my dad has one," I said, picking up a handful of the tapes. "I'll give him a ring later and find out."

Chapter 19

As usual, Steven answered on the first ring.

"Oh the pain," he groaned.

"Brain hurting, huh?"

"Yeah, so this better've been worth it. Out with it—what was on the tapes?"

"It appears that the previous owner was some sort of security freak," I said. "Every one of those tapes has two hours of closed-circuit video. There must be about six different hidden cameras in that house."

"Where?" Steven inquired. "We didn't see a single camera."

"Either they were removed at some point or they're well hidden. He's got one on each door of the house—"

"Inside or outside?" Steven interrupted.

"Inside each door, so he gets you when you enter. He's also got a few covering the backyard. And you'll be interested in this."

"What?" he asked.

"He's got one covering the library bookshelves, one covering the hallway behind the bookshelves, and one surveying the entrance to his panic room. All motion-sensor activated."

"Why would I be interested in that?" Steven asked earnestly.

"We've got tape of him opening the panic room."

"What? You're shittin' me! Can you see the keypad?"

"Not quite," I admitted.

"What does 'not quite' mean?"

"It means you can see the left edge of the pad, so we can see one of the six digits. It's a four."

"Better than nothing," said Steven, "but that still leaves the remaining five digits, which comes to . . . one hundred thousand possible combinations."

"There was one other thing I found interesting. I saw Lister use the mirror next to the panic room door."

"Use the mirror? Did he check his hair?"

"Nope."

"Look over his shoulder for burglars?"

"No."

"Well?"

"It was quite strange. Before he punched the code in, he leaned right into the mirror and pulled down his lower lip."

"He what?"

"He stretched his lower lip. With both hands. He stared at his mouth for a few seconds and then punched in the code."

"This is becoming more bizarre by the hour," said Steven.

"I'd have to agree with you, Holmes."

"How many times did he do this whole lip-pulling rigmarole?"

"I've fast-forwarded through two tapes so far, and he's five for five."

"And you couldn't catch any additional key-presses the other four times?"

"Only the one. But I've got a bunch of tapes left to look at, so who knows."

"So when can I come over to see the tapes?"

"Right now."

"I'll be there in twenty."

Steven arrived at my Northridge place fifteen minutes later.

"Take a seat," I said. I sat down on the couch, grabbed the remote control, and after a bit of wrangling, started the ancient VCR. Steven ignored me, instead crouching just to the right of the TV, a few feet back.

"It's pretty grainy," he said.

"Probably from being recorded over dozens of times," I offered.

The camera was mounted on the ceiling, to the left and back about four feet from the door; I was surprised we hadn't seen it. It had a pretty good view of the lower two-thirds of the steel wall, door, key-pad, and the mysterious mirror. A fraction of a second after the tape started rolling, a barrel-shaped, curly-black-haired man with a bald spot entered from behind the camera.

"Richard?" asked Steven.

"Must be. Kind of weird to think that the guy's dead now."

The figure walked up to the door, hesitated, turned about-face, and walked back out of the frame. A moment later, he returned.

"He looks jumpy," Steven said. Richard Lister gazed over his shoulder twice more before initiating his bizarre ritual.

"There he goes. Pause it," squawked Steven. "Interesting," he continued. "He doesn't touch the keypad at all. He goes straight for the mirror." Richard's hands stood frozen and shimmering, en route to his face.

"He's clearly not looking over his shoulder. He already checked the hallway three times. There must be something in his mouth."

"All right, let's continue. Can you play it in slo-mo?"

I looked at the remote. "Is it the wide circular dial?"

"Try it."

I placed my finger in the small depression and jogged the two-inch diameter wheel clockwise.

Over the course of five slow-motion seconds, Richard's stumpy fingers traveled from his chest to his lower lip. Our eyes shifted from his hands to the reflection of his face in the mirror.

"Slowly," reiterated Steven. I took it two frames at a time. Using both hands, Richard grasped either side of his lower lip with his thumb and forefinger and began leaning into the mirror.

"Stop!" Steven yelled. I'd gone too far, so I jogged the wheel back a few frames and brought the image to a shimmering pause.

"Let's look at his teeth," he said.

"The guy must be British." His teeth wore an uneven patina of tea-stained yellow. Steven turned and gave me a look.

"They're dirty, but there's nothing unusual about them," I said. "That can't be what he's looking at."

I continued shuttling through the frames, a few every second. After about sixty frames, Lister let go with his left hand and it began a ten-frame journey to the keypad; his right hand stayed put, still firmly clamped onto his stubbly lower lip. Richard started number punching in slow motion, tilting his head from mirror to keypad to mirror, but as I discovered during my first viewing, only the press of the four-key was visible behind his thick neck.

"What's the deal with the lip?" Steven asked, genuinely puzzled. "He's definitely looking at something in his mouth."

I shuttled through the frames until we arrived at the best view of his mouth in the mirror.

"As far as I can tell, there's nothing there."

"It's not the teeth. Definitely not the teeth."

"What about the lower lip?" Come to think of it, the exposed inside of his lip did seem to have an unusual texture.

"There's definitely something there, on the inside," said Steven excitedly. "Let me see the inside of your lip."

I repeated Richard's ritual and exposed my gums to Steven.

"Flesh-colored. Check mine."

I investigated the inside of Steven's mouth, as instructed.

"Rosy," I concurred.

"But his lip is definitely discolored. Grab the other tape." Steven pointed to a Post-It-covered tape on my coffee table. I inserted it and we repeated our frame-by-frame advance until Richard flashed his gums again.

This time, we had it.

Chapter 20

"THE GUY'S GOT DIGITS tattooed on the inside of his lip!" Steven ejaculated. "He can't remember the combination, so he keeps it where he'll never lose it."

"No wonder he's got such bad teeth. He didn't want anyone to know what was there. It's right out of a movie."

"They're not really that legible," Steven said, leaning forward.

"C'mon, for a five-million-dollar diamond, you can read them. But if you're not up to it, maybe I can."

I gave Steven a playful shove, crouched in front of the TV and stared for a good three minutes, but for the life of me, I couldn't pick out a single shimmering digit.

Rubbing my eyes, I said, "You take over. I'll be right back."

"Okay."

"I'll give you an extra five percent of the booty if you find the code before I get back." Steven had already returned to the screen, oblivious to my offer. If anyone had the patience and obsessive-compulsive personality to find this needle in a haystack, it was Steven.

After a brief visit to the bathroom, I grabbed my laptop and a bag of baby carrots and sat back down on the couch. While Steven continued his scrutiny of the videotapes, I logged into my Gmail account to check my mail. As usual, nothing. But that reminded me. I wondered if Richard had received any new emails in his ZeusMail account, perhaps containing new clues we could use to locate the diamond. I hadn't checked the account in days, so it was worth a try.

I pulled up the ZeusMail website into a fresh copy of the browser and keyed in Richard's credentials.

"I found another sequence of him opening the panic room," bellowed Steven.

"I'm right here, Holmes."

"Oh." He swiveled his head around and gave a sheepish grin. "Still no keypad though." He returned to the TV.

I directed my attention back to my laptop, and, now that the page had loaded, was ecstatic to find that Richard had received another email from the enigmatic Khalimmy: the buyer interested in the Florentine. It had been sent yesterday. I clicked to open it.

From: Spirited One <khalimmy@freemail.com>
To: Antique Collector <antique1@zeusmail.gr>
Subject: No more games

Clearly, you think this is a game. I do not share the same thoughts.

Just in case you need any motivation, your brother has decided to disappear for a while. If you don't deliver by Thursday, he may disappear for good.

"Oh shit. We have an unwelcome turn of events," I said seriously.

"Huh?" Steven mumbled, still fixated on the grainy video.

"Come over here. This is not good."

Steven rose from his haunches, walked over and plopped down on the couch next to me.

"What's wrong?"

"Take a look at this." I pointed at the email. "The bastard kidnapped Richard Lister's brother."

"Holy shit," said Steven. "This is bad."

"Yeah, but what can we do?"

"We have to go to the police."

"And say what? 'Excuse me Officer, I broke into a dead man's email account and read his private mail and found out his brother's been kidnapped? Oh and by the way, I bought his two-point-seven-million dollar house and am hunting for a black-market diamond'? That'll go over real well—"

Steven shoved his hand out. "Just give me the phone. I'll call Andy." Hillary's brother Andy worked for the rape unit down in Torrance.

"Okay, but I'm not telling him anything about the diamond," I said. "Just that we discovered a threatening email by accident."

Steven nodded, then dialed the eleven digits and hit the speaker-phone button. A few rings later, Andy picked up.

"Torrance Sex Crimes Unit, Officer Jensen speaking."

"Hey Andy, this is Steven."

"Oh, hey Steven. What's up?"

"Got a second? It's pretty serious."

"Yeah, shoot."

"Thanks. I've got Alex here too."

"So what did you want, guys?"

"Alex, you found it, you tell him."

As ordered, I proceeded to tell Andy about the threatening email.

"You found the email in the dead guy's computer you were fixing up? Seriously? That's right out of a movie."

"No kidding," I said.

"And it's clear that it's a kidnapping threat?"

"It's pretty unambiguous."

"You need to file a kidnapping report."

"But where? I have no idea where this guy Ronald Lister lives."

He hesitated. "You're still living in Northridge, right? Just go to Devonshire Station and report it there. They'll figure it out."

Steven dropped me off outside the front entrance to Devonshire Station.

"I'll wait for you in the car," he said. "No need to complicate things by involving both of us."

I nodded. "Wish me luck."

"Good luck."

I walked through the double doors and up to the department's front desk.

"I'd like to report a kidnapping," I said, choking on the last word.

"One second." The woman behind the desk, a middle-aged Latina decked out in a crisp blue LAPD uniform, picked up her phone, punched in an extension, and waited a few seconds.

"Hey Leonardo, someone here wants to give a kidnapping report." She paused. "Okay, thanks."

"Officer Flanco will be out in a second. You can sit over there for the time being."

I took a seat on the bench and began nervously picking at my cuticles.

"Excuse me, are you here to report a kidnapping?"

I jumped, startled.

"Uh. Yes."

"Hi, I'm Officer Flanco. You are?"

"Alex."

"Okay, please follow me."

Flanco led me through a security door, which he opened with a keycard, down a hallway and into a large room with six paperwork-strewn desks. He then walked to the farthest desk, by far the messiest, dragged a chair over and gestured to it. A half-finished cup of coffee sat on the tallest pile of manila folders, easily eight inches high and covered in a pattern of coffee rings strangely reminiscent of the Olympics logo. Flanco then eased down behind his desk, placed his hands on his keyboard, and said, "Okay Alex, who's been kidnapped."

"I think a guy named Ronald Lister was kidnapped."

"You think?" He took his hands off the keyboard and reclined in his seat, causing it to squeak. "Why do you think that?"

"A few weeks ago, my father bought a computer at an estate sale. I work with computers so he wanted me to refurbish it so he could give it to a needy family. So I started cleaning the computer up, cleaned some viruses from it, that kind of stuff."

Flanco reached for the coffee cup, sniffed, grimaced, and then took a hesitant sip.

"At some point I loaded up the web browser and accidentally pulled up the previous owner's email account. The owner was the guy that had died."

Okay, so technically "accidentally" was a fib. I continued: "So I pulled up his old email account and found this email." I handed Officer Flanco a printout of the kidnapping email. He leaned forward in his chair and lowered a pair of brown-plastic reading glasses from his forehead to inspect it.

"How do you know this email isn't a prank?"

"I'm pretty sure it's not. I googled the dead guy and he was apparently an antiquities smuggler, so it makes sense that someone might be trying to blackmail him."

"You're quite the Sherlock Holmes," he said facetiously. "What's the former owner's name? This antiquities smuggler?"

"Richard Lister," I said.

He jotted that down on a notepad, then reread the printed copy of the email. "That's all you have?"

"Yeah." I shifted uneasily.

"Nothing else you want to share with me?"

"No. Do you think you'll be able to help?"

"Alex, right?" he asked.

I nodded.

"Alex, first we've got to verify that this is real. We get hoax reports all the time. It could be two guys joking around." Flanco paused, saw the look on my face, and frowned. "Problem is, we've got seven kidnapping cases open right now." He pointed to the stack on his desk, and I wondered if Ronald Lister's folder would soon have coffee rings on it too. "I can't make any promises. But based on the amount of information we have, the odds aren't great. I'm going to need to talk with the LAPD Computer Crimes division, and since this is a potential kidnapping, the FBI."

Flanco spent the next ten minutes transcribing my story, then escorted me to the station's entrance.

"If we need any more information, someone from the office here will contact you. And if you think of anything else, please call me." He handed me his card.

Chapter 21

"How did it go?" asked Steven.

"As well as can be expected, I guess. But the cop was pretty skeptical, and based on the stack of files on his desk, I'm not holding my breath."

Steven nodded sullenly. "So that's it?"

"No way in hell." I shook my head. "There is no way I'm going to let Ronald Lister die."

Steven turned his head and stared at me.

"What are you thinking?" he asked. "Email Khalimmy from Richard Lister's email account and tell him we'll trade Ronald for the diamond, then bring the cops in?"

"No. The last thing I want to do is directly engage him. Plus, if we start sending emails from Lister's account and the police look into it, things get complicated."

Steven nodded and kept driving. "Then what?"

"We need to find out more about who we're dealing with before we go any further. I want to do some reconnaissance."

"Recon? Interesting!" he said, perking up, "But we have no idea where this guy lives."

"Digital recon," I said. "You remember that spyware we found on Richard's machine?"

"Yeah."

"I saved a copy before I removed it from the PC. You remember what it did?"

"Recorded everything you typed and sent it to Russia, right?"

"Right. It sent everything Richard typed to an email account—which, as you correctly remembered, was hosted in Russia. I'm going to modify the spyware software so it sends all of its recorded keystrokes to us instead. Then I'm going to send it to Khalimmy."

"How are you going to do that?"

"It's easy. The thing has the old Russian email address embedded inside it. I'm going to sign up for a new dummy email account and then reprogram the spyware so it forwards the transcripts to my dummy account instead of the account in Russia."

"It's really that easy?"

"It'll literally take about ten or fifteen minutes to change. Plus the five minutes it'll take to register for a new email account. That's where we have to be careful. I don't want this guy to be able to trace it back to me, so I'm going to register it under your name."

Steven gave me an "are you serious?" look.

"I'm just kidding. I'll sign up with a fake name."

"So once you jimmy the spyware, then you just send it to him in an email?"

"Well, I can't just send it to him from my email account, and he'd never click on it if it came from some random user. So I'm going to forge the *From:* address in the email so it looks like it's from a legit source."

"You can do that?"

"Why not?"

"You're shittin' me. It can't be that easy."

"Yes it can. You can do the same thing with snail mail. Anyone can write any return address they like on a piece of mail and drop it into a mailbox. Same with Internet email. You'd be surprised how much of the Internet is built that way—the thing was originally designed for nearsighted college professors to pontificate. Who needed security?"

"Seriously?"

"Trust me, that's just the tip of the iceberg. Actually . . ." I zoned for a second, the plan crystalizing in my mind. "Come to think of it, I don't think I'll even need to bother forging the return address. Anyway, I'll send the spyware to him in an email and make it look important. He'll double-click on the attachment, install it, and we'll be in business."

Steven turned his head from the road to look at me. "You think he'll bite?"

"Why not? Corporations get infiltrated that way every day. Then maybe we can get some information to help the police. And we can remain anonymous."

"I like it," said Steven.

"Good, then it's agreed. So now what are we going to do about that panic room?"

"No idea. Those tapes were next to useless." He pulled up to my house.

"All right, well, give it some more thought. Let's regroup in a few hours when I'm done sending the spyware."

"Roger," he said. "See you in a bit."

After grabbing a microwave burrito from my freezer, I logged into my laptop and began searching for foreign email hosting services. It took just a few minutes of googling to find a good candidate: a Brazilian email provider, Correio Brasil, that offered free, advertisement-supported email accounts with no phone number or address required to sign up. So, with the help of an online Portuguese-English dictionary, I created a new account and registered it to Fidel Castro. By three p.m., I was the proud owner of fidel2@correio.br—and untraceable. I'd use this account as a drop box for our kidnapper's keystrokes.

Next, I needed to doctor the spyware program I found on Richard's computer so it would forward its transcripts to Fidel's new email account. Using a program called a hex editor, I edited Richard's spyware file, searching for the original email address, OXOTHИK@flavmail.ru, and replacing it with my updated fidel2@correio.br address. The spyware would now send all recorded keystrokes to my Correio Brasil email account instead of its original mailbox at Flavmail. I also made one additional modification to the spyware program—I added several new instructions to the file so the first time it ran, it would pop up a window containing the words "Repairing virus infection," then show an hourglass for about ten seconds, and finally pop up a second window stating, "Your machine has been disinfected. Thank you for your cooperation—Freemail.com security staff."

Finally, to complete my digital ambush, I needed to send the spyware in an email that looked like it came from the security staff at Freemail.com—the email service used by the mysterious Khalimmy. I surfed to www.freemail.com and, after a bit of hunting, found and clicked the "Sign up for a FREE account" link. The new-user signup screen popped up and asked me to pick my new email address, so I entered "admin" on a lark and then clicked the "Submit" button. Predictably, the website returned quickly with "Another user has already reserved an email account with this name. Please try again." I tried several others including "administrator" and "support" with the same result—these email accounts had all been reserved, likely for the email provider's own staff. Finally, after about a dozen tries I picked a winner that hadn't been taken: "securityadmin." I then registered the new account to a Mr. Manny Vandervelde (that sounded like the name of a security administrator, didn't it?), typed in a random ten-digit number in the phone number field, and selected a password I'd remember. An instant later, Freemail.com greeted me regally: "Welcome to Freemail.com, Manny, where EVERYONE gets FREE mail! Your new email address is securityadmin@freemail.com! Tell your friends!"

Tell my friends? Maybe not.

Now all I needed to do was send the spyware file to our kidnapper, get him to double-click on it, and we'd be in business. This was the tricky part: the social engineering. Fortunately, I'd seen hundreds of these ruses during my time at ViruTrax, so I knew exactly what to do.

With a bit more sleuthing, I located the Freemail.com 1-800-number and jotted it down on a Regina Flowers Real Estate notepad; I also lifted the Freemail.com logo (an angelic-looking F with wings) from the website and saved it to my hard drive.

I clicked the "Compose a new 'freemail'" button and began writing my magnum opus, hoping our assailant's name was the same as his email address:

> *From: securityadmin@freemail.com*
> *To: khalimmy@freemail.com*
> *Subject: Infected computer*
>
> *Dear Mr. Khalimmy,*
>
> *Our email security filter has detected that your computer appears to be using our email service to send computer viruses to other users. As you may be aware, sending viruses through email is a violation of our licensing policy and also a vio-*

lation of the Federal Fair Computer Use Act. Therefore, we ask you to please remove the infection from your computer as soon as possible, or we will have to disable your account. We recommend a popular, freeware antivirus program like Dr. Finnigan's Antivirus, if you don't already have antivirus protection.

Manny Vandervelde—
Freemail Computer Security Manager

Freemail.com—where EVERY email is FREE

I finished it all off with a flourish, pasting the picture of the Freemail logo at the end of the email—I was all about the details—and then clicked "Send."

That was the teaser—just enough to get him worried, but not enough to raise any suspicions. Within seconds, the enigmatic Khalimmy would have a very authentic-looking yet disturbing email in his inbox from "securityadmin@freemail.com."

About two hours later, I finished the one-two punch with a follow-up email, again from the concerned Freemail security administrator:

From: securityadmin@freemail.com
To: khalimmy@freemail.com
Subject: Mass-infection of freemail users

Dear Mr. Khalimmy,

As we indicated earlier, we still believe that your machine was infected with a virus sometime during the week of the 20th. However, we have reason to believe that at least 60 other Freemail customers are also infected. Therefore, as a service to our customers, we have created a virus fix tool to clean up the infection (you will find it attached to this email). To activate

the program, please double-click on the provided repair pro-
gram.

I have asked my network security team to work overtime
today and tomorrow (Aug 29 and Aug 30) so if this tool fails
to resolve the issue, please feel free to call us for support. Our
twenty-four-hour support number is 800-555-4974.

Manny Vandervelde—
Freemail Computer Security Manager

Freemail.com—where EVERY email is FREE

With a few clicks of the mouse, I attached my doctored spyware program to the email and forwarded it on its way. The net was
unfurled, the chum dispersed, and all we had to do was wait for the
shark to take the bait.

Chapter 22

JUST AS I WAS ABOUT TO REACH for a half-dollar-sized rock, I felt a gentle vibration in my pocket. Dangling from my left hand, I extracted my phone. It was Steven.

"Hey," I said. "You coming by soon?"

"Yeah, I was planning on leaving in about twenty. But I just had an idea and I wanted to run it by you."

"One sec," I said, dropping four feet from my artificial rock wall onto the vinyl safety pad. "Okay, shoot."

"I think I've figured out a way into the panic room," he said.

"How? I've been racking my brain trying to figure out a way in and I've got nothing. I don't want to hire a locksmith. Not yet."

"Listen. I wasn't going to suggest a locksmith."

"Okay, what then?"

"We've got to get hold of Richard's b—" He cut out.

"What? I lost you."

"I said, I think we need to get a hold of Richard's body and get a look at that tattoo."

I did a double take. Had Steven gone mad?

"Wonderful! Let's just go dig him up. You practically had a heart attack visiting Richard's house at night, but you're fine taking a field trip to Forest Lawn and digging up his decomposing body. Are you frickin' crazy?"

"Hear me out!"

"And even if we were crazy enough to do it, what are the odds he hasn't decomposed into clam chowder?"

"Actually," said Steven.

"You've been smoking something."

"Actually," he repeated coyly, "if I were to bet, I'd guess he's in pretty good shape."

Steven wasn't crazy—he was obsessively rational; what was he getting at? I ruminated for a second.

"Alex?"

"One second, I'm thinking." I knew he was onto something, but wasn't sure why or how I knew this. What was it?

"The will," said Steven, as if responding to my thoughts.

The will! Richard hadn't been buried—he'd donated his body to science—to the UCLA Medical School.

"He was probably taken to the school and pickled the moment they found him." Not that this made things any easier.

"So we'll just waltz into the visitor's center at the morgue, buy a matinee ticket, and wait in line for a viewing?" I asked.

"Probably not." He hesitated. "But I figured maybe you could," he stuttered, "maybe you could ask your mom for some help."

"What? No way. She'd have a heart attack if she knew what we were up to. Plus she practices over at Northridge Hospital, not UCLA." I took a breath. "Plus, she spends most of her time curing fungal infections for old ladies—how the hell is she going to get us into the morgue?"

"I bet she could make some calls."

"No way. End of discussion."

Steven sighed audibly on the other end of the phone.

"Don't give me a guilt trip. No way."

"Okay, okay." He paused. "What about someone who went to UCLA med school? Know anyone? Someone who already has access and maybe could just take a quick look during their lunch break?"

I considered this for a second.

"I guess I could ask Linda," I said.

"Who's Linda?" he asked suggestively. Steven and my climbing friends traveled in different circles.

"Linda. You know, my climbing partner."

"Oh, her? She's a doctor at UCLA?"

"Not quite. She works in the campus hospital as an ER nurse."

"I forgot. Is she the hot one?"

"Why does that matter?"

"Answer the question," he pressed.

"You could say that."

"Then why aren't you dating her?"

"For God's sake, I thought we were talking about breaking into UCLA, not my love life. It's a long story."

"All right, all right. Touchy today. So you think she might be able to get us in?"

"Maybe."

"Well then, what've you got to lose?"

"Only my freedom, I guess." Was I actually considering asking Linda to break into the UCLA Medical School morgue? Worse still, breaking in myself? "I'll think about it and call you later." I hung up.

God help me.

Linda Reynaud. I'd fallen for her, or rather on top of her, during my junior year while struggling with a difficult overhanging boulder problem at the UCLA climbing gym. After an awkward disentanglement and a few choice words of scorn, we'd hit it off and had been climbing buddies ever since. With chestnut hair, a passable chest, long legs, and an all-American smile, Linda had a steady stream of suitors and even longer list of discards. When we'd first met, she was dating a guy named Larry (a royal loser) so we started off as friends, and given a series of unfortunately timed relationships and an unusual awkwardness on my part when it came to dating, that's the way things were destined to stay.

By the time I ascended my first route at UCLA, Linda had already been climbing for years with her father. Now, at twenty-six, she was one of the top two or three Southern California woman mountaineers, and even had a few climbs named after her on the local rock walls. For whatever reason, we'd limited our hanging out to climbing; we rarely saw each other outside of the local state parks. Actually, I guess all of my climbing friendships were like that. You had climbing friends and everyday friends, and the two didn't mix. Anyway, Linda was someone I could trust with the important things. She'd saved my life more times than I cared to recall. I shot her off a deliberately vague text from my smartphone (she never answered her phone), and headed back inside the house. It didn't take long for her to call me back.

"Hey Alex. It's Linda from climbing."

"Hey Linda from climbing. Thanks for calling me back so quickly."

"Trust me, it's my pleasure." Linda sighed. "I've been spit on twice and had a homeless patient almost bite me, just since lunch. I needed a break."

"Sounds exhilarating."

"That's one word for it."

"So how's Jim?" I asked, changing the subject.

"There is no Jim anymore." Her tone suggested "breakup" rather than "death." "Just me and Rusty." Rusty was her chocolate lab and a favorite among the regulars at the local climbing wall.

"Sorry—I didn't mean to—"

"Don't sweat it. And what about you? How's it going with," she paused a beat, "what's-her-name?" Always the tactful Linda.

"Julie," I said. "That ended a few months ago."

"Sorry, Alex."

"It's all good, trust me. Been climbing recently?"

"Not since we last went with Potter. My calluses are falling off and I'm starting to feel flabby."

"The calluses, I believe. The flabby part, not so much."

"Sweet talker."

"That's me. You're in for some serious pain next time you go out."

"I know. But with the overtime drying up next month, I'll be climbing a lot more now. So free up your calendar."

"Umm. That might be a bit difficult."

"Why? What's up, cowboy?"

"It's a long story. But right now, let's just say I need some medical advice."

"Having some health problems?" Her tone became more somber.

"No, nothing like that. Would you be up for some dinner? I'll tell you all about it, and it'll be my treat." *Our first date! Not.*

"I've got nothing planned. But do you mind if we eat here? With the long hours I've been working, Rusty's starting to give me dirty looks. What do you say you stop by at seven and bring over some takeout?"

"My pleasure. Just tell me what you want to eat."

Linda lived in the Topanga Canyon mountains southwest of the San Fernando Valley in a sixties-era ranch house that had seen better days.

I pulled down the graveled driveway off Topanga and parked in front of a dilapidated detached garage-turned-chicken coop next to Linda's Beetle. The main house wasn't in much better condition; curls of faded green paint flaked from its wood-slat walls and revealed years of dry rot. Linda stood in the door, grabbing Rusty's collar, a welcoming smile on her face.

"Long time no see, Alex."

"Yeah, it's been a while." She gave me a warm hug. Rusty showed a healthy amount of jealousy, jumping up and pawing at my hip.

"Hey boy!" I said, and after handing Linda the takeout, I dropped to the ground for a healthy face-licking.

A minute later, we were devouring Kung Pao shrimp at Linda's oak-stump kitchen table.

"Hear about Jotz?" I asked.

"No, what's with him?"

"He's got two broken legs and three cracked ribs." Jotz was an old-time climber—of the sixties variety—who thought that climbing with ropes was for sissies. At least the sissies didn't get broken femurs.

"Shit. What happened?" she asked, leaning in.

"He was free-climbing Monkey Sang, got about twenty-five feet up by the peanut-shaped hold, and put his hand into a hive of yellow jackets. About a dozen of them went straight for his face and he bailed."

"It was just a matter of time." Linda shook her head regretfully. "Jamie's been yelling at him for years."

"At least he's still alive," I said.

"He's lucky. Talking about cracked ribs, what's your medical problem, cowboy?"

"It's complicated."

"In that case," she stood up, "we'd better open a bottle of wine. Red or white?"

"Red."

Over the next hour, I delivered a synopsis of the past two weeks. Linda wasn't exactly a computer geek, so I skipped over the techie details.

"So you bought the guy's house?"

"Yeah," I said sheepishly.

"And you think this guy has the combination tattooed on his lip?"

"Yup."

"And you want to take a look at the cadaver?"

"That was the idea. Am I crazy?"

Linda took a sip of wine and gave me a subtle smile.

"Well, you're not Jotz crazy." Rusty arthritically hopped up onto the couch and put his head on Linda's lap. "The basement of UCLA Medical Center isn't exactly Fort Knox. If I were a betting woman, and assuming the body hasn't been cremated or buried, I'd give you good odds."

"How can I find out if the body's still there?" I asked, more excited.

"The school's got a database. They've got to track every donated body."

"Makes sense. I assume a family member could call them up and ask about a cadaver's status, right?"

"No idea." She hesitated. "But when a body's been donated, I think the family signs over all rights to the university. So maybe not."

"Hmmm. Are there any guards?"

"They've got one who patrols the whole lower level. Clarence. He's a little crotchety, but a nice guy."

I took my smartphone out and started typing in notes. "Do you mind?" I asked.

"Just don't put my name in there. Anyway, it's pretty busy down there, even at night. My guess is that as long as you look like you belong, no one's going to ask any questions."

I took a drink of wine. "Thanks for the info."

"My pleasure. Just do me a favor. If you go through with this little adventure, don't drag me into it. I like my job and I've got a mortgage now." She pointed at the ceiling.

"So responsible!"

"You got it. That's me, Ms. Responsible." She winked playfully. I didn't know if it was the wine, my repressed feelings for her, or a little of both, but like a fifteen-year-old on his first date, I felt my heart skip a beat. I closed my eyes and shook my head.

"What's wrong?"

"Nothing," I stammered. "So what else can you tell me about the morgue?"

"There are actually two morgues—one for the med school cadavers and the other for everyone else. Both are in the basement." Linda stifled a yawn. "Actually, come to think of it, the med school students also have a smaller freezer, up by their dissection rooms. There's a private elevator that connects the two."

"To avoid freaking out the patients."

"It's bad for business." Linda smiled.

"You're quite the treasure trove of information!" I smiled back. "When'd you become the morgue expert?"

"Remember when I wrecked my Gremlin?"

"How could I forget? I was your chauffer for a week."

"That's right!" She smiled reminiscently. "Anyway, I needed some extra money so I worked the morgue desk from eight until midnight for about six months. Got to know some of the students."

"So are the cadavers labeled?"

"Not with names. They're all anonymous. When we get them in, we put them in the database and they're assigned a ten- or eleven-digit ID code. They've got a number and a barcode on their big toe, just like on *ER*."

"I'll probably recognize his face. They look the same dead, right?"

"Generally. He wasn't bludgeoned in the face, was he?"

"Not as far as I know. I think he died from a heart attack."

"I guess I could look up his tag for you just in case."

"You still have access to the database?"

"No. But Karla owes me ten bucks from mahjong."

"I'd really appreciate it. You won't get in trouble, right?"

"I can't see why. As long as you keep your mouth shut and promise to pay for gas and margaritas on the next two trips to Tahquitz."

"Cross my heart and hope to die," I said. "Can I ask just a few more questions?"

Linda yawned again. I looked down at my smartphone—it was already eleven-thirty. "Actually, I'd better let you get to bed. I didn't realize how late it was."

Linda glanced over at a cuckoo clock on the wall. "Yeah. How about if I give you a call tomorrow," she said, standing up and displacing Rusty.

"Thanks Linda. The guy's name is Richard Lister." I jotted it down on a sticky next to her phone.

During the drive home, I brooded over a dozen unrealistic schemes. My sleep that night, if you can call it that, frothed with nightmares of every possible negative outcome, most resulting in my arrest.

Chapter 23

"Hello?"

"Okay, I've got three questions. First, where the hell have you been? Second, is she going to help us get to the body? And third and most importantly, did you get lucky last night?"

"What? What time is it?" I pulled the blanket from over my head and craned my neck to get a look at the bedside clock. 10:29 a.m. "Jesus. Sorry, I overslept."

"I guess that answers question number three," said Steven.

"Get your mind out of the gutter." I sat up in bed, rubbing my eyes. "Nothing happened. But I did get some useful intel."

"Out with it."

"Linda thinks she can find out if the body's still in the morgue." I yawned. "I'm hoping to hear back this morning."

"So assuming he's still there, what's the plan?" he asked. Then almost in a whisper, "And how can I help?"

"I've got no idea. I was up 'til five cooking up schemes, but they all seem too risky."

My phone beeped. Call waiting. "One sec. It might be her."

"Alex." It was my grandpa, in his usual hoarse, drawn-out voice, "*Aluuuhx.*"

"Hi Papa."

"How is my grandson this morning?"

"Fine, Papa. Can I call you back in a few minutes?"

"Certainly."

"Thanks Ingy. I'll call you in a few." I clicked back to Steven.

"So?"

"It was Papa."

"Say no more. Still sane?"

"As crazy as ever," I said.

"Anyway, back to the hospital—give me a few of your ideas."

"Right. The best I've got so far is: I'm going to throw on a pair of medical scrubs, hang right outside the morgue, wait for a student to walk in, and sort of tailgate in before the door closes."

"It could work," he said. "But it's risky. What if they ask who you are?"

"God only knows. You're the one who suggested this in the first place. Got any better ideas?"

Steven went silent for a second. "I need to think about it."

The phone beeped again. "Got another call," I said.

"You're not going to make me—" I clicked the flash button before he could finish.

"Hello."

"Hi Alex, it's Linda."

"Hey Linda. Any news?" I asked.

"Yeah. Listen, I haven't got long. I just wanted to tell you that Richard's checked in and enjoying the cool spa treatments. Not sure if the kiddies are taking him apart yet, but he's here somewhere."

"Thanks Linda!"

"Oh, you got a pen?"

"Yeah."

"Write this down: Oh-five-seven-seven-nine-six-oh-five-four-oh. That's his tag number."

"Thanks." I scrawled it down.

"One more thing. The door's unmarked, but it's hard to miss—it looks like a walk-in freezer. They used to change the security code every six weeks or so, so I'm not sure if this'll still work, but the morgue's door code was five-four-five-five when I worked down there. If that doesn't work, Clarence's got a backup key in his desk."

"How long ago was that?"

"About half a year ago."

"Wonderful."

"Look, it's the best I've got, and you still owe me two chauffeured trips to Tahquitz. And margaritas. Don't forget. I gotta run. And not a word to anyone."

"Thanks Linda."

"No problem. And good luck!"

I clicked back to Steven.

"Still there?" I asked the phone.

"Yeah, but a little bruised from this on-again-off-again treatment."

"Oh get over it. He's still at UCLA, in the med school morgue."

Steven whistled. "We've got to do it. Want to meet up to discuss the plan?"

Hillary's muffled voice came over the phone. "You're not thinking of breaking into the hospital, are you? You could go to jail. You go through with this and—"

"I'll call you back in a bit," mumbled Steven into the phone, and the line went dead.

A minute later, I had Papa on the horn.

"Hi Ingy, it's Alex."

"My lovely grandchild, I'm so glad you called."

"Of course. What's new with you?"

"Oh, I went over to Mama's and saw your dad. He bought a few cantaloupes for me, beautiful cantaloupes. Said they were only twenty cents a pound." It amazed me how excited grandparents got about cheap produce. Would I someday be just as excited about cheap smartphones?

"How's Hyman?" Hyman was the new buddy from the senior center.

"He's well. We went wading together yesterday." In the shallow end of the YMCA pool, no doubt, followed invariably by a trip to Denny's for eggs and four strips of bacon, extra crispy.

"Say, Alex, could you come over and help me with the sprinkler? It's been hot and it's only running three minutes per day." That was code-talk for "you haven't visited in a while, and that's as good an excuse as any."

"I'd like to, Papa, but I don't have any time today. Maybe next—"

A light bulb went off.

"Actually, will you be free in a half hour?"

"Sure!" he said excitedly. "What kind of fruit would you like?" Papa always felt he wasn't being hospitable if he didn't have some sort of fruit or nuts for me.

"I just ate," I fibbed, "save your money."

"All right. Then I'll see you in half an hour?"

"It's a date."

Papa's house had the usual old-person smell, topped 85 degrees, and was characteristically messy. I sat down at the dining room table, as I always did, and grabbed a handful of paper clips while he pulled up a chair. Papa was wearing thirty-year-old gray trousers cut at the knees into makeshift shorts and a loose tank top showcasing sheep-like tufts of gray hair from all exposed areas of his chest, arms, and back. A purple nipple stared at me from amidst the down.

"So what's new, my boy?" asked Papa.

"I've been involved in a little adventure recently." I gave Papa the now well-practiced, five-minute edition, sans the kidnapping part. He listened carefully.

"So you think there's really a diamond in this new house? And that this stiff's got the combination?"

"That's how it looks."

"How you going to get to the body?" asked Papa, unfazed.

"I don't know. Any bright ideas?" I shifted uneasily to avoid the lightning bolt I was sure was on its way down.

"You know, I used to work as an orderly in Mass General."

"That's right. You used to sew up the bodies after the autopsies."

"No," he leaned in and spoke more softly, "what I'm saying is I know my way around a hospital. I could help you get into the morgue."

"I don't know," I said. "Mom would kill me if anything happened."

"Your mother isn't my master." He dismissed her with a geriatric wave of his hand. "What the hell's going to happen, anyway? I'm eighty-eight. They going to throw me into jail?"

"Pop, you know how nervous you get." I paused for effect. "What if it takes four hours? Are you going to be able to sit for four hours? No bathroom breaks? No complaining that your leg is hurting?" He also had a bad case of sciatica.

"Ahh, shit," he said, suddenly irritated. "You never have any respect for me. For once, why don't you give me some respect? You always treat me like a child." He wiped a drop of spittle from his chin, bristling his three-day-old shadow of gray whiskers.

"All right, you want to come? You promise me now that you'll do whatever I tell you. And no complaining." I paused for effect. "Promise me."

"I promise."

"I need to go as soon as possible. Tonight. You can go tonight after ten or eleven?"

"Of course. What the hell do I have to do? I barely sleep anymore anyway."

"I still need to give it some thought. I'll call you in a few hours."

My trip home was punctuated by a quick visit to the medical supply store (which I'd been to a hundred times with my mom as a kid) and a call to Steven on my cell. As expected, Hillary had no intentions of budging, and in fact, the two weren't speaking. I couldn't remember the last time they'd been so angry. Steven merely grunted "good luck" when I told him I was bringing Papa. By two p.m., I'd formulated a makeshift plan and estimated the amount of time for each phase:

1. 15 minutes: I'd start by wheeling Papa back and forth through the basement to do some reconnaissance.

2. 5 minutes: Once I found the "freezer" door, as Linda called it, I'd drop Papa off in the lobby with ample reading materials to keep him occupied.

3. 10–20 minutes: Then I'd go back and enter Linda's code. If that didn't work (most likely scenario), I'd wait until Clarence went for a bathroom break and surreptitiously grab his master key.

4. 10–20 minutes: When the coast was clear I'd enter the room.

5. 20–30 minutes: I'd locate the body and copy down Richard's lip code.

6. 5 minutes: I'd pick Papa up from the lobby and we'd take off.

Assuming we started at ten p.m. we'd hopefully be done by eleven-thirty; I'd have Papa home and in bed by midnight, and I'd have the panic room open by one. At least that was the optimistic version. What could possibly go wrong?

By three, I'd reviewed the entire campaign half a dozen times. To be sure, there were lots of potential hiccups, but I resolved to abort, play dumb, and wheel Papa out the front door if I felt at any time I might get caught.

It just might work.

Chapter 24

PAPA LEANED EAGERLY ON HIS CANE as I pulled into his Reseda driveway. His blue-collar, twelve-hundred-square-foot house, circa 1960, had the distinction of being the only one on the block with a lava rock garden in the front yard. While my grandmother was alive, the yard was peppered with a variety of cacti; now, all that remained in the center of the field of red rocks was a single, four-foot-tall phallic specimen covered in gray hairs—the envy of the neighborhood, no doubt. Papa's lightly tattered United States and California flags tussled in the August breeze while I put my Outback into park and exited to assist him.

Now it was time for twenty questions.

"Did you use the bathroom before you came out?"

"Yes."

"Did you take all of your meds?"

"Yes."

"Do you have your house keys?"

"Yes."

"Show me."

He felt in his pocket, cursed, then ambled over to the kitchen table and grabbed them.

"Have you had dinner yet?"

"Of course." He began to get irritated. "Let's get going already." This was going to be an exciting evening. I'd fill him in on my plan in the car; we had a thirty-minute drive over to UCLA, plenty of time.

"Oh, where's your wheelchair?" I'd almost forgotten.

He pointed at the garage door. "It's next to my Jeep."

A few minutes later, I had the chair folded and packed in my trunk and Papa safely buckled into the front seat, clutching his seatbelt with shaky hands as he always did when I drove.

"So, ready to hear the plan?" I asked as I backed out of his driveway.

"As ready as can be!"

"When we get to the hospital, I'm going to wheel you in and we're going to take the elevator to the basement."

"That's where Radiology is," he said authoritatively.

"That and the morgue, apparently. When we get to the basement, I'm going to wheel you around until we find the morgue door. It looks like a big freezer door, so if you see it, holler."

"We're looking for a freezer door," he said as much to himself as back to me.

"If anyone asks what we're doing, I'm going to tell them you're recovering from surgery and I'm taking you for a walk because you couldn't sleep. What kind of surgery should we say you had?" I asked.

"A hernia," he responded. Not half bad, I thought.

"Sounds good. So if anyone asks, you tell them you're recovering from hernia surgery and are hoping to leave the hospital in the morning."

"Okay."

"Once we find the door, I'm going to wheel you up to the lobby, then head back down, go inside, and find the body. I'm hoping that'll take about an hour."

"I'd like to go with you into the morgue," he said deliberately.

"I'm not sure that'd be such a good idea, Papa. If I have to run, I don't want to have to worry about you."

"I don't know what there is to worry about."

What could go possibly go wrong? I thought again, rolling my eyes.

"No arguments," I said and continued without a beat. "As soon as I'm done, I'll pick you up in the lobby. No matter what, stay in the lobby and I'll pick you up. It might take a little longer than an hour, so you've got to be patient."

"I'll be fine."

"I've got plenty of reading material for you too." I pointed over my shoulder to a stack of large-print *Reader's Digest* back issues, Papa's favorite.

An hour later, I grabbed the parking ticket from the UCLA Medical Center parking kiosk and pulled my Subaru under the rising wooden arm into Lot 9. We'd forgotten to bring Papa's disabled-parking placard, so I wiggled into a skin-tight compact spot on the fourth level near the south elevator. Papa sprang from the car with an air of enthusiasm not befitting an eighty-eight-year-old, let alone one who just endured hernia surgery.

"Hey, you're supposed to be sick, Ingy," I said as I pulled his ride from the trunk and unfolded it. "Take a seat."

"I can walk on my own to the hospital," he said with mild resentfulness. This was true; he could still walk short distances without aid, but this was a moot point tonight. "You're supposed to be recovering. Ill. In pain. One foot in the grave. Sit." I pointed at the wheelchair, then steadied it while he gingerly lowered himself onto the worn green canvas.

"Ooh, I almost forgot the most important thing," I said. I popped open the back door, grabbed three magazines and plopped them into Papa's lap.

"Okay, let's review," I said, wheeling him to the elevator in my new set of scrubs. "You're recovering from hernia surgery, hoping to leave the hospital tomorrow. You couldn't sleep so we're taking a walk around the hospital."

"Right, ever sharp, kid."

Up to this point, my calm astounded me. I was about to brazenly walk into a hospital, break into the morgue and hunt for a corpse. Yet, somehow I was totally relaxed. Papa and I emerged from the elevator and navigated a zigzagging ramp toward the main entrance.

"Act sick, like a recovering patient," I murmured, bending over to his ear. He slumped and proffered a sickly look. "Genius!"

A blast of cool air hit my face as I pushed Papa past UCLA's sliding glass doors and into the hospital lobby; except for a guard and two tired-looking staffers behind the reception desk, the lobby was deserted. The guard, sixty-plus years old and balding in his navy-blue uniform, nodded at Papa as we strolled past him toward a bank of elevators.

"Catch any terrorists lately?" exclaimed Papa, to my horror. The guard swiveled around to face us, vaporizing any semblance of calm I'd enjoyed moments earlier. Gripping the handles tightly with frustration, I rotated the wheelchair.

"Excuse me?" he said, shooting a severe look at Papa. My grip tightened further, now visibly whitening my knuckles. "Caught a ninety-year-old trying to steal an extra helping of lime Jell-O from the cafeteria last week. That count?" He smiled.

"You old dog," replied Papa.

"He's always kidding around." I gave the guard a "sorry, this guy's a little crazy" look and swiveled Papa's chair around toward the elevators. "Good night," I continued.

The nearest elevator was waiting open, so I wheeled Papa in, facing the back of the elevator to prevent any further banter, and pumped the basement button. My left hand relaxed slightly on the handle as the door closed behind us.

"What were you thinking?" I asked, once the doors shut.

"Oh shithouse, I was just being friendly." He did have a way with words.

"Pop, you've got to try not to draw attention to us. I want to get in and out of here as quickly as possible—unnoticed."

Papa grunted and inserted the tip of his index finger into his right nostril.

A few seconds later, the elevator doors slid open. I rolled him into the corridor and then stopped at a T-shaped intersection connected to the main hallway. The basement was truly miserable; I could only imagine what it'd be like to have to wait down here in the gloom for an x-ray, nervous enough about having some horrible disease. Overhead, bank after bank of fluorescent tubes cast an austere tinge on the discolored, off-white walls and seventies-style speckled linoleum. For a school with so much funding, UCLA had obviously spent their money elsewhere.

A pointing hand stenciled on a green placard at the junction indicated that Radiology was to the left. Overhead, the tubes produced a dreary sixty-hertz hum. The place was totally deserted.

"That's where you go for x-rays?" I asked Papa, pointing down the corridor.

"For x-rays, and when they take blood."

"Ever see a door that looked like a freezer there?" I asked.

"No. Not that I remember," he said earnestly.

"Ever been down this way?" I asked, pointing toward the right.

"No."

"Well, what do you say we try the road less traveled, Ingy?"

"Sounds fine to me."

"Hold on!" Papa wisely grabbed the armrests (he'd learned from experience) and I accelerated the chair forward with both hands, momentarily kicking up the front wheels before rounding the corner toward the right hallway. The wheelie maneuver drew the ire of my parents, but always gave Papa a kick.

This hallway emanated the same depressing mood and continued another hundred feet, sprouting offshoot corridors every twenty-five feet. With a single glance, I could tell that none of the hallway's nondescript wooden doors met our criteria. Papa began humming softly to himself while I proceeded down the hall to check each of the branches. After another fifteen minutes of exploration, we finally hit a dead end with an alarmed emergency exit. It'd be easy to get lost here, and the experience now rekindled memories of UCLA Student Orientation where mischievous counselors told Edgar Allan Poe-esque stories of careless freshmen getting lost for days in the medical center's twenty-seven miles of hallways. Papa continued to hum, now with a more nervous tenor, or perhaps I was just projecting.

"I think we should've taken door number two," I said, dejected. I looked down at my watch; it was 10:15, way behind schedule.

"Its kind of frustrating when you're looking for something and can't find it," said Papa comfortingly.

"What do you say we head back and look on the Radiology side?" I said.

"Fine by me."

Seeking to raise my spirits on our way back, Papa entertained me with one of his many teenage orderly stories; remarkably, I hadn't heard this one. Responsible for removing dead patients from their hospital beds, apparently Papa had mistakenly wheeled the wrong patient (heavily sedated from surgery) to the morgue. The patient later woke up, nearly frozen and surrounded by corpses, and was only discovered three hours later, screaming, by the coroner. Sometimes I wondered if I was adopted. In any case, the story served its purpose, and by ten-thirty, we were back by the first set of elevators heading toward Radiology.

On the floor, a set of red foot-shaped stencils evidently led to the waiting room. Slowing my speed to a more casual pace, I pushed Papa along the footprints about twenty feet, past a pair of handicapped bathrooms, before pausing for a nonchalant look into the waiting room on our left. Along the wall, an elderly African American man in a ruffled tuxedo sat beside a younger woman, probably in her late fifties. The elder slouched forward, his face buried in his hands, crying quietly. The woman, probably his daughter, rubbed his back sympathetically. A male attendant sat at the counter reading a novel. No one bothered to look up at me, and before Papa could engage any of the visitors, I rolled him farther down the hall, leaving the footprints behind. Two more doors, both unmarked and with opaque glass windows, lined either side of the hallway before it terminated at yet another T.

"Let's hope we're getting close," I whispered into Papa's ear.

"Come again," he said, stopping his humming.

"I said I hope we're getting close." He nodded.

As we approached the intersection I closed my eyes, took a deep breath and offered a silent, nondenominational prayer.

"All the lights are off," he whispered.

I opened my eyes. He was right; someone had switched off the lighting on both sides of the corridor, doubtless to save electricity. It was impossible to see more than ten or fifteen feet down the right side of the hallway as it disappeared around another bend; however, about a dozen steps left of the intersection, a muted glow issued from the panes of a service alcove and the glass window set into its adjacent door. An empty gurney with a stack of folded white sheets and several boxes of surgical gloves sat against the far wall. Just as I was about to take a step forward to examine the placard next to the service window, someone inside the office cleared their throat, and, from the looks of the shadow cast on the hallway floor, stood up and began walking toward the door. Panicked, I accelerated the wheelchair down the opposite corridor into the gloom.

Chapter 25

I STOPPED JUST AROUND THE CORNER, breathless but ensconced in a comforting haze of darkness.

"What the hell?" Papa whined, vexed by my impulsive dash.

"Shhhhh," I whispered, gripping his shoulder firmly. "Someone's coming."

We both heard the door jerk open and a second later the squawk of a walkie-talkie.

"Just be patient. I'll be up in a minute," growled the voice. Whoever it was wasn't much younger than Papa and had soles worthy of a tap dancer. When the clopping receded I extracted my keychain from my pocket, careful to stifle the jangling.

"Let's see where we are."

I juggled my keys until Steven's inch-long lithium light settled between my thumb and forefinger, then depressed the button. About midway down, my beam illuminated the object of our expedition: a wide, stainless steel freezer door and an accompanying keypad. The door's twin sat embedded in the opposite wall. These had to be the two cadaver storage rooms.

"Eureka!" I whispered to Papa.

"Now we're cooking with gas, kid," replied Papa, equally excited.

I wheeled him between the two doors, both of which were clearly labeled: "Instructional Morgue" and "Hospital Morgue." That made things easier.

I pulled out my smartphone and looked up the code Linda had given me: five-four-five-five.

"Want to try to unlock it?" I asked Papa. Never mind the fact that if we did open the door, there was no way in hell Papa would agree to wait in the lobby. I'd worry about that on the off chance that the code still worked.

"How?" he said, looking up at me.

"I have an old code for the door. It might still work. Stand up and I'll give you the code."

Papa rose from the chair and scratched the back of his neck.

"The first digit is a five. Push five, Pop." Papa directed a shaky index finger toward the keypad and onto the five button, holding it down a good second before retracting his finger.

"Next hit four." Papa repeated the procedure. "Then five again," I paused. "And finally another five."

Papa released his trembling finger and looked expectantly at the door. A half-second later, the keypad emitted three rapid chirps. With my second prayer of the day, I grabbed hold of the hefty, stainless steel handle and tugged.

The handle refused to give. Fearing Papa's trembling hands might have inadvertently mashed an adjacent button, I re-entered the four-digit code. The door vetoed me once again.

"Damn," I whispered. Although I knew that the code had little chance of working, I'd still hoped.

"All right, Pop, I've got to get you back up to the lobby and find the combination." Pop turned, now partially stooped, and looked at me gravely.

"I don't want to go up. I want to help you here."

"Papa, I don't want you to get in any trouble."

"Ah, to hell with trouble. I'm eighty-eight years old, what are they going to do to me, send me to Leavenworth?"

I looked down at my watch.

"We don't have time for arguments. You want to stay? Stay. I need to get a look in the office around the hall. Do you want to stay here, or should I bring you over to the bathroom by Radiology?"

"I'll stay here."

"Fine. Don't move. Don't talk. Don't fart. I'll be right back." Papa eased himself back into the chair and began kneading his swollen, arthritic knuckles.

It had been a minute since the tap-dancing septuagenarian left his post. I didn't know how long before he'd return, so I walked briskly back down the hall, took a quick look toward Radiology—the hallway was empty—and over to the alcove. The door was closed. A carved wooden block resting just behind the service window read "Clarence."

Reaching for the doorknob, I was gripped by a surge of anxiety. I looked back over my shoulder, then leftward down the darkening hallway. Both clear. A single bead of sweat accumulated on my temple.

The doorknob to Clarence's station turned effortlessly and with infinite care I inched the door open just a hair, peered in to make sure there wouldn't be any surprises, then swung the door fully open and lowered the door stop. If the guy came back I'd say the door was open, that I was just looking for help.

The office consisted of a storeroom and the service alcove we'd seen from the hall. An old CRT monitor sat on a severely nicked, antique metal desk, along with a keyboard, a phone—its handset tagged "X7519," and coffee dregs in a formulaic paper poker-card cup. I held my breath, listened for footsteps, and then slid open Clarence's desk drawer. Aside from a handful of pens, a blank pad of stickies and a small notebook, the drawer was barren. The notebook—the miniature variety with the tightly wound spiral aluminum coil—had seen better days. I gently lifted its green cover, which remained attached by just the bottom few coils, to find a series of notes shakily scrawled in pencil. Unfortunately, neither the inside cover nor the first few pages offered any tantalizing clues—only a few phone numbers and a reminder to buy milk, denture cleanser, and walnuts. Later pages contained similar minutiae, coffee stains, and a creased gas station receipt.

Thirty seconds of additional flipping led me to the second-to-last page, which to my delight contained two columns of four-digit numbers. Though neither column was labeled, I knew these were the codes. The list ran the length of the page and from the spurious pencil marks on the opposite page, I guessed it also ran down its back. A flip confirmed my suspicion and simultaneously raised and dashed my hopes. Midway down the page, Clarence had decided to start concealing his codes, replacing the four-digit numbers with four-letter codes. This in itself didn't bother me; his unbreakable code was almost certainly just a substitution of the digits with letters from the telephone dial. What did bother me was that the last line of the right column didn't end in a four-digit code, but rather in the words "Andrea's birthday"—a mnemonic that was obviously trivial for Clarence to remember but utterly useless to me.

Loathe to waste any more time, I wrote the last four-letter code, "BYNE," on a stickie, dropped the notebook back into the desk and rushed for the doorway.

Papa's tightly cropped head bobbed from behind the corner three times before I completed the forty-odd-foot walk back.

"I told you to stay out of view!" I sniped.

"What did you find?"

"Cross your fingers," I said, meaning it. "Let's see." I approached the door to the student freezer and extended my finger to key in the code.

"Crap," I said.

"What?"

"I need to translate the letters into numbers." Papa grimaced uncomprehendingly. I whipped out my smartphone and pulled up the phone-dialing screen. "Okay, here we go. B translates to a two, Y into a nine, N into a six, and E into a three." I keyed in the four digits in rapid succession.

"*Beep beep beep*," whined the door. I tried the handle anyway.

"Shit." I reentered the code.

"*Beep beep beep*." No, no, no!

"Let's see if we're at least on the right track," I said to Papa, who was still thoroughly befuddled. I walked across the hall to the other door and punched in the code.

Before I could lift my finger from the final button the door issued a loud click. I grabbed the cool, steel handle and pulled, if only for a momentary sense of accomplishment.

"Wonderful!" said Papa enthusiastically.

"Not quite, Papa. This is the wrong door. I couldn't find the code for the other door." Papa just stared at me.

"That's the room we want to get into." I pointed across the dim hallway. "I only found the code for this door."

"The body we're looking for isn't in there?"

"No."

"Oh."

I collapsed onto the ground and grabbed my knees in a thinking pose; Papa, seeing that we weren't about to go anywhere, lowered himself back into the chair and stared at me.

"Why the hell can't they just use a key?" asked Papa rhetorically. "What's wrong with a cockamamie key?"

"Give me a few minutes to think," I said. So much for my carefully laid plan. What were my options?

"Why don't you bribe the watchman?" I looked up at Papa. "Offer him five bucks." I shook my head.

"Five bucks isn't what it used to be, Pop."

"The veterans used to offer me fifty cents to bring them whiskey. If the head nurse had caught me, that would've been it." He drew his finger across his throat.

"Give me a second." I had a kernel of an idea. "I'll be right back." I held up a finger indicating "stay put."

A moment later I'd returned with the gurney and one of the white sheets we'd found outside the alcove.

"I've got an idea. Up for a little adventure?" I asked Papa with raised eyebrows.

"Of course."

"Can you play dead? I mean really pretend you're dead?"

"Absolutely." Papa immediately dropped his head onto his shoulder, closed his eyes, and gently slacked his jaw. I had to admit, my grandfather had serious talent in this department. The sight also made me strangely nostalgic; at eighty-eight, I didn't know how much longer he'd have, yet I'd rarely given it any thought. I took a deep breath. "Impressive. Now do you think you could play dead like that for five or ten minutes? You think you could fool the watchman?"

"Absolutely."

"You're positive you can hold that look no matter what? Even if you have a sudden urge to urinate?" I tilted my head and looked him in the eye. "Even if you have a hot flash?" Hot flashes, Papa's latest affliction, were the result of the testosterone-depriving prostate cancer treatments he'd been receiving and which had recently taken him to the edge. "No matter what?"

"No matter what," he replied. I knew the odds of such resolve were roughly 100 to 1, but I was desperate, and I figured if all else failed, Papa could talk us out of the predicament, geezer to geezer.

"Okay. I'm going to call this guy's phone when he gets back to the office and tell him you just died. Follow me?" Papa nodded. "I'll tell him you died, and that you had indicated your body be donated to the medical school cadaver program. I'll tell him that I'll wheel you down right away from your room upstairs in the medical tower. So we'll put you on the cart," I pointed to the gurney, "cover you, and wheel you over to the office, and then have the guy escort us over to the morgue. I'll wheel you in, thank the guy, and then walk away. Once he goes back to the office, I'll come back, knock on the door, and you can let me in." I paused. "Make sense?"

"Sure."

"And if the guy pulls the sheet up—you're delivering a performance, right?"

"Say again?"

"If the guy lifts the sheet, you play dead—just like you did a second ago."

"Yeah sure."

"You want to use the bathroom first?"

"Ah shit," he said. "I can take care of myself. I'll tell you if I want to use the damn bathroom."

"All right, get up on the cart," I said doubtfully, one hand stabilizing the gurney and the other supporting Papa's arm. A few seconds later, I draped the sheet over his body and face. "Comfortable? Can you breathe?"

"Yes."

"Okay, I'm going to wheel you past the elevator back into the other wing. Don't forget, you're dead. No talking, farting, or any other noises."

Several hallways later and now in relative seclusion, I pushed the gurney up against a wall and drew the sheet from Papa's face.

"Here goes nothing." It took just a second to remember Clarence's extension, and another minute or two to look up the hospital's area code and phone prefix on my smartphone. I entered the ten digits and hit Send. Six rings later Clarence's voicemail answered.

"Not back yet," I explained. Papa nodded sullenly.

"What's wrong?" I asked.

"I'm just thinking about Mawtha." Martha—my maternal grand-mother had meant the world to my grandfather—and to me; she'd passed away of brain cancer ten years ago and Papa had never been the same. "Laying under the sheet just got me thinking."

"Mmm," I responded.

The next five minutes passed in contemplative silence, and jarred by a chirping reminder on my phone's calendar, I tried Clarence's extension again.

On the fifth ring, Clarence picked up.

"Hello?" Clarence's gruff voice boomed equally from the phone and from down the hallway. I froze.

"Hello?" A pause. "Dammit."

"Eh-excuse me," I stammered, "is this the morgue office?"

"Yes."

"Perhaps you can help me then?"

"I can try. What do you need?"

"I've got a patient here in the North Tower. The guy just passed away. Doctor . . . Doctor Pascul finished filling out the paperwork and asked me to wheel him down to the med school freezer."

"Okay. Bring him down quick then. I'm taking my lunch break in fifteen."

"No problem. I'll be right down," I said.

"So far, so good," I said to Papa. "Ready to play dead? Need to use the bathroom first? Pass any gas? Scratch?"

"I'm fine," he replied.

"Fine. For good measure, let's wait a few minutes. The North Tower is a good ten-minute walk from here." I looked down to Papa again. "You think you can get off of the gurney by yourself to open the door?"

"I think so."

"Give it a try." I lifted the sheet with a flourish. Papa sat up, slowly rotated his body and extended his legs off the side of the gurney, then gently lowered his feet six inches onto the floor.

"Genius," I said, helping him back up. "Just remember, wait until I knock on the door before you open it. Otherwise just stay put on your cart once you're in. It might take me five minutes to come back, so don't get nervous. Close your eyes."

I pulled the sheet back over Papa's face, and gave his slightly protruding nose a loving squeeze through the sheet.

Chapter 26

"Hello?" I addressed the empty service alcove.

"One second," replied Clarence. A moment later, he emerged from the storage room carrying a thick folded plastic tarp.

"Hi. I called a few minutes ago." I pointed toward the gurney. "I've got the body right here."

Clarence, easily seventy years old, bounded with unusual agility to the gurney and lifted the sheet, exposing Papa's thirty-year-old coffee-colored loafers. He gave me a confused look.

"What's with the shoes?" He lifted the sheet farther. "The guy's still fully clothed." This, from Clarence's voice, was not as expected.

"The doctor said to bring him right down," I muttered.

"He died in his shoes?" replied Clarence disbelievingly. "The guy's ready to go to a senior center dance, for God's sake."

"I asked the same thing," I improvised, "Doctor Pascul said the guy was a complainer, wanted to go home, wouldn't take no for an answer. He pulled on his clothes and a minute later keeled over from a massive infarction."

"Has he been added to the database? Where's his tag?"

"I assume Doctor Pascul added him." I ignored the second question.

"He needs to be processed before they put him in the med school freezer. You need to take him to Embalming."

"The doctor called Embalming first. They open at seven-thirty a.m. He said to throw him in the freezer until tomorrow."

"Incompetent. Either way, we can't put him in the freezer unless he has a tag. I'll get fired. Can't have untagged bodies sitting in the freezer." Clarence shook his head reprovingly. "Give me the guy's name. Then, go take off his shoes and put them under the gurney. And get me a temporary tag from the back." He pointed to the storage room. "Someone's going to have to take him to Embalming tomorrow morning. What was his name?"

"Melvin Stover," I responded, inadvertently providing my grand-father's real name.

"Stoufer?"

"S-T-O-V-E-R," I replied nervously. Clarence clacked away on a vintage IBM keyboard.

"Strange."

"What?"

"I found the guy. He's been a patient here, but he's not currently admitted to the hospital and the system says he's still alive. You sure you've got the right name?"

"Positive. If you need, I can get Doctor Pascul on the line." A bluff.

"Nah. But do me a favor and go grab his paperwork after we drop him in the freezer. And throw it on my desk. I'll take care of it after my break. Oh, go grab a tag from the back and get his shoes off." Clarence shot an impatient glance at his watch.

Several dozen stiff white plastic tags, each about the size of a busi-ness card, sat jumbled in a box just inside the door of the storeroom. Beside the box lay a bundle of clear zip-ties—like the ones they used on *Cops*—clumped together with a wide rubber band; under the assumption we'd need something to attach the tag to Papa's foot, I gen-tly shimmied one of the ties from the middle of the bunch and exited the small room. Clarence, obviously in a hurry to go on his break, had already removed Papa's left shoe and was working on the right.

"Here," he gestured, "finish taking his socks off while I get his ID." Clarence dropped the shoe atop Papa's covered legs, shuffled over and grabbed the tag from my hand, and headed back to his computer. A moment later he handed me the shakily stenciled tag. "My fingers are bad with the hog ties. Do me a favor?"

"No problem." Following his instructions, I threaded the zip tie through a punched hole in the tag and then fastened it loosely around Papa's right big toe—all the easier to remove it later for a quick get-away.

"I'm going to put a note in his file that he's in the morgue. He doesn't even have a morgue ID yet and I don't want him to get lost."

"What did you write on the tag?" I asked, confused.

"I just wrote his patient ID. There's a whole lot of paperwork they're going to have to do in the morning before he gets his country club membership." Clarence gave me an incongruous wink and then joined the two of us in the hallway. "This way."

A moment later, we rounded the darkened corner and I wheeled Papa up to the med school freezer door on the left. Unsettlingly, Clarence headed straight for the opposite door.

"I thought we were supposed to put him in the student freezer," I said nervously.

Clarence turned. "No way he goes in there until he's properly tagged. For all we know his family wants him buried. Last thing we need is some co-ed taking a Ginsu to his schmeckle and a nice big lawsuit." Clarence returned his attention to the door. "Dammit."

"What's wrong?"

"Forgot the code. One minute." The septuagenarian shuffled off, leaving the two of us in the gloom.

Dammit was right. I needed Papa in the hospital morgue like I needed a goiter. Somehow I needed to get Clarence to put Papa in the student freezer, and just about the only way I could think of was sabotaging the door to the main morgue. I could try smashing the keypad or shorting the keypad with some water, but I didn't want to cause any damage. Then it came to me.

"Hold tight Pop, we're getting close."

"What's going on?"

"Just hold on. Keep your mouth shut for another few minutes."

I walked up to the main freezer's keypad and rapidly punched in a four-digit code, then another, and another. Each time, the keypad chastised me with its three beeps. Undeterred, I entered five more random sets of digits, each with the same result. Finally, on my ninth attempt, the keypad flashed three times and stayed silent. Promising. I keyed in another four digits and to my delight, the keys no longer brightened after each press; nor did the keypad beep after my fourth digit. Now the question was whether my repeated failed attempts would attract hospital guards or just activate a temporary security-lockout in the lock. I was either the world's smartest treasure hunter or the world's dumbest grave robber. Literally five seconds later, Clarence rounded the corner with his notebook and a, "Sorry about that."

"No problem."

Clarence approached the door and then flipped open the crumpled notebook to the last page, angling it to catch the dim light of the adjoining hallway.

"Damn conservationists."

"Want me to turn on the light? Where's the switch?"

"Nah, I've got it." He tucked the book into his pocket and punched the four keys, again demonstrating dexterity befitting someone twenty years his junior. The keypad, still in lockdown, wholly ignored Clarence's key-presses. Clarence anxiously reentered the combination a second time with the same result, then withdrew his notebook, consulted the last page, and repeated the ritual—again with the same result.

"Dammit."

"What's wrong?"

"The damn keypad is busted. I'm going to have to get someone down here to fix it."

"This guy's going to start stinking soon," I suggested innocently.

"Dammit. One second."

Clarence approached the other keypad and without hesitation entered the four digits, his memory obviously jogged by the "Andrea's Birthday" hint that earlier stumped me. True to form, the lock clicked, prompting Clarence to grab the cold steel handle.

"Throw him in there for now."

"Yes sir."

I rotated Papa's cart lengthwise and, with a pair of thumps, wheeled it over the rubberized threshold into the frigid cadaver farm and against the right-hand wall. Papa certainly wouldn't be lonely during my absence; dozens of cadavers, or rather their sheet-covered forms, filled the vast refrigerator.

"I'll be back in five or ten minutes," I whispered to the sheet. "Open the door when I knock." With a quick snap of my foot I engaged the gurney's wheel lock and left the room.

"Thank you."

"No problem." Clarence secured the door and yanked on the handle, just to make sure. "I've got to go. I want to see this guy's paperwork on my desk when I get back."

I nodded. Clarence stared intently at my face, as if waiting for a verbal confirmation.

"Yes sir," I complied, and a second later, he disappeared around the corner.

I waited a good thirty seconds after hearing the last, distant scrape of Clarence's leather-soled shoes before knocking on the door. Nothing. I counted off another twenty seconds and then rapped again.

"Papa?" God forbid he'd fallen asleep. "*Paahpuuuh!*" I bellowed with my hands cupped up against the steel door. I took a step back and began pounding on the imposing door with both hands. Mid-strike, the door edged open and a whoosh of cold air poured through the crack. Papa stood hunched behind the door, barefoot and shivering, haphazardly bundled in the hospital sheet that moments ago had enshrouded his body. This certainly wasn't going to work. I flipped on a light switch, flooding the room with cold white light.

"Get your shoes on." Papa gave me a confused look. I gently took his arm and led him to the gurney.

"Sit," I said, and helped him up. A second later, I had the tag removed and his shoes on.

"Okay, do you think you can make it back up to the lobby by yourself?"

"I, I, I'm st, st, staying with you," he stammered.

"You're going to freeze to death."

Papa stared resolutely.

"One second." Using my wallet as a wedge to prop the door open, I dashed back to Clarence's storeroom, snatched a thick stack of hospital sheets, and sprinted back. In several minutes, I had Papa swaddled from head to ankle in six layers of hospital sheeting. I also wrapped a few layers around myself—an LA native, I was a lightweight and it was at most a few degrees above zero.

"Okay?" I asked, my words taking physical form via a whitish vapor in the refrigerated air. "Think you can last about fifteen or twenty minutes until I find the body?"

Papa nodded uncomfortably. At least now I could search without any risk of getting caught—that was, until Clarence returned from his break.

"Just do me one favor," said Papa.

"What's that?"

"Promise me you won't open the door to the, to the . . ." he screwed up his face in thought, "safe house without me." He meant the panic room, of course; it was an easy enough request.

"I promise," I said, "now give me a few minutes and we'll be out of here."

Free from immediate danger, nosy seventy-year-olds, and mischievous grandparents (Papa wasn't going anywhere), I surveyed the room. Unexpectedly, its contents were in disarray. Dozens of steel-framed gurneys and their enshrouded passengers were haphazardly strewn across the Olympic pool-sized room. Metal-grated drains, probably designed to collect biological effluent in the event of an accidental thaw, dotted the antiseptic white, inch-square tiles at regular intervals, and a floor-to-ceiling grid of brushed steel refrigeration shelves lined the two opposite walls down the length of the room. Overhead, banks of harsh fluorescent tubes gave an ashen tinge to the plastic-wrapped inhabitants. An acrid mélange of disinfectant and formaldehyde completed the effect.

I approached the nearest cadaver. Like each of his cohorts, he was wrapped in a form-fitting muslin cloth, soaked no doubt in embalming fluid, and covered with a thick discolored plastic sheet to keep things nice and moist. The cadaver's feet—and the toe-tag I'd need to identify Richard's body—were tucked beneath the two layers but clearly discernable; I'd need to unwrap the lot to find my golden ticket—like a morbid version of *Charlie and the Chocolate Factory*.

Gently, I grabbed hold of a crimp in the plastic and drew it from its tucked position beneath the feet, then unwrapped the damp fabric—which had a stiffness reminiscent of a used rag—from the right foot. There was no need to look at the tag; the yellowed, veined appendage was obviously a woman's. A quick poke, more out of curiosity than anything, gave the impression of a balloon filled with dense putty. After a quick wrap and tuck I proceeded to the next body. One down.

Fifty-some more to go. A few more awkward attempts were enough to perfect the procedure, and soon I had each evaluation down to thirty seconds.

Alas, none of our fifty-four companions proved to be Richard; nor was he hiding in any of the wall units. Papa looked up as I walked over.

"Get what you need?" he asked, oblivious to the glum look on my face.

"No. He's not in here. We've got one more place to look," I said, pointing at the service elevator set into the far wall of the room, "and then I'm giving up. I think that goes up to the dissection room. Do you want to wait here or come with me?"

Papa signaled his response by grabbing the side of the gurney with both hands and shimmying his buttocks over to the edge; I grabbed his arm and helped him back onto his feet.

"If we run into anyone, you let me do the talking."

A brief ride in the elevator deposited us at the far end of the student morgue, two floors above. As the doors parted, the elevator's overhead lighting revealed a room about the size of a large dorm room, just as cold and sullen as the main morgue. I groped along the right wall for the switch. The room's lighting flickered briefly and then dimly illuminated nine additional corpses. Most appeared hastily covered and, happily, all but one's feet and tags were directly visible through the plastic sheeting.

"Give me a sec, Pop."

It took just a minute to survey the remaining nine bodies—and to dash my hopes. Richard wasn't among the dead.

"Shit," I whispered. "Let's get out of here. He's not here."

I motioned Papa toward a door opposite the elevator and, upon reaching it myself, flicked off the light and quietly eased the door open. The room beyond, as I'd guessed, housed the dissection lab. What I hadn't guessed was that there'd be med students working overtime on a corpse; the body's chest cavity had been cracked open and peeled back into a gruesome maw. Two scalpel-wielding co-eds hovered over the remains.

I nudged the door a hair more to get a better view.

"Look. The guy had a small tumor." Student number one, a redhead with Pippi Longstocking freckles, pointed inside the cadaver's abdomen.

"I've seen enough tumors. I'll be right back, I've gotta pee," responded the second coed dismissively.

"How old are you? Five?"

"*Whatevah.*" The brunette exited stage right, revealing the corpse's pain-stricken face.

Richard's face.

Chapter 27

I EASED THE DOOR SHUT, temporarily plunging the two of us into frigid, inky blackness.

"He's outside," I whispered excitedly, "holy shit!" I flipped the lights back on.

"Who . . . who's outside?" asked Papa, shivering. I realized he hadn't also been peeking through the crack and explained.

"The corpse—our cadaver is on an exam table outside."

"Well then let's go already," Papa emoted, just a bit too loudly. I put my finger to my mouth and flashed the universal quiet sign.

"We can't. There're two girls in the room with him."

"Shit. Let's just go out, take a look, and leave already." There it was; he was finally getting antsy. But I had to admit, two hours thus far, some of it in near-zero temperatures without a single complaint, was a new North American record. Usually a half hour at the Reseda Denny's was sufficient.

"No, we'll get caught." I eased my back against the wall and slid down onto the floor. "We're not supposed to be in here. We'll be arrested if we go out. We've got to wait until they finish, and then we can take a look." I lowered my head to my knees and covered my eyes with my palms, creating a cathartic suction between them and my face. I pumped my palms in and out several times to repeat the effect. "It'll just be a few minutes. Let's go hide in—"

Before I could utter "the elevator," the door swept open with a whoosh of air. Caught—caught, after getting so close. A flood of adrenaline, and with it, a rush of feeble excuses raced into my mind, each less plausible than the last. I paused a beat, took a deep breath, and uncovered my now blurry eyes and directed them up at the students.

But there were no students in the doorway. What I did see increased my terror—if that was possible. Papa had thrown open the door and was clopping at a full geriatric gallop into the lab, with what purpose

136

I had no idea. Despite the intense desire to yell, no words came from my mouth, and despite my masochistic desire to view the impending calamity, my muscles refused to cooperate. So I sat on the floor, blurry and stunned.

"I'm not dead. They put me in the freezer but I'm not dead," croaked Papa. "Help me."

"How did you . . . what?" replied the redhead's stupefied voice.

"I didn't die. I'm not dead." He delivered a theatrical pause. "*Aaaugh*, I think I'm having a heart attack."

"Oh God. Oh God. One second."

The telltale clopping of Papa's coffee loafers filled a beat of silence.

"Where are you going?" I heard another door open.

"Where's my daughter?" He coughed. "I want to go home. I'm not dead." A second later, the door clicked shut.

"Oh fuck." This time it was the brunette. After a dash of footsteps, the out-of-view door again creaked open and a second later, it clicked shut. Holy Jesus.

Jolted to my senses, I staggered to my feet and dashed through the open door straight toward Richard's chopped-up corpse. Finally face-to-face with my anthropomorphic treasure map, I hesitated just a moment out of disgust before grasping Richard's bloodless lower lip and tugging downward. The flesh gave like a piece of rubbery leather, and, to my delight, revealed the six missing digits, tattooed backward in blue ink. Sans mirror, it took me a few seconds to reverse the digits in my head: seven, six, nine, five, four, two—I checked twice, and then grabbed a ballpoint pen from an instrument tray and jotted the numbers on my left palm. After an obsessive third check, I ducked back into the mini-morgue and rode the elevator to the basement—Papa would have to fend for himself for a few minutes. Fortunately, Clarence was either still on break or hiding within his alcove, for I didn't encounter a soul on my way back to the main elevator.

Back at my Subaru, I waited five minutes before dialing the main hospital line and asking to be transferred to the ER, the most likely place they'd take Papa after his miraculous resurrection—either there or the psych ward.

A Filipina woman answered the phone on the third ring.

"Emergency Room—how can I direct your call?"

"Melvin Stover, please."

"One second." I heard the requisite clicking on the keyboard. "I'm sorry, can you spell that?"

I did.

"No, we definitely don't have anyone by that name in the ER. Would you like me to transfer you to the main operator?"

I didn't have a chance to answer; someone was call-waiting my cell.

"One second." I tapped the switch-calls button.

"Hello?" I answered.

"Hi, can you please connect me to the front desk?"

"Dad? It's Alex."

There was a pause on the other end of the line.

"Alex? Isn't this . . . I thought I dialed the hospital. I must be losing my mind." He sounded half-asleep.

"What's wrong?" I played dumb.

"Your grandfather is over at UCLA Medical Center."

"What happened? Is everything okay?"

"The nurse says he came running out of the morgue screaming that someone mistook him for a cadaver and threw him in."

"What? How?" I barely contained myself.

"Lord only knows, but knowing your grandfather, it's not that surprising. I'm just glad your mother's not here. She'd die of humiliation. I don't know how he gets into these messes."

"It runs in the family," I joked uneasily.

"Well, fortunately your mother seemed to turn out fine. Anyway, I need to go pick him up. Get some sleep, I'm sorry I woke you."

I briefly considered informing my father that I was wide-awake, two minutes away from the hospital entrance, and could pick Papa up, but common sense prevailed.

"Good luck!" I said. "Give him my best and tell him I'm happy he's not a cadaver."

My father grumbled uncharacteristically and then said "Good-night, Alex," and hung up.

It wasn't quite the ending I'd planned for, but better than most of the alternatives.

Remembering my promise to Papa and the beating I'd take from Steven if I cracked the seal on the panic room on my own, I headed back to Northridge for a well-deserved few hours of sleep.

Chapter 28

By six I gave up on trying to sleep, and with infomercials hawking Abdominators on all my regular TV stations and Steven undoubtedly experiencing rapid eye movements, I grabbed my laptop off the floor and propped it on my lap. After an eternally long boot-up and a few clicks I'd checked my stocks and deleted three offers for "v1agra" and one email from a long-lost Nigerian uncle looking to help me collect my rightful fifteen-million-dollar inheritance from our mutual Peruvian cousin, Juan Carlo.

Juan Carlo from Peru, no—but I did know a Fidel in Brazil—and he hadn't checked his email in two days. In all of the excitement, I'd completely forgotten my electronic surveillance drop box.

The summary webpage read: "*25 emails novos.*" Twenty-five new messages. My heart jumped. I quickly clicked the inbox button only to be rewarded by an endlessly spinning browser progress icon. Frustrated, I clicked the link several more times in rapid succession, and a second later the site acquiesced and displayed a list of the first twenty emails. Not one was from my spyware—from their identical subject lines, all clearly contained Latin-language spam. Dejected, I selected the lot and clicked the "delete" button. The site refreshed the page and listed the remaining five messages. The first four, like those on the previous page, were clearly junk; the last, however, had a Russian-looking sender name in indecipherable Cyrillic and a subject of "30/08/15 8:00am." I'd netted my shark.

Eagerly, I clicked up the email and was presented with a transcript of Khalimmy's keystrokes. I scanned the first few lines:

google.com
Chinese takeout, 91601

Besides kidnapping, Khalimmy was also into Chinese food. A quick search of the accompanying zip code further revealed that he had a place somewhere in North Hollywood. Worth telling the police,

I thought. I continued scrolling down through the text when I found this:

> bash90266@vipmail.com
> We need to meet. Our supplier is not cooperating and we've got to decide what to do with our security deposit SOON. Usual place for breakfast tomorrow @ 8:00am? AK

More bad news. Khalimmy was getting restless, and if he was keeping to his timetable, his "security deposit," Ronald Lister, had less than twenty-four hours to live. Maybe less, if the email was any indication. But even if I handed the diamond over, what were the odds he'd keep his end of the deal? That was, assuming there was a diamond, and that it was in the panic room. Impulsively, I double-clicked the notepad icon and started constructing a forged reply from Khalimmy's associate:

> From: bash90266@vipmail.com
> To: Spirited One <khalimmy@freemail.com>
> Subject: RE: We need to meet
>
> The usual location is no good. I'll explain when we meet. Instead, meet at the Griffith Park Observatory at 2800 East Observatory Road–stand right in front of the stairway up to the right telescope. Carry a book in your left hand if you think you've been followed, in the right otherwise. I might be a bit late. Watch your back. Don't call.

A seedling of a headache began sprouting behind my right temple; I'd need some caffeine soon. Shaking it off, I proceeded to spend the next fifteen minutes scouring several of the more well-known hacker sites for a list of lax email servers—these improperly secured computer systems, usually located in Sub-Saharan Africa and other less tech-savvy areas of the world, were favorites of the hacker community because they would accept an email from anyone and forward it to anyone without any authentication. Many of these servers had been blacklisted, cut off from the rest of the Internet, because of the droves of spam they spewed. Others had gone largely unnoticed by the spammers and could still be used for occasional mischief. I picked one located in Zambia and sent my spoofed email to Khalimmy's email account, forging the "from" address as bash90266@vipmail.com—the address of Khalimmy's contact. I hit Enter and a few seconds later, the slipshod server reported the email's successful transmission. Now the only question was whether Khalimmy would see it before heading to his original rendezvous. This was my one chance to see the bastard, get his license plate number and if all worked out, save Richard Lister's brother. I crossed my fingers. Either way, my next stop was Griffith Park, hopefully with Steven.

By half past six, I couldn't contain myself any longer so I punched Steven's home number into my cordless and counted the rings impatiently. At four, his home phone answering machine picked up.

"Hi, we're not here—"

Dammit.

I hung up and keyed in his mobile number, but this too went immediately to voicemail. This time I left a message: "Hey Steven, give me a call as soon as you can. I need your help—it's urgent. I'm heading over to Griffith Observatory right now."

"Shit." I had no desire to do this alone. But what choice did I have?

I found a ratty Dodgers baseball cap in the closet and pulled on a pair of wraparound sunglasses. Fifteen minutes later I was flying down the 118, incognito in my hat, glasses, and scruffy jogger's attire.

Chapter 29

THE FIRST WAVES OF HEAT were already radiating from the Griffith Park blacktop by the time I pulled off Observatory Road and into the sparsely occupied lot. I was cutting it a bit close, my anticipated seven-twenty arrival dashed by a disemboweled purple couch occupying the third and fourth southbound lanes of the I-5 freeway. With no time to spare, I threw a small bottle of water into my shorts and began jogging toward the observatory. Aside from an early morning runner and his retriever, the park appeared deserted; only a few cars with staff decals peppered the lot, and as far as I could see, the mysterious Khalimmy had yet to take his place in front of the right-hand stairwell. Reaching the edge of the asphalt, I gingerly stepped over the foot-high wooden partition marking the start of the hike and continued up the dirt trail and around a loop-back until I reached an elevation that afforded me a comprehensive view of the building's grassy quad, the towering concrete Astronomer's Monument, and most importantly, the base of the rightmost stairwell.

Satisfied with my vantage, I leaned against a hollowed-out oak, donned earphones, and began playing Pink Floyd's *The Final Cut*. Within minutes, the back of my neck was hot to the touch and a film of sticky perspiration clung to my face; a quarter of an hour more of vicious heat convinced me that my skin was worth more than a perfect view of the stairwell, so I sat on an exposed, age-polished root along the shaded west side of the tree and rested against the weathered bark. From this position, I figured I could just see the head of anyone approaching the right telescope—it'd be good enough. Besides, it was already twenty after, and I was quickly losing hope that Khalimmy had received my early morning message.

At twenty past, a bald head—all I could see was a sunburned forehead—stopped by the stairs and faced the monument. Encouraged, I paused the album and rose to my feet. The head was attached to a pear-shaped specimen, late forties, wearing a white "Alaska" tshirt, gray floppy sweat-shorts, black socks and Birkenstocks. After a second of rummaging through a blue denim fanny pack, he withdrew a digital camera and motioned his children, who I'd managed to ignore in my initial excitement, toward Galileo's statue. Wearily, I settled back onto my root and continued listening.

Three subsequent sightings over the next twenty minutes were equally fruitless, and finally, certain of the failure of my last-minute plan and miserably hot and sticky, I rose to my feet, peeled the moist shirt from my back, and trudged back down the path. All went smoothly until about a swimming pool's length from the end of the trail. Here, the grade steepened, causing me to accelerate, and before I could react, I had snared my running shoe on the wooden partition. Try as I might to balance myself, my forward momentum was too great, my shoelace too strong, and the laws of physics immutable.

My body followed the path of a windshield wiper and a fraction of a second later I lay facedown on the ground with a throbbing right cheek and tingling, burning palms, no doubt shredded from grating over the coarse asphalt.

"Goddammit, you almost knocked me over!" shouted an irritated voice from a few feet away.

Roused from my shock but still unable to speak, I tried to prop myself up and look toward the voice but merely collapsed in the attempt. A moment later, I felt someone jimmy my foot from the partition.

"Here, take my hand."

"Okay," I think I managed to respond.

A pair of large hands assisted me until I rested more or less steadily on the pavement. Several constellations of red dots and scrapes covered my palms and I could feel trickles of blood running from my cheek. I looked up at the man, less stunned now.

"Sorry about that," I said. The man was in his fifties, a solid six feet, graying stubble adorning acne-pocked cheeks and a mess of thinning, wavy brown-gray hair. He wore an old pair of brown slacks and a white, short-sleeved dress shirt reminiscent of those worn by the NASA mission control guys in *Apollo 13*.

"Why don't you watch where you're going?" he spat. His accent was vaguely Middle Eastern. He looked down at his watch nervously.

"Sorry. I tripped," I said. "Thanks again for the hand."

He grunted, then took a step back, bent over and picked up a Stephen King paperback from the pavement. Jutting out from between its pages was a folded printout—I caught a glimpse of the top—a printout of my forged email.

Jesus Christ, it was him.

Khalimmy stared at me a long second, shook his head, then turned and hurried toward the quad. Then after a moment's hesitation, he made an about-face, walked up to a vintage red Mustang parked at the other side of the lot, and grabbed a bottle of water through the rolled-down passenger-side window.

Still perched on the wooden divider, I watched him make his way to the right stairwell and take a seat upon an adjacent concrete wall, and, after a brief scan of the area, with an obvious mocking "what kind of paranoia is this?" look on his face, he deliberately transferred the novel to his right hand and began reading.

Convinced he was now thoroughly preoccupied with his book, I hobbled over to my car and popped the trunk, which in addition to my climbing gear, held a case of water bottles, a first aid kit, and a gym towel. I uncapped a bottle, then another, and poured them over my stinging face, arms, and legs to wash off the blood and debris. Then I dried the scrapes with a roll of paper towels and shoved the blood-soaked lot into an old plastic bag. Once I finished, I shot a look back at Khalimmy, who was still engrossed in his book.

I needed to get a look at his license plate. I rose and made for a trail that skirted the edge of the parking lot, in an effort to surreptitiously gain a better view. Then my smartphone began ringing.

"Alex, where the hell are you?" asked Steven.

"Good morning to you too," I responded, still limping toward the trail. "It's about time!"

"What happened last night? You're obviously not in jail. Or are you?" he reconsidered.

"I'm here with the guy," I stammered. "I mean the kidnapper guy, the Khalimmy guy, he's thirty yards away."

CAREY NACHENBERG

"What?"

"Didn't you get my message?"

"No, we just got up."

"Listen, it's a long story, but I've almost got his license plate number—"

"Where are you?"

"Griffith Park."

"What? Why the hell are you at Griffith?"

"Later," I said. "I just wanted to get the guy's plate and take off, but now he's seen me. So it's a little more complicated. . . ."

"He what?" he yelled into the phone. "But there's no way he'd know who you are, right?"

"I don't know. I don't think so," I said uncertainly. I reached the trail and began hobbling counterclockwise around the lot.

"Can you get his license plate? The police could probably look up his address in a second."

"I'm working on it." I continued around the perimeter and limped nonchalantly toward a Park bulletin board until part of the Mustang's rear plate finally came into view. The plate's first four characters read "6CWH." I leaned in to try to catch the last three digits but they were obscured by a rusting metal pole. I needed to get closer. I shot a look back at Khalimmy.

"Crap."

"What?"

"He's getting up. One minute."

Khalimmy rose, followed the wall to a blue recycling container, and pushed his plastic bottle through the small round opening; then after a moment's hesitation, he walked purposefully toward the main entrance.

"I think he's going inside. Hold on, I've got an idea." I shoved the phone into my right pocket.

Once Khalimmy had disappeared behind the tinted glass doors I hobbled over to the passenger-side window of his Mustang, took a second glance over my shoulder at the entrance, and reached through the open window for the glove box latch. The small steel button stubbornly resisted a gentle push so I delivered it a second, less forgiving stab and with a crack, the latch gave and the door shot open and onto its hinges.

Ignoring Steven's mumbles from my pocket, I plunged my hand into the box and rummaged through the detritus until I found what I was looking for: a rubber band-bound, red-plastic-sleeved owner's manual. With a gentle tug, the band, crusty with age, snapped and fell to the seat. I'd worry about that later; right now I was interested in the registration slip, which to my satisfaction had been tucked into the inner pocket of the sleeve.

The white slip read:

Arnaz Khalimmy
19591 Gilmore Street
El Segundo, CA 90245

Sans pen, I recited the address three times until I figured I'd remember it, and then, after a final check of the observatory entrance, I tucked the slip back into the sleeve, replaced the manual in the glove box, and withdrew my head and arms from the car.

Free of the Mustang, I turned around and launched forward, practically smashing into a toned young blonde on her way to the grassy quad.

"Excuse me," I said, and then, "where did I put my sunscreen?" just loud enough to be heard but not so loud as to sound contrived.

Chapter 30

"ONE SEC," I SAID.

"What happened?" asked Steven anxiously. I ignored him and instead clicked up my phone's notepad application and typed in Khalimmy's address.

"Okay, back."

"What the hell happened?" Steven repeated, this time more emphatically.

"The guy went inside the observatory, so I popped his glove box and got his address from his car registration. Then I took a casual stroll over to the information kiosk in the parking lot. I'm pretending to read about the native plants of Griffith Park as we speak."

"You're crazy!" I was, and I could still feel my heart pounding.

"What if there was a cop, or someone saw you? What if *he* saw you?"

"Dude, they're going to kill Richard's brother. We need the guy's address."

"But the police could've looked the plate up in a second and—"

"It's done and I'm okay. It's not worth debating."

Steven started to speak but then censored himself. Then he said, "What are you going to do with the address?"

"I'm going to call the cop we met at Devonshire station."

Hillary's attenuated voice vaguely crackled over the smartphone's speaker; it sounded uncharacteristically whiny.

"One second, I'm talking to Alex," said Steven.

"Now," came a louder, more agitated response.

"Give me a minute." Steven cupped his hand over the phone. Muffled arguing ensued.

I used the breather to take a look around. Unfortunately, the kiosk obstructed my view of both the main entrance and the stairwell. I did, however, have a good view of the Mustang.

"Hello?" said a familiar, nearby voice. I turned to see who was addressing me but saw no one.

"Yes?" I returned reflexively, although I doubt so much as "yeh" left my mouth before the voice continued and I swallowed the word.

"Where the hell are you? I've been waiting here for forty-five minutes," continued the Middle Eastern voice—Khalimmy's voice. He was on the other side of the kiosk. "I know you said not to call, but . . ." He stopped.

"What do you mean what am I talking about? You told me to meet you at Griffith Park, no calls, double-oh-seven bullshit," continued the one-sided conversation. "Yeah, you're right, one of us is crazy. I can show you the email."

"I'm back," interrupted Steven. I smashed the End key on my phone and continued listening.

"I don't like this. I don't like this at all. I want to get this over with now."

The voice paused, then said, "All right, I'll stop by, but the moment we're done I'm going home to take care of it."

An instant later, my phone began vibrating. I barely stifled the follow-on ring with a quick press of the top button.

"Fine, thirty minutes," fired off Khalimmy, and a moment later he hurried to the Mustang shaking his head.

I yanked my Outback's door closed, pushed the lock button, and speed-dialed Steven. He answered before the first ring.

"What the hell happened?"

"They're going to kill him." I turned the key in the ignition. "Today."

"You've got to call the cops, man."

"I was just about to after I called you. You got a pen?"

"Yeah . . . one second . . . okay."

"Write this down: 19591 Gilmore, in El Segundo. That's Khalimmy's address, just in case anything happens. Are you familiar with that area?"

"No."

"I think it's industrial. Anyway, I'll give you a call once I figure out what's up with the cop."

A few minutes later, with business card in hand, I was on hold for Officer Flanco. At least he was in the office.

"Officer Flanco is on the phone," responded a female agent, "do you want me to transfer you to his voicemail?"

"No, I'll wait."

"Okay, please hold," and after a click, I was returned mid-advertisement to the mayor touting rewarding job opportunities with the LAPD Valley Division.

A few seconds later, the on-hold advertisements cut out. "Officer Flanco."

"Hi Officer Flanco, this is Alex Fife." I paused, waiting for a click of apprehension. "I reported the computer kidnapping threat last week."

"Oh, hello Mr. Fife. No progress so far, but I forwarded my notes over to the computer crime guys in West LA." He took a sip of something. "Have they contacted you?"

"No. Listen, I tracked down the kidnapper guy and I think he's going to kill this Ronald Lister guy today."

"Whoa. You tracked him down?" His voice more entertained than serious.

"I got another email. He said he wanted to kill Lister," I said, exasperated. "So I set up a meeting and . . . it's a long story . . . I got his address."

"You what?" Now he sounded infuriated. "You can't go around playing cop—you're going to get yourself killed."

I ignored him and continued. "I overheard him on his cell and he says he wants to kill Ronald Lister today."

"Alex, listen to me. What *exactly* did he say?"

"It's hard to remember. . . . He said something like he was going to take care of things today."

"Did he say 'kill,' 'murder,' 'harm,' anything explicit?"

"I don't think so."

"Are you sure?"

I reviewed the conversation in my head. "He wasn't explicit—but it was pretty damn clear what he meant."

"Did he mention Ronald Lister by name?"

"No," I admitted.

"That's pretty thin, Alex. You heard a conversation saying they were going to take care of something, but what it was they're going to take care of, you're not sure. Are you even sure this was the right guy?"

"Dammit. He's going to kill the guy."

"Listen, first of all, unless he explicitly says he's going to kill or hurt the guy, this won't even make it on the list. Those are our directives. You can ask my captain if you like. Second, and this is more important, you're," he paused, "you're a good kid but I think you've been a little obsessed with this whole thing. Don't you think this might be a prank, that you might be blowing this out of proportion? I mean, trying to meet this guy *in person*, reading his emails?"

"Listen to me. I'm not crazy. I'm not obsessed. This guy is going to be murdered."

"All right, Alex. Why don't you come down to the station at one-thirty and I'll take down your statement, and I'll try to conference in our local FBI kidnapping liaison. He'll give you a fair shot, and if he agrees, they can take over."

I banged the top of my dash with my fist.

"It can't wait. He said he would do it this morning, after he's done meeting God only knows who—his partner or someone. Can't you just send a car out to his address?"

"We can't—"

"Just to take a look?" I interrupted.

"Alex, unless you heard him explicitly say he was going to kill someone or have some other concrete evidence, we can't go barging into his home."

"This guy's death is on your head," I shouted and then threw the phone onto the seat, my raw palms throbbing.

"Screw it." I'd go on my own. If I got arrested searching Khalimmy's house, so be it.

Chapter 31

KHALIMMY'S HOUSE SAT AT THE END of a quiet cul-de-sac lined with remodeled fifties-era bungalows, reasonably well maintained lawns and mature, leafy trees in what had to have been one of the few upscale neighborhoods in industrial El Segundo. Just prior to reaching the house, I cancelled my phone's navigation system, took a U-turn, and parked a block away in the lot of a neighborhood playground I'd seen on my way over. I made a final call to Steven's cell, my sixth during the drive over, and was again sent to voicemail.

Skin is the most sensitive of organs, densely packed with nerves, and the otherwise mundane process of exiting my car took on a whole new meaning as my abraded, scabbing skin stretched and cracked, radiating needles of pain through my body. I winced from the initial shot of pain, threw on a clean shirt from my trunk, and then began walking at a brisk pace down the sidewalk toward Khalimmy's house.

Based on my earlier house-hunting experiences, the beige stucco-covered single-story house was of the Spanish Hacienda-style and looked to have been built in the early 1940s. Before me, a quaint brick walkway led across a scrubby, yellowing lawn peppered with clovers, through an archway to the front door. The matching brick driveway, to my right, was thankfully empty.

Despite my desire to look over both shoulders, I abstained and instead walked nonchalantly up the walkway until I reached a series of flagstones; these I followed left along the white rosebush-covered front of the house to the side yard. By the time I reached the gate just seconds later, my heart was hammering.

This was crazy.

But I had to do it.

I looked back, and to my surprise and relief the gate was obscured by an unruly ten-foot-tall bougainvillea and largely hidden from the street.

A nervous bit of blind fumbling for the latch revealed that the gate was padlocked from the inside, so I painfully mantled up the ivy-covered property wall and dropped behind the fence and into the backyard. The yard's rear walls were covered by dark, thick masses of overgrown vines and shrubs, many fifteen feet high, while creeping ivy covered the rear wall of the house, giving the whole yard an ominous dark mood, even in the now dreadful August sun.

This being my first and hopefully my last burglary, I had no desire to get caught—especially if Flanco was right and this was somehow a big misunderstanding. Yet deep down I knew it wasn't and everything in my core told me what I was doing was right. Improvising, I approached a curtained window just behind the gate, hoping to find it unlocked—I wasn't ready to start breaking glass just yet—then pushed my raw palms flush against the pane and attempted to use friction to slide the window open. After a few attempts, I gave up and walked around to the back to take a look at my other options. The rear of the house had two more windows, similarly shrouded in dark adobe-colored curtains, and a dilapidated back door with a doggie hatch.

Just what I was hoping for—I'd taken advantage of our own doggie door dozens of times as a teenager. I crouched down on the rear porch and tried to push my hand through the flap, only to find it had been blocked from the inside by a plastic security insert. Without a second thought I formed a fist and punched straight through the insert, sending it flying into the room. While my arm was long enough to reach the interior knob, I had to jam my shoulder deep through the portal just to make contact with the deadbolt, and it took an eternity of painful straining and fingering the edge of the bolt before I was able to nudge it to the vertical position and unlock the door. After a firm shove, the old door grudgingly disengaged from the jamb and swung open into a cramped laundry room whose every surface was blanketed in dust. Taking my first step into Khalimmy's house, and now surely guilty of committing a felony, I felt a surge of heat rush to my face and a wave of stress-induced perspiration. I took a deep breath and closed my eyes for a second.

The room was cool and nerve-rackingly quiet, the only noise a slight whistle from an air-conditioning vent set into the floorboard. I turned to lock the back door, then, after a second's thought unlocked and opened it a crack, just in case I needed a quick getaway.

Within a minute I had completed a circuit of the first floor, which was connected via a single rectangular hallway that visited each of the shared living spaces—kitchen, walk-in pantry, dining room, family room, living room, and entryway with a staircase to the second floor. Khalimmy was an obsessive-compulsive collector; every surface on every table and chair, not to mention most of the oak floor, was covered in stacks of old Arabic or Farsi-language newspapers, books, and magazines, leaving a foot-wide conduit through the dust-laden detritus. The chaos was made all the more eerie by a near total lack of outside light. Blackout curtains were drawn over every window; he obviously liked his privacy. Noticeably absent was any sort of windowless room—the better to hold a prisoner—or any door leading to a basement, where I'd envisioned Ronald Lister would be held.

Discouraged, I negotiated back through the stacks to the entryway and took the stairs two at a time up to the second floor. I cracked open the first of three doors accessible from the second-floor landing until it hit an obstruction, and peeking in, found it similarly packed to knee-level with thousands of books and periodicals. The second bedroom was similarly crammed, save for a six-by-four literature-free zone occupied by a card table, folding chair and old desktop computer, no doubt the one that had been sending me back electronic intelligence reports.

I completed my investigation of the upper floor with a visit to the master bedroom and bathroom. No Ronald Lister, no rooms where he could be held, no evidence of him—just a house filled with stacks and stacks of reading material—if Khalimmy had Lister here, he was well hidden.

A wave of nerve-induced dizziness overtook me. I steadied myself against the landing's wood railing, and for a second time my mind fixated upon the barely audible hiss of the air conditioning. The dizziness passed.

I worked my way down the stairs, through the entryway and back to the kitchen.

"Dammit!" I yelled at the top of my lungs. "Am I fucking crazy? Where . . . the . . . fuck . . . are . . . you . . . Ronald . . . Lister?"

The faint whistle of the air conditioning filled the void left by my outburst.

"Dammit!" I repeated, and looked around helplessly.

An instant later, a faint noise rose above the whistle, hopefully not from Khalimmy or the police, hopefully from some neighborhood kids playing hooky, or a dog. I dove into the pantry, closed the door to a crack, and tried to stifle my breathing so I could better hear.

The noise—maybe a muted voice—repeated, this time louder yet still unintelligible.

Then again: ". . . need water, plee . . ."

My heart jackhammered. Lister was in the house.

"Hello? Ronald?" I bellowed. "I've come to rescue you. Where are you?"

"Water, please," came the reply, this time less muffled and from directly underfoot. I pushed the door open an inch and fumbled for the light switch on the outside wall, then scanned the floorboards for a vent—the voice was obviously carrying through the vents, but there were none to be seen in the pantry.

I stepped from the small room, and, after making my way to a dusty floor vent, yelled again. "Hello Ronald? Where are you?"

Nothing.

I spun around and ran back into the pantry, nearly tripping on the head of a mop, and yelled again. "Hello Mr. Lister?"

"Please . . ." Lister's voice was muffled, but definitely discernable. Fifty bucks there was a trapdoor to the basement in the pantry.

Crazed, I dropped to my knees and began indiscriminately hurling the junk from the pantry into the kitchen until I'd cleared the floor. In retrospect, the three-by-three trapdoor should have been easy to pick out without my maniacal evacuation—the seams around it, while flush with the surrounding floor, were wide enough so as to be clearly visible. Only the door's latch, now exposed, had been concealed behind a stack of phone books. A Phillips screwdriver, serving as a poor-man's lock, had been inserted through the latch and a matching heavy-gauge steel bracket bolted onto the floor, effectively turning the basement into a cage. I withdrew the screwdriver, then grabbed hold of the latch and yanked open the door. A fetid combination of sour body odor and mustiness blasted up through the opening, nearly causing me to gag.

"Hello, Mr. Lister?" I yelled down into the gloom. "My name is Alex Fife. I'm here to help you."

"Thank you lord," he said, his voice parched.

"I've opened the door. Can you make it up the stairs?"

"No, I'm cuffed. . . . He cuffed me to a pipe."

"One second, I'm going to call the police and I'll be right down."

I extracted my cell from my pocket and punched in 911; after a brief recorded message telling me not to panic, they promptly put me on hold. I turned the speakerphone on.

"I'm coming," I said.

A steep set of wooden stairs led down into the darkness. Unable to locate a light switch in the pantry, I used the phone's screen to illuminate the stairs and took them down one at a time until my head was just below the floorboards. I then swept the screen to either side of the stairwell and up along the basement's ceiling, but the switch was still AWOL.

"Where's the light switch?" I asked.

"Oh God, I don't know. He turns on the light before he comes in. Just hurry."

It must have been behind something in the pantry.

"One second. I'll be right back. I'm going to find the light." The phone, still on hold, was now droning instructions on how to conduct CPR until an ambulance came.

Carefully, I rotated in place until I faced the stairs, then climbed back up until my head reached the floor level.

Two black shoes stood in front of me. My body went into shock—not fear but uncomprehending shock. I looked up.

Then everything went dark.

Chapter 32

"Oh God, please wake up."

Groggily, I opened my eyes and tried to turn toward the voice, only to be rewarded with a sharp twinge in my neck. I aborted the twist and instead squinted at the blurry bulb dangling from the ceiling.

"What happened?" I said, closing my eyes against the harsh light.

"Thank God. Are you okay?" asked Ronald. "I thought you were dead."

"I think so. I feel like I've been hit by a car. What happened?"

"I couldn't see in the dark, but from the looks of your face, that guy put a steel-toed boot in your cheek and sent you flying down the stairs."

"Where is he?" Given the shock of the event, I'd totally forgotten about the black shoes or the thug wearing them.

"I don't know. He took off about five minutes ago." That was at least an immediate relief.

"At least he had the decency to leave the lights on," I said.

I raised my right hand—fortunately it still worked—and gingerly touched my face.

"*Augh*," I screamed reflexively. I'd expected soreness but not daggers. Now lucid thanks to the sharp pain, I took inventory. Based on the throbbing, my left arm was going to be purple for a while, and both legs were bruised to hell—insult to injury after the morning's fall—but otherwise, I'd live.

"How long have I been out?"

"Around ten minutes. I've been trying to wake you since he took off. Listen, I want to get out of here now. Right now. Can you find something to get me out of these cuffs?"

"Dammit. I'm so damn stupid," I responded, dejected.

"Just find something to cut these cuffs, and please tell me someone else knows you're here."

"Yeah, I think so." I'd told Steven the address, hadn't I? The last

157

few hours were a blur. I thought about it for a few seconds. "Yeah, I'm almost sure. Let me get my bearings and I'll find something to cut you out. Give me a second."

"Okay, but please hurry. I don't know when that Arab bastard will be back, but I do know I want to be long gone by then," he said, then took a deep breath.

I tried to sit up. "Oh boy." A wave of dizziness hit me. I capitulated and lay back down.

"Here I thought I was saved," he wailed, "and then some fucking Russian thug out of nowhere fucks everything up."

"Russian thug?" What the hell? "What Russian thug? That wasn't Khalimmy?"

"Who?"

"The guy who abducted you. The Arab. Khalimmy. The guy who owns this house."

"No. This guy was new. I've never seen him before."

"So he wasn't the guy that abducted you?"

"No. At first I figured he was his partner or something. But he asked a lot of questions the Khalid guy already asked. I don't think they're working together. By the way, who are you anyway—a cop?"

"No. It's a long story. But I did come here to rescue you."

"What's your name again?"

"I'm Alex."

"Ronald Lister," he replied, then after a pause, "would you mind trying to get up again? I really want to get the hell out of here. The fucking bastard tortured me."

Summoning all my strength, I powered through the dizziness and sat up.

"Why didn't you just call the police when you heard I was kidnapped?" he asked.

"Whoa. One second." My head was spinning. Holding myself upright, I closed my eyes and responded. "I did, they said they couldn't help unless I had proof. The cop thought I was imagining it all."

The lightheadedness passed.

"Bastards. Well anyway, thanks for the attempted rescue," said Lister sullenly.

"No problem."

Using my good arm, I shifted onto my knees, this time thankfully without any real dizziness, and rose to my feet. Keen not to turn my neck, I shuffled my feet until I faced Lister, then walked over.

Ronald was a doppelganger of his brother: mid-fifties, about five foot eleven, barrel-chested, tight-curled black hair, and a week's growth of jet-black stubble on his face and down his neck. The untucked white dress shirt he wore was stained yellow around the armpits and smeared in filth, its unbuttoned collar exposing a tangle of black, sweat-matted chest hair. The skin area around his right wrist was chafed raw, the top layer presumably rubbed off from repeated struggling against the handcuffs that bound him to the water heater's piping. Khalimmy had yanked out two of his fingernails; I cringed involuntarily at the caked blood that covered the exposed nail beds.

"They don't hurt too much anymore," he said, following my gaze. "Can you get me some water first?" Ronald grabbed an empty cup from atop the water heater and pointed at an old-style washbasin with his free hand. "I'm about to pass out from dehydration."

"Thanks," he said as I handed him the cup. "Mind filling me up once more? And then there's got to be something over there to cut these things off." He gestured toward a cluttered workbench covered in boxes.

I rummaged through them and returned with a metal-cutting hacksaw.

"Thanks."

"If we're going to get out of here, we're going to have to hurry up. I'm pretty sure Khalimmy plans to kill you this morning," I said, turning my body back toward the hatch.

"Lovely," he said.

While Ronald hacked at the steel cuff, I walked over to the stairs, and, using my good arm, climbed until my head was just below the hatch. Then I slowly lifted my left arm up. A half-dozen curse words accompanied the pain.

"You okay?" He continued hacking behind me.

"Just dandy," I said. "I'll be even better when we get out."

I counted to three, gritted my teeth, and shoved the heel of my palm into the hatch. It gave, just a few millimeters, and then stopped dead.

"Mother Mary of Mercy!" I screamed. I followed up with a good ten seconds of Lamaze-style heavy breathing before gritting my teeth and trying once more with the same result. "It's locked. I bet he shoved that screwdriver through again."

"Sure he didn't just stack something heavy over it?" asked Ronald.

"Trust me."

I started down. Just a few steps from the floor, my heart jumped— my smartphone was sitting on the concrete between the stairs and an apple crate filled with garden tools. For whatever reason, the Russian had thankfully missed it.

"Thank God!"

"What?"

"I found my phone. The bastard didn't take my phone." I'd completely forgotten it in my stupor. Ignoring the pain, I crouched geriatrically next to the box and picked it up. Sadly, the screen was cracked and the battery had jettisoned to parts unknown. I grunted.

"What's wrong?" asked Lister, now from behind me.

"The battery popped out. Help me look for it?"

Ronald, far more mobile than I and intensely eager given his newly gained freedom, began searching through and between a cluster of boxes adjacent to the stairwell like a four-year-old on his first Easter egg hunt. Less able to dig between the boxes, I scanned farther afield.

Ultimately, I took the prize—I found the battery sitting eight feet from the stairs under the washbasin. Ronald scooped up the thin white battery, saving me the trouble of a painful squat, inserted it into the back of the smartphone, and placed the phone in my good hand. Then he gave me a "what next?" look.

"I've never used one this complicated," he admitted sheepishly. I offered the phone back to him.

"No problem, it's easy. Make sure the battery doesn't pop out and push the button on the top left—hold it in for a good second." He took the phone and pushed the power button. "Okay, in about ten seconds it should ask for my password."

Lister stared at the screen hopefully, but after a few seconds it was clear that the cracked touchscreen display had ascended to LCD heaven.

"Dammit. The screen is shot." Ronald drooped his shoulders dolefully.

"No, no. It might still work. These things are built like tanks. Bring the phone up to my mouth and hold in the bottom-middle button until you hear a beep."

He placed the phone right in front of my face and carefully placed his finger on the rectangular button. A few seconds later, the phone chirped.

"Dial Steven," I enunciated into the phone's mic. We waited a few moments, but nothing happened.

"Let's try once more," I said. "Hold the same button again until it beeps."

Again, he did as instructed.

"Dial Parents," I said.

Nothing.

"Shit."

Ronald laid the phone down on a card table and took a seat on the bottom stair.

"So much for that," he said.

"Well, like I said, my buddy knows we're here. Plus, Khalimmy doesn't know there's two of us." Of course the disarray I'd created upstairs wasn't exactly subtle. "We've got to find something to use as weapons. Then we kill the light, wait behind the stairs for him to come down, and whack him."

My MacGyver-esque plan didn't seem to motivate as intended. Undeterred, I gritted my teeth against the pain and began rummaging through the boxes for a makeshift weapon.

"So from what I understand, Khalimmy wanted to buy a rare diamond from your brother?"

Ronald looked up at me.

"Your brother passes away from a heart attack, Khalimmy doesn't know, and thinks your brother decided to renege on the deal." A few pokes with my good hand revealed a cache of used painting supplies under a decrepit spider web: brushes, a tarp, sandpaper and a few half-full cans of paint. I advanced to the next box. "Apparently he really wants the diamond. So he kidnaps you as collateral."

"This is the first I've heard of any diamond. The Khalid guy . . ."

"Khalimmy," I corrected him.

"Khalimmy," he said deliberately, "kept asking about a floral something or other."

"The Florentine. That's the name of a famous diamond. Your brother was trying to sell it from what I can tell."

Ronald stood up and walked over to the workbench. "Well apparently Khalimmy isn't the only one who wants it. Let him deal with the fucking Russians. Hopefully they'll all kill each other. How about this?"

I turned around to see him holding a weighty, three-foot piece of rusted steel rebar.

"Where'd you find that?" I hadn't seen it among the jumble of tools on the bench.

"It was in a box under the counter."

"Now we need one more for me." I rotated and advanced to the next box. "You had no idea at all what your brother was up to? He never mentioned the diamond?"

"I try, tried rather, to stay ignorant of his antiquities dealing. Once bitten, twice shy. I have no desire to go to prison." I assumed he was referring to his and Richard's indictments (and subsequent exoneration) on smuggling charges. The second crate held a few weathered leather gloves, pruning shears, and other gardening paraphernalia, but unfortunately nothing lethal.

"To be honest, before the funeral I hadn't talked with him in over a year, and then this Khalimmy guy puts a gun to my head in my garage and drags me here. I figured my brother had cheated him for some antique before he died. I kept trying to tell him that Rich was dead, but he didn't believe me, thinks he skipped town with this Florentine thing . . . will this do?" He held up a four-foot length of white PVC piping.

"Better than nothing, but I'd prefer something heavier." I returned my attention to the locker and lifted its latch.

Without warning, the chorus of Jethro Tull's *Thick as a Brick* filled the air. Ronald spun toward the sound, ominously swinging the crowbar in tight circles above his head.

"Steven!" I screamed—it was his personalized ringtone. Ignoring a thousand stabbing needles of pain, I spun and ran toward the card table. By the time I reached the table, my phone was vibrating madly across the vinyl surface in time with a second iteration of the chorus. I snatched it up, careful to prevent the battery from falling out of its bay, and placed it by my ear to answer.

Miraculously, the phone stopped ringing.

"Hello, Steven. Can you hear me?" I paused. No response. "Steven, my phone's busted. I can't hear you."

"Listen. If you can hear me, I found Richard Lister's brother but we're locked in Khalimmy's basement. The basement is accessible through a trapdoor from the kitchen pantry. Call the police as soon as you can. 19591 Gilmore. 19591 Gilmore in El Segundo. Call the police." I repeated the entire plea several times, then put the phone back onto the card table. Lister had dropped the crowbar to his side and looked longingly at the phone.

"Did it work?"

"I don't know, I couldn't hear him. Who knows if he could hear me."

"But you know it's your friend?"

"I programmed that ringtone for him. It's his favorite song. It's him."

Chapter 33

"All set?" I asked in a whisper.

"Yeah, I think so," responded Ronald. After finding a five iron in the locker, I'd unscrewed the basement's two bulbs and by the beam of my keychain flashlight, both of us had taken positions flanking the staircase.

"So the Russian is looking for the diamond too," I said. "It seems your brother was trying to find the highest bidder."

"No. He didn't say anything about a diamond. When I told him I knew nothing about this Florentine thing, he said he was looking for a flash drive that he said Richard had taken, or . . . rather . . . stolen."

"A flash drive? You mean like a thumb drive?"

"Yeah, I guess. He kept asking me if my brother ever sent me a flash drive to hold onto. 'Did your brother ever give you a flash drive? A portable hard drive? Did he ever give you a password to an account?' Flash drives and account passwords? My brother dealt in antiquities, not computers. I had no clue what the hell he was talking about."

Maybe the Florentine wasn't a diamond after all? Maybe Russian intelligence data? Or maybe it was a diamond and the drive held a digitized map of some sort?

"So what did you do?" I asked.

"I told him I had no idea what he was talking about. What else could I do?"

"And he believed you?"

"No." Ronald shuddered. "He pulled out a knife and threatened to remove my fingers if I didn't tell him. He said he'd work on you next."

"Me? He was going to question me about the Florentine?"

"Yeah. I figured that was it for both of us."

Jesus Christ. "Then what happened?"

"He grabbed my hand and pressed the edge of the blade against my finger. I nearly soiled my pants. And then his mobile rang. God help me, his mobile rang. He answered it, listened for a good thirty seconds, hung up, and began cursing. Then he bolted upstairs and took off. That was it," he crossed himself. "You woke up a few minutes later."

"Unbelievable," I said, "I wonder . . ." A noise. "Shhhh. Someone's upstairs."

"What?" he whispered.

"I heard the floor creak." The floorboards squeaked again, this time closer, louder.

"Ahh. I hear it."

"Aim for the shins. Hit as hard as you can as soon as you've got a good shot."

"Okay," he said.

After a nerve-racking minute of groans and creaks the hardwood floor's protestations ceased, plunging the basement into an unnatural silence.

"I wonder what the bastard's doing," commented Ronald in a full-volume whisper.

"Shhhh."

An instant later, the footsteps recommenced, this time from the far edge of the basement ceiling, and worked their way toward the trapdoor. Again, silence. I tensed. Then another groan, this time from shifting weight, followed by the unmistakable scrape of a screwdriver being withdrawn from the latch. I redoubled my grip on the leather-wrapped handle.

The hatch raised a crack, projecting a dim wedge of light along the stairs and directly in front of my feet.

"Alex? Tell me you're down there."

Steven!

"We're here!"

"Thank God." Steven grabbed the underside of the hatch and swung it open with a grunt. I'd never seen him so anxious; a dense film of perspiration covered his face.

"Did you call the police?" I asked, then gestured Ronald up the stairs. "Hurry."

"Yeah. They should be here soon."

"Last thing we need is Khalimmy throwing all three of us in the basement, covering the trapdoor with a rug, and telling the cops it's a false alarm."

"I don't think I want to wait around for the cops to arrive," replied Ronald uneasily.

"I don't blame you, this place is disturbing," responded Steven. "I say we get out of here and go straight to the police."

"Fine."

"This way," I motioned toward the front of the house. Ronald and Steven followed me down the entryway toward the front door. Like the rest of the house, the entryway's heavy curtains immersed the area in near darkness. With a quick twist, I rotated the deadbolt latch into the vertical position and then yanked the handle. The door stuck.

"Dammit." It was already unlocked, undoubtedly by the Russian. Exasperated, I grabbed the latch again, but before I could turn it, I heard a scratching noise and the latch began to rotate, of its own volition, between my fingers.

"Oh shit," I mouthed. "He's back." I tightened my grip to prevent the latch from turning. Khalimmy fought briefly with his key, then retracted it.

"Hold it," whispered Steven into my ear. "Don't let go." I reinforced my grip with my left hand.

A second later, Khalimmy reinserted the key, tried one more light turn, and then, failing, torqued it hard. Fortunately, my years of rock-climbing had developed cable-strength tendons and I had no problem immobilizing the latch; the key, however, was less fortunate and snapped immediately.

"*Ibn himar!* Goddamn lock."

I gently released the bolt and backed several feet from the door, followed by my companions.

"What now?" I whispered.

"Where are the fucking police?" whispered Ronald.

"They've got to be here soon. I called almost ten minutes ago," said Steven.

"Are you suggesting we just wait until they arrive?"

"I don't know. How should I know?"

"All right, calm down," I said. I tiptoed back to the door and peered through the peephole. Khalimmy had disappeared. "Shit, he's gone."

"What should we do?" asked Steven, panicked.

"I guess we could bolt out the front door."

"What if he's out in front of the garage or something? He'll kill us. What about the back? We could jump into a neighbor's yard."

"That could work—if he hasn't already gone back there. Shit."

"What?"

"Did you leave the back door open?"

"Crap. You think he'd go arou—"

Phut. Smoke emerged from a newly punctured, dime-sized hole in the doorjamb just left of Ronald's head. For a second, I stared dumbfounded at the wall, then at Ronald, wondering where such a smoking hole could have come from. I began to turn around, then heard a second *phut* and a sickening, organic crunching sound—the sound of splintering bone—and it clicked. I dove headfirst into a maze of waisthigh-stacked newspapers in the adjoining study, landing hard on my bad arm. Teeth gritted, I shimmied behind a heavy wood desk and out of sight of the hallway.

"Oh fuck!" screamed Steven.

Phut. A door slammed. *Phut.* A half-second delay. *Phut.*

I shifted onto the balls of my feet and surveyed what little of the room I could see from behind the desk's stacks of yellowing paper. Only one door: back to the entryway. A fireplace to my left—was there an iron poker? Something I could use as a weapon? I couldn't tell. A blacked-out window to my right.

My eyes returned to the desk. A grapefruit-sized glass paperweight sat partially hidden behind the piles at the edge. I grabbed it and ducked back.

"Please, my friends, it's time to stop playing." The hallway lights flicked on.

I said nothing. Neither did anyone else.

"All I want is what I've been promised. Give me . . . for God's sake, *sell* me the Florentine, and everyone lives."

He paused and again the house went silent, save for the subtle background whistle of the vent. I heard the stomp of a foot, then Ronald screamed.

"No more games or your brother dies. Right now. Your friend is next."

"Wait!" I yelled, still crouching behind the desk. "Don't shoot him. I'll get it for you."

The study's floorboards squeaked from several tentative steps, and a moment later the dim form of Khalimmy's shoes filled the gap beneath the desk's back paneling.

"Stand up, please. Hands above your head."

I rose to my feet, leaving the paperweight on the floor, palms out-facing above my head.

Khalimmy stared at me, clearly confused, and motioned me from behind the desk.

"Who the hell are . . . what?" Then, recognition. His eyes showed surprise, but recognition. "What the hell are you doing here? Where the hell is Richard?" He pointed the barrel of the pistol at the bridge of my nose. "Who the fuck are you?"

"I . . . we're . . ." I paused, befuddled by the prospect of my impending death. Then I heard it. The ever so faint, far-off wail of a police siren.

Undeterred by the siren, or perhaps still unperceiving, Khalimmy pressed the warm mouth of the silencer against my forehead and reiterated, "Let me repeat again, who the fuck are you?"

"I'm . . . I'm Alex . . . Fife," I responded, now completely distracted by the rapidly intensifying scream of the siren.

"Alex . . . Fife." He stared at me, utterly bewildered. The swelling sirens brought him back to his senses. "Did you call the fucking police?"

The screeching of car tires answered his question well before I could utter a word. Khalimmy twisted and shot a look back over his shoulder, inadvertently shifting his gun a few degrees from my face's midline. It was an opening . . . an opportunity, however small. Guided by the most basal, fight-or-flight regions of my brain, I balled my right hand into a fist and sent it flying upward toward Khalimmy's chin. My ring finger and thumb just barely caught his jaw, jerking his head sideways. Khalimmy staggered backward, his hand reflexively pumping several muffled rounds above my head into the ceiling's stucco, and fell with a crash between the yellowing stacks.

I dove just as another round left the chamber, my head smacking into something hard. I blacked out.

Chapter 34

"HELP!" I SCREAMED. "WE'RE BEING HELD HOSTAGE."

"He's coming to," said an unfamiliar male voice.

"Careful, he has a gun!" I shot up and opened my eyes. My head reeled. Had I been drugged?

"Relax, Mr. Fife, everything's okay." A hand gently eased me back down onto the pillow. "You're in the hospital."

A heart monitor's metronome-like beat started breaking through the haze. I tried to focus—it took a few seconds to reorient. I was in an eight-by-ten, beige-colored room, medical equipment everywhere. And tubes. Tubes taped to my arm.

"I'm going to go get the doctor, I'll be right back," said the male voice.

"You're in the hospital, Alex. Everything's okay now." It was Steven. That was Steven's voice.

"Steven? What? Where? Where are we?" My fingers found their way up to a bandage on my shoulder. "Was I shot?"

"No—it's nothing serious. Just relax, the doctor will be here in a minute."

I tried to concentrate, to remember what had happened.

"How did I . . . ?" I scanned the room. "What happened?" Things were coming back slowly. "I heard the police cars, then I think I hit Khalimmy and then I . . . I . . ."

"You're okay, Alex. Everything's okay. The police rescued us and the paramedics brought you here to Torrance Memorial."

"What about Ronald? Is Ronald Lister okay? He was shot. I think he was shot. I didn't see."

"I don't know. He was in a different ambulance. But he didn't look good."

"And Khalimmy? What happened to him? Tell me they caught him. Or better, killed him."

"I don't think so," said Steven, shrugging. "The way the police were questioning me, it sounds like they're still looking for him."

"Does Hillary know?" I asked, the blurriness abating. I noticed a pitcher on the bedside table and motioned for Steven to pour me a cup of water.

I downed the cup and handed it back.

"No way. I told her I was meeting you to go through more videotapes."

"I see the patient is recovering nicely!" came a voice from the door. A sixtyish woman with wiry graying hair, a genuine smile, and funky seventies glasses walked into the room and straight to the heart monitor.

"How are you feeling, Mr. Fife?" she asked, still staring at the LCD display.

"Not bad. I'm still a little hazy from whatever you're pumping into me." I lifted my right arm to highlight my many dangling tubes.

"That's saline." She smiled. "Salt water. You're probably feeling the sedative from earlier. It should wear off soon. That, and you took a nasty smack to the head."

"Is it bad?"

"Your MRIs are in Radiology right now, but I'm guessing you'll be fine after some rest. You were *very* lucky. The bullet just grazed your shoulder and took off the top layer of skin. You're going to have a good week or two of discomfort, but it's no worse than a first-degree burn." She walked over to my bed, pulled a pen flashlight from her pocket, and shined it into my eyes. "Good. And your vitals all look good as well."

I opened my mouth to speak.

"But," she interjected, seemingly anticipating my question, "I'd like to keep you overnight for observation, at least until we get your MRIs back. You should be able to leave sometime tomorrow."

"Okay," I acquiesced. "Do you know how Ronald Lister is doing?"

"Ronald Lister?" She hesitated. "Oh, the other gunshot victim from El Segundo?"

"Yes."

"Not well." She shook her head. "He lost a lot of blood before they

171

could stabilize him and went into a coma. He's out of surgery and in the ICU now. They're giving him a forty- to fifty-percent chance of surviving."

"Oh God. I hope he recovers."

"Yes, let's hope so."

Chapter 35

"THANKS FOR COMING EARLY," I SAID. I ushered Steven into my new home's entryway, then closed the door and spun the deadbolt.

"No problem man," he said, patting me on the back. "You feeling any better?"

"Physically, I'm fine," I said, heading down the hall. "Mentally, I'm a wreck."

Steven followed me into the kitchen and took a seat in one of the folding chairs.

"You're worried Khalimmy's going to come after you."

"The police spent two hours questioning me yesterday. They've got no idea where he is. But that's only part—"

"Alex, he's probably halfway to Cairo by now. The cops know who he is, where he lives, and probably his blood type. You really think he's a threat at this point?"

"Yeah, I do." My fingers tightened on the grip of Gennady's Ruger. "But, it's not just that. That's only part of the problem."

"What do you mean, part?"

"I mean that the Russians are after the Florentine too."

"What?" Steven closed his eyes to think. "You mean because of that Russian spyware we found on Richard Lister's computer? Aren't you jumping to conclusions? That's pretty thin."

"I wish it was," I said, briefly recounting my run-in with the Russian in Khalimmy's basement.

"Whoa, there was another guy in the house?"

"Yeah, before you came."

"And he was after the diamond too?"

"Yes and no. Ronald said he asked for a flash drive—he implied the Florentine was digital."

"A flash drive? Like one of those portable USB drives?"

"Yeah."

"I don't understand. So it's not a diamond?"

"At this point," I shrugged, "I've got no clue."

"What the hell? Why didn't you tell me this at the hospital?"

"Honestly, I was pretty out of it from the meds. I really didn't put everything together until this morning."

"Anyway," he shook his head, "go on."

"What if the Florentine isn't a diamond, but something much bigger? I don't know, like intelligence secrets."

"That's speculation," he said, shaking his head.

"I know, but let's say that's what it is," I pressed. "Then we're in deep shit."

"No. If that's what we find, then we just hand it over to the FBI or the CIA and let them worry about it. It's not the end of the world."

"But what if these guys still come after us? What if they think we still have it? Are you ready to disappear? Go into witness protection? It could come to that." I felt my face flush. "Then we're fucked!"

"Whoa!" Steven held up his hands. "Whoa! Alex, you're fixating on the worst-case scenario. Yeah, in the extremely unlikely event that it comes to that, maybe. But you're totally speculating." He took a deep breath and exhaled. "Look, let's figure out what this thing is before jumping to conclusions. Then we'll have a better idea of what to do. Take a deep breath and relax."

"You're right." I nodded. "You're right."

"It'll be okay."

"I just wish I hadn't invited everyone over. I'd rather the two of us just figured out what the Florentine is and get this over with."

"Just chill. It'll be fine," he said. "And look, the last thing we need is to freak out Hillary or Papa, so just keep quiet. Once we figure out what we're dealing with, we'll work through the options."

Hillary stepped through the door forty minutes later, a bottle of cheap champagne and a stack of plastic cups in her left hand, and a bag full of Tommy burgers in her right. Papa ambled in just behind her, leaning heavily on his cane; he looked exhausted.

"Hey Alex," she said, giving me a gentle hug, "feeling any better? Wow—that's some bruise."

"It's not as bad as it looks." I touched my cheek. "Thanks for picking up Papa."

"No problem." Hillary smiled. "We had a nice chat on the way over. I also explained how you had a little fall during rock-climbing."

"Alex, let me see your face," said Papa.

"It's okay, Papa," I said, smiling at him.

I eased the front door shut.

"Oh, my dear grandson," he said, gazing up at my cheek, "it kills me to see you in pain. How are you?"

"I'm feeling much better, Papa. How about you? Have you recovered from our little adventure?"

"Oh yes. That was quite something! The guys at the swimming pool aren't going to believe it."

"Let's hope not," I mumbled.

"So where's Steven?" asked Hillary. "After all the excitement, I can't wait to see this famous diamond, celebrate, and put this entire thing behind us."

"Amen," I said. "Your husband's in the kitchen. And Linda's hopefully going to make it as well."

"Linda? Then we finally get to meet the mystery girl?" asked Hillary. "You've been holding out on us."

"Really, we're just climbing friends."

A minute later, the three of us joined Steven in the kitchen. Papa eased himself precariously into a folding chair, falling the last few inches and nearly toppling. Steven grabbed his arm to steady him.

"I'm all right, I'm all right. Leave me be," he howled.

"Burger, Papa?" asked Hillary, ripping the grease-stained paper bag down its side.

Papa gazed hungrily at the paper-wrapped burgers—congealing flows of chili were now emerging from the seams of the wrapping.

"Don't tell your mother." Papa grabbed a burger from the table and tried to unwrap it. After a few seconds of arthritic fumbling, I removed the wax paper for him and put it on a Dixie plate.

"All right, everyone, while you're eating, I'll tell you my plan."

Hillary withdrew the iPhone from her purse and pointed its video camera at me.

"Shouldn't we wait for Linda?" she asked, tapping its screen.

I looked down at my watch—it was already two.

"She said to start without her if she was late."

I pulled a large plastic Fry's Electronics bag from the floor and sat it next to my laptop on the card table. "Since Papa's not in any shape to climb the ladder down into the 'dungeon,' I figured we could—"

"Ah shit, I can climb down a ladder just fine."

Steven rolled his eyes.

"Pop, I was thinking maybe you could man the headquarters up here. I've even got a video hookup so you can see the action live."

"I didn't spend an hour in a goddamn freezer to sit up here like a cripple."

"How about if I stay with you, Papa?" asked Hillary.

"Shit no. I deserve to go down with Alex and see our diamond, and no one's gonna stop me—"

Without warning, Papa grabbed the seat of his chair, leaned forward, and with a motion reminiscent of a leaping frog, jerked from the chair to stand. Before I could grab him, he toppled sideways to the floor. My heart jumped.

"God dammit!" he shrieked, rolling onto his back and rubbing his arm. He sucked in air through his teeth. "Damn it hurts."

After a few seconds of struggling, I took his shaking hands in mine and helped him back into the chair. He didn't have a chance in hell of making it down that ladder. But how could I go down without him now? And after all he'd done at the hospital? Every fiber in me wanted to open that door and find the Florentine, to get this over with. But I just couldn't do it.

I sighed.

"Whoa—I'm feeling a bit dizzy." I leaned forward, threw a hand on the table, and placed the other on my forehead. "On second thought, maybe I should stay up here and rest."

Steven shot me a "you've got to be kidding" look.

"Just go without me," I mouthed.

"What's wrong, Alex?" Papa asked, genuinely concerned.

"Just feeling a bit woozy from hitting my head, Papa. It's probably better if I rest for now. I don't want to pass out and fall down the ladder."

"Oh." Papa frowned. "I hope it's not a concussion."

"Will you stay here with me?" I closed my eyes and tilted my head back slightly. "I'm worried I might black out."

"Of course." Papa's shaky hand grabbed mine and squeezed.

"Maybe that's better. Thanks Papa." I slowly opened my eyes. "Steven, Hillary . . . do you think you guys could go down and open the room?"

"We'd be happy to, Alex," said Hillary knowingly.

After a few moments of faux recuperation, I pulled out a boxed TotCam 3300 wireless baby cam and laid it on the table. "All right, this way Papa and I can see the action. It's supposedly got a one-hundred-meter range, and plugs into a PC so you can watch the video on your screen."

"You take the cam. Papa and I keep the base station up here. And," I inserted my hand into the bag and pulled out my walkie-talkies. "Two-way communication, so we can communicate with you as well."

By the time the burgers had disappeared, I'd powered up the cam, hooked its base station up to my laptop, and completed a quick test.

"Here," I said, handing Steven a walkie-talkie. "I'll give you the panic room's security code once you reach the door."

"All right," he said. "Let's do this."

"After you, honey." Hillary gestured toward the library. "The date is Friday, August 26 and today we'll be unlocking the long-awaited subterranean vault. Will it hold the Florentine treasure? And for that matter, what is the Florentine treasure? Or will it hold something else entirely?"

Hillary panned the camera over to Papa. "Papa and Alex will be manning the operations center while we descend below ground level to the steel-encased vault."

"Hillary, enough with the narration," moaned Steven. "Let's get this over with."

"What's with him?" Hillary looked at me questioningly.

I shook my head. She shrugged and took off for the library loft.

"As we've seen," she continued, "the entrance to the hidden passage can be found behind this second-story bookcase." Her voice trailed off.

"Do you think there's really a diamond down there?" asked Papa.

"At this point, Papa, I'm not sure what's down there. But we'll find out soon enough."

"Steven is going down the ladder now," yelled Hillary.

"When is the," Papa pointed at the screen, "the, the teletype going to start?"

"Should be just a minute, Pop. They're climbing down the ladder now."

I depressed the walkie's button. "Papa wants to know when you're going to power up the cam."

"One second," yelled Steven.

A minute later, a grainy color image of Hillary's legs filled the screen.

"Pop." I tapped him on the shoulder; he'd momentarily closed his eyes.

"Da what?"

I pointed at the screen. "There's Hillary coming down the shaft."

Hillary turned from the ladder, waved, and mouthed something to the camera.

"What'd she say?" asked Papa.

"I couldn't hear either." I adjusted the volume of the laptop's speakers, then said into the walkie-talkie, "We couldn't hear that. Say again?"

"I just said Hi Papa—" Her voice cut out as a burst of static hit the display.

Steven started down the passage, the baby cam bobbing and panning rhythmically with his footsteps. One of the passage's bare light bulbs filled the camera's lens, temporarily blinding its digital CCD sensor and flooding my laptop screen with an intense white light.

"They're underground now, Pop—that hallway is ten or fifteen feet belowground. That's why it's a little static-y."

"Okay, now we're going to round the corner," said Steven, "and . . . and there's the door to the vault." Hillary walked next to the steel door and waved to the cam.

Papa waved innocently back at my laptop screen.

"Okay, Alex, we're ready for the unveiling," said Steven. "You ready up there?"

I gazed over at Papa: still awake, and focused on the screen. "We're all set."

"Okay, what's the code?" Steven handed the baby cam to Hillary. She stepped back a few steps and centered Steven, the keypad, and Richard's dinner-plate-sized mirror smartly in the middle of the frame. Steven's right hand remained poised over the keypad in anticipation. I pulled out my overstuffed wallet and extracted the green ViruTrax business card I'd jotted the code on after my escape from the hospital.

"Okay, here we go." I flipped the card and held it in front of Papa so he could see the numbers, then clicked on the walkie-talkie. "Seven, six, nine," Steven repeated each digit as he keyed it into the pad, and I continued, "five, four, and—everyone cross your fingers—two."

"I just heard the bolt click!" exclaimed Hillary.

"Here goes nothing." Steven grabbed the foot-long steel handle, rotated it counterclockwise, and then gave a tug. The door resisted stubbornly. Visibly aggravated, he squared his feet and redoubled his efforts, his biceps now clearly bulging from the effort. "It's stuck."

"Are you sure you turned the handle all the way?" asked Hillary from behind the camera. Steven shrugged, then gave the handle a hard shove with his palm, rotating it counterclockwise a few more degrees.

"All right, one more try," he said, grabbing the handle.

This time the five-inch-thick steel door capitulated and groaned as it rotated on its three massive hinges.

Chapter 36

Steven stepped tentatively over the inch-high steel threshold followed closely by Hillary and her twin cameras. The baby cam's cheap, charge-coupled sensor, unable to adjust to the room's relative darkness, momentarily transmitted undulating, indistinct shapes to the laptop's screen, each briefly materializing then fading back into the pixilated, mottled blackness.

"Lights," I croaked into the talkie.

"Working on it," responded Steven.

The laptop's LCD screen momentarily flared as the vault's overhead lights flickered to life. What filled the screen, amidst an almost intolerable degree of static, amazed me. Ten archaic gold coins rested on a dark, ruffled velvet matting beneath the pane of a curio cabinet. Papa whistled.

"What kind are they, Alex?" Hillary asked. "Roman? Greek?"

"It's hard to tell, but I'd guess they're Roman." The rich yellow glint of the ancient coins transported me back fifteen years to my coin-collecting adolescence and days of combing through numismatic catalogs. "If I'm not mistaken, those are the emperors: Alexander Severus, Hadrian, Marcus Aurelius. The one in the upper left is Julius Caesar."

Hillary panned closer in on the lustrous gold coin.

"You hit the jackpot," said Papa, in awe. My heart pounded as if I'd just cracked open the lid of a musty treasure chest and discovered a mountain of doubloons. What was all this?

"Could the Florentine be these gold coins?" asked Hillary. "Priceless Roman gold coins from Florence, Italy? Makes sense, right?"

"It's as good a guess as any," I said into the walkie-talkie. "Let's see what else is in there."

Hillary panned the cam over to the right side of the cabinet and onto a cache of silver coins, these more primitive looking—many had uneven borders and crudely stamped profiles. A particularly impressive example, separated from the others, featured an emperor on his throne, an eagle perched on the palm of his outstretched right hand.

"Wow, I wonder where those are from," said Steven.

Papa leaned inward toward the LCD screen to inspect the shining coin and raised his bushy eyebrows.

"There anything in this for me?" he asked.

"I don't see why not," I said, then, into the walkie, "Papa wants a cut of the booty. I hope there's enough."

"Oh, there's enough," said Hillary. She lifted her camera up, briefly exposing the bare steel walls of the vault, and walked over to another tall curio cabinet in front of Steven. "I think we're all rich."

Situated on the second shelf of the cabinet was a miniature Egyptian treasure trove. This time it was Steven's turn to whistle.

"Howard Carter would have been jealous," I said, my anxiety still quelled by the excitement.

"Who's Howard Carter?" asked Hillary.

"He's the archeologist who discovered King Tut's tomb," I replied.

At the center of the shelf rested a strikingly beautiful golden burial mask encrusted with gems. The mask's eyes, formed of what appeared to be inlaid obsidian and quartz surrounded by strips of deep blue lapis lazuli, stared off into the afterlife. To the left of the mask sat a collection of funerary jewelry, including a striking golden ankh, and a threesome of golden scarabs embedded within a golden frame, their wings inlaid turquoise. Right of the mask stood a ten-inch-high statue, sculpted from obsidian and inlaid with gold and silver, bearing the head of a bird and the body of a muscular man. Delicate gold and silver earrings, rings and bracelets, all decorated with gems, were scattered decadently across the shelf amongst the three larger antiquities.

"I think that's Thoth," I said of the statue. "Egyptian god of . . . I forget."

"The god of 'worth a lot of money,'" said Steven from outside the frame.

Hillary panned the camera clockwise and onto the opposing wall. A video surveillance recording unit, small CRT monitor, and a stack of VHS tapes like those we'd found outside in the subterranean hallway sat on a small wooden table in the corner. To their left, several paintings had been hung on the wall. Hillary approached the painting on the left and gasped.

"What is that?" I asked.

"If I'm not mistaken from my UCLA art history classes, it's an early Van Gogh," said Hillary from behind the camera. The painting depicted a group of parishioners in front of a dreary, three-windowed church amidst a series of dormant, leafless trees; drab oranges, olives and dirty blue hues gave the painting a profoundly depressing feeling. Hillary leaned forward and centered the cam squarely on the lower right corner of the painting, the signature, "Vincent," clearly visible. "That's how he signed. It could be a forgery, of course."

"Where's the diamond, already?" asked Papa impatiently, now seemingly bored by the procession of rare artifacts.

"Guys, Papa wants to know where the Florentine is." *That makes two of us.* "Anyone see it?"

"Let's see, Papa." Hillary swept the cam around the room past not-yet-scrutinized displays of medieval weapons, ancient pottery, and yellowing Renaissance manuscripts; the place was a museum.

"Could the Florentine be a manuscript?" she asked, focusing our static-filled ten-inch screen on a trio of vellum-bound volumes.

"I don't think so," I responded. One volume had been opened for display, depicting a bald friar, deep in prayer within a small window-less chamber; even given the cam's low image quality, the painting's vibrant colors popped from the laptop.

"I think I found it," yelled Steven.

"And whatever it is," Hillary abandoned the fifteenth-century man-uscripts and darted over, "it's not a diamond."

Steven stood in front of an old writing desk, in his hand a thick manila envelope with the word "Florentine" written in black perma-nent marker on its side.

Chapter 37

"ALL RIGHT, OPEN IT ALREADY," KVETCHED PAPA.

"One second, Pop," I said, examining the padded manila envelope in my hand.

"I wonder what it is," said Hillary. "Obviously not a diamond. Maybe a priceless document? Like an original copy of the Declaration of Independence?"

"I think Nicholas Cage already found that in *National Treasure*," snickered Steven. Hillary just shook her head.

"Perhaps something incriminating," I offered. "A damaging photograph of a politician?"

"Oh just open the damn thing already." Papa's arthritic hand shot out in an attempted grab. I yanked the envelope back reflexively.

"All right, all right." All four pairs of eyes focused on the tan envelope as I unwound the red drawstring and unfastened the stiff metal clasps.

"Thumb drives," I said, withdrawing a pair of gray, two-inch-long USB drives from inside. *The flash drives the Russian was after.* Each had the words "Florentine Controller" written in indelible marker on its side.

"That ain't no diamond," whined Papa. "What are they, suppositories?"

"They're thumb drives, Papa. They hold data for the computer."

Papa shook his head.

"Florentine Controller?" said Hillary, puzzled, "What the heck is a Florentine Controller?"

"God only knows," I said, equally perplexed. *Hopefully something we can hand over to the FBI and be rid of.*

"There's no reason to speculate," said Steven. "Stick one in your laptop and let's see what's on it."

"All right, here goes."

My hand shaking slightly, I inserted the first of the two drives into a USB slot on my laptop.

"Now what's supposed to happen?" asked Papa.

"Give it a second, Pop." With a few clicks, I brought up a window listing the contents of the drive.

"It's a movie?" said Steven.

Indeed, the only file on the drive was entitled "Florentine" and sported the ubiquitous triangular "play button" icon associated with video files.

I double-clicked the movie icon and, after a few moments of deliberation, the Windows Media Player window dutifully filled the screen. According to the progress indicator at the bottom of the window, the movie itself was sixty-five minutes long. After a few seconds of inky blackness, the videographer removed the lens cap and switched on the camera's lamp, barely illuminating the depths of a cave. Sans any narration, the videographer swept the camera in a horizontal arc past another hiker, clad in black, toward the cave's entrance. The last rays of the twilight sun flooded the cave's mouth, energizing a galaxy of fine dust particles and silhouetting what looked like the gnarled trunk of an oak just outside. The photographer pointed the camera back toward the cave's depths.

"Ready?" asked the darkly dressed companion from the lens's periphery. The voice was husky, thirties, African American.

"Yes, ready," answered the man behind the camera. His voice was deeper, late thirties, maybe forties, European accent. French, maybe. Not Russian. Too young to be Richard or Ronald at any rate.

"Who are they?" asked Hillary.

"More importantly, where are they?" added Steven.

"I can't tell," I whispered over the video. I paused the movie and dragged the progress indicator back with my mouse until the black-clad companion stood center-frame. The man's profile was a blur of darkly tinted flesh tones.

"The camera's moving too fast," said Hillary, "and it's too dark."

I hit the play button again. Papa began snoring softly.

The two walked a dozen steps deeper into the cave, then stopped.

"How's the picture?" asked the companion.

"I don't know. One second." The image instantly cut to black, then returned a millisecond later, far brighter. "Better."

The two followed the tunnel another thirty or so feet, then cut right; here, the cave had dead-ended. The videographer panned down to a three-and-a-half-foot-diameter hole at the base of the wall.

"Down there?" asked the videographer.

"Down there."

The companion moved into the frame, dropped onto hands and knees, then onto his stomach, and began writhing into the narrow channel, his pack almost instantly wedging against the edge of the aperture. He cursed, and with a tug, dislodged the pack and disappeared down the hole. Hillary shuddered.

"Claustrophobic?" I asked.

"Big time," she responded.

The videographer waited, camera aimed at the hole in anticipation. A few minutes later, the nearly inaudible voice of the companion whispered from the laptop's speaker.

"Okay, coming," responded the videographer. The man approached the hole, aimed the camera down the now-empty shaft, and cursed. The image cut to black.

"They're documenting where they hid the Florentine Controller," said Steven. "This is a video-graphic treasure map."

"You think so?" asked Hillary.

"What else could it be?"

"Let's keep watching," I suggested, "we'll know soon enough."

". . . second," muttered the European. The image returned. "There we go." A series of nearby stalactites sparkled in the pair's pivoting headlamp beams; however, the inky expanse of the room evaded the camera's reach.

"The next descent is left and up about thirty yards," said the companion, almost certainly a mountaineering or caving guide.

The two picked their way through a forest of person-height limestone stalagmites, some several feet in diameter and glistening with moisture. The guide, upon reaching a pair of particularly large specimens, held his hand up in caution, said, "Park it here," then threw his pack onto the ground and began extracting gear. Within a few minutes, a net of nylon slings had been affixed around the two limestone growths and a knotted rope dangled into the darkness from a gleaming pair of carabiners.

"Down there?" asked the European.

"Yes. You've rappelled before, right?"

"Yes."

"You first, then. You want me to film this?"

"No—I'll take the camera."

Again, the image cut, the tangle of webbing now replaced by a pair of undulating Day-Glo orange ropes that danced across the glistening, opalescent wall. The videographer panned the frame up just in time to catch the guide slithering smoothly down the rope and onto the ground.

"Pretty scary," commented Steven. "How do they get back up?"

I clicked the pause button. "They're probably going to use ascenders."

Steven stared blankly at me.

"I'll explain later. Let's keep watching, I want to see where they go."

Steven nodded and I resumed the video.

After a brief exchange, the videographer surveyed their position with the camera; the two had rappelled into a pocked, bowl-shaped depression, perhaps twenty-five feet wide. Its center was filled with a completely still, brackish pool of water.

"That way," said the guide from off-camera. The videographer walked along the edge toward the far end of the bowl. "And now, up." The camera panned up the slope, capturing a series of hand-sized depressions in the smooth rock, then cut to black.

The video, and their descent, continued for another fifty minutes. By the seventy-third minute of the recording, the two had traversed perhaps an eighth of a mile into the earth, with virtually every phase of their journey captured in exquisite detail, and if I'd had any clue where the cave was, I was certain I could retrace their steps.

At sixty-four minutes in, the guide, now seemingly soaked with water, stood impatiently, waiting for his orders. A five-foot-high tube-shaped tunnel ran off into the darkness behind him.

"Please wait for me here, I'll only be a minute," said the companion. The video ended abruptly.

"Interesting," said Steven contemplatively. He removed the first thumb drive from my laptop, laid it on the envelope, and replaced it with the second. A few seconds were enough to verify that its video was likely a duplicate, but he fast-forwarded several minutes just in case. The second copy was identical. He clicked the pause button and stood up.

"It's got to be a video-graphic treasure map," he said, looking to me for confirmation.

"Maybe," I mumbled.

"What do you mean, maybe?" he pressed. "What other possibility is there?"

None, I thought despondently. We were back to square one. No Florentine. No closure. Only a map showing a descent into a cave that could be anywhere. And worse, with nothing tangible to hand over to the feds, I still had two psychopaths potentially gunning for me with no discernable way out.

"The bigger question is this," Steven continued, "what *is* a Florentine Controller?"

I shrugged, too anxious to think clearly.

"Are you okay, Alex?" asked Hillary.

"Yeah, I'm just thinking," I stammered.

"C'mon Alex," Steven prodded, "just speculate. What could it be? What's a controller?"

"I don't know. I guess it's got to be small enough to fit in a backpack or they couldn't have dragged it down into the cave." I ruminated. "Maybe a microcontroller of some sort," I suggested.

"A microcontroller?" asked Hillary.

"A kind of microchip used to control electronics—they're used in consumer electronics but also in cars, planes, military systems, those kinds of things."

"That sounds feasible," said Steven, nodding. "Maybe someone's trying to hawk a prototype or the schematics for an advanced new chip? That could explain the five-million-dollar price tag. Any other ideas?"

"You know what I think?" said Hillary. "I think that it doesn't matter what it is. Look, whatever a Florentine Controller is, we know what it isn't, and that's a priceless diamond. Plus that cave could be literally anywhere—for all you know, it's in Pakistan." She drew a deep breath. "You guys have just found a fortune's worth of antiquities downstairs, so why not quit while you're ahead and put this whole thing to rest."

Steven opened his mouth to say something but I kicked him in the shin. He swallowed the word with a grimace.

She continued. "The last thing we need is for the two of you to get lost in some cave in God knows where. For heaven's sake, count your blessings and quit while you're ahead." She sighed. "Just let it go."

The room went silent save for Papa's soft snoring.

"You're right," I stammered a few seconds later. "At this point, there's no reason to go any further."

Hillary nodded and turned to Steven. "Agreed?"

Steven stared at my face a long second, then said, "Yeah. It's enough."

"Good." Hillary sighed. "I'm glad this whole thing is finally over."

Papa stirred, then opened his eyes and looked around the table.

"I want to go home," he moaned, "my elbow hurts."

"We should get going too." Hillary rose and motioned to Steven, who said, "I'm going to hang with Alex a while."

"Be my guest," said Hillary. "Alex, you mind dropping him off later?"

"Yeah, no problem. Can you take Papa back on your way home?"

"Sure. Papa, ready to go?"

"Yes." Papa reached for his cane, shuffled over, and kissed me on the forehead. "I'm proud of you, kid. That was a hell of an adventure."

And then he whispered softly in my ear. "And whatever you decide to do, just be safe. I love you."

Chapter 38

"I'M FUCKED." I walked over to the curio cabinet and picked up a mottled gold coin from the purple velvet matting. "That cave could be anywhere. And without the Florentine, I've got no options—I'm basically a sitting duck."

"Dude, you've got to relax. Khalimmy's probably in Beirut by now. And you've got no evidence that the Russians are after you."

"Wishful thinking," I said, spinning the antique coin in my fingers and appreciating its heft.

"Alex, just take a second and relax. Do you realize we've just found millions in antiquities? Millions. You should be ecstatic. You've got to trust me, you're overreacting."

"I hope you're right," I said, setting the coin back on its matting. "But—"

"Well, if you're still worried, just give the drives to the FBI and be done with it."

"And what? Ask them to go prospecting for the cave and send a crack team of government spelunkers in to hunt for the Florentine? They'll throw me in a psychiatric ward and shit-can the drives in the X-Files cabinet." I huffed. "And even if we did give the video to the feds, it does nothing to get Khalimmy or the Russian off my back. So when one of them is threatening to yank my eyeball out with a corkscrew, how exactly am I going to convince him I don't have the Florentine Controller anymore? Whatever it is."

Steven leaned against the wall by the weapons display and shook his head.

"Based on that line of reasoning, you've got two options," he said, "you either live in constant fear for the foreseeable future, or you track down the Florentine and execute our original plan. Find the thing and hand it over to the feds or to *60 Minutes* or something. Once it makes primetime TV, you'll be the last thing on Khalimmy's and the Russian's minds. Assuming you want to live a normal life, what other choice do you have?"

"Easy for you to say," I growled. "But, until we figure out where that cave is, the whole thing is moot."

Steven grunted.

A small red LED began flashing on the wall above the Van Gogh.

"What the hell is that?" asked Steven.

I stared at the light, bewildered. "A silent alarm? Maybe to alert Richard Lister if someone enters the house?"

The light stopped flashing.

"We'd better check what's going on upstairs." I grabbed the Ruger from the desk and shoved it in my pocket, then pointed to the weapons display next to Steven. "Grab that sword. We're not taking any chances."

"It's a doorbell," I said as I heard the knock at the front door. "The light's a silent doorbell."

I stepped through the secret bookshelf opening, descended the stairs, and soundlessly padded up to the front door for a look. Linda waved cheerily from behind the keyhole.

"Linda's here." I flipped the deadbolt and swung the door open. Linda stood in the doorway in a denim jacket, pink t-shirt and faded blue jeans, an apologetic smile on her face.

"Sorry I'm so late," she said, hugging me, "there was a nasty smashup on Wilshire and it was chaos in the ER." She stepped through the door.

"What's with the samurai sword?" she asked Steven with a wink. "You guys reenacting Pirates of the Caribbean or something?"

Steven blushed.

"If only," I said. "It's a long story. But before I explain, let me introduce my good friend, Steven."

Steven stared glassy-eyed at Linda. I couldn't blame him. With her slightly tousled damp hair, denim jacket, and teal sandals, she was stunning in her own totally casual sort of way.

"Holmes, this is Linda, my climbing buddy." *My stunning, totally platonic, out-of-my-league climbing buddy.*

"Nice . . . Nice to meet you," said Steven. "It's good to finally to put a face to your name. Alex's been talking about you for years."

"Funny, Alex never mentioned you before." Linda grinned, then said, "I'm just kidding, Steven. It's great to finally meet you, too." She stepped up and extended her hand while I shut and bolted the front door. "Alex—this place is unbelievable," she said, scanning the entry-way.

"Thanks," I said sheepishly. "Anyway, come on in."

Linda kicked her sandals off next to the front door and followed us in bare feet down the hall.

"So did the lip-code work?" she asked. "Did you find the dia-mond?"

"Yes and no," I said.

She looked puzzled.

"Just follow me and I'll show you."

"I'm dumbstruck," she said, walking from cabinet to cabinet in the panic room. She gingerly picked up the ankh to inspect it. "All this was just locked in here?"

"Trust me, we were totally stunned too. All along, we were expect-ing to find a diamond and we found this instead."

"No diamond?" she asked, surprised.

"No," said Steven, "that's a bit of a mystery."

Linda gently set the ankh back on the shelf, then leaned against the edge of the desk, an expectant look on her face. "Willing to share it with me?" she asked after a moment of silence.

Steven turned to me and raised his eyebrows questioningly.

"I'll trade you the story for some advice," I said.

"You want me to be brutally honest?"

"Do I have any choice?"

"None whatsoever. Now out with it."

"Okay. Bear with me." I paused to collect my thoughts. "So we originally thought the Florentine was a diamond and that Richard Lister—"

"The cadaver with the lip code?" Linda interrupted.

"Right. We figured Richard locked the diamond in here."

"I'm with you so far." Linda nodded.

"But now we're pretty sure the Florentine isn't a diamond—in fact, the only thing we found in here relating to 'the Florentine' was a pair of thumb drives labeled 'Florentine Controller.'"

"Florentine Controller?" she asked, shaking her head. "What the heck is that?"

"Exactly our reaction," said Steven. "But whatever it is, it's pretty clearly not a diamond."

Linda leaned in. "Okay, so what was on the drives?"

"A video documenting a descent into a cave."

"Come again, cowboy?" Linda looked perplexed.

"We think Richard Lister hid the Florentine Controller in a cave and documented its location with video."

"Kind of like a computer version of a treasure map?"

"That was my theory," said Steven.

"That cadaver's been busy," she nodded approvingly.

"I like her," said Steven.

"So are you thinking of spelunking for it? And if so, how do I get in on the expedition?"

"You may not want to when you hear the rest."

"There's more?" Linda motioned me to continue. "Keep going, then."

"Well, there's a hiccup. Remember that Khalimmy guy I told you about?"

"The guy who wanted to buy the diamond . . . or whatever it is, right?"

"Right. Well, he's still hunting for it, and now there's a Russian guy looking for it too. Bad people. They've already put Richard Lister's brother in a coma and nearly put us into body bags." I briefly filled Linda in on the latest about Khalimmy and the Russian.

"So they were after Richard Lister for the Florentine, and now that you've got it—or at least they think you've got it—you're worried they're going to come after you."

"You nailed it," I said. "I was hoping we'd find the Florentine locked in here. Then we could have just handed it over to the FBI and been done with this."

"Or given to the media to make a big stink about," added Steven. "Once the word is out that Alex doesn't have it anymore, these guys no longer have a motive to come after him."

"Okay, so why not just grab it from the cave and hand it over to Katie Couric?"

"Easier said than done," I said. "We've got no idea where the cave is. So now we're back to square one, with at least one and maybe two psychopaths stalking me."

"Not good, Alex," said Linda, pacing around the small room. "I had no idea this thing was so serious."

"Yeah, it's a big mess. I don't know what to do."

"And this Khalimmy guy and the Russian? You don't know anything else about them?"

"Nothing," said Steven. "Although Khalimmy's currently being hunted by the police, so I'm betting he's long gone."

"I'm not so sure," I said.

Linda bit her lip in thought. "I think your only out is to find this Florentine Controller thing and hand it over to the authorities. Or, like you said, Steven, to the media." She scratched her head. "Out of curiosity, have you thought about searching online for the cave?"

"How would you do that?" Steven asked.

"I've got to think you could find it on Spelunking.com or maybe on Rockclimbing.com. They've got thousands of caves cataloged. Members post photos and videos of their descents all the time. Unless the cave is totally unknown, which would be pretty surprising, it's just a matter of slogging through web pages. Or you could post a clip from the video onto their chat forum and see what people say."

"At this point, I'm willing to try anything," I said.

"Can you show me the video?" she asked. "Maybe I'll recognize the cave, or see something you guys missed."

I locked the panic room, then the three of us worked our way back up the ladder and into the library. It was getting misty outside, and as the last rays of the sun disappeared, curls of fog began to descend over the wall and amongst the ferns and bamboo.

I motioned for Linda to sit down in front of the laptop, then flipped on the kitchen lights.

"Here, take a look," I said, opening the clamshell and clicking on the Play button. After a brief pause, the computer resumed the video from where Steven had fast-forwarded it earlier. "This is a few minutes in. Let me back up to the start—"

"Wait." Linda grabbed my hand.

"You recognize it?" My heart raced.

"I'm not sure. Let me watch a little more."

Linda leaned into the small screen and stared intently.

"Those stalactites are pretty unusual. Somehow they look familiar—I'm pretty sure I've seen a photo of this place online before. Does the video show the outside of the cave?"

"Not really," I said, walking over to the sink for some water, "the footage starts just inside the mouth."

"Let's see," she said, swiping her finger and clicking the track pad. A beat later, the video began playing from the start. Again, she leaned into the laptop, chin resting on her fists, watching intently.

"The problem is they don't show the outside," I said.

"Shhhh!" Linda sat glued to the screen, watching and rewinding the video at least five times. Then with a vigorous nod of her head, she slid her chair back and stood up.

"Guys . . . I know where this is."

Chapter 39

"YOU WHAT?" ASKED STEVEN.

"That's the Cupeño Indian Cave!" Linda backed up the video a few seconds, then paused it.

"Cu-what?" I asked, running around the table to the laptop.

"Cupeño," she repeated. "It's supposedly an old Indian shaman cave." Linda pointed at the oak silhouetted at the mouth of the cave. "No mistaking it; I'm one-hundred-percent sure. Last week I was looking for new spelunking sites with Jamie. They had a photo almost identical to this shot on Climbing.com."

"Where is it?" I asked. "In Montana?"

"No! No, it's practically next door. According to the write-up, it's about a mile up the ravine in Malibu Creek State Park, an hour's hike past the rock pool, up on the left side of the canyon."

"Malibu Creek? Are you kidding?" I'd spent the last seven years of my life hiking and climbing every square inch of Malibu Creek State Park, but had never once heard of a cave system. "How come I've never heard about it?"

"You're not alone. The guy who posted the pictures is an old-timer, and he said he'd never heard anyone mention it either. He apparently found a reference to it in an old nineteenth-century naturalist book and decided to take a look."

"Have you been?" I asked.

"No. Jamie and I were planning on going in a few weeks."

"We've got to go, Alex," said Steven. "Let's settle this once and for all."

I gnawed on my thumbnail.

"Look," he said, "we know for a fact that we're the only people alive that have seen this video—no one else has a clue that the Florentine is hidden in a cave, or for that matter, where the cave is." He took a deep breath. "You could be in and out of there before anyone even knows it. And once you have the, the thing, you're in control. Give it to the FBI if you like. Or give it to the press. Either way, this whole thing could be over by tomorrow."

He was right. The only sure way to get closure was to find the Florentine and then expose it. And if we were going to go after it, now was the time.

"I . . . I can't do it alone."

"What do you mean, *I*?" asked Steven.

"There's no way you're going down into that cave. You'll get yourself killed. Even given my caving and climbing experience, I still wouldn't go more than ten feet into that tube without an expert partner."

"Okay, then who do you know who could go?" asked Steven.

"I don't know," I said, shaking my head. "This whole thing could be a deathtrap."

"I'll go with you, Alex." Linda twisted her chair to face me.

"No way. It'd kill me if anything happened to you."

"Alex, you're not going without me. I won't let you," she said, shaking her head. "If you want to drop this, that's okay, but there's no way I'll let you go in without me."

"I can't."

"Yes you can," she said. "I can take care of myself, Alex. And you need me."

I sat down and covered my face in my hands. Linda ignored me and plowed on.

"Like you said, you can't do this alone. You're going to need an experienced partner, one you've climbed with before. Someone who knows how you'll react—and what to do—when shit goes wrong."

"But," I stammered.

"How many times have we caved together, Alex? Ten? Twenty?" she asked. "Who knows you better than I do?"

I shook my head.

Linda stood up and began pacing. "We're going to need to round up a bunch of equipment and find a third. It's not safe with just two."

"I can be the third. You're both experts. I can be the backup."

Linda turned toward Steven, paused a beat, and looked questioningly at me. At two-twenty, Steven had put on a fair amount of weight since our college days—and he'd never set foot in a cave.

"Listen to me, Steven, you're going to be a liability," I said. "We need someone who can help us get out of trouble, someone who's caved before."

"I've climbed at least half a dozen times with you," countered Steven defensively.

"This is different," said Linda. "If someone gets injured down there, or we run into a gas pocket, or the headlamps die, or any one of fifty other things go wrong, we're going to want to have someone who knows exactly what to do."

Steven held up his hands. "Okay, okay."

"Alex, what do you think about Potter? He's caved for years."

"I couldn't drag Davis Potter into this."

"Why don't you let him decide for himself?" asked Linda.

"I wouldn't feel right," I reiterated. "It's just too dangerous."

"Just give him the facts and let him decide," she said. "You've been there for him, Alex, many times. And if he's not cool with it, we'll figure something else out."

"I . . . I guess I could ask him."

"Do you have any paper and a pen?"

"On the counter. One second." I grabbed the first thumb drive from the card table and slid it back in the envelope, then laid it on the counter to put back later.

"Here," I said, returning with a Regina Flowers notepad and pen.

"Let's watch the rest of the video and take notes," she said, "I want to make sure we know what equipment we'll need. Then we'll call Potter."

By the time the video had ended, Linda had a list twenty items long.

"Did you ever pick up a new set of Jumars and étriers?" she asked.

I nodded. "Yeah, they're in my garage with the rest of my spelunking gear."

"What's a Jumar and an . . . etr—" asked Steven.

"Et-tree-aye," said Linda in perfect French. "They're a set of devices that you use to ascend up a rope. You need them when you're caving and the rock's too wet or difficult to climb with your hands."

"Are they battery-powered or something?"

"Only in the movies," I replied with a smile. "They're muscle powered—they make it much easier, but you've still got to manually use them to pull yourself up the rope."

"That sounds like it would be a lot of work," said Steven.

"Trust me," I said, "it's exhausting."

Steven nodded nervously.

"Okay, I think that's it. Let's call Potter."

"You still want to go?" I asked Potter. "Even given all of the risks?"

"I do," said Potter over Linda's speakerphone. "I want to be there for you guys. You've saved my life more times than I care to remember, now it's my turn to repay the favor."

"Then we do it tomorrow morning—at eight—before the park gets busy."

"That works," said Linda.

"Sounds good," said Potter.

"All right, everyone knows what gear they're bringing," I said. "Let's call it a night and get some sleep, guys. We'll need it."

Linda hung up her phone, then stood to stretch while I packed my laptop for the trip back to my old place in Northridge.

"Actually, Linda, would you mind giving Steven a ride home? When I get back, I've got to dig up all my spelunking gear, and I want to transfer a copy of the video to my iPod so we can consult it on the way down. It'd save me some time if you could take him back."

"No problem," said Linda. "You cool riding in an old Bug without belts?"

Steven shot me a look that said 'I'd be cool riding with her without anything on,' then moderated his output: "Uh, yeah, that's fine."

"All right, cross your fingers, guys," she said, "tomorrow's the big day."

Chapter 40

MY STOMACH GROWLED as I turned left onto the Pacific Coast Highway from Latigo. I reached for the latch on my glove compartment—I usually had an energy bar in there for emergencies—then decided I was just too hungry. I'd stop at the Jack in the Box just before Topanga and load up before I headed back to Northridge to transfer the video. A delay, but I couldn't concentrate if I was hungry.

Then it hit me.

Shit. The video. I'd forgotten to lock up the other thumb drive—it was still sitting in its envelope, unprotected, on the kitchen counter.

The Pacific Coast Highway was nearly empty this time of night, so I slowed, checked for headlights in the fog, and, seeing none, cranked a tight U-turn and accelerated back up Latigo Canyon.

A minute later, I took the hairpin right turn onto the dense, tree-covered driveway and barreled over the uneven asphalt up to the gate. I clicked the remote on my sun visor and with a sudden creak, the iron gate shuddered and began rolling behind the estate's thick stucco wall. I edged the car past the gate and into the courtyard, then cut the engine and turned off the headlights. Two antique-style gas lamps mounted on either side of the front door flickered lethargically, illuminating wisps of marine fog and casting strange shadows through the yard's bushes.

I scanned the yard for any sign of movement, grabbed the Ruger, then exited my car and waded through the offshore mist toward the front door.

The key fit snugly into the lock. I twisted and shoved the door inward, clicked on the hallway lights, shut the door, and turned the bolt. I knew that no one could possibly be in the house—we'd left less than five minutes ago—yet I was oddly paranoid, alert.

"I've got a gun," I yelled. My fingers tightened on the pistol as I stood motionless, listening.

Nothing.

I took a tentative step, then another, my sneakers squeaking, echoing off the paneled walls and down the empty corridor. Again, I stopped to listen.

Silence. I lifted my foot to take another step.

Then I heard it. A footfall, tentative but unmistakable.

Shit.

I spun around and in one fluid motion, flipped the deadbolt, yanked the door, then slammed it shut. Taking the front steps in a single leap, I scrambled to the car and dug my hand into my pocket for my keys, fingers jamming in the tight fabric of my jeans. Pistol in my right hand, pointed shakily at the front door, I dug deeper with my left until my index finger caught the key ring. I yanked. The mass of keys jammed against my wallet and I tugged even harder, the thin steel ring slicing into the flesh of my index finger, stretching under the strain of my flexor tendon. I screamed from the pain, but continued pulling manically. The wire ring deformed further, then with a sudden, loud rip, the fabric tore and my keys went airborne.

I staggered over, grabbed the ring and jammed my thumb against the remote's unlock button. Nothing. I pressed harder, longer. Again, nothing. Key in hand, I closed the space to my driver's side door, rammed the key into the lock, and twisted. The lock clicked. I jumped in, inserted the key into the ignition, shifted the car into gear, and accelerated into a tight loop, past the gate and down the driveway. The undercarriage of the car scraped the curb as I skidded onto Latigo toward the Pacific Coast Highway.

"Hello? Steven?"

"Alex?"

"Fuck! They broke into the house!"

The line went silent for a long second.

"What? Where are you?"

I took a deep breath.

"In my car. I forgot to lock up the other thumb drive in the panic room, so I drove back. They must have been waiting for us to leave."

"Jesus Christ! Who was it? Was it the Russian?"

"How the fuck should I know?" I snapped. "I heard someone in the house and I bolted."

"Alex, just calm down and we'll figure this out." It was Linda.

My hands trembled visibly on the steering wheel. I concentrated on my heartbeat, inhaling and exhaling slowly.

"I'm not waiting until tomorrow morning," I said. "No way. No fucking way. If you found those cave photos on Climbing.com, then they will too. They're going to figure out where that cave is and I'm going to be fucked."

"Wait, Alex. Wait," yelled Steven. "This is the best thing that could have possibly happened."

"What? Are you crazy?"

"No. Hear me out. Now that they have the video, you're off the hook. Let them go after the Florentine. Once they have it, they don't need you anymore."

"Are you fucking crazy? This is the worst possible scenario. Maybe if there was just one of them, either Khalimmy *or* the Russian, you might be right. But they're both after the Florentine. If either one gets it and the other still thinks I have it, I'm fucked." I swallowed hard. "I want to get this damn thing over with tonight."

The line went silent.

"We can do that," Linda said after a few seconds, "but first you've got to calm down."

"I'll fucking calm down once the Florentine is sitting in front of fucking Wolf Blitzer on live TV. Then I'll calm down."

"Okay, okay. Let's—"

"Look," I interrupted, "between Potter, you, and me, we know every inch of that canyon. I want to be at the cave's mouth before sunrise."

I heard some mumbling on the other end of the line, then Linda said, "What time do you want to meet at the trailhead?"

"No later than four-thirty," I said.

"We'll be there. Just try to get some rest. I'll call Potter now."

Chapter 41

AFTER A TRIP to the park's lone remaining functional bathroom, I rejoined Steven, Potter, and Linda at the Malibu Creek trailhead. The three had their headlamps on, casting dim red beams of light onto the hard-packed gravel as they milled pensively around. In the background, the din of crickets filled the damp morning air.

"Before we start, I've got to say it again: this could be really dangerous, so if anyone wants to bail, I totally understand."

I shifted my beam toward Potter. "Not a chance," he said.

"Linda? Are you sure?"

"Stop asking stupid questions, Alex."

My head shot around, my eyes drawn to a pair of headlights. They quickly dimmed.

"It's probably just someone on the highway," said Potter. "We've seen a bunch of others come and go since we arrived."

"Okay," I continued, my heart still pounding. "Regardless of what we find, I want to thank you guys. I couldn't ask for better friends."

"Alex, you're like family," said Potter. "The Lord knows you've been there for us."

"Thanks, Potter." I nodded solemnly. "All right, let's go."

Everyone heaved their packs up onto their shoulders and began hiking down the dirt path. After a few minutes of silent walking, Steven and Potter began chatting softly, so I walked up ahead to Linda. She turned to acknowledge me with a warmhearted smile.

"I don't know how to thank you," I said. "For everything."

"Promise me you'll buy me that margarita when this whole thing is over," she paused, "and then keep your promise. That'll be thanks enough. I don't know what I'd do if anything happened to you."

I put my arm around her shoulder and squeezed. "That's a promise."

Twenty minutes later we reached the edge of the rock pool. Except for the cacophony of croaking toads and the occasional bug flitting on its surface, it was eerily devoid of activity, the usual crowds of cliff-diving weekend-goers still sound asleep at home. Our canyon lay beyond the brackish basin of water, sheathed in darkness.

After taking a moment to drink some water, Linda gestured silently, and we made our way like a quartet of spiders across the hundred-foot-long sheer left wall behind the rock pool: Potter first, followed by Steven, me, and Linda at the rear. Our hands shifted from pocket to pocket, feet balancing on a series of protruding rocks and ledges twenty feet above the waterline.

"I'm glad that's over," panted Steven as he stepped to the ground at the far edge of the pool. Even in the dim red light of my headlamp, I could see that his shirt was soaked in sweat.

"You did well," I said softly.

"Thanks," he said, wiping his brow. "Just tell me that was the worst of it."

I nodded. "That should be the worst of it."

I sat down on a rock and closed my eyes, then inhaled a deep, cathartic breath.

"Feeling a little safer now, cowboy?" asked Linda.

"Yeah. Now we're on our turf."

She sat down and gently placed her arm around me. "It'll all work out, Alex."

"I sure hope so."

After a brief rest we began the final leg of our trek, working our way over, around and under the forest of boulders, trees and bushes that littered the next mile of the canyon floor. Linda was the first to spot the cave's entrance. The four-foot-wide by twelve-foot-high undulating crack lay hidden behind a vertical fold of rock about twenty feet above the streambed. A series of large pockets in the face led up from the canyon floor to a natural shelf at its base.

"Wow, it's completely hidden," I said. "I've hiked past this spot at least half a dozen times and never noticed it. How did you spot it?"

"The oak," she said, pointing at the arthritic limbs of the gnarled old tree. "It looks just like the one in the video."

By the time we'd climbed up to the shelf and taken our packs off to rest, it was nearly six, and a faint morning glow tinged the sky. I reclined against the trunk of the old oak, while Potter and Linda found their own bean bag-size boulders and began soundlessly unpacking their food for breakfast. Steven sat down next to me, pulled a handful of energy bars from his backpack, and offered me a choice.

"So, based on the video," I said, breaking the silence, "I'm guessing we'll be down for about four hours, maybe five. It looks safe if you want to come with us to the first rappel point. Or you can stay here and keep an eye on things."

"After everything we've been through, I want to see the inside of that cave," said Steven.

"We'll give it a go then," I said. "But once we get to the first drop-off, we'll need you up here. Anything could go wrong down there, so we need a backup." I took another bite. "If we don't make it out in five hours, head back down the canyon to the visitor's center and get help."

"Will do."

We all chewed quietly for the next few minutes, each in our own world. When the last bites had been swallowed, I headed over to the edge of the cave.

"All right guys, it's now or never. Let's do this."

Chapter 42

"Word travels fast," said Linda, stooping down next to a makeshift stone fire pit about a dozen paces inside the cave's entrance. "At least it's not fresh," she said, nudging the remnants of a melted Corona bottle with a stick. "This is a few days old." She zoned out for a moment, then stood back up and unzipped her pack.

"All right gents," she continued, "make sure you know exactly where your backup headlamps and batteries are, and make sure you know how to put the batteries in—even if you can't see. Here's a little trick I learned recently from a spelunking blog."

She reached into her pack and withdrew three AA batteries that had been neatly taped side-by-side with a single layer of climbing tape. "Now if my batteries go, all I have to do is pull the old ones out and then slide this set in, bumpy side first." She wrapped the makeshift pack in a Ziploc bag and then buttoned them into her front shirt pocket.

"Clever," I said, grabbing my own backup batteries and a roll of athletic tape. After a moment of preparation, I slid the newly taped batteries into the top of my pack, then switched my headlamp to its brightest, white-light setting. Outside, it was beginning to get sunny— the old oak I'd leaned against cast a black silhouette against the brightening canyon wall.

"So you think this Florentine thing is actually hidden down there?" asked Potter.

"Let's hope so," I said, walking over to the three-foot-high tube.

"Either way, I'm glad I could help."

"We're lucky to have you, Potter," said Linda, who had lowered to her knees and was now peering down the dark shaft. "I think I'm going to leave my pack off and push it ahead of me. Less chance of getting stuck."

I lowered onto my haunches and gazed down the tube. "Ugh." I shuddered, just a hint of claustrophobia overtaking me. "Good idea."

"Well, here goes." Linda shoved her pack into the hole then followed behind it, shimmying forward on her elbows and knees. A moment later, her squirming feet disappeared, and it reminded me of the hind legs of a mouse being swallowed by a boa constrictor.

"Damn," said Steven, unconsciously backing up a step.

"You okay to go?" I asked.

Steven squatted to look down the hole, shot me an uneasy look, then peered down the hole again. "I think I'll stay here," he said, deflated.

"Don't sweat it, Steven," said Potter. "I had a panic attack the first time I went spelunking. Nearly lost it. It happens to everyone."

"Thanks, Potter," said Steven.

"No problem, man. It's the truth."

"All right, well in that case, I guess I'll go next," I said. "See you on the flip-side, Crouch." I swung the pack off my shoulder, dropped to the floor, and shoved it ahead of me. "No farting," I yelled into the tube.

"Too late, cowboy," chuckled Linda from somewhere deep inside.

"Here goes nothing," I said, pushing my unwieldy pack across the rough stone floor and into the shaft. With each shove of the pack, I shimmied a few feet deeper, braced one foot or another against a side-wall, then pushed again. After about fifteen feet, the tube craned right and constricted into a nearly impassible duct a mere foot-and-a-half high. I tried to advance, but recoiled each time the dozens of sharp rocks embedded in the tunnel's surface dug into my back.

"What was I thinking?" I mumbled, closing my eyes to avoid a wave of claustrophobia.

"What?" asked Potter from somewhere behind me in the shaft.

"Nothing," I yelled.

I lowered onto my belly from my knees and forearms and slithered forward like a snake, sending eddies of fine dust dancing through the shifting beam of my headlamp. Finally, after another five feet, the tube veered left and its outlet, and Linda's legs, came into view. Linda tugged my pack from the tube and extended me a welcoming hand.

"Thanks," I said. "Remind me to take a Valium next time."

"That makes two of us. That last part was claustrophobic as hell."

I wiped the dust from my glasses using my t-shirt and surveyed the cave. All around us, spiny stalagmites shot up from the ground, some reaching the level of my head or taller; their opalescent, mottled surfaces looked like the skin of some amphibian monster in my head-lamp's harsh LED beam. I tilted my head back. Overhead, an equally large number of stalactites dangled from the thirty-foot high ceiling, some with glistening drops of water pooling at their tips.

"It's beautiful!" I said.

"Yeah, who knew this was here all this time? These formations look a lot like the ones in Bishop's Cave. Remember?"

"How could I forget? I seriously thought we were going to die down there."

"That's right! Jotz ditched us a quarter-mile down to smoke some weed, then both of our headlamps died." She giggled. "You were as jumpy as a cat in a roomful of rocking chairs."

"That's right, I was," I said, nodding. "You know, we've had some good times."

"Yeah." She smiled nostalgically. An instant later, Potter's pack shot out of the tube like the head of a groundhog. I grabbed its straps and leaned it against the wall, then helped him out of the hole.

"Now I know what it's like to be a snake," he said.

"Can you imagine getting stuck in there and having your head-lamp go out?"

"I'd rather not think about it," said Potter, shuddering. "But actu-ally, that reminds me . . ." He stooped down to his pack and unzipped the top pouch. "Here, just in case." Potter handed each of us a pair of chemical glow sticks. "Snap one, and you've got four or five hours of light. You never know what's going to happen."

"Thanks Potter." It was actually a really good idea—no batteries required. I crammed them into a pocket of my nylon climbing pants and zipped it shut.

"All right, lead the way, Alex."

I pulled my Ziploc-wrapped iPod out of my backpack and used the touchscreen to advance the video to our current location.

"That way." I pointed. "According to the guide, it's about thirty yards down."

Our beams danced left and right across the forest of glistening stalagmites, casting an eerie kaleidoscopic lightshow as we probed deeper into the cave.

"No bats," said Potter, who was also scanning the periphery.

"Hopefully no Russians or pygmies with blow-darts either," I said, sinking up to my ankle in a pool of brackish water. "Dammit. Watch out, right here," I pointed, "it's deep."

Linda nodded and sidestepped the pool.

"Hey! I think that's where the first descent is," said Potter, pointing forty-five degrees right of our current trajectory. I turned my head and illuminated two towering stalagmites, each at least a foot and a half in diameter and ten feet high.

"I think you're right," I said. After I double-checked with the video, the three of us headed right, past a thicket of spiny growths, and toward the pair of megaliths.

"These should hold us, no problem," I said. Grabbing hold of the left stalagmite, I leaned forward to look over the edge, my head-mounted beam slicing through the blackness and illuminating a bowl-shaped landing at the bottom. "Looks like about a fifty-foot drop."

"Who wants to set up the rappel gear?" asked Potter.

"Go for it, Potter," said Linda. I nodded in approval and dropped my pack to the floor.

Within a few minutes, Potter's bright orange rope dangled from the two stalagmites, undulating into the darkness below.

"Should be safe and ready to go. Who wants to double-check?"

I stepped forward and inspected his setup. "It looks safe," I said. "Potter, you set it, you go first."

Potter hooked his harness up to the rope and turned to face us, his back to the chasm.

"All right guys, I'll catch you down below." And with just a hint of a smile, Potter shuffled his feet to the edge of the crag, leaned backward, and allowed gravity to do the rest.

"You next?" I asked Linda.

"Sure."

After Potter detached from the rope and gave us an A-OK, she stepped into position, fed the rope through her rappel device, and disappeared into oblivion.

Chapter 43

THE THREE OF US now stood along the edge of a hole-pocked, water-smoothed bowl a good thirty feet wide. A brackish pool of water—I had no desire to plumb its depths—filled its bottom. The air here was heavier and had a distinctly musty, sour smell.

"Take a look," said Linda.

"What?" I asked. Linda tilted her head back and panned her beam across the near sixty-foot-high wall we'd just descended.

"This definitely looks climbable if we had to. What do you think? The holds look reasonable and are spaced pretty close together. Humph . . . except for that run up near the top." She pointed. "That looks thin."

"Next time we come out, we can give it a go," said Potter.

If there is a next time. "Okay," I said. "Let's keep going. So far we're making good time." I withdrew the iPod from my pocket and fast-forwarded it just past our current position. "Looks like we want to head straight up over the far edge of the bowl, and then down the canyon a long ways to a second pool of water." I gestured to Linda.

"Onward, then," she said. We sidestepped left along the edge of the bowl, careful to avoid the stinking pool of water, then shuffled up its far side using a series of natural pockets in the smooth rock. Ahead of us, two towering walls, seemingly formed of melted wax, created a narrow canyon that extended from the edge of the bowl off into the darkness.

The three of us cleared the edge of the bowl, scrabbled down a short slope, and then made our way down into the canyon. Down we traveled, deeper and deeper, our beams slicing through the darkness, dancing across the translucent walls as we snaked left and right through the narrowing ravine. At about thirty minutes in, the canyon forked into two separate channels. Following the video's cue, we veered left into the narrower of the two outlets, then right, down a second fork into an underground slot canyon that, at its tightest, tapered to just a foot wide. At this point, we had to remove our packs, holding them above our heads, and sidestep between the walls to pass. Finally, after traveling nearly a quarter mile in total, we found the canyon's terminus: a large, semi-cylindrical cistern, roughly thirty feet long by twenty feet wide by fifteen feet high. Knee-deep, algae-covered water filled the boulder-strewn reservoir.

I pulled the iPod out of my pack, and together we watched the next five minutes of the video at double-speed. After arriving in the cistern, the two explorers had waded through the muck to its far end and crawled through the cavern's solitary outlet, which to my chagrin was another narrow tube. Even more horrifying, however, was the fact that the tube was almost completely flooded, leaving just a few feet of breathing room between its ceiling and the putrefying, algae-laden water below.

"Lovely," said Linda.

"Let's get this over with," I said, cringing. I walked over to the chute, dropped my pack on an algae-covered rock, and eased my knees through the cool water until they settled on the bedrock. Then I grabbed my pack and manhandled it, half-sunken, into the hole.

"Careful, Alex!" said Linda. "Can you see the outlet?"

"Not yet."

The first few feet on hands and knees were bearable and while the water drenched my pants and the lower half of my shirt, my face was at least a foot above the sour-smelling muck. I edged forward two more feet, pushed my pack forward, and to my dismay it began sinking lower into the water; the tube was sloping down. I turned my head around as far as I could manage in the cramped space.

"Shit! The water is getting deeper!"

"How deep?" asked Linda, her head poking into the hole.

"I'm not sure, one second." I extended my right hand forward along the bedrock until I felt the change in grade, then inched the rest of my body forward. "It's hard to say. I'm just going to go for it." Again, I pushed my pack forward, only this time the water swallowed it whole. I cursed and pushed on, my chin now just two or three inches above the muck's surface.

"Are we sure this is the right way?" I called back, nearly gagging from the fumes of the decaying algae.

"I think so," yelled Potter from behind.

"Okay," I said, peering forward, "I hope it's not too far. I'm going to try to swim underwater the rest of the way."

"Careful, Alex," said Linda nervously, "it's easy to get disoriented underwater. Whatever you do, don't panic. Just stay calm."

"Thanks for the heads-up," I said, "I'll be okay."

The ceiling lowered sharply just ahead, leaving barely an inch of breathing room above the water's viscous surface. Keeping hold of the straps, I shoved my pack forward as far as I could, inhaled a mixture of oxygen and fumes from the decaying muck through my nose, and ducked under the surface. Eyes and mouth clamped shut, I shoved off of the rough walls with my hands and propelled myself forward. My body almost instantly ran into my pack, so I heaved it forward again then launched forward a second time. Totally blind and nervous that I'd soon run out of oxygen, I eased my head up until I felt the welcome coolness of air on my scalp, then on my eyes and nose. I raised my head farther, just exposing my mouth, and gulped a deep, though rancid breath. I tried to relax—at least I had oxygen for the moment—and used my left hand to wipe the muck from my eyes. I opened my lids to absolute blackness: my headlamp had shorted out underwater.

I panicked and took another gulp of intensely putrid air. A surge of stomach acid, bile, and partly digested food rushed up my esophagus and into the back of my throat. I swallowed hard, but my gag reflex was just too strong and a second esophageal spasm ejected a spray of vomit onto the water just inches from my face. The smell of half-digested food and rotting algae caused my stomach muscles to lurch and I gagged again, shooting a further surge of vomit from my mouth and causing me to rear reflexively. My head cracked against the ceiling, and as a shower of flitting stars streaked across my retinas, I collapsed face-first into the water.

Chapter 44

"Alex! Alex! Are you okay? Alex! Where are you?" Linda's screams sliced through the blackness and echoed anxiously off the walls. "Where are you? Potter! Where the hell is Potter?"

I opened my mouth to respond but managed only to discharge a lungful of rancid water in a painful spasm of coughing. Panicking from the lack of oxygen, I involuntarily gasped for air, choked on my own saliva, then retched again.

"Here," I said, panting. "I'm sitting . . . on a rock."

My lungs heaved and I gagged again. "Oh God that's painful," I said, grabbing my chest.

"Alex," she said in a more relieved voice, "are you okay?"

"Yeah, I think so. I must have a guardian angel or something. I'm amazed I didn't drown."

"Just give me a second and we'll check you out. Damn, it stinks in here," said Linda. "*Augh*, smells like . . ." She hesitated. "Vomit and rotten vegetables."

"Your sense of smell is accurate," I said into the darkness. "My vomit, to be exact."

"One second," she said. I heard her sloshing through the water toward me.

"You trash your headlamp too?" I said.

"Potter and I bagged them before going through. He yelled to you right before you disappeared, but I guess you'd already dived under." I heard a zipping noise and a second later the beam of Linda's headlamp crisscrossed the room in search of me. "Jesus, you look horrible," she said.

"I'm feeling all right. Now."

Linda walked over and gently wiped the algae from my face with her hands, then examined my scalp.

"You've got another bump to add to your collection," she said. "Are you feeling dizzy?"

I shook my head.

"Good. Look into my eyes."

She shined her headlamp at my eyes; my lids shut reflexively.

"Open up," she said. Then, after a few more seconds she smiled and said, "You'll live. But if you pull something like that again, it's not going to be the drowning that kills you. I'll take care of it myself."

That smile—at once both loving yet hopelessly platonic—made me want to die. It made me want to kiss her more than anything else in the world, to tell her how I felt—how I'd felt for more than five years— but I couldn't. I didn't have the courage. I'd never had the courage. "Thanks," I said, swallowing the emotion.

Linda panned her beam around the cave, which was small and dome-shaped, maybe ten feet high and just as wide, and filled with water.

"Oh, were you lucky," she said.

"Huh?" I said dazedly.

Linda shook her head and pointed behind me. I twisted to follow her index finger—the boulder I sat perched upon rested at the edge of a good twenty-foot drop. A few more feet of blind, semi-conscious stumbling and I'd have been lunchmeat.

"Holy mother of Jesus!" wailed Potter. I spun back around to see him emerge from the water covered in gray, rotting algae strands like the Creature from the Black Lagoon. "What is that . . . that . . . stink?"

"Fife had a gastric spasm," replied Linda.

After wading over to my boulder, Potter withdrew his headlamp from a plastic bag in the top of his pack and patted me on the shoulder. "Doing okay, man?"

"I've been better, Potter," I said.

"Your pack's about five feet back. I kicked it walking over."

"Thanks. Any remedies for a waterlogged headlamp?"

"Use your backup," said Linda, "you can fix that one later."

"Good point. Where was my pack, Potter?"

Potter pointed and I slogged through the water to retrieve it. In a minute, I'd swapped my primary and backup lamps, and was ready to go.

"All right, let's get this over with," I said, after a few more minutes of rest. "If I'm not mistaken, this is our last rappel."

While Linda set up the last rope, I reviewed the remainder of the video with Potter. Then, the three of us, in turn, slid down the twenty-foot length to the landing below.

"There's the final cave, just like in the video," said Potter.

"After you, Fife," said Linda, holding out her hand.

Needing no encouragement, I dashed through the ankle-deep pool of water to the mouth of the cave, and, stooping to avoid hitting my head, ducked into the shaft. And there, upon a boulder just feet from the mouth, sat a reinforced aluminum box the size of a cigar case.

"Holy shit!" I stared at the box, disbelieving.

"What are you waiting for?" asked Linda from behind. "Open it."

"Here goes nothing," I said. I dropped onto my knees, and, using both shaking hands, released the two latches and opened the box's lid.

Chapter 45

MY JAW DROPPED. The box contained a red plastic Slinky, a costume jewelry bracelet studded with fake glass gems, a small stuffed teddy bear, a cheap ballpoint pen, and a plastic freezer bag containing a diary.

"What the hell?" Potter and Linda crowded beside me to see. "Toys?"

"It's a geocache," said Potter.

"A what?" I asked.

"It's a geocache, Alex," Linda said calmingly, "you've found a geocache. It's a hobby. People place these objects in obscure places, in the middle of the forest, behind a park bench at Disneyland, and, I guess, deep in caves. Someplace where they're not easily discovered. Then they leave hints on the Internet for people to find them." She picked up the plastic bag and began to open it.

"I don't understand," I said. "This doesn't make any sense. So there's no Florentine? Where the hell is the Florentine Controller then?"

Linda and Potter stared blankly at me.

"Could it be a hoax?" asked Potter.

"No way. Ronald Lister wouldn't be in a coma right now if this was a hoax. Maybe the diary has the location of the Florentine?" I muttered to myself, unconvinced. I seized the small leather-bound book from Linda's hand and opened its clasp. Its first entry was dated June 5 of 2009 and read:

> *Congratulations! If you are holding this diary, then you are indeed a true adventurer and are to be applauded! You have descended hundreds of feet, braved stalactite mazes, water-filled tunnels and of course your own fear—and you've made it in alive. Take an object in the treasure chest as your prize, but be sure to leave one of your own for the next explorer. And of course, please sign the guestbook. If you enjoyed the adventure, drop me a note: Salzo Kaza skaza1971@gmail.com.*

I flipped through several pages. Just two others had signed their names in the intervening years—both offered a description of their descent but neither left anything resembling a clue to the Florentine's location. The rest of the pages were blank.

"This makes no sense."

"The guy on the video must have been a geocacher," said Linda. "He's probably some wealthy guy. He hires a guide, has the adventure of his life, and makes a video."

"I'll buy it, but then how is the video tied to the Florentine?"

"You found the video in the vault?" she asked.

"Yeah. And it was labeled 'Florentine Controller.'"

"Maybe the guy hid it somewhere else nearby?" suggested Potter.

I gazed down the tunnel, which dead-ended in a sheer wall less than a dozen paces away. "Not here." I shook my head. "It wasn't meant to be, I guess. Maybe someone got to it before us?"

She patted me on the back. "I don't think so. Whatever the Florentine is, I don't think it was ever here. The more I think about it, the more I'm sure that video was just a travelogue."

"Then what are we missing?" I asked.

Both stared blankly at me. I sat down and began to run through the possibilities.

"I'm totally confused," I said, after several minutes of thinking. "It just doesn't make sense."

Linda patted me on the back. "Let's reason through it on the way up," she said. "Maybe we'll see something we didn't see before."

"Yeah, let's go," I said dejectedly. "On second thought . . ." I grabbed the diary and shoved it into my pocket. "Just in case."

Chapter 46

WE'D JUST COMPLETED THE HIKE up through the winding slot canyon and my lower back and legs were screaming. Linda and I collapsed at the edge of the bowl as Potter investigated the periphery.

"Give me five to rest," I said, exhausted by a mixture of physical fatigue, lack of sleep and melancholy. Neither Potter nor Linda said anything, so I found a passably flat area at the edge of the bowl, lay down, doused my headlamp, and fell instantly asleep.

"Alex." Potter shook me. "Alex, wake up. We should get going."

"Whuh?"

"You slept nearly half an hour," said Linda.

I rubbed the sleep from my eyes and sat up. Linda lay next to me, head on her pack and face pensive.

"You get any sleep?" I asked.

"Nah. I've been trying to figure this whole thing out," she said. "But I'm not making any progress."

"Join the club." I frowned. "I don't know what I'm going to do at this point."

"We'll figure something out, Alex. Hell, if it comes to it, I'll go with you to Thailand for a few years to disappear. We can climb at Railay Beach and drink margaritas until things cool down." She tussled my hair gently and my heart skipped a beat.

"Don't go promising anything. The way things are looking, I may take you up on it."

"I'm going up, guys," said Potter. "I want to get this last ascent over with."

"Go for it," I said, then I turned back to Linda. "Hey, can you go next? If I'm going to be dodging killers for the next six months, I want to get at least one last climb in before we go topside."

"You're incorrigible," she said, a sad smile on her face. "No problem. You deserve it."

I rummaged through my pack and dragged out my climbing shoes while Linda readied herself for the ascent. Then, after I'd laced them, I stood up and swept my beam across the wall, selecting a pair of shoulder-height pockets to start with. Hand over hand, I methodically worked my way up and right along the face.

"Ready for number two," yelled Potter from between the anchoring stalagmites.

Linda patted me on the calf, threw her pack over her shoulders, and hooked herself up to the rope. I continued rightward until I'd traveled up about ten vertical feet, then followed the pockets back down and took a seat near my pack.

"You're up, cowboy," yelled Linda.

I opened my eyes.

"Already? All right, I'm coming," I said with a yawn. I grabbed my pack, slung it over my shoulders, and then headed back over to the rope and connected my ascending gear.

"Here goes," I mumbled. Slowly, I worked my way up the rope using the Jumars, sliding one up, then the other, my feet dancing back and forth between the dangling nylon étriers.

About thirty feet up I paused for a breather, dangled from the Jumars, and panned my beam over the rock's mottled face. "Under better circumstances, this would have been a killer route," I yelled. I waited for a response, but got none.

"Linda?" I yelled. "Did you hear me?"

". . . the hell?" her voice echoed down.

"I'm sorry?"

"What the hell?" screamed Linda. I jolted my head back, tried to see above the ledge but they were too far from the edge.

"What's going on?" I asked. "Is everything okay?"

I waited a beat.

No reply.

Fighting the fatigue, I began double-timing up the rope. Then I saw her. Linda backed up between the two stalagmites, and her hand concealed behind her back, began furtively waving me away.

"I don't know," Her voice trailed off, then, "talking about. I'm telling you." Her hand signaled again. Something was very wrong.

I looked down, my heart hammering, trying to figure out what to do. I was thirty-five, maybe forty feet above the ground and locked to the rope. Pistol buried deep inside my pack. As good as dead, a sitting duck. Noiselessly, I unclipped my harness from the ascending gear, careful to maintain my grip on the pair of aluminum Jumars still locked to the rope. Now totally untethered, I could wrap my legs around the rope and lower myself down, hand under hand. If I could just reach the bottom, I could hide behind . . .

"You can stop now, Mr. Fife."

I looked up, stunned, both hands still clutching the Jumars.

Khalimmy leaned over the edge, a gray steel gun gripped tightly in his right hand, a Maglite aimed at my torso in his left. Potter stood next to Linda between the two towering stalagmites that anchored the rope.

"Please stop, Mr. Fife, or I'll have to shoot one of your friends." He turned momentarily. "Both of you, turn your lamps off and throw them here." He gestured at his feet. Both complied. "And you, Mr. Fife. Drop your lamp." I removed my headlamp and dropped it as instructed. Its light disappeared a second later with a crack, leaving the room totally dark save for the beam from Khalimmy's lone Maglite.

"How?" I stammered. "How could you possibly . . ."

"We simply followed you here." He paused to scan the room. "And I must say, this remote location does simplify things greatly. Now, Alex, I'm going to ask you a question, and I need an honest answer. If you give me an honest answer, no one will get hurt. Otherwise, I *will* shoot your friends."

I swallowed hard and felt a drop of sweat run down my right temple.

"Just tell me what you want. I'll give it to you."

"Thank you," he said mildly. "Now I need you to tell me the password for the video."

I thought for a moment: video . . . password . . . What password?

"Do you mean for the Florentine video?"

"Yes."

"But there wasn't any password. It wasn't password-protected."

"Come now, Alex, you don't take me for a fool, do you?" He raised the gun a few degrees toward Potter.

"I don't know what you mean. The video wasn't password-protected. Let me come up and I'll just give you the damn thumb drive. Please."

"I have the video—you graciously left it out for me on your counter," he raised his gun farther, pointing it at Potter's face, "but what I need is the password."

"I just . . ." I stammered, "I don't have any password. There wasn't any password on the video."

Khalimmy's muzzle flashed and before the event registered in my brain, Potter's body flew past me. Below, I heard the sickening crunch of bone impacting rock. No screams, no whimpers, just stillness.

"What the fuck did you do?" I screamed, "What the *fuck*?" Linda sank to her knees and began sobbing.

"Alex, I don't want to have to ask you again. I don't want to have to kill either of you, but I need the password." Khalimmy walked up to Linda and pointed the muzzle at her forehead. "You have three seconds."

"Three."

"Two."

"Wait!" I yelled. "Stop! I'll tell you."

Khalimmy withdrew the gun an inch. "Yes?"

"The password is 3729724, three-seven-two-nine-seven-two-four," I screamed, rattling off my childhood phone number.

Khalimmy took a step back from Linda and stared at me contemplatively.

"Now, Alex, there are two possibilities. One is that you're lying to me to save yourself. The other is that you've finally come to your senses." He scratched his grizzled chin with the tip of his gun. "The problem is that I can't tell which is which. So I think I'm going to have to turn the screws just a little tighter and make sure you're not lying to me."

"I told you the password. Please, just go, leave us."

"Not quite yet, Alex." Khalimmy lowered the gun and fired. Linda's body spasmed.

"Fuck!" I screamed, spittle shooting from my mouth. "Why? What did she do to you? I told you the fucking password."

"It was just a kneecap," said Khalimmy, "now I'm going to ask you one more time. Tell me the correct password or I'll just kill both of you right now."

"I told you, it's 3729724, I swear to God."

Khalimmy lowered the gun to Linda's head, which bobbed lightly as she sobbed.

"What more can I do to convince you?"

"Are you sure, Alex? Because I will put a bullet into her head if you're lying."

"3729724," I sobbed, "3729724!"

"Well, I have to say, I believe you, Alex. At first I doubted, but now I believe you. Thank you, Alex." Khalimmy raised the gun from Linda's head and aimed it at my chest. "But even given your cooperation, there is no way I can afford to let either—"

Linda threw her shoulder sideways into Khalimmy's leg, sending him staggering backward into the darkness.

"Go!" she screamed, "jump!" Khalimmy cursed, then fired again— this shot purposeful and deadly. Linda's silhouetted figure slumped to the ground.

"God help me," I murmured. I closed my eyes, released both hands from the Jumars and launched backward.

Chapter 47

MY MUSCLES TENSED in anticipation of the impact, of the jarring crunch of bone, but as the heels of my feet connected, it was with water, not rock. My body plunged deep into the inky pool until its liquid surged into my wide-open mouth and down my windpipe. Choking, I thrashed for the surface, my lungs begging to evacuate the asphyxiating fluid, the need so primal it overrode any fear of Khalimmy or his bullets. But my body refused to rise. The weight of my pack was dragging me down. I wriggled from the shoulder straps, jettisoning the pack into the void, and kicked upward. As my head breached the surface, a bullet whistled by my ear and into the water.

My mind willed me to dive back under as another bullet slammed into the water centimeters from my face, but my lungs revolted. A third bullet punctured the water's surface somewhere behind me mid-cough, then another torpedoed through the water, grazing my arm painfully. Amidst my violent coughing, I somehow managed to tread toward the edge of the pool, and just as a final shot ricocheted off the volcanic rock, I climbed from the water and staggered toward the safety of the overhanging wall. Khalimmy cursed from above and swept his beam along the bowl's pocked edges for a target.

Leaning against the wall, I grabbed my chest and heaved, then finally took a full breath. I coughed, ejecting the final vestiges of water from my lungs, then inhaled again. Khalimmy's beam zagged closer to the wall and scanned right. I edged left, toward the cover of a dense colony of stalagmites just beyond the edge of the bowl, my body in the shadows, pressed hard against the cliff face.

Khalimmy's beam passed behind me and left. Reaching the edge of the wall, I waited until the beam reversed its course, then spun and dove into the thicket of rocks. Khalimmy screamed and sent a pair of slugs ricocheting off the towering rocks.

"Fuck you!" I spat. "You're going to fry."

"Hardly." His footfalls echoed off the cave walls. "But I can't say the same for you." I peered from behind a stalagmite. Khalimmy had rested his gun and flashlight on a boulder and was now rapidly retracting the rope.

"Thank you for the password, Mr. Fife," he said, as the tail of the rope cleared the overhang and disappeared. "I'm afraid I won't have the satisfaction of seeing you die myself, but I'll revel in the knowledge that you'll soon suffer a painful death from hunger or thirst. Good enough."

The sound of Khalimmy's footsteps receded, as did his flashlight's illumination, until finally the cavern settled into complete darkness and stillness.

I crouched behind the rock formation and tried to calm down, tried to put my situation into perspective but my brain refused to focus. I closed my eyes and zoned out, breathed in deeply, then out, in and out for five minutes. Slowly, my heart rate moderated and I remembered that I'd been shot. I carefully touched the wound on my left arm. My finger came away slick, but the wound was shallow, just a skin abrasion.

"Potter?" I spoke softly, fearful Khalimmy might still be hiding up above. No response, no movement. I stepped from behind the stalagmites and yelled this time. "Potter?" Again, no response. "Linda?" I waited, then shouted her name again.

"What a fucking mess!" I screamed. "What a motherfucking mess!"

Slowly, sweeping my hands for obstacles, I made my way over to the wall. Given the total lack of light, gear, water, and food, Steven, if he were still alive, was my only chance for survival. I leaned back against the wall and sank to the floor.

Over the next half hour, I called out for Steven every few minutes, hoping that he'd somehow evaded Khalimmy and come to find me, but each passing minute of silence brought more despondence. I rose to stretch my legs and relieve the growing ache in my lower back. What could I do? What were my options? My backpack and all its gear were a lost cause, waterlogged and submerged beyond my reach, my headlamp God knows where, Potter's and Linda's packs—and their spare headlamps—sixty vertical feet of advanced climbing above me. If I had a headlamp I might be able to make it up, but given the utter lack of light, it was suicide. I sank back down to the cave's floor and my mind wandered. Hours passed. Steven wasn't coming.

"Why did Khalimmy need a password for the video?" I asked myself. I wasn't sure—my memory of the preceding hour and a half was a hazy blur—but I thought Khalimmy said he had the copy of the video. But if he had a copy, he'd know the thing wasn't password-protected. If he had a copy, he could have gone after the Florentine himself. But he didn't ask for the Florentine. He didn't expect us to have it—he didn't expect it to be here. He just wanted a password. The password. There were no other files with the video—I'd checked multiple times. It just didn't make sense.

I took a deep breath and stretched my arms upward, then reached down to scratch an itch on my thigh through my moist nylon climbing pants. As I dug my fingernail into the material I noticed a crinkling sound, the sound of a plastic wrapper, and I remembered Potter's glow sticks. The things had been sitting there the entire time, my leg numbed to their presence the same way one learns to ignore a ring or a pair of glasses over time.

Electrified by the renewed prospect of an escape, I shot to my feet, unzipped the zipper, and ripped one of the sticks from the pocket along the front of my leg. The plastic stick bent with a crack as the glass ampoule holding one of the stick's two chemicals fractured, releasing its contents to mix with the other compound in the stick's interior. A moment of shaking mixed the reactants together, generating a surprisingly bright green iridescence.

I had to find Potter, to see if he was still alive and see if I could help. After a minute of searching I found his body along the right edge of the bowl, partially hidden by a pair of short stalagmites. His head was twisted at a grotesque angle, his legs and arms unnaturally splayed like that of a carelessly dropped puppet. Potter didn't deserve any of this and I'd caused it. I was the reason he was dead. My eyes welled with tears. I closed them and cursed.

I had to climb out; rope or not, I wasn't going to die here, alone in the darkness. I was going to get out and make Khalimmy pay. I wiped my eyes dry with my forearm and returned to the wall.

I replayed our hours-earlier rappel of the wall in my mind's eye, trying to recall its topography to come up with a general plan of attack. My best shot was generally up and to the right—that was where I'd seen the most promising holds on my way down. Of course, this route would take me over the stalagmites and away from the safety of the pool, but what other option did I have? I scoured the face for a good starting point, and found a reasonable hold that resembled the interior of a small cup of yogurt, mid-wall, about a foot above my head. I clenched the glow stick firmly between my teeth then slotted the fingers of my left hand into the pocket. The hold was solid, so I lifted my right foot from the floor and directed my gaze to the base of the wall to locate a foothold.

While the area above my head was sufficiently illuminated from the stick, its green glow only radiated down as far as my knees, leaving my feet shrouded in darkness. Undeterred, I dropped back to the narrow floor at the bowl's edge and removed the second stick from my pocket. I cracked the ampoule and after a moment of vigorous shaking, loosened the laces of my right climbing shoe and inserted the stick between the alternating cords. It did the trick; a quick sweep of my foot highlighted a chain of charcoal briquette-sized stones embedded in the wall's base, a foot from the floor. Again I reached up for the yogurt cup, then, guided by the illumination of the second stick, placed my feet on the briquette protrusions.

Feet firmly planted, I shifted my attention back above my head. The greenish glow highlighted a triplet of closely spaced, thimble-sized holes. Maddeningly, the trio lay inches from my outstretched fingertips; to reach them, I'd need a foothold at least a foot above the briquettes, yet the green glow revealed only smooth, vertical rock. It would have to be enough. I raised my right foot and smeared it against the slab, actively applying pressure much like a masseur might press his palm against a tensed muscle. Under my leg's pressure, the climbing shoe's rubber dug into the rock's minute grooves and held fast, giving me enough height to reach the three dime-sized holes. I slotted my three middle fingers into the thimbles, and, with a look downward, was able to drag both feet up onto a wide, quarter-inch-deep ledge.

I breathed a breath of relief and focused on the dull ache in my arm and the growing burning of my fingers' tendons. Slowly and method-

ically I ascended the route, up and right, up and right, lightly test-
ing each new hold before committing my weight. I wasn't a religious
person, but I considered that I might have to reevaluate my beliefs if
I survived; the holds were almost too good—well spaced, deep and
positive.

Thirty feet up, I cranked my right bicep tight to pull my body into
the rock and reached up, left, for what looked to be the lower, semi-
circular rim of a natural jug. My fingertips just barely rounded its lip,
but it wasn't enough; my hand didn't have enough contact surface area
to hold on, and my engorged right bicep, now supporting virtually all
of my body weight, burned painfully.

I closed my eyes, inhaled deeply through my nose, and wriggled
the pad of my left index finger a hair farther around the rim until,
unexpectedly, it caught a little divot along the lip's interior. Anything—an increase in perspiration, a poorly planned shift in balance,
or an inadvertent twitch, would compromise the friction bonding my
skin to the rock and send me careening down into the water, or worse,
into a sharp stalagmite. I needed a better foothold to improve my grip.
I craned my neck and scanned the porous wall by my feet for poten-
tials until my eyes locked onto a pocket the size of an eggshell near my
left knee. With glacial slowness I raised my left leg until the tip of my
foot hovered in front of its target, then carefully inserted the toe of my
climbing shoe into the cavity. That gave me the extra reach I needed.
I dug my left hand deep into the jug and breathed a sigh of relief. For
the moment, I was free of imminent danger.

After two minutes of alternating grips and shaking out my arms,
the burning in my arms abated. Against my better judgment, I gazed
down to gauge my progress—the light from my shoe's glow stick was
dwindling prematurely and now penetrated just inches below my
footholds. Probably better that I couldn't judge my true height, but I'd
need to reach the top soon. At least my teeth-clenched glow stick was
still burning bright.

I scanned the area above my head—a cue ball-sized pocket sat a
few feet up at ten o'clock; at two o'clock, a shallow, sloping shelf rose
diagonally up and into the darkness. I liked shelves, even narrow ones,
so long as they angled upward. I extended my right hand and slid it

up and right along the two-inch-deep outcropping for a grip. Nothing solid, but nothing to sneeze at either. I tightened my fingers on the ridge and adjusted my feet. Hand over hand, I worked my body up the diagonal shelf, two feet, then four feet, then six. And hold after hold, the shelf improved, offering an almost rain gutter-like rail to ascend.

After a blissful twelve feet, the shelf disappeared into the face, ending at a pair of large gouged pocks. I was getting close. I could feel it. Perhaps it was the cave's acoustics or maybe subtle changes in the air currents, or something subconscious. I worked my hands into the higher of the two natural scars, feeling the increasing burn in my forearms, then rose up and scanned the wall's face. The glow stick dangling from my mouth illuminated a scene that was at the same time terrifying and gruesome. I was just four feet from the top, from surviving the horror of the last few hours. Yet, between my hands and the ledge above, not a single pocket, shelf, or nub graced the smooth wall—I'd reached a dead end. Dead in more than one way. Linda's limp, lifeless arm dangled sickeningly over the edge, her body wedged between the two stalagmites above. My mouth opened in an involuntary gasp, and before I could shut it, the glow stick slipped from my teeth, bounced off my foot, and careened into the darkness below.

Chapter 48

MY LIMITED OPTIONS HAD, in an instant, been reduced to one. With no light to direct my hands, any attempt to retrace my way downward would be a death sentence. And the featureless wall above was not an option. My choice, therefore, was to either let go (and pray I'd land somewhere in the pool) and then attempt the climb again with just a single, dim glow stick, or make one last go at it.

"Sorry, Linda," I murmured.

I closed my eyes tight and like an apparition, the outline of Linda's arm glowed in an afterimage on my retinas. Without shifting the angle of my head, I edged my feet higher, then, with both feet smeared high against the wall, I launched up through the darkness toward Linda's iridescent, outstretched arm. Just as my body reached its apex, my fingers clamped around Linda's wrist and her tendons and muscles groaned sickeningly under my full hundred-and-sixty-five-pound load. Linda's body jerked forward, the friction of her corpse against the rough rocks above battling against gravity's pull on my body. I threw my right hand around her forearm, then used my stomach muscles to steady my swinging feet and draw them in up against the smooth cliff wall. The shoe's rubber gripped; all I needed was just a second of friction, enough to throw my right hand up to the ledge above. I hiked my feet higher, released the grip of my right hand, drew my body up high with my left bicep, and lunged.

Linda's body jerked forward under the increased tug just as my right hand hit its mark and locked onto an uneven volcanic outcropping atop the ledge. I realized I was holding my breath, so I inhaled, and then pulled myself up and onto the ledge.

My entire frame shook as I collapsed on the floor next to Linda.

"Why?" I screamed, tears streaming from my eyes. "What have I done?" My body convulsed in sobs.

"I'm so sorry, Linda," I stammered. "Potter . . . I've been the cause of so much death." I shook my head. "So much. I'm so sorry."

I lay there in the dimming green light, weeping, my mind numbed by guilt. And then, when the tears refused to flow further, I rose and gently lifted Linda's body and drew it away from the edge.

"Why couldn't it have been me?" I asked, my eyes welling again with tears. "I'm so sorry."

I leaned in to kiss her forehead.

And then I felt her breath.

Chapter 49

"Linda?" I pleaded. "Linda, can you hear me?"

Nothing.

I leaned in closer, placing my face just a fraction of an inch from her nose, and felt it again, shallow and slow. But how? How could she have survived? Agonizingly, I directed my gaze down at her blood-soaked shirt, at the bullet hole. The slug had entered just over her left breast—through her shirt pocket—and traveled directly into her chest.

I ripped the dimming glow stick from my shoe and clamped it between my teeth, then carefully unfastened Linda's top two buttons and peeled away the blood-soaked fabric. The bullet had penetrated Linda's chest four inches below her clavicle, its entrance hole pooled with coagulating blood. But why hadn't it killed her? A shot like that from less than five feet away?

Then it dawned on me.

Her backup battery pack!

I hurriedly unbuttoned Linda's breast pocket and withdrew the trio of batteries. There it was—a dime-sized hole punched through the tape, midway between the rightmost two batteries. The pack hadn't stopped the bullet but had slowed it. Just enough.

I needed to get her medical attention immediately, but I had to stabilize her first. There was nothing I could do about her chest wound other than to keep her still, so I shifted my gaze down to her right knee. Tourniquets were only called for if there was uncontrolled bleeding, and while her knee was pretty mangled, the blood had stopped flowing.

There was nothing more I could do.

"Linda," I squeezed her hand gently, "if you can hear me, just hang on. And if you need some motivation, just remember that margarita I owe you. If nothing else, hang on for that margarita. Just for a few more hours. I'm going to bring help."

I kissed her forehead and headed for the entrance.

———

Resting on my hands and knees, just hidden from view, I surveyed the dimly lit cavern from within the tube, listened for any movement. Nothing. It was empty. Khalimmy was gone.

I shimmied through the shaft's remaining few feet, then stood up and ran to the mouth of the cave. As I reached the entrance, the intense afternoon light blinded me and I staggered back reflexively into the darkness.

"Steven!" I yelled.

Nothing.

"Goddammit, where the hell are you? Crouch, it's Alex!"

I cupped my hands over the top of my eyes and stepped from the cavern and into the full daylight, squinting painfully up and down the canyon. Was he still alive?

"Or dead?" I mumbled. "God help you Khalimmy, if you even touched a hair on him. God help you."

"Steven," I screamed again.

"Alex?" The voice was faint and distant but unmistakable. "*Auuughh,*" he groaned.

"Where are you?" I yelled.

"Over here." He was upstream.

"I'm coming," I responded.

I carefully picked my way through and over the nearest group of boulders, then yelled again, "Where are you?"

"I'm not exactly sure," he groaned. "I'm injured."

"Just take it easy," I said. I worked my way up the canyon and scrambled onto the top of a boulder the size of a VW Bug.

"Marco," I yelled.

"Polo," he replied feebly. His voice seemed to project from a narrow crevasse separating two massive boulders, each easily fifteen feet tall.

"I'll be right there," I said. Steven groaned more persistently while I worked my way up a series of pockets to the top of the nearer boulder and to the edge of the fissure. I cupped my hands and yelled down, "Marco."

"Polo," he sputtered from the shadows below.

"Thank God," I said. "Are you okay?"

"I've got a broken leg." I could hear him wince.

"Do you have your phone?" I asked. "We're going to need a helicopter."

"Yeah, but I can't get a signal."

"One second, I'll see if I can find a safe way down."

I backed off from the edge and worked my way down the back side of the boulder and to the edge of the creek. Then I waded upstream through the shallow water until I reached the nearer of the two boulders.

"Marco," I yelled.

"Polo." His voice was louder. I rounded the first boulder and shimmied several feet through a narrow, water-smoothed gap into a darkened grotto. I could just hear his breathing over the trickling stream outside.

"I'm so glad you're still alive," I said, near tears.

"So am I," he grunted. "Now just do me a favor and get me to a hospital."

"Give me your phone." I waded slowly over toward Steven's voice until I bumped into his foot and he screamed.

"Sorry," I said.

"Shit it hurts. The bone's sticking out."

"Jesus. Give me your phone."

"Here," he said a moment later. I cautiously waved my arm through the air until it bumped into his outstretched hand.

"Got it?" he asked.

"Yeah." I tightened my fingers around the handset. "Give me a second. I'll try it on top of the boulder. If I can't get a signal, I'll head down to the canyon, to the visitor's center." I thought back to Linda. *Will she last that long?*

"Don't worry," he called out, "I'm not going anywhere."

I pocketed the phone and then climbed atop the VW Bug boulder, stopping once I'd found a safe place to make the call. Disregarding the phone's weak signal indicator, I punched in 911.

After about ten seconds of silence, the phone flashed a "No signal" message and issued a beep. It was a long shot—this far back, the canyon had notoriously bad reception. I pushed the talk button again, with the same result. I pocketed the phone again and worked my way back atop the closer of the two huge boulders.

Again, I tapped the three digits in and hit the talk button. A few seconds later, I heard a garbled ring from the handset.

"Got it," I yelled. The line rang once more and picked up. "911 Emergency. Please—" the signal cut out, "—nature of the emergency."

"Can you hear me?" I asked.

"Yes sir. Please state the nature—" The phone cut to static again.

"I've got two injured people a little more than one mile beyond the rock pool in the canyon at Malibu Creek State Park."

"Excuse me? You broke up. You're where?"

"In the canyon beyond the rock pool in Malibu Creek State Park. We're about one mile up the canyon from the rock pool area."

"Let me confirm. You've got two injured hikers one mile up the," the voice descended into digitized fuzz, "ool in Malibu Creek State—"

"Correct, one mile up the canyon from the rock pool area," I repeated. "One person with a serious gunshot wound, the other with a broken leg, maybe other injuries. I can't tell."

"A gunshot wound?"

"Yes. A woman's been shot in the chest and leg. Two injured people, one critical."

"Okay, I'm going to dispatch Search and Rescue now. Make sure to stay where the helicopter can see you. Do not try to mov—" she cut out, "—injured."

"Hold tight, Steven." I worked my way back down and around to the base of the two boulders. "They're coming. Just hold it together."

"Okay."

"What happened to you?" I asked.

"I was looking around up here when I saw Khalimmy and this other guy," he sucked air through his teeth in pain, "so I backed up to hide and tripped." He paused. "I'm so glad you guys are okay. Where are Linda and Potter?"

"Potter is dead," I stammered, trying but failing to suppress tears. "Linda was shot in the chest. I don't know . . . I can't tell how bad it is."

"Oh shit."

We sat in silence for a minute, Steven waiting for me to calm myself.

"All right," I said, wiping my eyes, "I'm going to go up top to wait for the helicopter. Just hold it together for another twenty or thirty minutes. And pray."

My ears registered the powerful *thwapping* of the rotors nearly half a minute before the rescue helicopter rounded the bend and came into view. I waved my arms frantically from atop the boulder until the chopper, now one hundred yards away, slowed in recognition. After a moment of hesitation, the machine inched forward, hovering directly above us, the wash from its powerful rotors overpowering in the narrow canyon. Instinctively, I sat down, plugged my ears, and squinted to avoid the vortex of dusty air.

A Search and Rescue ranger descended via a winched steel cable, landing about a dozen steps away on top of the adjacent boulder. The ranger detached the cable from his harness and gave a hand signal to the winch operator above; immediately the cable began to rise. The man worked his way onto my boulder and stepped up to my ear.

"Where are the injured?" he yelled.

"There's a gunshot victim inside that cave," I responded, pointing at the narrow crevasse in the rock. "I think she's lost a lot of blood. And the man with the broken leg is down there." I pointed between the two boulders.

"Got it," he said. Then, into his walkie-talkie, he yelled, "I've got two injured, one critically inside a cave. Ask Lee to come down with the second med-kit and tell him to bring ten units of blood." He hesitated, holding his hand over his earpiece. "Well then send whatever we've got. And then request another chopper, stat—we're going to need backup."

Chapter 50

"Any news on Linda Reynaud?" I asked, still sniffling.

"Reynaud? R-E-Y?"

I nodded.

"One second, I'll check." The diminutive Filipina nurse keyed Linda's name into her terminal. A few clicks later, she said, "Nothing yet, she's still in surgery."

"She's been in there for hours. Can't you find out her status?" I asked.

"Not until the surgery is done. Will you be in the waiting room?"

"Yes."

"I'll come get you the moment they take her to the ICU for recovery."

I nodded, then walked back to the sitting area. My bench had been taken by a man in his early thirties and his five-year-old. I crumpled onto the lone empty seat across from them and closed my eyes. After two hours of interrogation by the police, an hour in the ER getting sutures, a violent confrontation with Hillary that resulted in me being bodily shoved from Steven's hospital room, and nearly forty hours without sleep, I was emotionally drained and running on fumes.

"What's that one with the spines on its back?"

"Huh?" I asked, opening my eyes.

The man sitting across from me pointed at a page in the thin picture book.

"Mmmmmm." The boy shifted on his father's lap as he noodled over the image.

"Starts with an S," hinted the father.

"Stoopidosaur?" The kid giggled infectiously. I sighed. Potter would never experience the joy of fatherhood, of dinosaurs, of father-son outings. And what about Linda? I shivered.

"Steg . . ." the dad hinted.

"Stegosaurus!" screamed the kid.

"Correct!" He flipped the page. "And that one?"

The kid giggled. "Tyrannosaurus Rex! *Rawr!*"

Click. All of a sudden, something went off in my head. I couldn't quite place it, but my subconscious had sent a signal-flare up. Tyrannosaurus Rex? It made no sense but I took a mental note anyway.

"Spot-on," said the father. "And this one?" He flipped the page.

"Tri. Ser. Ahh. Tops!" screamed the kid.

"Right again!"

The boy jumped to the floor, placed his hands on his hips, and asked, "When are we going to see Mommy?"

"In just a little bit, Tyler. The doctors are working with her now to bring you a new baby sister."

"Excuse me."

"I'm sorry?" I gazed up. It was the nurse. "Is she okay?"

"I don't know her status, but you can visit her now. They've taken her to Recovery Room 5 in the ICU." She pointed down the hall.

"Thank you so much," I said.

She nodded once, wordlessly, then headed back to her station.

Linda lay unconscious in a railed hospital bed in the narrow ICU bay. A menacing chest tube poked from beneath her gown and led down to a plastic bag, its interior tinged with fresh blood. An IV drip connected her wrist to three hanging bags of fluid, and a pair of oxygen tubes fed into her nostrils. Her chest rose and fell weakly as the heart monitor droned on. She looked bad.

I stepped from the bay and scanned the hallway for someone who could tell me more. No one. I walked over to the ICU desk.

"Excuse me," I said.

The attendant, a fortyish man in blue scrubs, glanced up from his paperwork. Dark bags sagged from beneath tired eyes.

"Yes? How can I help you?"

"I'm Linda Reynaud's f–" I hesitated, "fiancé. Can you tell me how she's doing? Will she be okay?"

"They just wheeled her into bay five. She's in critical condition. If you'd like to talk to the attending physician, I can page him."

"I'd appreciate it," I said.

The man nodded and returned to his paperwork. After ten seconds, he looked up, an impatient expression on his weary face.

"Why don't you go back and keep her company? I'll page him in a minute."

I dragged the plastic chair from the corner of the alcove to Linda's bedside and sat down.

"Well, Linda, I'm crossing my fingers and praying for you. As you know, I don't believe in God, but I'm praying just in case. I don't know what else I can do."

Her body shifted slightly.

"I'm so sorry I dragged you into this. I just . . . I just don't know what to do. How to end it."

I leaned forward and rested my face on my palms, exhausted.

"God, I hope you make it. I don't know how I'm ever going to cope with Potter's death, but if I lost you too . . ."

I wiped my eyes on the sleeve of my blue loaner scrub shirt, then laid my hands on the bed's railing.

"Assuming you do make it through," I continued, "and assuming I do, I've got some things I want to tell you. Things I've never had the guts to say that I should have said a long time ago. So, if some part of your brain can hear me right now, now you've got something to look forward to." I paused. "Or not." I laughed cynically. "Either way, I just hope you make it."

"Hello."

Startled, I looked up.

"You must be Ms. Reynaud's fiancé?"

"Yes. I'm Alex," I said, standing up and extending my hand.

"Hi Alex, I'm Doctor Weinstein." He shook my hand.

"Will Linda be okay?" I asked nervously.

He stared impassively at me. "I'm hopeful, but it's touch-and-go at this point. The bullet collapsed her lung and caused a large amount of internal bleeding. She's lucky the EMTs got to her when they did." He pointed to her chest tube. "We drained her chest cavity to help the lung reinflate, but it's going to take time."

"Could you give me odds?"

He grimaced and shook his head. "It's just too early, but we're doing everything we can."

I nodded somberly. "Thanks."

"You're welcome. We'll have a better idea tomorrow. Why don't you try to get some sleep and come in first thing in the morning. There's nothing more you can do right now."

I nodded again. "Do you have the time?"

"Yeah," he glanced down at his watch, "it's ten 'til nine."

"Thanks," I said. "Thanks for everything."

I wanted to see how Steven was doing before visiting hours ended, even if it meant another confrontation with Hillary, so I steeled myself and headed for the elevator. When I reached the fourth floor, I walked down a long hall, past a nurses' station and into a wing of patient rooms. Steven's was 401, the first door on the right. I knocked softly.

"Come in," said Hillary.

"Hi guys."

Hillary eyed me malevolently.

"I shouldn't let you in here," she said, fuming. "How could you just go off on your own without telling anyone? You . . . you almost got my husband killed today," she spat. "And your friends, Alex. One is dead, and Linda . . . it's all on your head. All your fault."

I closed my eyes and inhaled, tried to maintain my composure, but the tears began streaming uncontrollably down my face.

"Can I have some water?" asked Steven, groggily.

"Here you go, honey." Hillary inserted the straw into his mouth, then returned her gaze to my face and shook her head furiously. "So, Alex, is this obsession finally over? How many more people will have to die before you give up this madness?"

I grabbed a tissue and blew my nose. "I'm not sure I have any control at—"

"Of course you do!" she interrupted. "You've always had total control over this wild-goose chase." A tear streaked down her cheek. "And look where it's gotten us."

"I'm sorry, Hillary, but—"

"Don't apologize to me. Go apologize to the families of your friends."

"I'm not apologizing," I countered.

She lifted her finger to make a point.

"Wait!" I said. "I'm not apologizing, because I'm not the one doing the killing. And Hillary, whether you like it or not, Khalimmy is still out there. And he still doesn't have the Florentine, and he wants it, Hillary. He wants it bad. Bad enough to murder Potter, and Linda, and me. And if I can't give him what he wants, where do you think he's going to look next? Oh, and by the way," I blurted, "there's another guy after the Florentine as well. He likes to remove fingers to get what he wants. So unless we all want to pack up and go into permanent hiding, this problem isn't going away. So for God's sake, enough with the blaming. At this point I need your help. Help me. Help *us*."

Hillary brooded taciturnly; Steven shifted his gaze between us, flustered by the silence, but didn't say a word. She wiped away a tear.

"Well, if," she sniffled, "if they're not going to leave us alone until they get it, what can we do?"

"I don't know," I said. "We were hoping to find the Florentine Controller in the cave and give it to the FBI or to the media. We hoped once it was out in the open they'd all go away. That's why we went to the cave last night."

"But it wasn't in the cave," confirmed Hillary, blowing her nose.

"No, it wasn't," I said. "And the more I think about it, the more I think it was never in the cave."

"But then why did Lister have the video? Why label it Florentine Controller?"

I shook my head. "I wish I knew. Khalimmy has a copy of the video now too, and apparently it hasn't helped him get any closer to the Florentine either."

"He has a copy?" She looked startled.

"Yeah, he broke in and stole it last night after we left Latigo."

She paused a moment in thought. "But I don't understand. He obviously thinks the video is important or he wouldn't have stolen it."

"It doesn't make any sense, does it? The only clue I have is that he kept asking for a password for the video." I began pacing the room. "But the video wasn't password-protected, so I don't know what he's talking about."

She looked at me quizzically.

"I know, I'm totally confused too," I admitted. "Hill, I know you're really angry with me and probably not in the mood, but can I at least run some of my thoughts by you? It'll help me get my head around things, and maybe you'll see something I missed."

She took a deep breath, then said, "Go ahead."

"So we thought the video was a digital map to the Florentine Controller, right? But it looks like it's just a video of someone documenting a descent into a cave."

"And you're sure there wasn't anything hidden down there?"

"No way—we triple-checked. The floors of the cave down there were solid rock. There wasn't anywhere to bury or hide anything."

"So you went back up," said Hillary. "And then what happened?"

"When we got back near the entrance to the cave, Khalimmy ambushed us and asked for the password to the video."

"He didn't ask you for the Florentine?"

"No. That's why I think it wasn't hidden in the cave. If he thought the Florentine was hidden down there and that we'd found it, he would have just asked for it, right? But he asked for a password. He just wanted a password."

Hillary stared at me a moment, then said, "You're sure the video's not password-protected?"

"We all watched it together. It didn't have a password."

"So why would he need a password for it?"

I paused a beat. "You know, while I was in the waiting room, something sparked a thought and I had this hunch I was getting close. But then it passed a second later."

"What brought it on? Maybe we can recreate the moment."

"This father and his kid were reading a book on dinosaurs."

"Dinosaurs? What does that have to do with the video?"

"I'm not sure," I admitted. "But there was definitely something there that got me going."

"Why don't you review the conversation with me?"

"There wasn't much. The guy was pointing out pictures of dinosaurs in a children's book. Then the kid mentioned something about Tyrannosaurus Rex and something clicked. That was it."

"Hmmm. Dinosaurs. Fossils. Tyrannosaurus Rex?" She looked at me expectantly—I shook my head. "Extinction? Evolution? Triceratops? Jurassic Park?"

"Velociraptor," added Steven, joining the conversation.

"Nope."

"Archaeopteryx? Brontosaurus? Stegosaurus? Allosaurus? Brachiosaurus?" he slurred.

"No . . ." There it was again—that feeling. "Wait . . ."

"Say those again, Steven."

"I don't remember exactly what I said."

"Brontosaurus, stegosaurus," Hillary jumped in, "allosaurus, brachi-something and," she considered for a second, "archaeopteryx."

I lowered my head and gazed down at the floor, repeating each to myself. And then it hit me.

"Stegosaurus . . . Stego," I murmured. "Steganography! That's got to be it!"

"What?" asked Hillary, befuddled.

"They've hidden a secret message in the video file. They're using steganography to hide the Florentine."

"Stega-what?" asked Hillary. Steven shook his head in medicated puzzlement.

"Steganography. It's when you embed a secret message into digital content—like into an image file, a movie file, or an MP3 music file. Spies use that kind of thing to transmit secrets in plain view."

"You can do that?" she asked.

"Yes. There's freely available software to do it. Al Qaeda has supposedly been doing this kind of thing for years to hide its communications. You take a standard picture, music file, whatever, and use steganography software to embed your secret data into the file. The picture will look slightly different after the secret data's been embedded inside—the colors change just a small shade from the original picture. But the typical person, at least one without anti-steganography tools, would never be able to detect a thing."

"So you're saying there's something hidden in that cave video?"

"Yes. For example, if Richard Lister had hidden the Florentine Controller somewhere, he could have embedded the directions to it inside that video. And no one would have a clue."

"A map inside a map!" said Steven with awe.

"That's got to be it. That would explain Khalimmy's interest in a password. Most of the steganography systems allow you to encode the data with a password before embedding it inside a media file. He must know that the Florentine, or something that helps him find the Florentine, is hidden inside the cave video, but he doesn't know the password." I paused. "Then again, neither do we."

"What if Richard Lister used his lip password?" asked Hillary.

"There's only one way to find out."

Chapter 51

Tom opened the door clad in a pair of boxers, half-asleep.

"Alex?" he said, clearly confused by my midnight arrival. "Uhh. Come on in."

"Thanks." I stepped in through the door, closed it, and locked the deadbolt.

Tom gave me a strange look. "What brings you here . . . so late?" He paused, looking me over. "Jesus, Alex, are those sutures on your scalp? What happened?"

"Does Gennady have another gun?" I asked, ignoring his question.

"I think so. Why? What's going on?"

"Gennady," I yelled. I heard a sleepy groan from the other room. "Gennady! Wake up now and get your gun." I paused. "Now!"

"Alex, what's going on?"

"It's a long story. Right now, I need somewhere safe to decode this." I held up my remaining thumb drive.

"Safe? Slow down. What's going on?"

"I've got Arab and Russian killers after me. That Florentine thing I told you about—it wasn't a diamond. It's almost certainly some type of state secret. Whatever it is, it's on this drive."

"What's on the drive? I'm totally confused," said Tom.

"I don't know, but I'm going to find out. I need to use your computer."

Gennady came down the stairs, bleary-eyed. "Alex? What the hell is going on?"

"I'll tell you in a minute. Just go get a gun."

"Where's the one I gave you?" he asked, rubbing his eyes.

"It's at the bottom of a cave. I'll explain later. Just go get your gun and make sure it's loaded."

Gennady focused, took in my disheveled state, and nodded. "I'll be right back."

"Where's your computer?" I asked. Tom pointed upstairs.

"This drive holds a video," I said, walking up. "And I'm pretty sure that the video contains a hidden, embedded file. Probably state secrets or schematics for some military system, God only knows. I need to decode it, figure out what it is, and get it to the authorities."

He considered this for a second, then said, "What can I do to help?"

"Can you get me some caffeine? This might take a while."

Tom logged me into his computer and went downstairs to put on a pot of coffee.

I pulled up the browser and began googling for steganography software. My search turned up three major packages: StegoSoft, Stego-Crypt, and Secrify. StegoSoft and StegoCrypt each offered trial versions, but Secrify only offered a pay version. I'd start with the trials.

While the two freeware versions were downloading, I inserted the thumb drive into Tom's computer and initiated a copy of the large video file down to the hard drive. Windows popped up an hourglass with a countdown timer indicating the copy would take another fifteen seconds.

"What's going on, Alex?" asked Gennady, gun in hand. I briefly repeated the explanation I gave Tom.

"Christ. And you think there's a hint in the video?"

"No, not a hint. Not something visible in the video," I said. "If I'm not mistaken, this video has a secret file steganographically embedded inside of it."

"Stego-what embedded inside?" Gennady lowered onto his knees next to me and stared at the screen.

"I think the Florentine is a secret document of some sort. And I'm betting that Richard Lister actually hid that data file inside this video using steganography software."

Gennady shrugged. Tom walked into the room carrying a coffee-pot and three mugs.

"Thanks," I said. Tom placed the tray on the desk and pulled up a chair for himself.

A few seconds later, the first of the free-trial steganography packages finished downloading. I double-clicked on the icon to install it, then pulled up a picture from Tom's photo folder and pointed to the upper-leftmost pixel in the image. "Each dot in this picture is represented by a number between zero and 16 million. Zero represents the blackest black, and 16 million represents the whitest white, one million might represent a reddish-blue color. Each picture is just a series of rows of numbers, one number for each colored dot. When the computer displays the picture on the screen, it translates each number into a color, and that's what you see."

"Okay, that makes sense," said Tom. "But how do you encode a file inside a picture?"

"I'm getting to it, one second. The human eye can only see several thousand different colors. It definitely can't tell the difference between color number 0 and 1, or 1 and 2, for example. All three are so dark, so close to black, they all look identical to the human eye. So the steganography software uses this flaw in the human vision system to encode secret messages."

I flipped back to the installer and then clicked the "next" button. The first steganography package began copying its files to Tom's hard drive.

"So it does something like this," I said. I pulled a pad of paper and a pen out of the desk drawer. "It starts by taking every number in an original picture file—the one we want to use to conceal our secret—and it converts each number to the nearest even number." I wrote the numbers 101, 200, 521, 36, and 95 on the pad. "Imagine these five numbers represent the colors of five consecutive dots in an unprocessed picture file. The software would first convert these five numbers to 100, 200, 520, 36, and 94, leaving each even number alone, and converting each odd number to the even number just below it. This produces a second image made up entirely of even-color numbers. Now if you were to view the two images side by side, you wouldn't notice any difference—your brain can't detect such minor changes in color. So now imagine that the user wants to secretly encode the digits 1, 1, 0, 1, 0 inside of this image." I drew these five digits under the original numbers:

$$100 \quad 200 \quad 520 \quad 36 \quad 94$$
$$1 \quad\quad 1 \quad\quad 0 \quad\quad 1 \quad\quad 0$$

"All the software needs to do is add these ones and zeros to each of the even-color numbers. This would give us the following numbers."

$$101 \quad 201 \quad 520 \quad 37 \quad 94$$

"These numbers represent a slightly different series of colors than the original ones in the picture, but again, the human eye can't tell the difference since the numbers are still so close to the originals, so this new image will look identical to the original. Yet there's now a secret message encoded in the picture. Now every odd number in the picture represents a secret 1 value, and every even number represents a secret zero value. The typical image file contains millions of pixels, so you can encode a heck of a lot of ones and zeros in it. You can encode even more data in a video."

"Unbelievable," said Tom. "How come we've never heard of this?"

"Most people haven't, but it's pretty prevalent. Spies use this kind of technique to encode messages to their handlers. The terrorist networks are rumored to use it too. You've probably seen dozens of stenographic images and had no idea. Anyway, I believe this video has hidden data encoded inside of it. I'm downloading several of the most popular steganography software packages to see if I can decode it."

I double-clicked on the newly installed application and selected Richard's cave video file. The software instantly popped up a window stating: "This video file has not been encoded using StegoSoft."

"Crap. Strike one." I double-clicked the second installer and followed the prompts to install the second steganography application.

"How many different packages are there?" Gennady asked.

"Dozens, probably. I'm hoping he used one of the more popular ones or we're going to be here all night." A moment later the second package finished installing. I launched it and, again, asked it to decode the cave video.

The software displayed an hourglass on the computer screen for several seconds, then popped up a window: "This video contains a password-encoded file. Please enter the password to proceed with decoding."

"That's it!" I yelled. "Okay, cross your fingers. Hopefully Richard

Lister was a creature of habit, or else we're back at square one." I gazed up at the ceiling, conjuring up Lister's inner-lip code from memory: seven, six, nine, five, four, two. I keyed the six digits into the window and hit Enter. After a brief delay, the software popped up a window titled "Decoding . . ." and displayed a progress bar. Three minutes later, as the bar reached 100%, the software proclaimed "Decoding complete. Please select a folder to hold your decoded file."

I selected the computer's Desktop, and within a few seconds, Stego-Crypt had created a new icon called FLORENTINE.ZIP on my home screen. Two additional clicks extracted the ZIP's archived contents, a document file named Florentine.pdf, a data file named Florentine. keys, and a program file named Florentine.exe.

"All right, let's figure out what this thing really is."

"It's software application." Tom pointed his finger at the Florentine. exe file listed on the screen.

"Yeah, that's surprising. I'd just expected a document file of some sort, not a program file," I admitted. "Let's see if the PDF explains what it is."

I took a sip of coffee and double-clicked on the Florentine.pdf file. The document instantly rendered on the screen.

"What language is that?" I asked.

"Russian," said Gennady.

"Can you read it?"

"I'm a bit rusty, but it shouldn't be a problem," he said. "Move." He tapped me on the shoulder and I vacated the chair.

"Well, this first part is easy—it says 'state secret, top-most level.' Something like top secret."

"Holy shit. This explains why the Russians are involved." Things were crystalizing in my mind. "This makes a lot more sense now— the spyware on Richard Lister's computer was sending everything he typed to a Russian email address. They were bugging his computer to get the Florentine back. The guy who attacked me in Khalimmy's cellar," I pointed at my cheek, "was supposedly also Russian." I paused for a breath. "Khalimmy was trying to buy Russian state secrets from Lister, and the Russians are busy trying to tie up loose ends. They're doing damage control."

Gennady picked up his gun and turned to Tom. "Go double-check the doors and all the windows."

Chapter 52

By THREE A.M., Gennady had completed a translation of the document's first section:

> Security Clearance: Top Secret, Level 3
> Categorization: Information cyber-warfare
> File Number: SVR-11-1078-52
> Codename: Florentine

> Background

> Between 2001 and 2005 the SVR placed six assets within Microsoft's Redmond, Washington and Bangalore, India engineering centers. Since their introduction, these assets introduced back doors into a series of Microsoft products and systems that enable the SVR to covertly broadcast attack commands to Windows computers, worldwide, and then execute these commands on preset trigger dates. This system was designed to enable Russia to launch Internet-scale attacks on hostile nations or blocs, and provides Russia with an unrivaled cyber-warfare capability.

> SVR studies estimate that roughly 85–90% of the world's computers now run on Florentine versions of Windows. Roughly 82%–87% of these computers are permanently or semi-permanently connected to the Internet and may be targeted. This gives Russia control over between 69% and 78% of the world's computing infrastructure and the ability to launch massive-scale digital attacks.

> Due to the immense strategic advantage conferred by the Florentine system, it has been classified at the highest level of

secrecy. Disclosure of this document, project, or any related materials to those with less than a Level 3 security clearance has been categorized as an act of high treason under Russian law.

The remainder of this document describes the technical nature of the Florentine system and provides specific details on the following items:

1. *Attack logistics (launching, targeting, and timing attacks, payload creation)*

2. *Attack management (monitoring attacks, cancelling attacks)*

3. *Florentine distribution statistics, by country*

4. *Attack propagation/saturation estimates*

"I'm willing to bet that the Florentine.exe file we found inside the video is a Command and Control program," I said.

Gennady looked at me questioningly. Tom looked up, shaking his head. "What? Sorry, I'm spent."

"If what this document says is true, most computers around the world have this back door built into them. So let's say the Russians want to launch an attack. How do they go about doing it? They need some way of contacting all those computers and unlocking their back doors to send them the attack. I'm betting that's what the software on the thumb drives is for—it's a Command and Control program. Some disaffected Russian intelligence guy must have figured he could take an early retirement by selling a copy of it to the highest bidder. I wonder how Richard Lister got hold of it—this is big-time stuff."

"If you're right, and the wrong people got control of this thing . . ." Gennady's voice trailed off.

"We need to get this to the NSA as soon as possible," I said, glancing over at the clock. "Gennady, do you think you can translate the rest by morning? I can help with any technical terminology that doesn't make sense."

Gennady nodded warily. "Yeah. Let's do it."

When I woke up, I found Gennady sitting at Tom's computer desk perusing a stack of printed pages. He looked exhausted. Next to the stack sat his gun, an empty coffee cup, and a half-eaten plate of scrambled eggs.

"What time is it?" I asked, bleary-eyed.

He consulted his watch. "Seven-thirty. You fell asleep around three, and I figured you needed the rest. I finished a rough translation of the rest of the document." He shook his head wearily. "This is either the world's first digital atomic bomb, or the world's most elaborate hoax. I can't figure out which."

"Based on recent events, I'm guessing it's the former."

After using the bathroom and grabbing a plate of cold eggs from the kitchen, I reviewed the rest of Gennady's translation. He was unable to translate some of the more arcane technical terms, but overall, the nature of the Florentine project was crystal clear.

The Florentine's design, frightening in its simplicity, effectively granted the Russians the ability to take control of virtually any and every Windows-based computer on the planet—without being discovered and blocked in the process.

"The brief said something about using Windows Update to distribute attacks," said Gennady. "Does that make sense to you?"

It did. And it scared me. "The Russians knew in order to launch an attack, they couldn't just directly connect to the world's billions of computers and send each of them the attack. That would fail. Most of the computers they'd want to target would be protected by firewalls."

Gennady looked confused.

"A firewall is the digital equivalent of a security guard. It blocks all unauthorized attempts to contact the computers that it protects. Most computers are shielded behind some type of firewall, so any attempt by the Russians to initiate contact to them would be blocked immediately. Not to mention that to attack that many computers, they'd have to generate an immense volume of network traffic. That would stand out like a sore thumb to the NSA. But it looks like the Russians found a way around both problems by leveraging Windows Update."

"How?" he asked.

"Microsoft uses the Windows Update system to distribute new updates and fixes to computers around the world. Once per day, at an essentially random time, each Windows computer wakes up and contacts Microsoft's Windows Update website to check for new updates. If it finds any, it downloads and installs them automatically."

"Okay, but how does that help the Russians?"

"I'm getting to it. While Windows Update was designed to deliver official software updates, the system is in theory capable of sending down any type of data. And if an attacker—for instance, a Russian mole inside Microsoft—somehow obtained control over the Windows Update website and could post an attack payload file, all those billions of computers would happily download it along with their legitimate updates."

Gennady nodded in dawning understanding. "It's like poisoning a waterhole—you don't have to hunt down the animals, they die when they come to drink."

"It's a reasonable analogy," I replied. "When an attack payload makes it down to a computer, the Florentine back door they've built into Windows immediately intercepts it, verifies its authenticity, and detonates it. Based on your translation, these payloads could do anything—steal confidential information, delete all your files, anything."

"Is it realistic?" he asked. "Could that actually work?"

"Unfortunately, yes. Like I thought, that executable file we found in the video is essentially a Controller. It's used to post attack payloads on the Windows Update website. The other file, Florentine.keys, contains the cryptographic authentication keys required to unlock and gain access to the system. Whoever's in possession of these two files can distribute and launch an attack on virtually every Windows computer in the world in less than twenty-four hours."

The phone rang three times before Rod Sanders, a former ViruTrax colleague in the Washington, DC sales office, picked up.

"Hi Rod, Alex Fife here. Have a minute to chat?"

"Alex Fife. It has been a while. You enjoying your retirement in, where, the Bahamas? Monte Carlo? While the rest of us still have to work to make a living?"

"Sorry to be blunt, Rod, but I've got an emergency."

The line went silent for a beat. "Shoot."

"You still work with our special friends over in Baltimore, right?" I was referring to the NSA, who was headquartered in Baltimore, Maryland. Rod, an ex-military officer, had a top-secret security clearance and was one of a handful of ViruTrax engineers with sufficient clearance to consult with the government's three-letter agencies on their internal cyber-security-related affairs.

"Yes."

"I've got some information that they need to hear about. It's urgent. Would you happen to have a contact there that could get me to the right person, ASAP?"

"Cyber-intel?" asked Rod.

"Yes."

"And this is urgent? You believe there is a material threat to national security?"

"Yes."

"Give me a number where I can reach you. I'll make some phone calls and get back to you within the hour."

I gave him Tom's number and hung up.

Five minutes later the phone rang.

"Hello," said Gennady and I simultaneously.

"Hello," responded Rod.

"I'll take it," I said. Gennady hung up. "Sorry, Rod, I'm at a friend's place."

"No problem. I chatted with one of my friends in Baltimore and they're going to have someone call you at this number in about ten minutes." He coughed up some phlegm. "These are good guys. Just tell them what you know and leave it to them."

"I will. Thanks Rod."

"No problem. If someone doesn't call you in the next ten minutes, call me back and I'll follow up. And good luck."

"Thanks."

———

The phone rang five minutes later.

"Hello."

"Hi, I'm calling for Alex Fife."

"This is Alex."

"Hi Alex, this is Jon Whitehouse. I've been asked to call you to follow up on some information you have."

"Thanks for calling so quickly." I turned on the phone's speaker-phone so Gennady and Tom could hear.

"It's my pleasure. Actually, you may not remember but you came to present to my team a few years ago. Your new malware detection method was groundbreaking, and actually influenced some of our data collection approaches."

"Thank you," I said, "I'm humbled I was able to help."

"You did. All right, what did you want to discuss? This is not a secure line, so I'm going to ask you to provide me with only high-level details. Once I understand the nature of your problem we can figure out how to proceed."

"Okay." I took a deep breath. "I have credible evidence that the Russian FSB has introduced a back door into Windows that will allow them to control virtually any or every Windows PC and server connected to the Internet within a twenty-four-hour timeframe. It's code-named Florentine."

"The FSB? Do you mean the SVR?"

"SVR?" The initials pinged something in my memory, but I couldn't place the reference.

"The Russian Foreign Intelligence Service: Sluzhba Vneshney Razvedki, the SVR."

"That rings a bell."

"Okay. And the project's codename is Florentine?"

"Yes."

"Can you briefly tell me how it works?" Whitehouse paused a beat. "Scratch that, we're not on a secure line. What evidence do you have?"

"I have documentation, written in Russian, describing how the system works, a Command and Control program supposedly capable of launching the attack. And a set of cryptographic keys that can be used to authenticate the Command and Control program to the system."

"Okay. And how did you obtain access to this system?"

"It's a long story. But the important thing is that the Florentine was being sold on the black market by a guy named Richard Lister. A guy named Arnaz Khalimmy was trying to buy it from him—"

"Spell that for me, please," Whitehouse interrupted, "Arnaz what?"

I did, then continued, "But Lister died before completing the sale. Now that I've got hold of it, Khalimmy's after me."

"Has he obtained control of the system?" Whitehouse asked.

"He's got an encrypted copy of the file, but doesn't have the password. But not for lack of trying—he's already murdered at least one person trying to get it."

"I'll be right back." I heard a muffled discussion on the other end of the line, then Whitehouse continued: "Okay Alex, here's what I want you to do. Gather up all the computers that hold a copy of the Florentine system and power them off. Unplug them. Gather up all media, thumb drives, portable hard drives, printouts, anything with Florentine data, and keep them safe until we come and pick them up. Make sure you get everything." He paused. "Any questions?"

"No."

"Okay, give me your address."

I quickly recited Tom and Gennady's address.

"Okay. I'm going to have someone over there in the next hour. One of our team just arrived in LA to attend the USC Crypto Conference. We'll have him head straight over from the airport."

Someone mumbled something to Whitehouse. He hesitated a beat, then continued, "Alex . . . does anyone else know about this system? Who else knows you have it?"

"Just the two of my friends here and Khalimmy." I thought a second. "And I'm not sure, but I think there's also a Russian guy trying—"

"The Russians?" He whistled. "They must have discovered the leak."

"That's what I'm guessing, but honestly, I've got no idea."

Whitehouse went silent for five pregnant seconds.

"Okay, Alex, listen to me very carefully. Do not discuss this with anyone else. Make sure your friends understand. Not a word to any-one. I'm going to have the local FBI office send over a car to pick you and your friends up. I need you all to pack for a few days of travel—clothes, any medications, enough for three or four days. And if you have any protection, a gun, a baseball bat, arm yourself. And lock your doors and windows until my colleague arrives. He'll stay with you until the FBI can take you into custody. His name is Arnold Altschiller." My heart skipped a beat. Arnold Altschiller was one of the fathers of modern cryptography—a seventies computer-science genius-hippy, an icon in the computer security industry.

"I'm going to give you my cell phone number and also his num-ber," Whitehouse said. "Call him first if you have any trouble. If you can't get through to him or he doesn't arrive within an hour, call me immediately or call 911." He gave me the two numbers. "Do you have any questions?"

"No."

"Good. Just hang in there and we'll fix this thing."

Chapter 53

WHILE TOM AND GENNADY PACKED, I downloaded a freeware encryption program off the Internet and used it to encrypt copies of the original Russian document, Gennady's English translation, the Command and Control program, and the Florentine authentication keys, then uploaded the encrypted files into my DropBox.com file-sharing account. Just for safekeeping. Not that I didn't trust the NSA, but I wasn't about to take any chances. Then I deleted all the decoded files from Tom's computer, and packed the chassis into a cardboard box from Tom's closet. I slipped Richard's thumb drive and Gennady's printed translation into a manila envelope and dropped that into the box as well, then carried the box over to the front door.

We waited at the kitchen table with a carafe of coffee, a box of Danishes, and Gennady's semi-automatic. The doorbell rang exactly one hour and five minutes after my call to the NSA. I walked to the door, Tom, Gennady, and his pistol in tow.

"Who is it?" I asked, peering through the keyhole.

"Arnold Altschiller," replied the man nonchalantly, "I'm here to see Alex."

"That's him," I said. "No mistaking it." I unlocked the door and motioned him in.

Altschiller stood five-foot-seven-inches tall, clad in Bermuda shorts, a Hawaiian shirt covering a developing potbelly, and gnarled Birkenstock sandals. Underneath a Mets baseball cap he sported a long, frizzy mane of white hair and a matching five-inch beard. The guy was one-hundred-percent seventies computer hippy.

"It's an honor to meet you," I said, shutting the door and engaging the deadbolt.

"Get to know me a little better and you'll change your mind, Alex," said Altschiller good-naturedly. "By the way, do you have a bathroom I could use? My flight from Germany just landed when I got the call, I'm about to explode."

"Down the hall and left." Tom pointed.

As soon as the bathroom door closed, Gennady looked at me questioningly. "That's the guy who's going to save us from the Russians?"

"He's the father of modern cryptography," I said. "Like the Einstein of cryptography."

"Right now I think we need Mike Tyson, not Albert Einstein," he replied.

"Back!" Altschiller said jovially, water dripping from his hands, face, and beard. "Pardon me, I should have introduced myself. I'm Arnold Altschiller."

Tom extended his hand hesitantly. "Tom Chien."

Gennady followed suit. "Gennady Cheryenko."

"Nice to meet you both. Okay gents, have you packed everything up?"

"Yes," I pointed to the box on the floor next to the front door. "Every copy we have is right here. Khalimmy—the guy who's been trying to get the Florentine—has an encrypted copy too, but as far as we know, he hasn't figured out the password."

"Good. Okay, we've already called the FBI, so they should be here soon. Alex, I'm going to ask you to come with me to brief our team in Baltimore." He turned to Tom and Gennady. "Gentlemen, you're going to have to go into protective custody until we get a handle on this thing."

"Is that really necessary?" asked Gennady.

"Yes," said Altschiller, stroking droplets of water from his beard. "If what your friend has discovered is authentic, there are a lot of bad people who will go to great lengths to obtain it. Your knowledge of the system makes you both targets."

A beat later, Altschiller's mobile rang with a digital rendition of Handel's *Messiah*. He pulled the phone from his belt, and, after checking the caller ID, casually stepped into the other room to talk. The doorbell rang a few minutes later. Altschiller walked briskly to the front door and stepped up to the keyhole, cell still to his ear.

"Who is it?" he asked.

"FBI. Special Agents Velasquez and Snyder," came a voice from behind the locked door.

"Please hold your badges up to the keyhole," said Altschiller. Then, to us, while still peering through the hole, "Those are the names the field office provided, but it doesn't hurt to make sure." Then, to his phone, "They've arrived."

A moment later the two beefy agents stepped through the front door.

"Agents, thank you for coming. I'll need you to take these two into protective custody," said Altschiller, gesturing to Tom and Gennady, "and once I complete this call, Mr. Fife and I are going to need an escort to the airport."

"No problem, sir," said Velasquez. "Gentlemen, I'll be taking you to our field office, and after a debrief, to a local safe house. Do you have a change of clothes and toiletries for a few days?"

"Yeah," said Tom. "We're all ready."

"Okay. Let's get going then," said the agent.

"Good luck, man," said Gennady.

Tom stepped up and gave me a hug. "Somehow it's always an adventure with you. See you on the flip side, Alex."

"Thanks, guys," I said.

"All right, let's go," said Velasquez. "Snyder, once you get them to the airport, we'll regroup back at the office."

Snyder nodded, then turned to Altschiller. "Sir, I'll be waiting outside the front door. Just tell me when you're ready."

Altschiller signaled his approval, then returned to his call as Tom, Gennady, and Velasquez stepped out the front door and into a black Lincoln Town Car. Snyder stepped out onto the porch a moment later and withdrew a cellphone.

"The friends are safely on their way," said Altschiller, locking the front door. After a few more minutes of discussion, he said, "Yes, I can do that. I'll call to confirm receipt as soon as I'm done," and ended the call.

"Okay, slight change of plans." Altschiller turned to face me. "They want me to upload the Florentine files over a secure link before we leave, so the techs in Baltimore can start looking immediately. Once we transmit the data, we'll pack up and head straight over to the airport."

"Makes sense," I said.

"Good. Let me go get my laptop—I'll be right back." Altschiller took another look through the keyhole. "You have Internet here, right?"

"Yes."

"Good," he said. Then he unlocked the door and stepped outside.

"I'll be in the kitchen grabbing some food before we leave," I said. "The thumb drive with the Florentine file is in the manila envelope." I pointed at the box.

A brief inspection revealed nothing but beers in the refrigerator, so I began rummaging through the pantry.

Then I heard it.

The *phut* of a silenced gun, then the thump of a body collapsing to the floor. A second later, the gun spat again, and I heard another body slam into a wall.

Fuck.

It had to be Khalimmy. But how could he possibly know I was here? That I'd made it out? Had he had me tailed?

Nausea seized my stomach. I had no way of escaping out the front or the back without heading through the main hallway, right past Khalimmy. I could duck into the guest bedroom next to the kitchen, but without any place to hide, I had no chance. I scanned the counter-tops for some means of defense.

Nothing. Dammit!

No time. I slipped around the center island and slid underneath the large kitchen table, shimmying beneath its center to hide from view.

Step by step, Khalimmy's cautious footfalls grew louder. I gazed helplessly toward the hallway, waiting for him to round the corner.

After ten excruciating seconds, his black slacks slid into view. He took a tentative step forward, hesitated a long moment, then walked up to the sliding glass door leading to the backyard and gave it a tug. Satisfied, he turned to face the kitchen and took a few tentative steps toward the counter. Then he stopped, his slacks and brown loafers just feet from my face.

I held my breath, my heartbeat hammering in my ears.

Then I saw it. Just inches away from Khalimmy's outstretched hand.

Gennady's pistol.

He'd left it on the granite counter covered by a newspaper, the circular mouth of the barrel barely visible from my vantage on the floor.

Khalimmy stood there, immobile, completely silent.

Had he seen me? Heard my breathing?

Five agonizing seconds later, he took a first tentative step toward the guest bedroom, then a second and a third.

He disappeared through the door.

I readied myself.

The guest bedroom's bathroom door creaked open.

It was now or never. I shifted out from under the table and rose to my feet, then, taking one long stride, reached the counter and quietly slid the gun from beneath the newspaper.

I had it.

Hands shaking, I carefully wrapped my index finger around the trigger, and then, with the gun's barrel centered on the bedroom's doorway, began inching back toward the hallway. Just as I reached the edge of the kitchen wall, Khalimmy reappeared in the doorway, his silenced pistol pointing straight ahead. Directly at my chest.

"Drop it," I yelled.

"It seems we have a stalemate," he said calmly.

"Drop the fucking gun!" I screamed. "Now."

"You can't win this, Alex," he said, immobile, his gun still trained on my chest.

"No, but if I'm going to die anyway," I spat, "at least I'm going to get even."

I pulled the trigger.

Chapter 54

AND DOVE RIGHTWARD, down the hallway and onto the floor.

I scrabbled to my feet and immediately fired again, sending a warning round smacking into the kitchen ceiling, then backed up a handful of steps and pumped another round down the hallway.

Step by step, I backed up, gun trained down the hall, until my backside pressed into the brass handle of the front door.

I reached behind me, clicked the latch, and tugged the door open. Gun still aimed toward the kitchen, I sidestepped through the doorway, then yanked the door shut.

Safe. For now, at least.

I spun around to bolt.

The fist caught me squarely in the solar plexus and I collapsed to the ground, gasping for oxygen. Then, as in a nightmare, unable to breathe or lift my arms to defend myself, I saw the butt-end of a gun fly in an arc toward my temple.

Chapter 55

I CAME TO SLOWLY, confused and physically uncomfortable—my temple, neck, right shoulder and lower back throbbed angrily and my right arm had fallen asleep. I opened my eyes to total darkness; the air, hot and stuffy, smelled of gasoline and old rags.

The bastards had locked me in a car trunk. After a moment to clear my head, I shifted my body left and dislodged my right arm, unleashing a thousand excruciating pins and needles. Once the feeling had returned, I probed with both arms to gauge the space and quickly ran into a jumble of boxes, cables, and a plastic gas can, its contents sloshing from the sudden shift.

I rotated my body, making every effort not to generate additional noise, shifting my feet to the rear of the car and my head toward the front, then pressed my ear up against the rear of the backseat and listened. If they were in the front of the car, they weren't making any noise. They probably locked up the car in a garage and were waiting until after dark, when they could safely drag me out. Again I shifted, placing my ear up against the metal trunk lid. No one within earshot.

Reassured, I rummaged through the boxes, feeling around for tools: a crowbar, screwdriver, a jack, anything I could use to escape. Nothing. Well, at least I knew my situation. Locked in a trunk, probably inside a garage, hopefully out of earshot. I rearranged my body into a less cramped position, reducing the strain on my neck and lower back, and ruminated.

I could try kicking out the lid of the trunk but that would make noise. I could also try kicking the backseat into the front of the car. That would be quieter. I'd try that first.

I rotated and wedged my frame against the rear of the trunk, then using my arms to steady myself, launched a devastating kick at the rear of the backseat. This, to my stunned disappointment, sent searing pain through the heels of my feet yet did absolutely no damage to the car's rear seating. After the pain subsided, I steeled myself and kicked again.

The seat didn't budge. I tried once more, this time kicking toward the top of the seat. Nothing.

Dammit.

I had to try the lid, even if it meant they might hear me. I wiped the layer of sweat from my forehead, took a few deep breaths, and positioned my body for an attack on the trunk's hatch.

Over and over I slammed my palms up through the suffocating darkness against the trunk's lid. The lock felt like it was starting to give, ever so slowly, but I couldn't keep it up. The temperature had risen noticeably in just the past few minutes, and whether it was the heat or the dwindling oxygen, I was starting to get dizzy. I had to stop or I'd pass out.

Shit. That was the last thing I needed.

I laid my head down on what felt like a clump of oily rags. I'd rest a minute. Slow my breathing. Let . . . let the dizziness pass. Just for a minute. Because if I were still here when they got back, I was dead. They'd torture me for the password, and then they'd . . . and they'd kill me . . . and I wasn't . . . I . . .

I slipped into unconsciousness.

Chapter 56

I AWOKE CONFUSED and sore on the dusty linoleum floor of a small, drably furnished bedroom—a children's room, at least at one time. Flaking hand-painted clouds and biplanes ornamented the scuffed, gray-hued walls. A cot with a rumpled army surplus blanket lay in one corner, a shabby children's dresser next to it, and opposite them, a door and a sliding mirrored closet. A lone window, boarded from the inside, covered the wall nearest my feet. After gaining my bearings I tried to shift my arms, which had been bound behind my back, to alleviate the stress on my shoulders. The exercise was futile; I instantly recoiled in pain—savagely tightened plastic cable ties, the kind police use to incapacitate protesters, sliced into the flesh of my wrists. I looked down at my ankles. They too were fastened, with no less than three of the nasty bindings. The bastards weren't taking any chances.

I lay still on the filthy floor, listening and staring intently at the dim sliver of light beneath the door for any sign of movement. None came. After several minutes of waiting, I shimmied my rear along the floor and inched my body backward, using my bound feet, until my back rested against the wall. Drawing my feet in close, I pushed my heels against the floor, extended my legs, and gently slid my body up the wall.

Once I'd gained my feet, I hopped over to the door, then shuffled in place until my hands contacted the knob. It was locked, as expected. Undeterred, I worked my way over to the dresser, backed myself up to it, and pulled the drawer open a few inches.

I hit pay dirt. Among other items, the top drawer contained a Zippo lighter, a flat-head screwdriver, and a bunch of pens. I bent forward, extending my bound arms back to pull the drawer open farther just as I heard footsteps in the hall.

"Let's get this over with," said Khalimmy.

Shit. Hands caught in the cookie jar. I jerked backward in an attempt to shut the drawer, lost my balance and slammed shoulder-first onto the dusty linoleum floor.

The lock clicked and the door edged open a few seconds later.

"How do you like the accommodations?" asked Khalimmy.

I rolled onto my stomach and gritted my teeth to stifle the searing pain.

"Not feeling too talkative, I guess. Unfortunately, I've got a few questions for you." He prodded me with his foot. "Would you rather answer lying there on your face, or on the cot?"

"C-cot," I stammered through the pain.

Khalimmy grabbed my left arm and tugged me upright, then escorted me over to the cot, his pistol trained on my chest.

"Better?"

"Better," I replied, noticing for the first time the bloodied bandage on his right ear.

"I must give you some credit," he said, observing my gaze. "I never expected you to pull the trigger."

Silently, I shook my head in anger. If only I'd aimed a few more inches to the right.

"Good. All right, Alex. I'll make this simple. I'm going to need the password for the video. The last time you stalled, two people died." He scratched his graying, stubbled chin wearily. "I have no qualms torturing you for it. But understand one thing, I will get that password."

As if on command, Khalimmy's partner walked up to the door with a spool of nylon cord, a rusty pair of pruning shears, and a ball peen hammer.

"Over there," he said, motioning casually at the drawer with his gun. His eyes didn't leave my face.

The man dropped the tools into the drawer and mumbled something in what must have been Arabic. Khalimmy replied, and the stocky man walked over to the cot, grabbed the mass of cable ties securing my ankles and yanked my legs toward the edge of the cot, then knotted my legs to the cot's aluminum frame with the cord. He then looped the cord several times around my neck and knotted it around the other end of the frame. I was, for all intents and purposes, immobilized.

"Thank you, Sami," said Khalimmy, then he asked something in Arabic. The man responded in kind, then left the room.

"You were sloppy," he said. "Sami tells me that you didn't properly wipe the Florentine files from your computer when you deleted them. He thinks he might be able to recover them."

"So you don't need the password after all," I said.

"No. I didn't say that. I'm not going to take any more chances, Alex." He walked over to the drawer, laid the gun down, and picked up the shears. "I am not going to wait while Sami plays Steve Jobs. You're going to tell me now, and get this over with. If you don't give me the password, or you give me the wrong password, I will inflict enormous pain on you."

Khalimmy walked over to the cot and kneeled next to my head. "I'm sure many things are going through your mind right now, so what do you say I give you thirty seconds to think it over. To give you some incentive, I intend to start with your nose."

He waved the shears inches from my face, then stood up, walked over to the closet, and dragged out a large roll of plastic sheeting.

"This kind of thing can get messy," he said as he lifted his shirt-sleeves and stared at his watch.

Capitulate now, or suffer immeasurably and then capitulate? The choice was easy.

"I'll give you the password."

"Good. You won't regret it." Khalimmy pulled a small spiral note-pad from his slacks and a pen from his shirt pocket, then stared at me expectantly.

"Seven, six, nine, five, four, two."

"Thank you, Alex." Khalimmy jotted down the digits, then slipped the pen back into his pocket. He had just reached the door when Sami yelled something incomprehensible. Khalimmy yelled back, then rotated in the doorway, a large grin exposing his yellowing teeth.

"Sami just finished recovering all of your deleted files. We didn't need the password after all. In any case, you just saved yourself a great deal of unnecessary suffering, Alex."

Several hours later, Khalimmy returned with a paper plate of Chinese takeout and plastic fork.

"No monkey business, please."

He placed the plate on the dresser, loosened the cord binding my neck, and used the shears to cut through the plastic ties around my wrists. Fighting extreme stiffness in my shoulders, I brought my arms forward and accepted the sagging plate of food. It was cold and congealed into a takeout-box-shaped clump, but edible. Khalimmy leaned up against the dresser and stared pensively at the wall as I ate.

"The beginning of the end . . ." he mumbled to himself.

"What?" I asked, looking up from the plate.

Khalimmy straightened, his eyes focused, and he studied me.

"This will be the beginning of the end for America and Israel," he said after a moment. "A suitcase nuclear bomb can kill thousands, maybe tens of thousands of infidels, but this is ultimately insignificant. The sting of a hornet to a bear. Bin Laden never recognized this, and this was his fatal flaw. He measured success based on the count of bodies.

"But the reality, one that few in my world are able to appreciate, is that west's strength is built upon a flimsy house of cards. Your banks, hospitals, stock markets, your electricity and traffic grids, your military—everything is computerized. Everything. You are dependent on computers as much as any organism is dependent on oxygen. Take away this oxygen and the organism dies. It will asphyxiate and collapse.

"The challenge, of course, was how to destroy your hundreds of millions of computers without being discovered and blocked in the process. Our academics suggested that we use a sophisticated computer virus." He snorted condescendingly. "Fools. Even the fucking Israeli pigs, with their trillions of stolen wealth, were able to impact only a tiny fraction of our uranium enrichment with their *advanced* Stuxnet virus." Khalimmy scratched his chin. "But then we learned of the Florentine, and its remarkable potential." He shook his head. "You must give credit to the Russians. They are godless and corrupt, but they are also brutally clever."

Sami called from some other part of the house. Khalimmy stepped out into the hall for a few minutes, then returned.

"Allah is smiling upon our efforts. Sami has almost finished preparing a test payload for dispersal with Florentine."

"A test payload?" I asked.

"A benign payload, Alex. We must make sure the cryptographic keys from Lister's flash drive are valid, and that the distribution system is functioning properly," he responded matter-of-factly. "Allah willing, within a few days, we will be safely back in Iran, and your people will be looting and killing each other."

I finished the food and laid the soggy paper plate on the floor next to the cot.

Khalimmy stifled a yawn, backed up to the door, and yelled something in Farsi. Sami responded gruffly, and then lumbered in a moment later with a handful of the vicious plastic cable ties. While Khalimmy aimed his pistol at my head, Sami affixed the restraints around my wrists, dumped me roughly back onto the cot, and then attached my leg cuffs to the cot's aluminum frame.

"Sweet dreams, Alex," he said, then the two of them left.

Chapter 57

I AWOKE FROM A FITFUL SLEEP with an unbearable stiffness in my neck, the taste of morning breath, and an uncomfortably full bladder. Aiming to relieve the pressure on both, I fought my foot restraints and twisted my body as far as I could manage. All night my mind had fixated, both willingly and later involuntarily, on Khalimmy's plan.

It was simple yet potentially devastating: all Khalimmy had to do was create a destructive payload and specify the targeting parameters, and the Florentine would do the rest; the Russians had solved all the intractable distribution issues.

Creating a destructive payload, likely a disk-scrambling program, would take a competent programmer literally an hour or two. Identifying which computers to target was also an unnervingly simple task—when the payload arrived upon a computer, it could easily check the computer's time-zone setting to identify its location. If it matched one of Khalimmy's five targeted time zones—Pacific, Mountain, Central, Eastern, or Jerusalem—whammo, the payload would trigger. Or if that didn't work, I was certain they'd identified a dozen other ways to accurately recognize and target American- and Israeli-owned computers.

Such an attack would certainly be devastating and painful. It would take large swaths of infrastructure, banks, businesses, and the Internet off-line. But big businesses and government agencies made continuous backups of their most critical data and files, and as hard as Khalimmy tried, my bank account would still have all of its money, my prescriptions would still be filled, and my power would be back on within a few days or weeks of the attack. It would be painful, but we would persevere.

I turned my thoughts to a more important subject: how I was going to stay alive, and if possible, stop the attack. I shifted my body again and had begun contemplating escape plans when Khalimmy cracked the door open, checked that I was still on the cot, and then walked inside, a sickening look of delight on his face.

"Good morning, Alex," he said. "Would you like some food, maybe use the restroom?"

"Yes to both, restroom first."

"You'll be happy to know," he said while he cut the restraints from the cot, grabbed my triceps, and roughly hoisted me onto my feet, "we have successfully tested the Florentine distribution mechanism. Last night at two a.m., Sami uploaded a software payload that simply beeps twice at four p.m. Greenwich Mean Time, or eight a.m. Pacific, on computers bearing either of two serial numbers—those of two of our laptops. This morning at eight a.m., after Sami manually ran Windows Update on the computers, both beeped just as planned."

"Congratulations," I said sardonically. Khalimmy ignored my sarcasm and led me to the bathroom, cut the cable ties binding my wrists and sat me on the toilet, waiting guardedly just outside the open door.

"After one more test, our wait will be over, as will your captivity."

"One more test?" I asked.

"We have to make sure our final payload works when distributed through the Florentine. We wouldn't want anything unforeseen to go wrong."

"What could go wrong with deleting files or formatting the hard drive? Any teenager can write that kind of attack in a matter of minutes."

"This is true, Alex. But our attack doesn't simply delete files or format hard drives." I could hear pride in his voice and had an intense desire to kick the door into his face with my bound feet.

"What does it do?" I asked, genuinely surprised. *Is he bluffing?*

"Come," he said gruffly once I'd finished. After I'd zipped up, he manhandled me into the kitchen and sat me in front of a dilapidated card table. A microwave-style burrito still in its wrapping sat on a paper plate in front of me. "Eat." He pointed, eyeing me warily from the kitchen sink. "Our engineers have created a very special payload," he continued, "which I'm sure, of all people, you will appreciate. It annihilates the flash firmware on each motherboard by writing a random stream of garbage over the existing instructions."

I dropped the burrito onto the plate.

"Like I said, I knew you would appreciate the brilliance of our plan.

It did take a while for our researchers to prepare the payload to work on most major brands of American and Israeli computers—all of them require slightly different parameters, as you'd expect. But that work was completed over the past few years in anticipation of a viable distribution mechanism. Which, thanks to you, we now have. All that remains is verifying that the two pieces of the puzzle work together on a few test computers, and then we will share our creation with your hundreds of millions of countrymen."

"The firmware instructions can't be modified," I stammered uncertainly, "only older computers are susceptible to that kind of attack. That won't—"

"Incorrect," Khalimmy interrupted. "You are wrong. With the proper digital certificates, the majority of firmware chips can be easily re-flashed. And I assure you, Alex, I have those certificates." Khalimmy walked over to the greasy, dented refrigerator and pulled out a bottle of water.

This was bad. Every computer in the world had a special microchip soldered onto its motherboard that held the firmware instructions required to drive the computer. Trash the firmware, and the computer would go into the digital equivalent of a coma. Permanently. Unlike a deleted file, which could be restored from a backup in a matter of hours or days, a computer with corrupted firmware could only be repaired by physically unsoldering the damaged microchip from the computer's circuit board and soldering in a replacement. Practically, this meant the destruction of hundreds of million computers. How long would it take to manufacture that many replacements? Months? Years? I shuddered.

"Yes," said Khalimmy appraisingly. "Now you appreciate the magnitude of the attack."

I looked up at him; his gaunt, stubbled face showing only weary determination.

"Assuming all proceeds well with our second test, Sami will launch the attack this afternoon. By ten a.m. Pacific Time on Wednesday morning, most of your nation's hundreds of millions of computers will have connected to Microsoft's website to check for their daily update, and in the process, all will become infected with our payload. And at ten a.m., Allah willing, your country will take the first step toward its proper place on the ash-heap of history. The Russians, they will take all the blame."

Then, without hesitating, he slammed his fist against the table and yelled, "Eat your fucking food." He considered. "Or don't. It doesn't really matter."

My stomach lurched. "I don't see what good it does. You're going to kill me anyway."

"You should be so lucky," he sneered. "That would be the easy way out. The thugs at VEVAK have demanded to *interrogate* you."

I stared at him, confused.

"The Iranian Ministry of Intelligence and National Security," he said. "I'm sure they'll be considerate when questioning and disposing of you."

He paused, then yelled, "Sami!"

Khalimmy removed the gun from his pocket and pointed it at me. Sami lumbered in and bound my wrists under the cover of Khalimmy's aimed weapon, then shuffled me back to the makeshift cell and slammed the door. I heard the distinctive click of the steel padlock they'd bolted to the door and its jamb, receding footsteps, and then silence.

I wasn't going to die. I also wasn't going to let any of this happen.

Latching my bound feet behind the cot's steel leg, I tugged my torso upright, and with a bit of effort lurched onto my feet and hobbled over to the dresser. I rotated my body, leaned forward and extended my bound hands back and under the drawer's lip, then shuffled forward on my feet, dragging the drawer outward a good eight inches. Bucking the pain in my shoulders, I raised my arms behind my back until they just cleared the lip of the drawer, inserted them, and groped amid the drawer's mess for the lighter.

After what seemed like an eternity of fumbling, I found it. I snatched it and shuffled forward until my hands cleared the edge of the drawer. I gripped the Zippo lighter firmly in my right hand and flicked the flint wheel with my thumb. Nothing happened. I flicked it again, and then again. Finally, the propellant caught. My heart leapt as soft bluish hues danced upon the walls and ceiling behind me. The plastic cuffs sliced deeper into the raw layers of skin around of my wrists as I struggled, blindly, to orient the lighter's flame beneath the plastic. If I could position the flame below the tough plastic bands for just ten seconds, I was sure I could melt the plastic enough to snap it. Dissatisfied with the flame's position, I swiveled the lighter again, disregarding the growing heat beginning to singe the skin above my left thumb. The smell of burning hair wafted sickeningly up to my nose, but still I held the lighter steady for two, three, and then four seconds.

The pain became too intense. My hands shot open reflexively and the lighter dropped to the linoleum with a soft thud.

But the flame had not extinguished with the fall. The cool blue cone continued to dance from the nozzle. Thank God Khalimmy had expensive taste in lighters.

Using the cot, I eased my body onto the linoleum and wriggled backward toward the lighter until my fingers could feel its heat. I grabbed and righted the lighter on the floor and then, using the warmth to guide my movements, squirmed to position the cuffs over the now-vertical blue flame. The pain was agonizing but I held my hands steady, encouraged by the wonderful, acrid smell of melting plastic that had joined odors of singed hair and skin. Then, using every ounce of strength my shoulders could muster, I strained until the cuffs severed with a pop. Once my arms were free, I similarly disposed of the ankle cuffs, stood up, and pocketed the screwdriver from the drawer.

Khalimmy had bolted the door from the outside with a steel plate and padlock, and the windows were similarly unassailable—any attack on either would take too long and be way too noisy. I could wait until he returned and stab him with the screwdriver, but with Sami in earshot, the situation would likely quickly deteriorate. I could also electrify the doorknob using the ceiling bulb's socket—assuming I didn't electrocute myself first. But I'd need a long length of wire and a lot of luck—my only electrical training came from reruns of *MacGyver*. Neither option gave me much confidence. I quietly slid open the closet door in search of other alternatives.

Other than a few open boxes crammed with books, the floor of the closet was empty. I shifted my gaze up to the closet's top shelf and almost shrieked—there, set into the ceiling above the shelf, was a trap-door to the house's attic.

Chapter 58

TAKING CARE NOT TO MAKE ANY NOISE, I stacked two boxes on the floor directly beneath the hatch, then using the shelf to balance myself, stepped up onto the unsteady mound. The hatch resisted my first gentle shove, probably welded to its frame by years of disuse. I reoriented my weight and thrust my palm upward. Following an instant of resistance, the layers of paint along its edges cracked and the hatch popped up into the darkness.

I paused to listen for signs that I'd been discovered, but heard nothing but the faint sound of a radio, so I lifted and shoved the hatch to the side, grabbed the hatch's wood frame and heaved myself up through the aperture and into the stifling crawlspace. Now perched on the frame, I probed the scratchy fiberglass insulation in search of wood beams that would support my weight. When I had found two that felt sturdy, I shifted both feet onto them and then reseated the hatch on its frame. The attic descended into midnight blackness.

My heart sank. I'd hoped for an attic window, a vent, some potential means of escape, but based on the total absence of light, I was out of luck.

I'd need to find another way out.

I flicked the Zippo's blue flame to life, and moving slowly so as not to cause the beams to creak, worked my way to the center of the stuffy cavity. Pink fiberglass insulation covered the entire thirty-by-thirty-foot attic surface, and a triangular roof rose above me to a height of six or seven feet at the center, tapering to just a foot or two at the edges. Over in the far left corner, several dust-covered apple crates sat upon a makeshift platform of plywood. In addition to the hatch I'd just passed through, two others poked up through the pink wadding, offering potential escape routes. I worked my way over to the crates.

The first was filled with useless odds and ends—a sixties-era swan-neck lamp, several dusty hardcover books, a heavy iron pot, cheap ceramic plates, and a collection of dull kitchen knives. I grabbed the largest and least dull of the lot and put it to the side, then began rummaging through the second box. It contained more garbage: a stack of old paperbacks, a handful of sports trophies, and an autographed baseball. The knife would have to do. Below, snatches of conversation mixed with the jabbering of an AM radio talk show; based on the noises, I was near the main living area—perhaps above the kitchen pantry or a laundry room.

I grabbed the heavier of the two boxes, and using the noise of the radio to cover any groaning of the beams, deposited it squarely on top of the hatch above my improvised cell. Then I traversed the rafters to the second trapdoor and put my ear to it. Based on my limited familiarity with the house's layout, I was guessing this one led to the second bedroom. I heard no voices from below—only the muffled prattling of the radio. I listened again, longer this time, until I was certain neither of them were nearby, and then applied just a hair of upward pressure on the hatch. As with the other hatch, this one resisted, welded to its frame by disuse. Masked by the radio, I tugged at each corner until one finally yielded, then shifted the cover a hair and put my ear to the gap.

Khalimmy and his subordinate were no more than a dozen steps from the second bedroom's closet, so I could hear their goings-on below. I extinguished the flame and lay down on one of the beams to listen.

Over the next hour, the two conversed in a largely incomprehensible mixture of Farsi and English, but from their tone and a few comprehensible words, it was clear that Sami had completed the second validation—well ahead of schedule.

"I celebrate with smoke," said Sami in broken English.

"Be my guest," replied Khalimmy, "you deserve it." The back door creaked open then closed with a thump. Khalimmy, based on the noises below, had remained in the kitchen.

Now that they had tied up their loose ends, I had an hour and a half, maybe two, before they'd come to feed me and discover I was missing, but with Khalimmy still just a few steps away and probably armed, I had no choice but to wait.

My predictions were off by an hour. Khalimmy unlocked the door to my cell just thirty minutes later.

"*Bokon*," he screamed, "the bastard is gone. Sami, *inja bya*, get the gun."

Sami mumbled something in return.

"Yes! In the attic. Get the flashlight. *Ajale kon! Bokon!*"

The old hardwood floors groaned chaotically beneath their pounding feet. I lifted the hatch and set it to the side, then waited, knife in hand. A sliver of light slipped through the door and illuminated a cramped three-by-four-foot closet precariously heaped with junk. No way I'd be able to lower myself without knocking over half of it and risking discovery.

The first hatch creaked, then slammed down under the weight of the crate. "Fool, *shoma ra cheh mishavad*?" yelled Khalimmy. "*Bokon*. He has blocked it. Get the ladder from the garage! Go!"

More groaning of floorboards. A door wrenched open and then slammed shut.

It was an opening—as good as any I'd ever get. I placed the knife between my teeth and lowered my legs through the hatch, braced both forearms on the frame and began easing my torso through.

Then the doorbell rang.

"*Bokon*. What the fuck now?" Khalimmy snarled. The bell rang again.

"One second," he yelled. I heard a door open, whispering, and more creaking of floorboards—someone, Sami by the sound of it, positioned himself just outside my closet door and cocked a gun. Still dangling half in and half out of the attic, I willed my arm and stomach muscles perfectly still against the increasing burn.

"I'll be right there," yelled Khalimmy.

Another door opened. More mumbling, this time faint, deep.

"I'm sorry, I'm not interested. Thank you." The front door slammed shut.

"They're gone," said Khalimmy, "just get the fucking ladd—"

The crash came suddenly, cutting him off mid-sentence. An instant later, the door slammed shut and I heard a spat of air. Khalimmy moaned.

Sami cursed under his breath and I could hear him shifting, perhaps orienting his body for an assault. Then, a second later, I heard the clicking of keys on a keyboard.

"Is there anyone else here?" asked a deep Russian voice.

Khalimmy didn't reply. I heard a dull impact and then another moan. The deep voice said something in Russian, then said, "But don't kill him."

The door creaked just barely, and instantly another volley of gunshots—these unsilenced—slammed into it, sending vibrations through the wooden trapdoor frame and into my arms. The Russian howled in pain and collapsed heavily to the floor. A new burst of clicks assaulted the keyboard as Sami murmured.

The floorboards in the main area creaked, the clicking paused a beat, and two more rounds pounded through the door; then the staccato of taps resumed. Two seconds, then five seconds passed, the frenetic clicking of keys now joined by the nearby barking of dogs.

The tapping stopped, replaced by the unmistakable ejection of an ammunition clip and the click of another shoved home. Sami's faint prayers mingled with louder, agitated Russian voices and squeaking floorboards.

Abruptly, the bedroom door crashed open. Three, four, five muffled rounds thumped into flesh and bone. A body hit the floor hard.

The Russian's footsteps paused just outside the closet, and Sami's gurgling, rapid breathing ceased with a final, silenced round. I held my breath and body perfectly still, my muscles screaming in pain.

"Check the other room," came the other, strained voice. A curt reply came back in Russian. "What did you do with the Florentine?" asked the same voice.

"Fuck you," spat Khalimmy weakly.

"*Nechevo*," said the other.

"What the fuck did you do with it?" repeated the strained voice.

"Fuck you, you fucking godless—" The bullet silenced Khalimmy.

"Fuck it! Grab the computer and help me up—the police will be here any minute."

The front door slammed shut.

Heeding the screaming pain in my arms, chest, and stomach, I eased myself down and around the masses of junk and onto the floor of the cramped closet. Two, then three minutes passed uneventfully. They weren't coming back.

I hesitated when the closet door resisted, instead peering cautiously through the narrow gap. Sami's bullet-riddled corpse lay sprawled against the closet door, the fresh pool of blood still growing and, to my horror, flowing under the closet door and around my feet. His bloodless face held a waxy, almost theatrical grimace of pain and anger. I shoved my shoulder against the door and when the aperture had opened wide enough, gingerly stepped through it and over Sami's body, leaving a trail of bloody footprints in my wake.

I needed to get out—fast. Sami had almost certainly launched the attack. Or had he? Maybe he didn't think he had enough time? Had he just spent his last few seconds sending the decoded Florentine files to his compatriots, deleting them from his computer, a last-ditch effort to conceal the botched attack? That was a possibility too, but one thing was clear: If I was around when the police arrived, I'd be detained for days, and by then, it would be too late to stop an attack. I worked my way over to Sami's desk. A confusion of handwritten scraps of paper and Post-Its littered the desk, the Farsi script unintelligible. I poked through the pile, grabbed several with the most writing and shoved them into my pocket, then worked my way to the main room.

Khalimmy had propped himself against the living room wall prior to his execution. His body now slumped sideways, mouth ajar, a single, narrow bullet hole adorning his graying left temple. Good riddance.

I twisted the knob to the front door and took off.

Chapter 59

"HILLARY?"

I nodded to the gas station attendant in thanks.

"Alex, we've been worried sick. Where the hell have you been?"

"It's a long story. I need your help. Can you come pick me up? I'm in North Hollywood."

"North Hollywood? One second." In a more muted voice she asked Steven, "Will you be okay by yourself for an hour or so?"

Steven mumbled something unintelligible.

"Okay, where are you, Alex?"

I cupped my hand over the phone and asked the attendant.

"The corner of Lankershim and Victory. At the Shell station," I said.

"I'll be there in thirty minutes."

Hillary arrived in forty-five, her face a conflicted mixture of anxiety and relief.

"What the hell happened, Alex?" She frowned at me as I buckled the seat belt. "What happened to your wrists? Jesus!"

"I'll tell you everything. But right now I need you to get me to UCLA. As quickly as possible."

Hillary nodded uneasily, then signaled and turned right onto Victory.

"Yesterday after I left the hospital, I picked up the thumb drive, then went over to Tom and Gennady's place to try to decode the video file. I was right, the video held a bunch of hidden files."

"What was in them?" she asked, switching into the left lane.

"It's hard to explain," I said, "but basically, the files are the digital equivalent of a key."

"As in lock and key?"

"Yeah. The files in that video are capable of unlocking and controlling a Russian cyber-weapon. That's what the Florentine is, Hillary. It's a Russian cyber-weapon."

"A cyber-weapon?" she repeated, shaking her head.

"Like a computer virus, only orders of magnitude worse."

She gazed at me in amazement. "This whole thing, all this violence, was over a stupid computer virus? You've got to be kidding."

"It's *not* a computer virus. The Florentine is a back door that's embedded into every computer running Windows on the planet. Those thumb drives we found hold the key that can unlock that back door, and whoever controls it has the power to decimate the world's computers."

"Holy shit," she said, "that's why everyone's after it."

"That's right. Khalimmy's an Iranian agent, Hill. Iran wants to use the Florentine to nuke the US computing infrastructure."

"But where have you been?"

"It's a long story. Basically, Khalimmy kidnapped me to get to the Florentine, and I'm pretty sure one of his guys used it to launch their attack. And meanwhile, the Russian intelligence service is trying to cover the whole thing up."

"Jesus. We've got to get you back to the NSA, Alex."

"I'll call them as soon as I can, but right now I need some advice. I need time to think."

"What's there to think about? Just call the NSA and let them take care of it."

"It's not so simple, Hill."

"I hope you know what you're doing, Alex."

Hillary pulled into the right lane and slowed for a red light. When the signal turned green, she turned right and accelerated onto the 101 Freeway onramp.

"Any news about Linda?" I asked.

Hillary hesitated.

"What?" I probed. "Just tell me."

"She's not doing well. Her lung was improving yesterday, then all of a sudden this morning she started wheezing." Hillary grimaced. "I just don't know. They rushed her back into surgery right before you called."

"Oh God."

"We're praying for her, Alex." Tears began streaking down her cheeks.

"Me too," I said. "Me too."

"I'm sure they're doing everything they can," she continued, wiping tears. "But right now, I'm worried about you." She paused. "Just for God's sake, try to stay safe. I don't know what I'd do if anything ever happened to you."

Twenty minutes later, Hillary pulled up to the UCLA turnaround in front of Engineering IV, then gave me a kiss on the cheek and another admonition to be safe. I took off for Boelter Hall with a promise to call and report my status later that evening.

Boelter Hall, the home of UCLA's Computer Science Department, was also my home away from home during my four years studying at UCLA. Built in 1959 and showing its age, Boelter had a long and storied history. Its rooms had not only housed countless generations of engineering students, but also the first computer routers of the ARPANET, predecessor to the Internet, and even a small nuclear reactor.

Amir Taheri opened the door to his third-floor lab on the fifth knock and stared at me for a long second. Then his face lit up.

"Alex . . . Alex Fife! How long has it been?" Amir embraced me warmly. "Three, no, four years since you graduated? Come in, come in!"

Amir Taheri, aka the "Hardware Guy," was a Comp Sci department fixture, the kind of guy who never seemed to age, always had a smile on his face, and somehow managed to help generations of pimply-faced undergrads with their advanced algorithms homework while still putting in an honest nine-to-five day fixing department computers. I'd served as Amir's intern and chief gopher during my junior and senior years, but hadn't seen him since. My faced flushed in a mild pang of guilt for not visiting the man who most helped me cope with the death of my grandmother during my college years.

"I hoped you'd be here," I said earnestly. "I figured you'd retired by now but it was worth a shot."

"Well, you've come just in time, Alex. In fact, I retire next Friday after forty-five years of service. I hear they give you a UCLA Engineering watch at forty-five. I could use it," he said, tapping the old Mickey Mouse-themed timepiece strapped around his wrist. "I've had this one since you were solving integrals down in thirty-four hundred."

"Good timing then!" I said, momentarily cheered. Amir's tender smile at once rekindled the warmth I'd felt for him during my time at school. "You look exactly the same," I said. It was mostly true; prematurely gray, he'd looked in his fifties as long as I'd known him, and with the exception of a few new wrinkles, he looked just as I recalled.

"Would you like some coffee?" he offered.

"Please. I could use some." I nodded, leaning up against his workbench.

Amir filled a Styrofoam cup with instant black coffee and deposited it next to me. "So what brings you here, Alex? Just reminiscing? You know, three of your classmates have come to visit—with darling children of their own, no less—in the last few weeks. When it rains it pours, I guess!"

"It's strange how that happens, sometimes," I said, "but I've come for a different reason. I need your help. Do you have an hour to hear me out?" I withdrew Sami's notes from my pocket and laid them on the table. "It's literally a matter of national security."

Amir's smile melted and his face inspected me with a look of incredulity.

"I have time," he said. "What's this about, Alex? And why me?"

"May I?" I asked, walking over to lock his door. "I've become more paranoid over the past few days."

"Go ahead," he said, easing himself into his cracked leather desk chair.

Over the next hour, I downloaded and decrypted the files from DropBox, then brought Amir up to speed on the nature of the Florentine, briefly going over each section of Gennady's translated document.

"Let me summarize my understanding for you. Please correct me where I'm wrong," he said once I concluded.

"Sure."

"The Russian intelligence service has embedded a back door inside every copy of Windows running today." He touched his laptop. "This laptop, for example, has the back door."

I nodded, and Amir took my cue and continued. "Each back door gets its commands from Microsoft's update servers, which are traditionally used to distribute legitimate bug fixes and security updates to Windows computers."

Again, I nodded.

"The Russian intelligence service also added a back door to Microsoft's update servers, which allows anyone with the Florentine Controller tool to submit attacks to the update servers without Microsoft's knowledge. Once the attack is sent to the update servers, anytime a Windows machine connects to a server to retrieve the latest, legitimate updates, it will also retrieve the attack commands, if any are present—"

"That's my understanding," I interrupted.

"Okay. Let me finish." Amir stood up and began pacing. "In their default configuration from the factory, each Windows computer is configured to contact these update servers once every twenty-four hours, to download these legitimate updates. So within a twenty-four-hour period, all machines that are turned on and connected to the Internet will contact Microsoft's update servers as a matter of course and unknowingly retrieve the attack—along with any other legitimate updates posted by Microsoft—if an attack has been submitted for distribution. Is this correct?"

"Yes."

"Okay. And finally, every attack must be encoded with a special cryptographic authentication key provided by the Russians, or the attack won't be accepted and executed by the back door in Windows. This limits someone who discovers the Florentine system from abusing it, since they won't have a valid key. Is that right as well?"

"Yes."

"Okay. I think I've got it." He paused. "And you are certain that this man, Khalimmy, used the Florentine to launch an attack?"

"Not positive, but I'm pretty sure. They had the entire attack prepped and ready to go. They were waiting for the results of a test run on their own, guinea pig computers, before launching the full-scale attack. When everything went to hell, the other agent began pounding away at his keyboard, and I don't think it was to eliminate evidence. He knew what was coming. I took these from his desk." I pointed to Sami's notes. "Any clues?"

Amir picked up the clutter of college-rule notebook pages and Post-Its and diligently reviewed each.

"This essentially confirms some parts of the attack," he said, shaking his head. "These people are sick, they . . ." He grunted. "When the payload software arrives on a new PC, it goes to sleep," he rifled through the sheets until he arrived at a stained sheet of notebook paper, "until ten a.m. Pacific Time on Wednesday morning. It doesn't say anything about what it does after it triggers. It also lists two Windows settings values. One has a value of 'en-us,' and the other 'he-il.'"

"Ring any bells?" I asked.

"Yes, yes, this makes sense. You said their goal was to attack American and Israeli computer systems. This is how they identify which machines to attack. They are checking to see if the currently configured display language in Windows is either American English—that's the 'en-us' setting—or if it's 'he-il'—that almost certainly stands for 'Hebrew-Israel.' In fact, I configured these very settings for a recent visiting Taiwanese professor who wanted his computer's language changed from English to Traditional Chinese. We set his computer to 'zh-cn.' But with this program, if the machine is configured to use either the English or Hebrew languages, they launch the attack."

"Well, at least that clears up how they identify target machines," I said. "I had assumed they'd use the time-zone setting to decide what computers to terminate."

Amir set down the pages and stared thoughtfully into space.

"You need to contact Microsoft and get them to shut down their update servers, immediately. If, as you say, the Florentine distributes attacks through Microsoft's Windows Update servers, then the faster you shut down those servers, the fewer machines will be able to contact them over the Internet and retrieve the attack program. As for those computers that are already infected, I'm at a loss."

"I agree, but I can't just call Microsoft and ask them to shut down thousands of servers. They'll think I'm crazy, assuming I could even find the right people to call."

"Call your contacts at the NSA then." Amir grabbed his phone and deposited it at the edge of his desk. "Call now."

I habitually reached into my pocket for my smartphone and came up empty.

"Dammit. I don't know how to contact the NSA people I talked to earlier." I picked up Amir's phone and called my old boss at ViruTrax. His voicemail picked up immediately—he was on the phone with someone—so I left a brief message, recited Amir's number into the handset twice, then hung up.

"He'll call right back. He's obsessive about checking his voicemail."

"In the meantime, we must think of a backup plan for those computers that are already infected," said Amir, glancing down at his watch. "On the typical computer, Windows checks the Microsoft Update servers once per day, so roughly one-twenty-fourth of the affected computers would check every hour. So if this man launched the attack three hours ago, up to twelve percent of American computers may have already been infected. Fewer in Israel, where it is in the middle of the night and many computers will be turned off. Even if the NSA can shut down Microsoft's update servers, it won't do anything for those that have already been infected."

"So the question is," he continued, "how can we use the Florentine to cure these infected computers? Could we send a cancellation message—tell the infected computers to abort the attack?"

"Not without the right password." I paged down through Gennady's translation and pointed. "Here. 'When launching an attack with the Florentine, the operator must specify a password and an authentication key in addition to the attack instructions and targeting parameters. After the attack has been launched, it may only be cancelled or have its parameters adjusted by an operator in possession of this original password and the authentication key of the original attack.'

"Any hint on possible passwords or keys in Sami's notes?" I asked.

Amir sat up in his chair and rifled through the crumpled sheets. "The password could be anything. . . . I don't see anything that stands out. There is a number circled here," he held up a Post-It "which could be the authentication key."

"But that's worthless without the password," I lamented.

Amir began pacing the room in thought, then stopped. "Ah!" he said brightly. "I have a solution. We can use the Florentine to send a new command to all of the computers, and instruct them to rewind their internal clocks backward a few days, perhaps even a week or a month back. Say we set the internal clocks of all those computers back forty-eight hours. When the trigger time on Wednesday comes around, all the computers will think it's still today, preventing them from launching the attack. That will give the NSA two extra days to properly fix the problem. Or you could fast-forward the clocks to Wednesday, after ten a.m., and bypass the trigger date completely."

"I considered both options," I said, "but the document says that the Florentine back door in Windows intercepts all attempted changes to the system clock, and adjusts the trigger time of existing payloads accordingly. So rewinding or fast-forwarding the time won't have any effect."

Amir's smile dimmed. "Back to the drawing board then." He glanced at his watch. "Maybe you should try contacting your boss again? Or asking another colleague for the NSA contact number? And perhaps we should experiment with the Florentine software now. That way, should we identify a weakness, we can use it to deploy a cure immediately."

"Okay," I said nervously, "but I feel like we're playing with live explosives. We've got to be extremely careful."

"Don't worry," he said, "I have no desire to be known throughout history as the man who accidentally destroyed the Internet."

I pulled up a plastic chair and sat down next to Amir, launching a second round of calls to every ViruTrax extension I could remember, while Amir began his detailed review of the translated document and the accompanying files. John Wong, one of my first mentors at the company and now the company's oldest engineer at seventy, answered just as I was about to slam the handset down on my ninth attempt. I dispensed with pleasantries, asking immediately for Rod's number. Sensing my urgency, John suppressed his usual chatty repartee and pulled up Rod's page in the corporate directory, repeated both his extension and private cell phone number twice for me, and then forwarded me to his work number.

Rod's work extension reverted to voicemail after four rings, so I left Amir's number and was about to try his cell when Amir raised his finger in warning. I cradled the receiver and gestured for him to talk.

"I've changed my thinking. Hear me out. If the NSA shuts down the update servers, there will be no way to distribute a cure using the Florentine system. That means the tens of millions of computers that have already received the attack command will be damaged permanently. That's not acceptable. We have the means to restore all of those computers, if we can just identify a clever cure. You could call your friend Rod, but even if he were able to get hold of the NSA, it would take them hours to safely retrieve you and the Florentine, then additional precious hours to debrief you and understand its operation and attempt to use it to deploy an antidote. By that time, it will be too late. If, as you say, Windows systems check Microsoft's update servers once every twenty-four hours, most of the infected systems wouldn't have a chance to receive the cure until well after the detonation event. No," he continued after consulting his wristwatch, "the only viable solution is to do this ourselves."

I considered his argument and came to the same conclusion. He was right; the timing was just too tight, and even a couple hours of delay would subject tens of millions of computers to assured destruction. But the thought of placing hundreds of millions of both nations' computers in the hands of two private citizens was madness. I opened my mouth to raise my objection, but Amir shook his head.

"No, Alex. There is no other option." Amir took my silence as agreement and continued.

"Now, as we reviewed earlier, the software requires three different parameters to launch a new attack." Amir double-clicked an icon, and a command shell window popped up on his desktop; he then keyed in "florentine.exe" and hit the Enter key. The computer paused briefly, then a firewall alert popped up:

> *The software Florentine.exe is attempting to connect to the Internet. Do you want to [Allow once], [Allow always], or [Block]?*

Amir ignored the warning, clicking "Allow always" as fast as his aging hands could manage. An instant later, the program printed the following on the screen:

Использование: florentine.exe ключи.dat пароль нагрузка.dat
florentine.exe -o ключи.dat пароль нагрузка.dat

He said, "When you run the software without the proper parameters, it prints out a line that explains what parameters the tool expects the operator to provide. According to your friend's translation, the first parameter," he pointed to ключи.*dat*, "specifies a data file that holds an authentication key. Without a proper key, the back door in Windows will ignore the attack command. This prevents the system from being hijacked by an adversary. Each cryptographic authentication key can be used just once to launch an attack, and once, if necessary, to cancel a previously launched attack prior to its execution." Amir clicked his mouse and brought up a second window containing nearly a dozen 256-digit sequences. "Fortunately, the Florentine package came with ten such cryptographic keys—enough to launch ten attacks. These were in the Florentine.keys data file."

"Like launch codes the President carries around for arming our nukes," I said.

"Yes. And based on what you've told me, I assume the first few keys have already been used by the Iranian agents, to prepare for and launch their attack." He picked up one of Sami's yellow Post-Its and pointed to an eight-digit number scrawled at the top. "See. These digits here match the first eight digits of the first key in the file. So my inclination is to start with the last key and work our way up."

He clicked back on the original window, bringing it into focus. "The second parameter," he pointed his finger at the пароль, "specifies the cancellation password. When you launch a new attack, you must specify a new password. The password is then required, along with the original key, to cancel the attack at a later time. And the third parameter specifies the name of a payload file that contains the details of the attack timing, machine targeting, and the attack program itself. The Controller tool connects to the Microsoft Update servers over the Internet and sends the key, password, and payload to them for distribution."

"What's the 'dash-o' for?" I asked.

"That's the cancellation command. If you add a '-o' to the command line with the proper key and password, it transmits an abort command to the server. Unfortunately, even though we have the keys used by the Persian operatives, without their password, there will be no way to cancel their previous payload. Our only option is to send a new attack that somehow negates the earlier one."

We next reviewed how to create a Florentine attack program. Each attack program included a series of instructions that would be executed on each computer at the designated trigger time. An attack program could check conditions on the computer, such as the computer's display language, its address on the Internet, the names of users on the machine, and dozens of others, and then conditionally perform or exclude parts of the attack based upon those conditions.

"There are several example programs in the PDF file—I found them while you were making calls," he said. "And if necessary, you can launch more-complex attacks using an embedded machine code module."

"That's probably what Khalimmy and Sami used to trash the firmware chips."

"Yes, there's no evidence of any built-in commands to alter or destroy the contents of the firmware. They almost certainly had to add a special module of their own to do this."

Amir consulted his watch again. "So we have roughly nine or ten hours of remaining time to come up with an antidote and upload it to the update servers. If we can do so before ten a.m. tomorrow, that will give the population of machines exactly twenty-four hours of time to retrieve our antidote commands, the minimum duration required for all the machines to connect at least once to the update servers, at least those that are powered on during this period."

"The big question is how we cancel the attack," I said, just as a knock came at the door. I spun around in alarm.

"It's okay, Alex. I'm sure it's just a student." Amir patted me on the back and then walked over to the door, turning the knob three-quarters of the way to the open position, before hesitating and asking, "Who is it?"

"It's Terry. Have you got a second? Johan forgot his password again."

Amir pulled the door open a crack. "I'm sorry Terry. I've got an emergency I'm dealing with right now. Can you have Johan call up the Engineering helpdesk?"

"I'll tell him but he won't be happy. Last time he spent two hours on hold before someone picked up."

"I understand. Please apologize for me, and tell him I'll try to stop by later if I have time." Amir eased the door shut and returned to his chair. "These emeritus professors can't tie their own shoes without assistance," he snorted, "let alone operate modern computers."

"Amir, is there any chance we could move to a more secure location?"

"Why? We're perfectly safe here. And no one knows you're here. Correct?"

"Only a close friend. But Khalimmy managed to locate me at my friends' house, and the Russians managed to locate Khalimmy's hideout as well. So I'm not so sure . . ."

Amir considered this. "I have a small hardware storage room in the Cellar. It's not very pleasant, but it's got power, and only a few people know I've taken over the room."

"The Boelter Cellar?" I asked. A graveyard for maintenance equipment and other digital detritus accumulated during Boelter Hall's fifty-plus years of existence, the Cellar would be a perfect hiding place. Accessible only from the seldom-visited second-floor atrium area in the middle of Boelter Hall, most students didn't even know the cavernous junkyard existed, or for that matter, how to reach the atrium.

"That would be perfect. Does it have an Internet connection?" I asked.

"No direct connection, but we can use the department's Wi-Fi network. The area is directly underneath the large Boelter 3400 lecture hall."

"It's settled then. Let's grab some food from the Engineering café and head down."

Chapter 60

LADEN WITH LAPTOPS, power strips and bags of plastic-wrapped pre-made sandwiches, protein bars, and energy drinks, Amir and I rode the southwest Boelter elevator down to the second floor, rounded the corner, and then stepped down into the atrium. The courtyard's fallen leaves crackled under our feet as we moved silently, both in brain-storming mode, across the open space and to the Cellar entrance.

"Hold this." Amir handed me his laptop and fished in his pocket for a keycard.

"Wow. This never used to be locked. Hell, the doors used to always be propped wide open when I was a student."

"Times have changed, Alex." He shook his head disappointedly. "They put card readers on all of the doors after a rash of comput-er-equipment burglaries last year."

Amir slipped the card from his pocket and waved it past the card reader along the right side of the gray metal door; the electronic door lock clicked immediately. Amir gazed suggestively at the handle, so I grabbed it and eased the heavy warehouse-style door open.

"One second," he said, navigating around a heap of sixties com-puter equipment, "hold the door until I find the light switches."

Amir knocked something over, cursed in Farsi, and a few seconds later, a seemingly random collection of overhead fluorescent lights began flickering listlessly, emitting just enough illumination to cast the helter-skelter graveyard of discarded engineering equipment in ominous shadows.

"Spooky," I said. "Looks just like it did five years ago when we used to go dumpster diving in here. Only dustier. You know, back during junior year, we found parts of the control panel of Boelter's original nuclear reactor in a pile over there. Just sitting there, totally covered in dust. My friends also used to enter the underground steam tunnels from here. That door over there at the far end," I pointed into the back wall, "supposedly leads to a tunnel under the Court of the Sciences."

"It's amazing you and your crew were never expelled," he said, piloting around an engineering desk covered with stacks of dust-covered PDP-11 mainframe manuals. "Follow me. Carefully."

Amir wended his way through the islands of discarded equipment, heading toward the right wall of the fan-shaped room. He stopped at a metal door set into the grimy concrete wall and pulled out an enormous key ring.

"Welcome to my vault," he said, fingering through the two dozen keys decorating the ring. "It's not much but it's all mine." He stopped when he reached a hexagonal brass key, and unlocked the door.

Amir's vault stood in stark contrast to the chaotic main storeroom, clean and bright. He'd removed the depressing overhead fluorescent bulbs and replaced them with four large halogen floor lamps. Rows of individually labeled cardboard boxes with names like "Ethernet Cables," "Ethernet Cards," "Wi-Fi Cards," "SATA Cards," and "Cabling Tools" lined wire-mesh shelves along the left and right walls. Along the back wall, a sixties-era desk held several neat stacks of paperwork, and to its side a half-height dorm-room refrigerator hummed softly.

"Dump the computer over there," he pointed at the desk, "and throw the drinks and food in the cooler, please."

He dropped his load onto the desk as well, propped the metal door open, and disappeared into the ersatz equipment graveyard. He returned a minute later with a dust-covered leather desk chair.

"This was Dean Boelter's, believe it or not. For the next twenty-four hours, it will be yours. Grab a paper towel from the roll on the cooler and wipe the dust off outside, then it's back to work."

"I've been thinking," he said while I wheeled in the wiped-off chair. "We know that the Florentine has a module that runs inside of Windows on every PC. That module is responsible for monitoring for incoming attack payloads from Microsoft's update servers, then launching each attack at its designated trigger time. If we can't trick this module by changing the time, could we possibly send a command to delete the module altogether? If we could remove the time-triggering module itself, this would solve all our problems."

"Like removing the timer from a time bomb." I chewed on my lower lip and considered the idea. "Even though the bomb is still functional, it can't trigger without the timer, and is rendered benign. It's a good idea. The challenge is, this module could be hidden anywhere inside of Windows. Even if we found it, it could take days to figure out how to safely disable it."

Amir shook his head glumly. "Back to the drawing board."

"Not a bad idea though, just not practical given our tight timing. But it does give me another idea, a plan of last resort, really."

"What's that?" he said, swiveling his chair around.

"Well, even if we can't figure out how to locate and disable the Florentine component that's hidden *within* Windows, we can easily attack Windows itself. We could delete essential Windows system files so it simply can't function. Like ripping the spark plugs out of a car engine. And if Windows can't run, then the Florentine module hidden inside it can't run either: or for that matter, activate its payload."

A puzzled look materialized on Amir's face. "You're suggesting that we attack every computer in the United States and Israel, and kill Windows on all those computers, before the Florentine has a chance to do so itself? The cure is as bad as the disease, no?"

"No. Deleting a few Windows files is temporary. That can be fixed in just a few hours or days. Khalimmy's firmware attack is permanent—those machines will be turned into paperweights."

"But the devastation . . ."

"Yes, it's an option of last resort. It would cause a massive disruption—probably billions in lost business during the outage. But it would be temporary. Everything would be back up and running in a few days. And if we scheduled such an attack to trigger at 9:55 a.m. on Wednesday morning: say, five minutes before Khalimmy's attack, then his payload would never get a chance to run. Meanwhile, that would give the NSA, or Department of Homeland Security, or whoever, time to come up with a permanent cure."

Amir mulled over the idea some more, then nodded. "You're right, it is an option, but it should be our last option." He cleared his throat.

"Agreed," I said. "Let's create the attack and keep it in our back pocket for now."

I sat down at the desk and motioned for Amir to join me.

"Now if I recall correctly from my virus analysis days, there are about four or five key files that are involved in the boot-up of Windows—after each one starts up and performs its task, it proceeds to load the next file in the series, until Windows is fully up and running. All of them are critical. If even one of them is missing, Windows won't start. These files are often targeted by viruses, because if the virus can inject its logic into one of them, it gets control of the entire computer immediately when it starts up."

As Amir processed this, I pulled up the network settings on his laptop and connected it to the Computer Science Wi-Fi network; the signal was extremely weak—just one bar—but sufficient for our purposes.

"So if we delete one or more of these files, the computer crashes?" he said.

"Not quite. Once the computer is up and running, deleting these files probably won't cause any problems: Windows will continue to run normally because the files are only involved in the startup process. But the next time computer is restarted, it'll crash immediately, certainly long before the Florentine component has a chance to load."

"I see. So we need to not only remove these files, but also reboot the computer to ensure that it crashes."

"Correct," I replied. "Now if I'm not mistaken, each version of Windows uses a slightly different set of files to start up. So, to make sure we can cause all versions of Windows to crash, we're going to have to identify a different set of files to delete for each major version of Windows."

Amir eyed his watch nervously.

"We'll have time." I pulled up Google in Amir's web browser and searched for "windows startup process." After a few minutes of hunting, we found web pages that described the boot-up sequences for Windows XP, Windows 2000, Windows Vista, Windows 7, and Windows 8: all the major versions. I cut-and-pasted the names of the operating system files involved in starting up each version of Windows into a document file, so we could see them all in one place.

"Each version of Windows uses a slightly different set of files to start up," commented Amir.

"Not quite. If you look closely," I pointed with my finger, "all of them share one file in common: NTOSKRNL.EXE. If we delete that file, I believe we'll be able to crash all versions of Windows, at least all the major ones."

Amir considered this, then nodded in agreement. I opened up the Notepad application on Windows and began to type in the payload script, consulting the example attack payloads that were included in the Florentine PDF. Amir leaned in and watched from behind as I typed.

```
TRIGGER-CRITERIA-BEGIN
    DATE=09/06/2015
    TIME=17:55:00GMT
TRIGGER-CRITERIA-END
PAYLOAD-PROGRAM-BEGIN
    IF (oslang == "en-us" OR oslang == "he-il")
        THEN DELETE %SystemRoot%\system32\
        ntoskrnl.exe
    ENDIF
PAYLOAD-PROGRAM-END
```

"That should do it," I said. "This will trigger at 5:55 p.m. GMT this coming Wednesday, which is 9:55 a.m. Pacific Standard Time, five minutes *before* Khalimmy's attack is supposed to trigger."

Amir lifted his glasses and reviewed the trigger criteria. "I concur."

"Good, let's review the payload now. Our payload first checks to see if the system is configured to use either English or Hebrew. This is the same criteria Khalimmy used, as far as we know, to identify which machines to target. If a machine uses either language, then our payload deletes the ntoskrnl.exe file. Otherwise our payload does nothing. Did I make any mistakes?"

Amir leaned in and studied the three-line program.

"No," he said, running his index finger down the screen for a second review. "There are no problems I can see." I moved the mouse over the Save button and clicked.

"Wait," he said. "You're missing the reboot command that will cause the machines to restart and then crash."

"Good catch," I said, adding a line with the word "REBOOT" after the "DELETE" line. "Look okay now?" I asked.

"Yes," he said, after pausing to reread the entire program. Receiving his blessing, I saved the payload into a file called Antidote.dat.

"Now let's reserve one of the authentication keys and pick a password."

He shook his head. "You know, it's scary that in just ten lines, you've got the power to crash hundreds of millions of computers, to potentially alter the path of entire economies . . ."

"It is scary," I agreed.

I switched windows to the file containing the ten Florentine authentication keys and copied the last 256-digit key into a new file called Key.dat. Finally, I opened up a command shell where I could type in the command to launch the attack.

"Okay, pick a password we can use to cancel the attack, if need be."

"Shamshiri," Amir said.

"Like the restaurant?" I asked, referring to the popular Persian eatery near campus.

"Yes, it means 'sword' in Farsi. We are the defensive sword."

"I guess we are," I said, typing in the command line:

```
C:\TEMP>  FLORENTINE.EXE  KEY.DAT  SHAMSHIRI
ANTIDOTE.TAD
```

"Don't hit Enter!" said Amir nervously.

"Don't worry." I swiveled the chair around and patted him on the shoulder. "I intentionally misspelled the name of the payload file, Antidote.tad—it should be '.dat', not '.tad'. If and when we're ready to launch the attack, I'll fix the spelling and then hit Enter."

"I am getting slow in my old age." He patted my back reciprocally. "So if we are to give all of the machines at least twenty-four hours to retrieve our Shamshiri payload, we need to launch the antidote before ten a.m. tomorrow morning, at the latest?"

"At the latest. Plus there's a chance we'll run into some problem or other, so I'd suggest we limit our launch time to no later than eight a.m. tomorrow morning. And the same holds true if we want to send a cancellation command. In order for the cancellation to reach every machine, we also have to launch it at least twenty-four hours prior to the original payload trigger time. Otherwise, there's no guarantee all the machines will check the update server and see it."

Amir reflected. "I hadn't considered that. It's another good point. Well, hopefully we won't have to launch this attack in the first place, let alone send out a cancellation." He stood up, stretched, and yawned. "So now we must focus on a less destructive solution. There must be something we're missing, some clever fix."

"Occam's razor," I suggested.

"Yes, exactly, an Occam's razor solution but without the sharp edge." Amir put his hand over his pocket. "Hold on a second." He pulled out a cell phone. "Hello?" . . . "What? Nelson's hurt?" . . . "Oh God. Is he okay? Did you call an ambulance?" . . . "Good, good. I'll be right up."

Amir clicked off his phone and took a step toward the door. "Professor Keller was found wandering aimlessly on the seventh floor with a bruise on his forehead. He must have fallen. He's been having balance problems. Can you manage for fifteen or twenty minutes without me?"

"Go," I said. "I'll keep brainstorming."

Amir dashed out of the room. I stood up and began pacing in thought.

After a few minutes of fruitless ruminating, I propped open the door and stepped back into the main Cellar area. Perhaps a walk between the old stacks of junk would help stimulate my creative juices.

I wandered through the mounds, stopping at an eighties-era metal desk entirely covered with thick textbooks. Crouching down on my haunches, I began dusting off their spines one at a time with my finger. *Introduction to Bioengineering*, *Organic Chemistry II*, and *A History of Life* successively emerged from beneath the filth. I flipped open the top cover of *Introduction to Bioengineering* in search of an inscription. A label on the first page read "From the library of Irving Whitman."

"Probably long dead," I muttered, "otherwise maybe you'd have some ideas for me."

I scraped the dust from my finger on the underside of the desk, then tried its drawers: all locked. A challenge. My first-year UCLA roommate had taught me how to pick simple locks with a couple of heavy-duty paperclips, so I grabbed a handful from the desk in Amir's vault and returned to test my skills.

"How is defending against Khalimmy's attack like picking a lock?" I asked myself. I'd found that out-of-the-box questions like that sometimes resulted in interesting insights. This one did not, but after a bit of fumbling in the wavering gloom of the overhead lights, the lock clicked anyway. I pulled the left drawer open and rummaged inside. The drawer held a spare pair of thick-rimmed, black plastic glasses with quarter-inch-thick bifocal lenses, a half-full bottle of Jameson whiskey, and a tumbler.

I tried the right drawer and found a stack of yellowing exams. A thin, shiny-covered picture book sat partially covered at the base of the drawer under the stack. I pulled it out. *How Animals Hide: Camouflage Techniques of the Animal Kingdom* read the title. I flipped through the glossy color photos, catching successive glimpses of a salamander, a stick insect, and a flounder in the blur of pages. Who knew that flounder could change their skin colors? Not me.

I dropped the book back on top of the stack and eased the drawer shut.

Then the solution hit me like a load of bricks, or rather a net full of flounder.

Chapter 61

I RACED BACK TO AMIR'S LAPTOP, grabbed a soda from the refrigerator, and in just five minutes had created a new payload, actually two new payloads—my plan required a two-phase approach—and saved them under the names Flounder1.dat and Flounder2.dat. In another three minutes, I'd selected two new authentication keys—the next two from the bottom of the list of ten—picked a new cancellation password, and prepared the two command lines to submit my new payloads to the Microsoft Update servers. Eight minutes flat: an Occam's razor solution if there ever was one. Assuming the approach was sound—and this, I wanted Amir to corroborate—all I needed to do was hit the Enter key twice to submit the two payloads, and Khalimmy's impending attack would be fully neutralized, with little collateral damage, by five minutes after ten a.m. on Wednesday morning.

But where was Amir? I had no way of contacting him without leaving the Cellar, so I returned to the laptop and began reviewing my logic, running through every possible contingency. I couldn't find any flaws, but I needed him to double check. I rubbed my eyes and looked over at the wall clock. He'd been gone for nearly two hours.

Something was definitely wrong.

I tucked the laptop under my arm, then worked my way around the piles to the Cellar's exit. Amir hadn't left me his keycard, so I grabbed several thick manuals from the nearest desk and propped open the door as I left. Just in case.

If I wasn't mistaken, and it *had* been a long time, Nelson Keller's office was in a suite on the fourth floor. The emeritus professor, who was considered prehistoric when I was an undergrad and prattled incessantly about programming with punch cards, was almost certainly near death at this point. I took off toward the northwest stairwell to head up.

I reached the pair of glass doors leading from the atrium to the second-floor hallway, pulled the door open halfway, and stopped cold;

standing no more than ten feet down the hall was a solid-looking guy in a blue suit, a cellphone at his ear, talking in what could only be described as agitated Russian.

How the hell did they find me? I eased the door closed, and just as I released the handle, the man turned around and headed for the elevator. He nodded to me curtly as he passed. I nodded back, as nonchalantly as possible, then did an about-face and began walking unhurriedly back to Cellar. At about ten steps from the Cellar door, I heard his voice again. I turned my head reflexively to look back; his eyes stared intently at me as he continued talking calmly into the phone in Russian. I kept walking.

When I reached the Cellar door, I took another look back—the phone was gone and the guy was surveying the atrium warily. Then his right hand reached inside his navy blue coat.

I wrenched open the door, kicked the manuals out of the way and slammed it shut behind me. I'd be safe for the time being—the guy wasn't going to raise hell blasting through the metal door with a pistol. I scanned the dimly lit grotto for a campus phone to call 911. Nothing. Nor did Amir have one in his vault.

My mind blanked as I tried to concentrate, to identify my options. Then I heard it: the click of the metal door's lock. Somehow the guy had obtained a keycard. Shit.

The door opened slowly, just a crack, casting a narrow strip of light along the right wall. Acting entirely on instinct, I threw my body up against the door, slamming it shut, then slapped my hand down on the light switch and dashed around the back of the closest heap of junk. The room was now totally dark. Laptop under my left arm, right hand out in front, I edged forward on my knees toward the back of the room.

The door clicked again, then opened. An instant later, the overhead fluorescents flickered back to life. This was it. I was dead.

"Excuse me," came a voice—Amir's voice—from outside. "Can I help you?"

"Building maintenance," said the man in brusque, Russian-accented English.

"I'm sorry, but this is a restr . . ."

I didn't wait for Amir to finish. I rose, fumbled left around a dented, six-foot-tall metal-mainframe chassis, and sprinted toward the rear door.

Expecting it to stick from years of disuse, I wrenched the handle and the door flew outward, nearly slamming into my face as I reeled backward. I dropped down and inched through the doorway, yanking the door shut behind me.

The cinderblock walls of the tunnel stretched off a good fifty or more feet without any obvious hiding places so I took off, sidestepping down the corridor to avoid the angry-looking plumbing, wiring, and electrical boxes strapped along both walls. After about thirty seconds of gentle uphill travel, the narrow passage opened up into a four-way intersection.

I was now almost certainly under the Court of the Sciences, or maybe a bit farther east, under the Geology building or Young Hall. While I hadn't navigated the steam tunnels before, I'd heard endless stories about ways to access the network of passageways, and if my memory served me, a doorway in the basement of Franz Hall was my closest option for escape. I turned left into the wider artery, heading toward north campus and Franz Hall, Amir's laptop cradled under my left arm. With each step, the heat increased. It was now easily eighty degrees and uncomfortably humid; overhead, bare light bulbs hung from aging PVC piping bolted into the concrete ceiling, painting the tunnel's walls a harsh, artificial white.

The passage took a hard right turn after another hundred and fifty feet or so. I turned to look back but as I did, the cement wall to my left exploded in burst of tiny fragments.

Shit. I dashed right and sprinted about fifteen feet, then hit another T-shaped intersection. If my mental map was correct, I was either under or nearly under Franz Hall. I turned right toward the south, hoping to find an exit into Franz's basement. Behind me I heard echoes of running footsteps—he was getting closer. The passage veered left again. I followed the bend, walked four steps, and ran into a solid wooden door bearing a plaque labeled "Franz Basement."

I grabbed the metal doorknob and cranked it counterclockwise. The knob hesitated a millisecond, then twisted clear off the door and into my hand. "Dead end," I whispered to myself, "literally." A large drop of sweat trickled down from my right temple onto my cheek.

Louder footsteps, more hesitant now. He couldn't be more than fifteen or twenty feet away. I had a fifty-fifty chance. If he veered left at the T, he'd almost certainly get lost in the larger network of tunnels heading to the north campus. If he chose right, it was game over.

Even odds were unacceptable. I edged up to the bend and hurled the doorknob north, past the last intersection, then backed up and stood deathly still. Before the knob finished clattering along the floor, the Russian bolted northward after it. I lingered until his footfalls faded and then walked stealthily back around the loop, sprinting once I reached the main north-south artery.

One thing was clear. Whether or not I ultimately survived, I needed to launch the antidote as soon as possible. With God-knows-how-many other Russian agents patrolling the Engineering school, I couldn't afford to vet my solution with Amir, assuming he was even still alive. Any delay, and I might not get a second chance.

I slowed as I approached the four-way intersection, turned right, and began sidestepping down the middle of the narrow passage back to the Cellar.

I reached for the door handle, then jerked reflexively as a pipe a few feet behind my head exploded in a blistering burst of steam. A second bullet smacked into the wooden door in front of me. I pulled the door open and jumped through, slamming it shut behind me, then made a split-second decision—I needed at least thirty uninterrupted seconds to launch the attack, and while Amir's storage vault was a dead end and a likely death sentence, the atrium offered no cover whatsoever; I'd be a sitting duck. I slalomed around the piles toward Amir's vault, kicked up its doorstop, and slammed the door closed.

The first of the shots smacked into the metal door just as the laptop finished waking from its hibernation mode. The Russian rattled the door, then fired another shot into the lock. A combination of fear and adrenaline caused my fingers to shake near uncontrollably, but I managed to switch windows and hit the Enter key to launch the first phase of my antidote. The program launched and quickly printed "обработка . . ." then paused a second, then two, then three.

Why was it taking so long? Was it working?

I heard a kick, then another, and turned to see the metal door crash open. I returned my gaze to the screen and switched windows to launch the second phase of my cure but before I could hit the Enter key, my body lurched forward and onto the desk. No pain, somehow, but the gunshot's blast registered a millisecond later in my ears. I heard a second blast and a scream, probably my own, as my vision grayed and I lost consciousness.

Chapter 62

"ALEX, CAN YOU HEAR ME?"

"Mmmmmm?"

"I think he's awake," said my mother, excitedly. "Alex?"

"Yes," I said, my mouth unbelievably dry. "Can I get some . . ." The word wouldn't come.

"Water?" responded my mother. I felt a hand, her hand, squeeze and then let go of mine.

"Yes."

My mind latched on to the rhythmic beeping of a heart rate monitor—I was in a hospital. Again. I tried to sit up but was rewarded with searing pain in my back and stomach. I groaned and tried to open my eyes. That lasted all of about two seconds.

"Don't move, Alex." It was my father.

"Here," said Mom. She inserted a straw into my mouth and I sipped weakly. When she removed the straw, she continued. "Need anything else?"

"No," I said, again fixating on the pulsating beeps. Beep . . . Beep . . . Beep . . . "What . . . what happened to . . ." The name wouldn't come.

"To who, Alex?"

I couldn't remember. "The world is going to end," I mumbled.

"No, everything's going to be fine, honey. Just rest and everything will be fine."

I tried to concentrate. Why was the world going to end? "The world is going to end at . . . ten. What time is it?" I tried to sit up again. Again, stabbing pain. The monitor's beeping quickened.

"No honey, everything's going to be fine. Just relax."

I was certain she was wrong, but I wasn't sure exactly why. "*Moooommmm*," I pleaded.

"It's actually a few minutes before ten, Alex. You'll see, everything will be just fine. You're just a little sedated right now so you're having strange thoughts. It will pass soon."

"Amir!" I cried. It was slowly coming back. I opened my eyes again. My mother and father blurred in and out of focus. "Can I get some more water?" Mom placed the straw between my lips and I drank again, this time until I was sucking air. "More?"

"Who's Amir?" asked my father.

"Amir is . . . Amir . . ." I couldn't quite find the words to explain. "But is he okay?"

I heard a pouring noise and shifted my gaze over to Mom, but couldn't focus on her.

"We don't know who Amir is, honey," she said. "Can you tell us?"

I couldn't. I shook my head weakly. Beep . . . Beep . . . Beep . . .

"The world is going to end at ten a.m. . . . . on . . ." then it came to me, "Wednesday."

"No, honey, everything will be fine. Here, take another sip."

Again, she placed the straw between my lips and I sucked.

Then the heart monitor stopped beeping.

Three seconds later, the lights went out.

Chapter 63

"I THINK WE'RE READY TO BEGIN, MR. FIFE."

I gave a thumbs-up to the agent. Amir, seated next to me in an ill-fitting gray suit, an arm sling, and his signature Mickey Mouse watch, patted me on the back with his good arm and delivered the proud smile of a father as I rose to take my place behind the podium.

"Good afternoon, everyone." The agent tapped on the microphone several times to quiet the audience, then continued, "Good afternoon. Today I'm pleased to introduce our speaker, Mr. Alex Fife. Mr. Fife will be briefing our team on the recent Iranian-initiated Florentine cyber-attack. Before we begin, I needn't remind any of you that this briefing has been classified top secret. Alex," he smiled at me, "your reputation already precedes you here at the NSA, but for those who have been conducting signal intelligence in Antarctica over the last few years, let me give a brief bio. . . ."

"Thank you, that was very kind," I said once he finished. I removed a stack of notecards from my suit pocket and walked behind the podium. Before me sat nearly two dozen agents from various three-letter American and Israeli agencies. I smiled at the crowd.

"Hello everyone. I'm excited to be here, and frankly happy to be alive at this point—the past month and a half have been quite harrowing. Before I begin, I'd like to say a few words about your colleague, Doctor Arnold Altschiller. By now, you all probably know that Doctor Altschiller was murdered four weeks ago, while in service to his country. While Doctor Altschiller was obviously one of the world's, no, *the* world's most influential cryptographer, he was also an inspiration and role model. And in fact his career—his discoveries and innovations—are what inspired me to pursue my career in cyber-security. So I owe Doctor Altschiller a great personal debt, as does our country." I took a sip of water, then cleared my throat and continued.

"Four weeks ago, on Wednesday, September 6, at 9:55 a.m. Pacific Standard Time, the United States and Israel experienced the largest computing outage in the history of the world. As I'll discuss in more detail shortly, hundreds of millions of computers in our two countries simultaneously reset themselves at this exact moment, creating a major hiccup in cyberspace and temporarily taking large swaths of our nation's physical infrastructure offline. Of course, as most of you also know by now, I was responsible for this 'hiccup.' But in my defense, the alternative would have been much, much worse."

My host nodded; the rest of the audience stared stoically.

"So how did we get here? My understanding is that you've all been briefed on the Russian Florentine document, so I'll skip over the background and go straight to the timeline.

"As early as six months ago, a leaked SVR software package that granted access to the Florentine system found its way onto the black market. For purposes of clarity, let's call this software package the 'Florentine Controller.' An attacker in possession of the Controller could use it to upload up to ten attack payloads to Microsoft's update servers, for immediate worldwide distribution and activation via the Florentine back door.

"Shortly after the Controller's initial availability on the black market, members of the Iranian intelligence services contacted the broker, Mr. Richard Lister, with an offer to purchase it. Their goal? To decimate computing infrastructures of the United States and Israel.

"Okay, so here's the detailed timeline." I clicked my presentation remote. The screen cleared and an empty timeline appeared.

"Over the past few years, a small team of hackers led by Iranian operative Arnaz Khalimmy engineered a software payload capable of scrambling the firmware chips of most major computer models." I clicked my remote and an Iranian flag jutted up from the timeline. "Needless to say, this would turn most PCs and servers into paperweights. The team apparently experimented with using computer viruses, or more likely, worms, to deliver their payload, but quickly found these vectors inadequate. So until their discovery of the Florentine, they had no means of widely distributing their attack.

"By Sunday, September 3, roughly four weeks ago, I had obtained a copy of the Florentine Controller software, and immediately after determining its nature, contacted the NSA. Unfortunately, shortly after my call—"

"Excuse me," interrupted a man in a dark green cardigan. "Before you continue, can anyone from NSA briefly explain why we didn't just shut down the Florentine system when Mr. Fife first reported it?"

"I'll field this one." Jon Whitehouse raised his hand. "Sorry for the interruption, Mr. Fife. In answer to your question, Phil, at the time Mr. Fife reported the Florentine system to NSA, we had no intel of any in-progress or imminent attacks. Nor could Mr. Fife communicate any details about the system, since he was calling on an insecure line. So when he disappeared, all we could do was dispatch a team into fact-finding mode. Let's take this one offline, but I can fill you in later if you'd like."

"I would, thank you," said the man in the cardigan. "The Senate Subcommittee on Cyber-security is on the verge of conducting an inquisition, and we'd better have our story straight." He paused a beat for others to comment. "Sorry Mr. Fife, please continue."

"As I was saying," I continued with a frown, "shortly after my call to the NSA, Arnaz Khalimmy kidnapped me to obtain a copy of the Controller software. And by late Sunday night, his team had completed a benign, dry-run test of the Controller to ensure its authenticity."

I clicked my remote and a flag bearing the words "Iranian Dry Run Test Launched" appeared on the timeline at eleven p.m. on Sunday.

"Now, unbeknownst to the Iranian team—and to us at the time—the Russians had embedded a tracking beacon into the Controller software. Not surprising, given its immense strategic value. We now know that this beacon activates and sends geo-location data back to a Russian-controlled server any time a user activates the Controller software.

"By all accounts, the Russians were alerted by this beacon at the time of the Iranian dry run, and by ten-thirty the next morning, an SVR 'cleaner' team arrived at Mr. Khalimmy's base of operations, a safe house in North Hollywood, California. The SVR operatives quickly neutralized the Iranian team, but not before the lead Iranian engineer had uploaded the live firmware-killing payload to the Microsoft Update servers for distribution. I don't believe the Russian team realized this, and even if they had, they lacked the password required to cancel the attack."

Another click of my remote caused a flag to appear on the timeline at ten-thirty a.m. Monday, bearing the words "Iranian Live Payload Launched."

I took a sip of water, scanned the room for questions, and finding no hands, continued.

"So what were the timing and triggering criteria of the live Iranian attack? First, the Iranian team chose a payload trigger time of ten a.m. Wednesday—two days later. This deadline was chosen to ensure ample time—nearly forty-eight hours—for the world's population of computers to download the attack payload from Microsoft's Windows Update servers prior to the payload's trigger deadline. We now know, thanks to assistance from some of your colleagues, that during this forty-eight-hour period, the Florentine system distributed the Iranian attack to nearly one-and-a-quarter-billion computers of all makes and models around the world."

A hand shot up, this one from a woman dressed in a prim navy skirt and white blouse. "I'm sorry, you said the attack was distributed worldwide? Not just to American and Israeli computers? I thought that the attack was just targeted at computers in our two countries?"

"Good questions. The Florentine was designed to launch large-scale, blitzkrieg-style cyber attacks, not conduct pinpoint cyber espionage. As such, the way the system works is that every Windows computer around the world downloads every available Florentine payload from the Windows Update servers. Once a payload arrives on a computer, it's responsible for checking whether the machine meets its criteria, and if so, it activates. If not, the payload silently self-destructs. The Iranian payload checked the language settings of all 1.25 billion computers it landed on, and only launched its firmware attack on those bearing a language setting of American-style English, or Hebrew."

"Very interesting. Thank you."

"Not a problem." I continued. "So at ten a.m. Wednesday, the Iranian payload activated on machines around the world." I clicked the remote and two laptop computer icons, one labeled "American" and the second labeled "Israeli," appeared on the timeline. A beat later, a mushroom-cloud graphic rose atop both computer icons.

"Of course, as we all know now, the attack largely failed. However, it did not fail due to any programming errors on the part of the Iranians. Their payload, we now know, was perfectly lethal. Nor did it fail because of SVR intervention."

A few members of the audience nodded energetically in dawned understanding; others regarded me with confused stares.

"With the help of my good friend, Amir Taheri," I smiled at Amir in the front row and he returned a gentle wink in return, "I identified a flaw in the Iranian payload's targeting approach and created my own Florentine payload, an antidote if you will, to stave off the attack. Actually, technically I created two payloads—a two-part antidote."

I paused a moment for questions, then continued. "So how did my two-part antidote work?"

I clicked the remote and an animated flounder swam onto the screen.

"Of all places, I got the idea from a children's book on animal camouflage, from the flounder fish—also known by its taxonomic name, *Bothus mancus*. This remarkable animal is capable of temporarily changing the color and pattern of its skin to match those of the sea floor when it senses danger. This gave me an idea: if the Iranian payload was looking for American and Israeli computers, or to be more precise, computers with English or Hebrew language settings, then why not camouflage all those computers—just prior to the Iranian payload's trigger time—to look like computers from a different country?

"And that's exactly what the first part of my antidote did. My first payload, which I called 'Flounder1,' started by checking to see if each computer was configured to use either English or Hebrew, the two languages I knew the Iranian payload targeted for its firmware attack. If a computer used either language, my Flounder1 payload first created a backup of the computer's original language setting so this could be restored later. It then changed the computer's language setting to Japanese, effectively camouflaging the computer to look like one from Japan rather than one from America or Israel. Finally, Flounder1 forced a reboot of the computer, to ensure the changes took effect. I programmed Flounder1 with a trigger time of 9:55 a.m. Pacific Standard Time on Wednesday morning, ensuring it would run exactly five minutes prior to the Iranian payload's trigger time."

I clicked the remote; the large flounder swam off the right side of the screen and the timeline returned. Then a small flounder icon animated at 9:55 a.m., just to the left of the laptop computer icons and mushroom cloud at ten a.m. on the timeline.

I looked around the room for other questions. None came, so I continued.

"The second part of my antidote, my 'Flounder2' payload, was responsible for reversing the camouflage. I programmed it to restore each disguised computer's language from Japanese back to its original setting of either English or Hebrew. I programmed Flounder2 so it would activate at 10:05 a.m. Pacific Standard Time, five minutes after the Iranian attack had triggered."

I clicked the remote, and a second small flounder icon animated at 10:05 a.m. on the timeline, just right of the two computers and their accompanying mushroom clouds.

"So, in essence, my two antidote payloads were designed to sandwich the Iranian payload in time, temporarily disguising all the targeted computers during the instant of the Iranian attack.

"Unfortunately, as they say, 'man plans, God laughs.' While I was able to submit my Flounder1 payload to Microsoft's update servers, an SVR agent shot me before I could upload Flounder2 for distribution."

With a click of the remote, the second flounder faded from the timeline.

"Any questions so far?" I scanned the room. "Everyone following?" Several agents nodded.

"Good. So to recap, that Monday morning, the Iranians used the Controller to post their payload on Microsoft's update servers, and just hours later, I followed suit, posting my Flounder1 payload.

"Now, within minutes of each payload's transmission to Microsoft's servers, Windows computers around the world began down-loading them just as they would any newly available, legitimate soft-ware update. A substantial fraction, roughly fifty-two percent of the world's estimated two-point-four-billion computers, connected to Microsoft's update servers at a rate of roughly fifty million per hour, and by Wednesday at 9:55 a.m., most of them had retrieved both the Iranian payload and my Flounder1 payload. If you do the math, that's about one-and-a-quarter-billion computers. Of course, some comput-ers only downloaded the Iranian payload, and some just downloaded my payload, but most downloaded both."

"Only fifty-two percent?" asked a polo-clad, middle-aged man in the back row. "Why so few?"

"That's what your colleagues estimate," I responded. "The remain-ing forty-eight percent were either off, or had no connection to the Internet during the period of time when the payloads were posted. Or," I said, flipping an imaginary light switch off with my right hand, "it's possible that these computers simply had their auto-update fea-ture turned off by their owners. Many corporations disable the Win-dows Update feature on their corporate PCs. They manually distribute new updates to their machines on their own schedule."

"Interesting. I had expected the percentage to be much higher. Thanks."

"It surprised me too, frankly." I paused. "Now at five minutes before ten a.m. Pacific Standard Time, the Florentine back door acti-vated my Flounder1 payload on every one of those 1.25 billion com-puters. Of these, roughly 304 million computers were American or Israeli computers, and on these computers, my Flounder1 payload proceeded to back up their original language setting and then switch their language to Japanese." A click of my remote control morphed the captions under the laptops from "American" and "Israeli" to "Jap-anese" and "Japanese."

"A microsecond later, Flounder1 rebooted those 304 million com-puters. Of course, I don't have to tell any of you about this. That simul-taneous reboot caused the blackout most of you experienced firsthand. The Department of Homeland Security recently released an estimate that over seventy-five percent of all US and Israeli power plants, traffic grids, hospitals, and police stations went dark, as both their primary and failsafe computers simultaneously reset. Fortunately for me . . . and our two countries . . . these systems quickly came back to life. Over the next few minutes, give or take, those 304 million computers restarted themselves and resumed their normal operation. With one notable exception: all of them now attempted to display their user interface in Japanese rather than English or Hebrew.

"Minutes later, at ten a.m. Pacific Standard Time, the Florentine back door inside those same 1.25 billion computers activated again, this time launching the Iranian payload. But by the time this payload activated, only a minute fraction of the 304 million potential targets still retained their original English or Hebrew personas. All of these un-camouflaged machines predictably suffered an untimely and permanent end—without functional firmware chips, they were turned into paperweights. However, the vast majority of computers—your colleagues estimate as high as 99.8% of the potential targets—escaped destruction due to their new Japanese identity."

A final click of my remote control caused the mushroom clouds to fade from the screen.

"Of course, my intention was to reset these 304 million computers back to their original English and Hebrew personas with my Flounder2 payload once the Iranian Angel of Death had 'passed over,' but as they say, stuff happens." The audience chuckled at my euphemism. "As a result, all 304 million of these computers retained their new Japanese identity until either their owners manually switched them back—no doubt with a confused look on their faces and the help of a Japanese-speaking neighbor—or a day later when Microsoft, at the urging of the NSA, released their own traditional Windows Update to restore those computers back to normal.

"Of course, unless you have been holed up in a cave," I nodded to my host, "you know that rumors have abounded about the cause of the mass outage. My favorite was the space alien-generated computer virus hypothesis in the *Enquirer*. Oh, and in a moment of supreme irony, the official Iranian Fars News Agency blamed Israeli agents for the outage.

"So where are we now? Well, I'm happy to say that the Florentine system is no longer functional. The weekend after the attack, an NSA team worked around the clock with Microsoft to remove the Florentine back door from their Windows Update servers. Without the update server back door, attacks could no longer be uploaded and distributed, effectively neutering the Florentine system. And, as I understand it, this morning Microsoft released a 'critical' patch that they claim addresses a serious flaw in Windows. They have urged users to download and install the patch as soon as possible, lest they be susceptible to a new super virus. The cable news shows are all over the story. Of course, in reality, this patch simply expunges the Florentine back door from Windows.

"So at this time, as far as we know, the world's computers are safe from further attack."

Chapter 64

One week later
Los Angeles

"Sit, boy."

Eyeing the box of fresh doughnuts in my hand, Rusty eased onto his haunches and then, shifting his gaze to my face, fixed me with a pair of sad eyes.

"Don't worry, I'll give you one," I whispered. "Just wait until we get inside."

"Alex!" admonished Linda, ambling over on her crutch, "If you give that dog so much as a crumb, you'll be the one on crutches."

"You're out of luck, pooch," I said, ringing the doorbell. Rusty's eyes continued to bore into mine. "Don't give me that look. Give *her* the guilt trip."

A few seconds later, Pippin began barking maniacally from behind the door.

"Who's that outside, Pipp?" asked Steven. "Could that be Alex?"

Pippin responded with a fresh bout of yelping, his tail thumping wildly against the inside of the door.

"I've never seen him this excited." Steven eased the door open a hair. "You bring a pound of bacon or something?"

"Something like that."

"Okay, here goes."

Pippin came flying through the doorway like a bat out of hell and scampered straight past me and up to Rusty. A frenzied bout of mutual sniffing and tail wagging ensued.

"Welcome back, Alex! Hi Linda!" Steven shifted his gaze down. "And who's this?" he asked, extending his hand for Rusty to sniff.

"That's old man Rusty," said Linda.

"Nice to meet you, Rusty," he said, scratching the dog behind the ear. "Well come on in. Hildegard! Linda and Alex are here."

"Hey guys!" yelled Hillary from the kitchen. "I'm almost finished cooking breakfast, come on in and take a seat."

Upon reaching the kitchen, Linda propped her crutch against the wall, grabbed my arm, and limped over to the table to sit down. I took a seat next to her and deposited the box of doughnuts on the table.

"Those smell great," said Steven.

"Have one," I offered, sliding the pink box across the table. "They're your favorite, chocolate with rainbow sprinkles. Fresh out of the deep fryer."

"Linda, you're looking much better," said Hillary from the stove. "You had us worried there for a few days."

"Thanks, Hillary. It helped to get out of that hospital and back home with Rusty." She patted him on the head, then reached over and squeezed my hand. "And Alex has been a real help these past few days, too."

"Now I understand my place. Just below the dog," I joked.

"I wouldn't say *just* below," said Linda with a grin.

"So, Alex, fill us in," said Steven. "That power outage a few days after the cave—was that the Iranian attack?"

"Top secret, man," I said. "But let's put it this way . . . your computer still working?"

"Yeah," said Steven.

"Still getting water and power to the house?"

"Yeah."

"Well then, it probably wasn't the Iranian attack."

Hillary deposited a large bowl of scrambled eggs, a stack of toast, and a heaping plate of bacon on the table, then took the seat next to Steven. "Tuck in," she said.

"So you stopped it?" he persisted, picking up several strips of bacon.

"More or less."

"Then why the disappearing act for the last five weeks?"

"Days and days of meetings and debriefings with lots of three-letter agencies and VIPs," I said, "including one with a pretty powerful guy."

"No!" said Hillary.

I smirked.

"Unreal!" said Steven, scooping out a heaping mound of eggs. "Did you mention my Oscar-winning performance as a house inspector?"

"How could I not?"

Hillary shook her head in mock disapproval. "Well, in any case, I'm glad it's finally all over." She looked at me questioningly. "It *is* finally over, right? No more violence?"

"It's over," I said, nodding. "The FBI's been in cleanup mode all month. Two weeks ago they arrested a group of Russian engineers at Microsoft. Then last week, they rounded up another two Iranian agents who'd been working with Khalimmy. And, most important, the back door's been totally deactivated, so technically, we don't know anything that could make us targets."

"Good riddance," said Hillary.

"Well, here's to normalcy." Steven held his coffee cup up for a toast. "And we've got something else to toast!"

"Yeah? What?"

"We're the proud owners of nearly four-point-six-million dollars in loot. Everything but the Van Gogh is ours to keep. The painting was stolen several years ago from a private collector, and has to be returned."

"Wow! That much?" I exclaimed.

"That's what Sotheby's thinks. I've got a meeting scheduled with Christie's tomorrow."

"So, Alex, what are you going to do with your share?" asked Linda.

"You mean after covering all your medical bills? After that, I don't know. I've been thinking of using it to honor Potter, maybe establish a charity for homeless kids. Something he'd have been proud of."

"That's so nice of you, Alex." Hillary's eyes began to tear.

"It's the least I can do for him," I said, tearing up myself.

"Anyway, guys, we should probably get going," I said, standing up. "Linda and I were thinking of driving up to the park at the north end of Wellingsworth Canyon for some fresh air, maybe playing some catch with Rusty. Isn't that right boy?"

The old hound stared at me for a moment, then let out a hearty "woof" and rose to his feet.

"Got room for three mo— Ouch!" Steven looked under the table. "Why'd you do that?"

Hillary shot him an exasperated look.

"Oh," he said, "on second thought, we're busy this afternoon. But have fun."

"Thanks for being so transparent, Steven," chuckled Linda.

"What are friends for?" Steven smiled. "You know, Alex, they say there's treasure hidden somewhere in that canyon."

"That's what I hear. Maybe once your leg's all better—"

"Alex, don't even think about it!" shrieked Hillary.

"Now Hill." I winked. "What could possibly go wrong?"

About the Author

Carey Nachenberg is a leading cyber security expert and a co-inventor of Norton Antivirus, the world's most popular computer security product. Nachenberg was named one of *Computerworld* magazine's "40 Under 40: 40 Innovative IT People to Watch," and was awarded the *Wall Street Journal*'s 2010 Technology Innovation Award for his innovations in the security field. Nachenberg holds a master's degree in computer science from UCLA, where he continues to serve as an adjunct assistant professor. In his free time, he enjoys rock climbing at the local crags with students and friends. He lives in Southern California.

OPEN ROAD

INTEGRATED MEDIA

Open Road Integrated Media is a digital publisher and multimedia content company. Open Road creates connections between authors and their audiences by marketing its ebooks through a new proprietary online platform, which uses premium video content and social media.

Videos, Archival Documents, and New Releases

Sign up for the Open Road Media newsletter and get news delivered straight to your inbox.

Sign up now at
www.openroadmedia.com/newsletters

CPSIA information can be obtained
at www.ICGtesting.com
Printed in the USA
BVOW08s0605071117
499752BV00001B/30/P